Avon Books by
Lisa Kleypas

LISA KLEYPAS

STRANGER IN MY ARMS

AVON BOOKS
An Imprint of HarperCollins*Publishers*

This is a work of fiction. Names, characters, places, and incidents are products of the author's imagination or are used fictitiously and are not to be construed as real. Any resemblance to actual events, locales, organizations, or persons, living or dead, is entirely coincidental.

AVON BOOKS
An Imprint of HarperCollins*Publishers*
10 East 53rd Street
New York, New York 10022-5299

First Avon Books special printing: June 2007
First Avon Books paperback printing: July 1998

Printed in the U.S.A.

10 9 8 7 6 5 4 3 2 1

Chapter 1

"LADY HAWKSWORTH, YOUR husband is not dead."

Lara stared at James Young without blinking. She knew she had not heard the estate agent correctly . . . or perhaps he had been drinking, though she had never known him to tipple before. It was possible that he had grown a little dotty from having to work in the service of the current Lord and Lady Hawksworth. They would surely drive anyone mad, given enough time.

"I know it is a great shock to you all," Young continued earnestly. Concern flared in his bespectacled eyes as he glanced at Lara. "To you in particular, my lady."

Had the news come from a less reliable source, Lara would have dismissed it immediately. However, James Young was a cautious and trustworthy man who had served the Hawksworth family for at least a decade. He had done an excellent job of managing her trust property's income since her husband's death, no matter that there was precious little money to oversee.

Arthur, Lord Hawksworth, and his wife, Janet, regarded Young as if they, too, doubted his sanity.
They were an ideally suited couple, both of them
blond, tall, and spare of frame. Although they had
two sons, the boys had been packed off to Eton and
were seldom seen or even mentioned. Arthur and Janet seemed to care about one thing only—to enjoy
their newfound wealth and status as conspicuously
as possible.

"Preposterous!" Arthur exploded. "How dare you
come to me with this nonsense! Explain yourself at
once."

"Very well, my lord," Young replied. "I received
word yesterday that a frigate recently arrived in London carrying a most unusual passenger. It seems that
he bears an uncanny resemblance to the late earl."
He glanced respectfully at Lara as he added, "He
claims to be Lord Hawksworth."

Arthur exploded with disbelieving scorn. His lean
face, carved with deep lines of cynicism, flushed a
vivid shade of red. His long beak of a nose twitched
angrily. "What sort of outrageous hoax is this?
Hawksworth has been dead for a year. It's impossible
that he could have survived the shipwreck off of
Madras. My God, the vessel literally broke in half!
Everyone on board was lost. Are you telling me that
my nephew somehow managed to survive? The man
must be a lunatic to think that any of us would believe him."

Janet's thin lips tightened. "He'll be proved an impostor soon enough," she said crisply, smoothing the
toothlike points of dark Vandyke lace that trimmed
the bodice and waist of her emerald silk gown.

Ignoring the Crosslands' furious disdain, Young

approached the widow. Larissa sat in a gilt-wood armchair near the window, her gaze fixed on the carpet covering the floor. Like everything else in Hawksworth Hall, the Persian carpet was opulent to the point of tastelessness, woven in a fantastical design of surreal flowers spilling from a Chinese-style vase. The worn toe of a black leather shoe protruded from beneath the hem of Larissa's mourning dress as she absently traced the edge of a scarlet flower with her foot. She seemed lost in memories, not noticing Young's approach until he had reached her. Abruptly she straightened like a chastened schoolgirl and lifted her gaze to his face.

Even in her dark bombazine dress, as high-necked and pristine as a nun's habit, Larissa Crossland possessed a soft, elegant beauty. With her dark sable hair always seeming on the verge of tumbling from its pins, and sultry pale green eyes, she was original and striking. However, her looks generated little heat. She was often admired but never pursued . . . never flirted with or desired. Perhaps it was the way she used cheerfulness like a weapon, if such a thing were possible, keeping everyone at a distance.

It seemed to many in the town of Market Hill that Lara was an almost saintly figure. A woman with her looks and position could have managed to snare a second husband, yet she had chosen to stay here and involve herself in charitable works. She was unfailingly gentle and compassionate, and her generosity extended to nobleman and beggar alike. Young had never heard Lady Hawksworth utter an unkind word about anyone, not the husband who had virtually abandoned her nor the relatives who treated her with contemptible stinginess.

But for all her apparent serenity, there was something unsettling in her translucent green eyes. Some quiet turbulence that hinted at emotions and thoughts she never dared express. As far as Young could tell, Larissa had decided to content herself by living vicariously through the people around her. It was frequently said she needed a man of her own. However, no one could ever seem to think of a particular gentleman who was suited to her.

That was undoubtedly a good thing, if it turned out that the late earl really was alive.

"My lady," Young murmured apologetically, "I did not want to distress you. But I felt you would want to be informed immediately about any matter that concerns the late earl."

"Is there any chance it could be true?" Lara whispered, her face shadowed with a frown.

"I don't know," came Young's careful reply. "As they never found the earl's body, I suppose there is a chance that he—"

"Of course it isn't true!" Arthur exclaimed. "Have you both taken leave of your senses?" Brushing by Young, he assumed a protective expression and settled his hand on Lara's narrow shoulder. "How dare this scoundrel put Lady Hawksworth through such torment!" he exclaimed with as much false pity as he could muster.

"I'm fine," Lara interrupted, stiffening at his touch. A frown knit her smooth brow. She pulled away and went to the window, longing to escape the overdecorated parlor. The walls were covered in bright pink silk and heavy gold scrollwork, the corners filled with vases of exotic palms. It seemed that every inch of available space was taken up with a collection of what Janet referred to as "friggers," concoctions of glass birds and trees covered with clear protective domes.

"Careful," Janet exclaimed sharply, as Lara's heavy skirts brushed the side of a glass bowl set in a tripod mahogany stand, causing it to wobble.

Lara glanced down at the forlorn pair of goldfish swimming in the bowl, and then back at Janet's pinched, narrow face. "They shouldn't be placed in the window," Lara heard herself murmur. "They don't like too much light."

Janet let out a contemptuous laugh. "You would know best, I'm sure," she said acidly, and Lara knew she would make a point of keeping the fish exactly where they were.

Sighing, Lara turned her gaze to the fields surrounding Hawksworth Hall. The land extending from the former Norman stronghold was studded with groves of chestnut and oak, and cut by a wide and flowing river. The same river provided a millstream and shipping channel for the nearby town of Market Hill, a bustling and prosperous port.

A flock of mallards settled on the artificial lake in front of the Hall, disrupting the regal progress of a pair of swans. Past the lake was a road leading to town, and an ancient stone bridge known to the locals as the "bridge of the damned." Legend had it that the devil himself had placed the bridge there with the stated intention of collecting the soul of the first man who crossed it. As the story went, the only one who dared to set foot on the bridge was a Crossland ancestor, who had defied the devil and refused to hand over his soul. The devil had placed a curse on all his descendants, that they would always have difficulty producing male issue to carry on the line.

Lara could almost believe the tale. Each generation of Crossland men had produced very few children, and most of the males had died at a relatively young age. Including Hunter.

Smiling sadly, Lara forced her thoughts back to the present and turned toward Mr. Young. He was a small, slight man, his face nearly level with her own. "If this stranger is indeed my husband," she asked calmly, "why has he not returned before now?"

"According to his story," Young replied, "he floated in the ocean for two days following the ship-wreck, and was picked up by a fishing vessel en route to Cape Town. He was wounded in the wreck, and had no recollection of who he was. He didn't even know his own name. A few months afterward his memory returned and he set sail for England."

Arthur snorted contemptuously. "Not remember his own identity? I've never heard of such a thing."

"Apparently it is possible," the estate manager countered. "I've discussed the matter with Dr. Slade, the family physician, and he confirms that such cases, though rare, have been reported."

"How interesting," Arthur said sarcastically. "Don't tell me you give any credence to this sham, Young."

"None of us can determine the truth until the stranger is interviewed by those who knew Hawks-worth well."

"Mr. Young," Lara said, concealing her inner tur-moil, "you were acquainted with my husband for many years. I would appreciate it if you would go to London and meet this man. Even if he is not the late earl, it sounds as if he could be troubled and in need of help. Something must be done for him."

"How very like you, Lady Hawksworth," Young remarked. "I dare say most people wouldn't conceive of helping a stranger who is attempting to deceive them. You are a kind woman indeed."

"Yes," Arthur agreed dryly. "My nephew's widow is the patron saint of beggars, orphans, and stray dogs. She can't resist giving away whatever she has to others."

"Which is why we haven't seen fit to supplement Lara's annuity," Janet added. "The extra money would only slip through her fingers, as even the smallest child seems able to take advantage of her. She's given everything she owns to that shabby orphanage."

Lara's face burned at their snide remarks. "The orphans need money far more than I do," she said. "They need a great many things that others could provide quite easily."

"I have been charged with preserving the family fortune for future generations," Arthur snapped. "Not to squander it on parentless children."

"Very well," Young interceded hastily, interrupting the brewing argument. "If it pleases all of you, I shall depart for London along with Dr. Slade, who knew the late earl since birth. We will see if there is any truth to this man's claims." He gave Lara a reassuring smile. "Do not distress yourself, my lady. I'm sure all will turn out for the best."

Relieved to escape the Hawksworths' presence, Lara went to the old gamekeeper's cottage, which was set at a distance from the castle along the willow-lined riverbank. The cottage was a far cry from the large timbered Elizabethan gatehouse that had once been used as separate quarters for guests or visiting relatives. Unfortunately the interior of the gatehouse had been ruined by fire the previous year, when a careless visitor had overturned an oil lamp and set the place ablaze.

Arthur and Janet had seen no reason to have the place restored, deciding that the unoccupied cottage was sufficient for Lara's needs. She could have cast herself on the mercy of other relatives who might have offered her more comfortable lodgings, or even accepted her mother-in-law's offer to serve as her traveling companion, but she treasured her privacy too much for that. Better to remain near familiar surroundings and friends, despite the discomforts of the cottage.

The stone dwelling was dark and damp, with a moldy smell that no amount of washing could banish. It was rare that a meager ray of sunlight entered the lone casement window. Lara had sought to make the place more habitable by covering one wall with a patchwork counterpane, and filling it with a few simple pieces of cast-off furniture from Hawksworth Hall. The chair by the fireplace stove was draped with a blue and red lap blanket knitted by some of the older girls at the orphanage. A carved wooden salamander was placed near the hearth, a gift from an elderly man in town who had assured her that it would protect the cottage from harm.

Closing herself in solitude, Lara lit a tallow-dipped candle and stood in the glow of its sputtering, smoky light. Suddenly her body was racked by a hard shiver.

Hunter . . . alive. It couldn't be true, of course, but

the very idea filled her with unease. Going to her narrow bed, she knelt on the floor, reached underneath the creaking ropes that held the mattress. She tugged out a cloth-wrapped parcel and undid the coverings to reveal a framed portrait of her late husband.

Arthur and Janet had offered her the painting with a show of generosity, but Lara knew that they were eager to be rid of the reminder of the man who had held the title before them. She hadn't wanted the portrait either, but she had taken it, acknowledging inwardly that Hunter was part of her past. He had changed the course of her life. Perhaps someday when time had softened her memories, she would hang the portrait in full view.

The painting depicted a large-boned, stocky man in the company of his dogs, one huge hand casually clasped around the butt of his favorite gun. Hunter had been handsome, with thick gold-brown hair, intense dark brown eyes, and a perpetually arrogant expression.

It had been three years since Hunter had set sail for India on a semidiplomatic mission. As a minor stockholder in the East India Company, and a man of some political influence, he had been appointed to advise the Company administrators in India.

In reality, he had been one of many hangers-on eager to join the crowd of idle debauchees in Calcutta. They lived like kings there, indulging in endless parties and orgies. It was said that each household contained at least a hundred servants who saw to every detail of their masters' comfort. Moreover, India was a sportsman's paradise, abounding in exotic game—irresistible to a man like Hunter.

Remembering her husband's enthusiasm upon his departure, Lara smiled sadly. Hunter had been more than eager to leave her. England had begun to pall for him, and so had their marriage. There was no doubt that he and Lara had been ill matched. A wife, Hunter had once told her, was a necessary nuisance, useful only for the sake of bearing children. When Lara had failed to conceive, he had been deeply injured. For a man who had prided himself on his strength and virility, the absence of children was hard to bear.

Lara's gaze fell to the bed, and cold knots formed in her stomach as she remembered Hunter's nighttime visits, his heavy body crushing hers, the painful invasion that seemed never to end. It seemed like an act of mercy when he had begun to stray from her bed and visit other women to satisfy his needs. Lara had never known anyone so physically strong and vital. She could almost believe he had lived through a violent shipwreck that no one else had managed to survive.

Hunter had so dominated everyone around him that Lara had felt her spirit withering in his shadow over the two years they had lived together. She had been grateful when he had departed for India. Left to her own devices, Lara had become involved in the local orphanage, giving her time and attention to improving the lives of the children there. The feeling of being needed was so gratifying that Lara had soon found other projects with which to occupy herself: visiting the sick and elderly, organizing charitable events, even trying her hand at a bit of matchmaking. Upon being informed of Hunter's death, she had been saddened, but she had not missed him.

Nor, she thought guiltily, did she want him back.

For the next three days there was no word from Mr. Young or the Hawksworths. Lara did her best to go about her activities as usual, but the news had traveled all through Market Hill, spread by the excited gossip of the servants at Hawksworth Hall.

Her sister, Rachel, Lady Lonsdale, was the first to visit. The black-lacquered barouche stopped midway up the drive to the Hall, and Rachel's slight form emerged to walk unaccompanied along the cottage path. Rachel was Lara's younger sister but gave the impression of being the elder, possessing greater height and a sweet solemnity that lent her an air of maturity.

They had once been proclaimed as Lincolnshire's most attractive sisters, but Lara knew that Rachel's beauty eclipsed her own. Rachel possessed perfectly classical features: large eyes, a small rosebud mouth, and a narrow, slightly upturned nose. By contrast Lara's face was round instead of oval, and her mouth was too wide, and her straight dark hair—fiercely resistant to the curling tongs—was always slipping from its pins.

Meeting her sister at the door, Lara eagerly welcomed her inside. Rachel was expensively dressed, her brown hair pulled back to reveal the delicate point of a widow's peak. The sweet scent of violets clung to her hair and skin.

"Dear Larissa," Rachel said, glancing about the cottage, "for the thousandth time, why don't you come live with Terrell and me? There are a dozen rooms to spare, and you would be much more comfortable—"

"Thank you, Rachel." Lara hugged her sister. "But I couldn't stay under the same roof as your husband. I can't pretend to tolerate a man who doesn't treat you properly. And I'm certain that Lord Lonsdale holds me in equal disaffection."

"He isn't that bad—"

"He's an abominable husband, much as you try to pretend otherwise. Lord Lonsdale doesn't give a fig about anyone but himself, and he never will."

Rachel frowned and seated herself by the hearth. "Sometimes I think the only person, man or woman, that Terrell ever truly liked was Lord Hawksworth."

"They were cut from the same cloth," Lara agreed, "except that at least Hunter never raised a hand to me."

"It was only the once," Rachel protested. "I never should have told you of it."

"You didn't need to tell me. The bruise on your face was evidence enough."

They were both silent, remembering the episode two months before when Lord Lonsdale had struck Rachel during an argument. The mark on Rachel's cheek and eye had taken weeks to fade, causing Rachel to hide in her home until she could venture out without causing suspicion. Now Rachel claimed that Lord Lonsdale deeply regretted his loss of self-control. She had forgiven him, she said, and she wished Lara would do the same.

Lara couldn't forgive anyone who had hurt her sister, and she had the suspicion that it would happen again. It almost made her wish that Hunter really were alive. In spite of his faults, he would never have countenanced hitting a woman. Hunter would have made it clear to Lord Lonsdale that such behavior was unacceptable. And Lonsdale might have heeded him, as Hunter was one of the few people on earth whom he respected.

"I didn't come here to talk about that, Larissa." Rachel's gaze was loving and concerned as she watched her older sister seat herself on an upholstered footstool nearby. "I heard the news about Lord Hawksworth. Tell me . . . is he actually coming back to you?"

Lara shook her head. "No, of course not. Some crackbrain in London is claiming to be my husband. Mr. Young and Dr. Slade are visiting him, and I'm certain they'll have him confined in either Bedlam or Newgate, depending on whether he's mad or a criminal."

"Then there's no chance that Lord Hawksworth is alive?" Reading the answer in Lara's face, Rachel sighed. "I'm sorry to say it, but my mind is relieved. I know that your marriage was not a good one. All I want is for you to be happy."

"I wish the same for you," Lara said earnestly. "And you're in far worse circumstances than I ever was, Rachel. Hunter was far from the ideal husband, but he and I got along well enough, except for . . ." She stopped and blushed suddenly.

It wasn't easy for her to speak of intimate matters. She and Rachel had a puritanical upbringing, their parents kind but distant. It had been left to Lara and Rachel to learn about the act of physical intercourse on their respective wedding nights. For Lara, the discovery had been an unpleasant one.

Rachel seemed to read her thoughts, as always.

"Oh, Lara," she murmured, the color rising in her own face, "I think Lord Hawksworth must not have been as considerate of you as he should." Her voice lowered as she continued. "Lovemaking isn't so terrible, really. There were times with Terrell, early in our marriage, when I actually found it rather pleasant. Lately, of course, it's not at all the same. But I still remember how it once was."

"*Pleasant?*" Lara stared at her in amazement. "For once, you've managed to shock me. How you could have liked something so embarrassing and painful is beyond me—unless you're trying to make a very bad joke."

"Weren't there occasions when Lord Hawksworth kissed you, held you close, and you felt rather warm and . . . well, womanly?"

Lara fell into a perplexed silence. She failed to see how lovemaking—ironic term for such a repulsive act—could *not* be painful. "No," she said thoughtfully, "I can't ever remember feeling that way. Hunter wasn't fond of kissing or embracing. And when it was over, I was glad of it."

Rachel's face was soft with pity. "Did he ever say that he loved you?"

Lara gave a hollow laugh at the idea. "Goodness, no, Hunter would never have admitted to such a thing." A bleak smile curved her lips. "He didn't love me. There was another woman whom he should have married instead of me. I think he often regretted his mistake."

"You never told me that," Rachel exclaimed. "Who is she?"

"Lady Carlysle," Lara mumbled, vaguely surprised that after all this time, the name still caused a sour taste in her mouth.

"What is she like? Did you ever meet her?"

"Yes, on a few occasions. She and Hunter were discreet, but it was obvious that they took enormous pleasure in one another's company. She liked all the same things he did—riding, hunting, horses. I've no doubt that he visited her often in private after we were married."

"Why didn't Lord Hawksworth marry Lady Carlysle in the first place?"

Lara hugged her knees and lowered her chin, unconsciously drawing herself into a ball. "I was much younger, whereas she was past childbearing age. Hunter wanted an heir . . . and I suppose he thought he could mold me to his liking. I did try to please him. Unfortunately I couldn't seem to give him the one thing he wanted from me."

"A child," Rachel murmured. From the expression on her face, Lara knew that Rachel was thinking of her own miscarriage, which had occurred only a few months ago. "Neither of us has had much success in that regard, have we?"

Lara's face burned as she continued. "At least you've proven that you're able to conceive. With God's blessing you'll bear a child someday. I, on the other hand, have tried everything—I drank tonics and consulted moon charts, and put myself through any number of ridiculous and humiliating exertions. Nothing worked. When Hunter finally left for India, I was so glad that he was gone. It was a blessing to sleep alone and not have to wonder each night if I would hear his footsteps approaching my door." Lara shivered at the memories that flashed through her mind. "I don't like sleeping with a man. I never want to again."

"Poor Larissa," Rachel murmured. "You should have told me these things long before now. You're always so eager to solve others' problems, and so reluctant to discuss your own."

"Had I told you, it wouldn't have changed anything," Lara pointed out, making an effort to smile.

"Had it been left to me, I would have chosen someone far more appropriate for you than Lord Hawksworth. I think Mama and Papa were so dazzled by his position and wealth that they overlooked the fact that you didn't suit."

"It wasn't their fault," Lara said. "The blame was mine . . . I'm not really suited to be anyone's wife. I should never have married at all. I'm much happier on my own."

"Neither of us landed the kind of match we hoped for, did we?" Rachel reflected with sad irony. "Terrell with his moods, and your lummox of a husband . . . hardly the stuff of fairy tales."

"At least we live close to each other," Lara pointed out, trying to dispel the cloud of regret that seemed to hang in the air. "That makes everything bearable, at least for me."

"For me as well." Rachel left the chair and went to hug her tightly. "I pray only good things will happen to you from now on, dearest. May Lord Hawksworth rest in peace—and may you soon find a man who will love you as you deserve to be loved."

"Don't pray for that," Lara said, her alarm half feigned and half real. "I don't want a man. Pray instead for the children at the orphanage, and poor old

Mrs. Lumley, who is going blind, and Mr. Peacham's rheumatism, and—"

"You and your ever-expanding list of unfortunates," Rachel commented, smiling fondly at her. "Very well, I'll pray for them too."

The moment Lara ventured into town, she found herself inundated with questions, everyone demanding to know the details of her husband's return from the dead. No matter how often she stated that "Hawksworth's" appearance in London was most likely a hoax, the citizens of Market Hill wanted to believe otherwise.

"Well, if 'tisn't the luckiest woman in Market Hill," said the cheesewright as soon as Lara entered his shop, one of many that lined the town's primary street of Maingate. The air was redolent with a pleasantly milky, tangy smell that wafted from the slabs and rounds of cheese stacked on the wooden tables.

Smiling halfheartedly, Lara set her willow basket on a long table and waited for him to produce the round of cheese she came to collect each week for the orphanage. "I'm fortunate for many reasons, Mr. Wilkins," she replied, "but if you're referring to the rumor about my late husband—"

"A lovely sight you'll be," the cheesewright interrupted heartily, his jovial, big-nosed face glowing with good humor. "The lady of the manor again." He hefted a cheese that measured nearly a foot across into her basket. The soft curds had been salted, pressed, wrapped in muslin, and dipped in wax to ensure a mild, fresh flavor.

"Thank you," Lara replied evenly, "but, Mr. Wilkins, I must tell you I'm sure you that the story is false. Lord Hawksworth is not coming back."

The Misses Withers, a pair of elderly spinster sisters, entered the shop and tittered in pleasure as they saw Lara. Identical flower-trimmed bonnets covered their small gray heads, which bobbed together in a swift exchange of gossip. One of them approached Lara and laid a frail, blue-veined hand on her sleeve. "My dear, the news reached us this morning. We're so happy for you, so happy indeed—"

"Thank you, but it's not true," Lara insisted. "The man who claims to be my husband is undoubtedly an impostor. It would be a miracle if the earl had managed to survive the shipwreck."

"I say hope for the best until you're told otherwise," Mr. Wilkins said, while his stout wife, Glenda, emerged from the back of the shop. Eagerly she reached out and stuffed a bunch of daisies in the corner of Lara's basket. "If anyone deserves a miracle, milady," Glenda said merrily, "it's you."

They all assumed that she was hopeful about the news, that she wanted Hunter to return. Flushed and uncomfortable, Lara guiltily accepted their good wishes and hurried out of the shop.

She started on a brisk walk along the winding riverbank, passing a small, tidy churchyard and a succession of white-walled cottages. Her destination was the orphanage, a decaying manor situated on the east side of town. Set back among stockades of pine and oak, the orphanage was a distinctive place built of gritstone and blue brick, with a blue-glazed tile roof. The method used to make the special frost-resistant tiles was known only to the village potter, who had stumbled across the recipe by accident one day and swore he would someday take it to his grave.

Puffing from the exertion of walking a long distance with a heavy basket on her arm, Lara entered the building. Once it had been a fine manor, but after the last occupant's death, the place had been abandoned and had fallen to ruin. Private donations from the townsfolk had restored the structure until it was suitable to house two dozen children. Further gifts had provided annual salaries for a handful of teachers.

Lara ached with regret when she thought of the fortune she'd once had at her disposal—what she couldn't have done with such money now! There were many improvements she longed to make to the orphanage. She had even swallowed her pride and gone to Arthur and Janet to ask if he would make a donation for the children's sake, but she had been coldly rebuffed. The new Earl and Countess of Hawksworth were firm in their belief that the orphans must learn that the world was a harsh place, and they must make their own way in it.

Sighing, Lara entered the building and set the basket just inside the door. Her arm trembled from the strain of carrying its weight. She caught a glimpse of a curly brown head as someone ducked behind a corner. It had to be Charles, she thought, a rebellious eleven-year-old boy who constantly searched for new ways to cause trouble.

"I wish someone would help me carry this basket to the kitchen," she said aloud, and Charles promptly appeared.

"You carried it this far by yourself," he observed sullenly.

Lara smiled into his small, freckled, blue-eyed face. "Don't be surly, Charles. Help me with the basket,

and on the way to the kitchen you can tell me why
you aren't in class this morning."

"Miss Thornton sent me out of the schoolroom,"
he replied, lifting one side of the large basket and
eyeing the cheese hungrily. Together they carried it
down the hall, their steps softened by the threadbare
carpet. "I was making too much noise, and paid no
mind to the teacher."

"Why is that, Charles?"

"I learned my maths before everyone else. Why
should I have to sit still and do nothing just because
I'm smarter than the rest of 'em?"

"I see," Lara replied, reflecting ruefully that it was
probably true. Charles was an intelligent child who
needed more attention than the school was able to
provide. "I'll speak to Miss Thornton. In the meantime, you must try to behave yourself."

They reached the kitchen, where the cook, Mrs.
Davies, greeted her with a smile. Mrs. Davies's
round face was rosy from the heat of the stove,
where a large kettle of soup was kept warming. Her
brown eyes were bright with interest. "Lady Hawksworth, we've heard the most astonishing rumor from
town—"

"It isn't true," Lara interrupted ruefully. "It's
merely some troubled stranger who has convinced
himself—or is trying to convince us—that he is the
late earl. If my husband had survived, he would have
come home long before now."

"I suppose," Mrs. Davies said, seeming disappointed. "It would have made a romantic story,
though. If you don't mind my saying so, milady,
you're too young and pretty to be a widow."

Lara shook her head and smiled. "I'm quite content with my situation, Mrs. Davies."

"I want him to stay dead," Charles announced, causing Mrs. Davies to gasp in horror.

"What a wee devil you are!" the cook exclaimed.

Lara bent until she and the boy were at eye level, and smoothed his unruly hair. "Why do you say that, Charles?"

"If he *is* the earl, you won't come here anymore. He'll make you stay at home and do his bidding."

"Charles, that's not true," Lara replied gravely. "But there's no reason to argue the point. The earl is gone—and people don't come back from the dead."

Dust from the road coated Lara's skirts as she returned to the Hawksworth estate, passing tenant farms bordered with wattle-and-daub fences made of woven branches and mud. Sunlight glittered on the water that spilled lavishly beneath the bridge of the damned. As Lara neared the stone cottage, she heard her name called. She stopped in surprise at the sight of her former abigail, Naomi, running from the Hall with her skirts lifted to keep from tripping.

"Naomi, you mustn't run like that," Lara exclaimed. "You'll fall and hurt yourself."

The plump lady's maid gasped with exertion and feverish excitement. "Lady Hawksworth," she exclaimed, struggling to catch her breath. "Oh, milady . . . Mr. Young sent me to tell you . . . *he's* here . . . at the castle . . . they're all here, and . . . you must come at once."

Lara blinked in confusion. "Who is here? Mr. Young has sent for me?"

"Yes, they've brought *him* from London."

"Him?" Lara asked faintly.

"Yes, milady. The earl has come home."

Chapter 2

THE WORDS SEEMED to hover and buzz around Lara like gnats. *The earl has come home, come home* . . . "But it can't be," she whispered.

Why would Mr. Young have brought the stranger here from London? She licked her dry lips, the inside of her mouth feeling like parchment. When she spoke, her voice didn't sound like her own. "H-have you seen him?"

The maid nodded, suddenly bereft of words.

Lara stared fixedly at the ground and forced out a few halting words. "You knew my husband, Naomi. Tell me . . . is the man at Hawksworth Hall . . ." She lifted her beseeching gaze to the maid, unable to finish the sentence.

"I think so, milady. Nay, I'm certain of it."

"But . . . the earl is gone," Lara said numbly. "He drowned."

"Let me help you to the castle," Naomi urged, taking her arm. "You look all queer and white, and 'tis no wonder. 'Tisn't every day a woman's dead husband comes back to her."

Lara pulled away from her with a jerky movement. "Please . . . I need a few minutes to myself. I'll walk up to the Hall when I'm ready."

"Yes, milady. I'll tell them to expect you." Throwing her a concerned, excited glance, Naomi retreated and hurried along the path leading back to the castle.

Stumbling into the cottage, Lara went to the washstand and poured lukewarm water into the chipped earthenware basin. She splashed the dust and perspiration from her face, her movements methodical, her mind whirling with frantic thoughts. She had never found herself in such an impossible situation before. She had always been a practical woman. She didn't believe in miracles, had never asked for one. Especially not this one.

But this wasn't a miracle, Lara reminded herself, letting down her disheveled hair and trying to coil and pin it back in place. Her unsteady hands wouldn't obey, fumbling with pins and combs until they fell to the floor in a delicate clatter.

The man who waited for her at Hawksworth Hall was not Hunter. He was a stranger, a cunning one if he had managed to convince Mr. Young and Dr. Slade that his claim was true. Lara would simply gather her composure, go to assess him for herself, and assure the others that he was certainly not her husband. Then the matter would be over. She took several breaths to restore herself and continued to stick pins haphazardly in her hair.

As Lara stared in the square Queen Anne mirror poised on the chest of drawers in her room, it seemed that the atmosphere changed, the air suddenly heavy and pressing. It was so quiet in the cottage that she could hear her own mad heartbeat. She caught sight of something in the mirror, a deliberate movement that paralyzed her. Someone had entered the cottage.

Skin prickling, Lara stood in frozen silence and stared into the mirror as another reflection joined her own. A man's bronzed face . . . short, sun-streaked brown hair . . . dark brown eyes . . . the hard, wide mouth she remembered so well. Tall . . . massive chest and shoulders . . . a physical power and assurance that made the room seem to shrink around him.

Lara's breath stopped. She wanted to run, to cry out, faint, but it seemed that she had been turned to stone. He stood just behind her, his head and shoulders looming far above hers. His gaze held hers in the mirror . . . The eyes were the same color, yet . . . he had never looked at her like this, with an intensity that made every inch of her skin burn. His was the hard gaze of a predator.

She shook in fright as his hands moved gently to her hair. One by one he slipped the confining pins from the shining sable mass, and set them on the dresser before her. Lara watched him, quivering with each light tug on her hair. "It's not true," she whispered.

He spoke in Hunter's voice, deep and slightly raspy. "I'm not a ghost, Lara."

She tore her gaze from the mirror and stumbled around to face him.

He was so much thinner, his body lean, almost rawboned, his heavy muscles thrown into stark prominence. His skin was tanned to a copper blaze that was far too exotic for an Englishman. And his hair had lightened to the mixed gold and brown of a griffin's feathers.

"I didn't believe . . ." Lara heard her own voice as

if from very far away. There was a pinching sensation around her chest, and her heart could no longer sustain its own violent rhythm. Although her lungs moved in painful spasms, she couldn't seem to get enough air. A thick mist rolled over her, covering all sight and sound, and she sank swiftly into the dark abyss that opened beneath her.

Hunter caught her as she fell. Her body was light and lush in his arms, conforming easily to his hard grip. He carried her to the narrow bed and sat on the creaking mattress, cradling her in his lap. Her head tilted back, her ivory throat encased in the banded black fabric of her mourning gown. He stared intently at her, riveted by the delicacy of her face. He'd forgotten a woman's skin could be so fair and fresh.

Her mouth in repose was soft and a little sad, her face as vulnerable as a child's. How strange for a widow to look so unawakened. She had a tidy bandbox prettiness that appealed to him tremendously. He wanted this small, neat creature with her dainty hands and forlorn mouth. With the cold calculation that had always been integral to him, he decided he would take her, and all that came with her.

Her eyes opened, and she stared at him gravely. He returned her wondering gaze with an opaque one, letting her see nothing of the man inside, and he curved his mouth in a reassuring smile.

She didn't seem to notice the smile, however, only stared at him with those unblinking eyes. And then a strange softness entered the pools of translucent green, a curious, pitying tenderness . . . as if he were a lost soul in need of salvation. She reached up to his neck and touched the edge of a thick scar that disappeared into his hairline. Her fingertips sent fire racing through him. His breathing deepened, and he went very still. How the hell could she look at him this way? To her knowledge, he was either a stranger or a husband she hated.

Bewildered and aroused by the compassion in her face, he fought the insane urge to bury his head against her breasts. Hastily he dislodged her from his lap and put a few necessary yards of distance between them.

For the first time in his life, he was afraid of his own emotions—he, who had always prided himself on iron self-control.

"Who are you?" she asked softly.

"You know who I am," he muttered.

She shook her head, clearly dazed, and tore her gaze from his. She made her way to a set of shelves where she kept a few dishes and a small teapot. Taking refuge in a commonplace ritual, she fumbled for a parcel of tea leaves and pulled the little porcelain pot from its place on the shelf. "I-I'll make some tea," she said faintly. "We can talk. Perhaps I can help you."

But her hands were shaking too badly, and the cups and saucers clattered as she reached for them.

So she had decided he was some poor desperate fool or scavenger who was in need of her aid. A wry smile twisted his mouth, and he came to her, taking her cold hands in his warm ones. Again he experienced the sweet, unexpected shock of touching her. He was fiercely aware of the delicacy of her bones, the softness of her skin. He wanted to show her his gentleness. Something about her seemed to pull the last bitter dregs of his humanity up to the surface.

She made him want to be the kind of man she needed.

"I'm your husband," he said. "I've come home."

She looked at him dumbly, her limbs stiff and her knees trembling.

"I'm Hunter." His voice turned soft. "Don't be afraid."

Lara heard her own gasping, incredulous laugh as she stared into his features, a devastating mixture of the familiar and the unknown. He looked too much like Hunter for her to dismiss him summarily, but there was a foreignness about him that she couldn't accept.

"My husband is dead," she said tightly.

A small muscle twitched high in his lean cheek. "I'll make you believe me."

He reached for her swiftly, both hands wrapping around the back of her skull, gently gripping as he brought his mouth to hers. Ignoring her cry of alarm, he kissed her as she had never been kissed before. Her hands came up to his muscle-roped wrists, trying in vain to pry herself free. The sensation of his mouth, incendiary, delicious, stunned her. He used his teeth and lips and tongue, seducing her in a blaze of sensuality. She floundered for purchase until he let go of her head and gathered her against the hard surface of his body. She was held tight and secure in his embrace, thoroughly possessed . . . utterly desired. Her nostrils were filled with the scent of him: earth and air and the mild, pleasant bite of sandalwood.

His lips slid downward, finding the sensitive place on the side of her neck. He took a deep, luxurious breath and fanned it over her skin, and pressed his face close until she felt the sweep of his lashes against her cheek. She had never been held like this, touched and tasted as if she were some exotic spice to be savored.

"Oh, please," she gasped, arching as he touched his tongue to her frantic pulse.

"Say my name," he whispered.

"No—"

"Say it." His hand cupped her breast, long fingers shaping the sensitive mound. Her nipple hardened in the warm cove of his palm, searching for more stimulation. In one violent movement Lara twisted out of his arms, tottering away a few steps to create a necessary space between them.

Clasping a hand over her aching breast, Lara stared at him in astonishment. He was expressionless, but the jagged sound of his breathing revealed that he was struggling for composure just as she was.

"How could you?" she gasped.

"You're my wife."

"Hunter never liked to kiss."

"I've changed," he said flatly.

"You're not Hunter!" The words were tossed over her shoulder as she fled to the door.

"Lara," she heard him say, but she ignored him. "*Lara*, look at me."

Something in his voice made her pause. Reluctantly she stopped at the threshold and glanced at him.

He was holding something in his palm.

"What is that?" she asked.

"Come and see."

Reluctantly she crept forward, transfixed by the object in his hand. Using his thumb, he pressed the tiny catch on the side, and the flat enameled box snapped open to revealed a miniature portrait of her.

"I've stared at this every day for months," he murmured. "Even when I didn't remember you in the days right after the shipwreck, I knew that you belonged to me." He closed the box in his hand and tucked it back into his coat pocket.

Lara lifted her incredulous gaze to his. She felt as if she were in a dream. "How did you get that?" she whispered.

"You gave it to me," he replied. "The day I left for India. Remember?"

Yes, she remembered. Hunter had been in such a hurry to leave the estate that he'd nearly been too impatient for good-byes. But Lara had managed to draw him aside for a private moment, and had given him the miniature case. It was common for a wife or sweetheart to bestow a memento on a man going abroad, especially to a dangerous place like India, where he had an excellent chance of being killed by wild game or bloodthirsty rebels, or dying of a fever. However, the risks had appealed to Hunter, who had believed himself to be invincible.

Hunter had actually seemed touched by Lara's gift, enough to press a careless kiss on her forehead. "Lovely," he had muttered. "Thank you, Larissa." The atmosphere had been thick with the memories of their unhappy two-year marriage, the mutual bitterness and disappointment of two people who had found no common ground to sustain even friendship. Yet Lara had still worried for him.

"I will pray for your safety," she had told him, and he had laughed into her concerned face.

"Don't waste your prayers on me," he had said.

The man before her seemed to read her thoughts. "You must have spared me a prayer or two after all," he murmured. "It's the only thing that brought me back home."

Lara felt the blood drain from her face, and she staggered beneath the weight of sudden realization. Only her husband would have known their parting words to each other. "Hunter?" she whispered.

He caught her elbows, steadying her, and ducked his head to stare at her with teasing dark eyes. "You're not going to faint again, are you?"

She was too overcome to reply. She allowed him to guide her to a nearby chair, and sat with an abrupt collapsing motion. Sinking to his haunches, the man brought their faces level. He brushed a lock of hair behind her ear, his roughened fingertips skimming the fragile curve. "Starting to believe me?" he asked.

"F-first tell me something else that only my husband would know."

"Good God. I went through enough of this with Young and Slade." He paused and glanced at the widow's weeds that covered her body, and she flinched at the intimacy of his gaze. "There's a small brown mole on the inside of your left leg," he said softly. "And a dark freckle on your right breast. And a scar on your heel from when you cut your foot on a rock one summer when you were a girl." He smiled at her dumbfounded expression. "Would you like me to go on? I can describe the color of your—"

"That's enough," Lara said swiftly, blushing hard. For the first time she allowed herself to really look at him, at the dark grain of his shaven whiskers, the hard jut of his chin, the lean hollows where his cheeks had once been round and full. "The shape of your face has changed," she said, timidly touching the edge of his high cheekbone. "Perhaps I would have recognized you if you hadn't lost so much weight."

He surprised her by turning his mouth in to her palm. As Lara felt the heat of his lips against her tender skin, she snatched her hand back reflexively.

"And your clothes are different," she continued, staring at the gray trousers stretched taut across his thighs, the worn white shirt, and the unfashionably narrow cravat around his neck. She had always seen Hunter dressed in the finest garments: broadcloth coats, embroidered brocade vests, breeches of leather or fine wool. His evening attire had been equally superb: crisp black coats, streamlined trousers or pantaloons, gleaming white linen shirts, stiffly starched collars and neckcloths, shoes polished with champagne.

Hunter smiled wryly at her close scrutiny. "I wanted a change of my old clothes at the Hall," he said, "but they seem to have been misplaced."

"Arthur and Janet disposed of everything."

"Including my wife, it seems." He glanced around the gamekeeper's cottage, his brown eyes turning cold. "My uncle will pay for putting you in such a place. I would have expected better of him than this, though God knows why."

"It's been comfortable enough—"

"It's not fit for a washwoman, much less my wife." Hunter's voice was as stinging as a whip, making Lara jump. Seeing the involuntary movement, he softened his gaze. "Never mind that. You'll be taken care of from now on."

"I don't want..." The words slipped out before

Lara could stop them. Horrified, she clamped her lips together and stared at her lap in silent misery. It was incredible, something beyond a nightmare. Hunter was home, and he would take charge of her life as he had before, crushing her independence like a flower beneath his booted foot.

"What is it, my love?" he asked quietly.

Startled, Lara stared into his serious face. "You never called me that before."

His hand slid around the slim curve of her throat, his thumb caressing the line of her jaw. He ignored the way she shrank from his touch. "I've had a great deal of time to think, Lara. I spent months convalescing in Cape Town, and then I went through the damned long voyage here. The more I remembered about you and our marriage, the more I realized what a selfish bastard I'd been. I promised myself that as soon as I returned to you, we would begin again."

"I don't think that's p-possible."

"Why not?"

"Too much has happened, and I . . ." Lara paused, swallowing hard, and tears sprang to her eyes. She struggled to keep them back, while guilt and unhappiness welled inside her. Why did Hunter have to come back? With one stroke of fate she had been sentenced once again to a life she had hated. She felt like a prisoner who had been set free, only to be closed behind bars again.

"I see." Hunter's hand fell away from her. Strangely, he was looking at her as if he *did* understand, though he had never been remotely perceptive.

"It won't be like before," Hunter said.

"You can't help what you are," Lara replied, a tear spilling down her cheek.

She heard Hunter's swift intake of breath, and felt his fingers brush away the salty drop. Lara jerked away, but Hunter leaned forward to close the distance between them. She was imprisoned in the chair, her head and neck wedged hard against the back of it.

"Lara," he whispered, "I would never hurt you."

"I'm not afraid of you," she said, and added with a touch of defiance, "I just don't want to be your wife again."

The old Hunter would have been annoyed by the sign of rebellion, would have subdued her with a few cutting words. Instead he looked at her with a calm calculation that made her unbearably nervous. "I'll see if I can change that. All I ask is that you give me a chance."

Lara gripped the arms of the chair tightly. "I would prefer to lead separate lives, as we did before you went to India."

"I can't oblige you, sweet." His reply was gentle, but she heard the finality in it. "You're my wife. I intend to resume my place in your life . . . and in your bed."

Lara blanched at that. "Why don't you go to Lady Carlyle?" she said desperately. "She'll be overjoyed at your return. She was the one you wanted, not me."

Hunter's expression became guarded. "She means nothing to me now."

"You loved each other," Lara said, wishing he would move away from her.

"It wasn't love."

"It was quite a convincing imitation!"

"Wanting to bed a woman isn't the same as loving her."

"I know that," Lara replied, forcing herself to look straight into his eyes. "You made it clear to me on many occasions."

Hunter absorbed her statement without comment. He rose to his feet in one smooth movement. As soon as she was freed, Lara sprang from the chair and went to the other side of the room, distancing herself from him as much as possible in the confines of the cottage.

Grimly Lara vowed to herself that she would never again welcome him into her bed. "I'll try to accommodate you in every way possible," she said, "except one. I can't see any reason for us to be intimate with each other. Not only did I fail to please you, but I'm barren. It would be better for us both if you found someone else to satisfy your needs."

"I don't want anyone else."

"Then you'll have to take me by force," she said, blanching as he approached her. It was impossible to read his expression. Was he angry? Was he contemptuous, or merely amused? His hands closed around her upper arms in a gentle but firm grip. Lara stared into his implacable face and felt all the old suffocating misery sweep over her.

"No," he replied softly. "I won't come to your bed until you're ready."

"That will be a long time. Forever."

"Perhaps." He paused and considered her thoughtfully. "Has there been another man in my absence?"

"No," she said with a choked laugh, stunned he would think that was the reason she didn't want him.

"My God, I wanted nothing to do with men after you left!"

He smiled ironically at the unflattering comment. "Good. I wouldn't have blamed you for turning to another man—but I can't stand the thought of anyone else touching you." He rubbed the back of his neck in a weary gesture, and Lara's attention was caught once more by the raised discolored line that betrayed a recently healed wound.

"Your head . . ." she murmured.

"The shipwreck," he said warily. "There was a powerful gale. We were tossed about until the ship was driven against a reef. My head hit something, but I'll be damned if I remember what it was. I couldn't recall my own bloody name for weeks afterward." He held still as she came closer.

Against her will, Lara experienced a great wave of sympathy. She couldn't help it—she hated the thought of him in pain. "I'm sorry," she said.

He grinned. "Sorry the wound wasn't mortal, I suspect."

Ignoring his mockery, she couldn't resist touching the ridged scar. Her fingers slid into his thick hair, exploring his scalp. The scar was a long one. The blow that had caused it must have nearly split his skull open. As she touched his head, she heard his breath catch. "Does it hurt?" she asked, instantly removing her hand.

He shook his head with a short laugh. "I'm afraid you're causing me another kind of pain."

Perplexed, Lara stared into his eyes, and her gaze dropped to his lap. To her mortification, she saw that her innocent touch had aroused him, causing a heavy, unmistakable ridge to strain against his trousers. Lara flushed and jumped back from him.

The remnants of his grin lingered. "Pardon, sweet. A year of celibacy has erased whatever self-control I may have once possessed." He gave her a look that made her insides knot with tension, and he extended a hand to her. "Now come with me, Lara. I want to go home."

Chapter 3

LARA WOULD HAVE liked to change into a fresh gown, but she had no intention of disrobing with her husband—for she was nearly certain he told the truth—present. She pinned up her hair as neatly as possible, conscious all the while of his intent gaze on her. When she had finished, he crossed the room and proffered his arm. "Shall we?" he asked with a quirk of one thick brow. "They're all waiting with bated breath to see if you'll come with me."

"Do I have a choice?" she asked.

He gave her a sardonic glance. "I'm not going to drag you there kicking and screaming."

Lara held back, sensing that if she took his arm and left with him, she would be committing herself to a course from which there was no retreat.

Dropping his courtly pose, Hunter reached for her hand, his long fingers wrapping around hers. "Come," he said, and they began the walk to Hawksworth Hall.

"It will take some time for the earl and countess to move their belongings," Lara said.

"They're not the earl and countess," he said shortly. "You and I are. And I'll have them out of Hawksworth Hall by this evening."

"Tonight?" Lara was stunned. "But you can't possibly send them away so soon."

"Can't I?" His face hardened, and he suddenly looked far more like the man she had married five years earlier. "I won't allow Arthur and Janet to disgrace my home another night. You and I will stay in the private family rooms."

"And Arthur and his wife will occupy the guest rooms?"

"No," he said inflexibly. "Let them stay here or find lodgings elsewhere."

Lara gave a spurt of horrified laughter at the thought. "That's going too far. We must offer them the guest rooms at the Hall."

"If this old gamekeeper's cottage was suitable for you, it's a damn sight too good for them."

"You won't get them out, in any event," Lara said. "They'll do everything in their power to paint you as an impostor."

"I'll get them out," he said grimly, and turned her to face him. "Tell me something before we reach the Hall," he said. "Do you still have doubts?"

"A few," Lara forced herself to admit, trapped by his smoky dark gaze.

"Do you intend to express them to the others?" There was no expression on his face.

Lara hesitated. "No," she whispered.

"Why not?"

"Because I . . ." She bit her lip and searched for a way to explain the inner sense that it was wrong somehow to deny him. The wisest course, it seemed, was to wait and see. If he wasn't the man he claimed to be, he would make a mistake sooner or later. "Because if you're not my husband," she said, "I will find out soon enough."

He smiled, though it contained no warmth. "Indeed," he said tersely, and they walked the rest of the way in silence.

"I'm impressed with what they've done with the place," Hunter said brusquely as they entered Hawksworth Hall. The antique Flemish tapestries and side tables bearing French porcelain vases had been replaced by nude marble statues and silk hangings in garish shades of peach and purple. The medieval fireplace, large enough to fit a dozen men inside, had been stripped of its original carved Flemish overmantel. Now a heavy mirror framed with golden trumpeting angels towered over the hearth.

Hunter paused to survey the full effect with a scowl "It's not everyone who can take an elegant home and decorate it like a brothel in such a short time."

"I wouldn't know," Lara replied. "I'm not as well acquainted with brothels as others are."

He grinned at the crisp rejoinder. "As I recall, you were more than happy for me to spend my nights in brothels rather than visit your bed."

Uncomfortably Lara returned her attention to the vulgar decor. "Unfortunately none of this can be changed now."

"Why not?"

"It would be wasteful."

"We can well afford the expense."

"You had better look through the estate books before you make any assumptions," Lara said in a low voice. "I suspect that our accounts have been depleted in your absence. Your uncle has extravagant habits."

Hunter nodded grimly and took her elbow as they went through the hall. He had an air of calm authority, seeming entirely comfortable in his surroundings. Surely an impostor would have displayed some sign of uncertainty, but he showed none.

Lara had never dreamed they would be together in this house again. She had closed away the memories of her life with him. But now he had come back with a suddenness that left her reeling. It was impossible to believe that he was here, even with his large hand on her arm and the taste of him lingering on her lips.

The area surrounding the double curving staircases was filled with at least fifty servants: housemaids, underbutlers, footmen, kitchen staff, hallboys and odd-job men. The servants greeted them with wondering exclamations, realizing that Lara's presence beside Lord Hawksworth was a positive confirmation of his identity. No doubt they were thrilled at the prospect of getting rid of Arthur and Janet, who were demanding and impossible to please.

The housekeeper stepped forward with a smile. "Lord Hawksworth," she said, her round, middle-aged face glowing, "I suspect we'll all need second and third glances to assure ourselves that it's really you. I find it nearly impossible to believe my own eyes. Welcome home, sir."

Her sentiments were echoed by the other servants, and Hunter smiled. "Thank you, Mrs. Gorst. After being away for so long, I doubt I'll ever want to leave

England again." He glanced over the crowd inquiringly. "Where is Mr. Townley?" he asked, naming a butler who had been in the Hawksworth service for at least a dozen years.

"I'm afraid he has engaged himself with another household, sir," came the housekeeper's cautious reply. "He didn't wish to remain in the employ of the current earl."

Hunter scowled and remained silent, while Mrs. Gorst continued hastily. "I hope you don't blame Townley overmuch, my lord. He was quite distressed at your death . . . that is—"

"I don't blame Townley," Hunter assured her, and guided Lara to the family receiving rooms. "Come, sweet. It's time I set my house in order."

"There he is!" a voice exclaimed as they entered the upstairs receiving room, and there was a chorus of excited cries. Arthur and Janet were there, of course, as well as Mr. Young, Dr. Slade, and some Crossland relatives who had come to see the stranger for themselves.

Arthur came forward before anyone else, regarding Hunter with contempt. "It seems you've gotten Lara to side with you." He turned his attention to her and sneered. "An ill-advised move, my dear. I'm surprised that you would be so easily convinced to help this scoundrel in his charade. You've revealed a weakness of character I hadn't suspected until now."

Lara returned his gaze without blinking. "It is no charade, my lord."

Mr. Young interceded calmly. "I assure you, Lord Arthur, in my opinion this man is indeed Hunter Cameron Crossland, Lord Hawksworth."

"No doubt he is paying for your support," Arthur

snapped. "Well, I intend to take up the matter with the courts. I will not allow an impostor to come forth and proclaim himself as the Earl of Hawksworth. To begin with, he bears only a passing resemblance to Hawksworth, who would have outweighed him by at least three stone!"

The man at Lara's side smiled. "It's no crime for a man to lose weight, Arthur."

Arthur gave him a derisive stare. "It must have been damned convenient for you to suddenly 'remember' that you were the inheritor of a large fortune."

Mr. Young interceded calmly. "All the evidence confirms this man's identity, Lord Arthur. We have tested his memory and found it to be accurate. We have identified special marks on his body, including the shoulder wound from a hunting accident when he was a boy. We have even examined samples of his handwriting, which closely resembles Lord Hawksworth's. His appearance, though altered, is consistent with the late earl's, and that, combined with the recognition of everyone who has seen him so far, proves that he is Hawksworth."

"*I* do not recognize him," Arthur said hotly. "Nor does my wife."

"But then, you have the most to lose if he *is* the earl," Dr. Slade pointed out, a cynical smile appearing on his leathery face. "Besides, his own wife accepts him, and a woman as honorable as the countess would never accept a stranger as her husband."

"Unless she stands to profit by it," Janet sneered, pointing a bony finger at Lara. "She would bed down with the first man available if it meant regaining the Hawksworth fortune."

Lara gasped in outrage. "I don't deserve such an accusation—"

"A young, pretty widow, starved for a man's attention," Janet continued sharply. "You've fooled a great many people with all your noble prattle about the orphanage, but I know what you really are—"

"Enough," Hunter said. There was a murderous gleam in his eyes that unnerved them all. He stared at Arthur with a vengeful gaze that caused the man to sweat visibly. "Get out of my sight," Hunter said. "Your belongings will be sent to you, unless you dare set foot on the estate. In that case, they'll be burned. Now leave—and count yourselves fortunate that I don't pay you back in full for what you've done to my wife."

"We've been nothing but generous to Lara!" Janet burst out. "What lies has she been spouting?"

"Out." Hunter took one step toward Janet, his hands raised as if to throttle her.

Janet hurried to the door, her eyes bulging with fear. "You have the manners of an animal," she spat. "Don't think your ruse will fool anyone—you're no more the Earl of Hawksworth than one of the dogs in the kennel is!" Arthur joined her in the doorway and they both left while excited murmurs rippled through the assemblage.

Hunter bent his head, his mouth close to Lara's ear. "I never meant for you to be left at their mercy. Forgive me."

Lara turned to stare at him in wonder. Hunter had never apologized to her for anything—he hadn't been capable of it. "There are moments when I almost agree with Janet," she whispered. "You're not at all like the man I married."

"Would you rather have me back the way I was?" he asked, too quietly for the others to hear.

Lara blinked in confusion. "I don't know." She backed away as the crowd swarmed around him, exclaiming over the miracle of his return.

The servants were in a muddle, scurrying to obey two masters as they packed some of Arthur and Janet's belongings. Hunter had not retreated from his position that the Crosslands must leave the estate at once—a humiliation that Lara knew they would never forgive. Janet stormed about Hawksworth Hall in explosive wrath, hurling orders and insults at everyone in her path.

Feeling lost and uneasy, Lara wandered through the house. Some of the upstairs informal rooms had been left in their original condition, serene and tasteful, the windows swagged in pale watered silk and velvet, the French furniture light and clean.

"Taking stock, are you?" came a silken voice from the doorway of the ladies' reading room, and Lara turned to see Janet standing there. With her thin frame held so stiffly, she seemed as hard and sharp as a knife blade.

Lara felt a twinge of pity for Janet, knowing that the loss of the title and estate was a devastating blow. For a woman of such overweening ambition, returning to the modest life she had known before must be difficult to bear. "I'm sorry, Lady Crossland," she said sincerely. "I know how unfair the situation must seem—"

"Spare me your false pity! You think you've won, don't you? Well, one way or another, we'll get the title back. Arthur is still the heir presumptive, and we have two sons—and as everyone knows, you're barren. Have you told *that* to the impostor claiming to be your husband?"

Lara's face turned white. "Have you no shame?"

"No more than you, apparently. How willing, how *eager*, you are to climb between the sheets with an absolute stranger!" Janet's face twisted into an ugly sneer. "For months you've played the martyr, with your angelic face and ladylike manners, while in truth you're nothing but a cat in heat—"

Her tirade was interrupted by an angry growl, and both women froze in surprise as a lean male form entered the room with the speed of a striking cobra. Hunter seized Janet and shook her, his countenance dark and wrathful. "Be glad you're a woman," he advised, "or I would kill you for what you just said."

"Let go of me!" Janet screeched.

"*Please*," Lara said, hurrying forward. "Hunter, don't."

His back stiffened at the sound of his name.

"There's no reason for a scene," Lara continued, approaching him. "No harm was done. Let her go, for my sake."

Suddenly he released Janet with a sound of disgust, and the woman fled the room.

Lara blinked in amazement as her husband turned toward her. It seemed that his entire body was filled with bloodlust. She had never seen such a savage look on Hunter's face. Even at his angriest, he had never lost the polished veneer that had been his birthright. But sometime between the day he had left for India and now, his civilized facade had cracked . . . and a very different man was emerging.

"Janet is a vindictive bitch," he muttered.

"She was speaking out of anger and pain," Lara said. "It meant nothing to me—" She broke off with a gasp as Hunter came to her in a few strides. One huge hand settled at her waist, while the other grasped her chin and tilted her head back. His assessing gaze moved over her face.

Lara moistened her dry lips with the tip of her tongue. She was aware of a disquieting pleasure that uncurled low in her stomach. Her breath turned choppy, and she stared at the broad chest before her face, remembering the solid feel of his body against hers, the exciting way he had kissed her.

Janet's accusations had hit their mark. Lara couldn't deny that she was attracted to this man, and that she had never felt this way about her husband. Was it because they had both changed? . . . or was it proof that this man wasn't Hunter?

Everything was happening too quickly. She needed to be alone to try to make sense of things. "Don't touch me," she whispered. "I can't bear it."

Hunter released her, and she fell back a step. His eyes were the most remarkable color, a glimmering shade of brown that appeared black in certain lights. Without doubt, they were Hunter's eyes . . . but they were filled with an intensity she had never seen before.

"How could you be my husband?" she exclaimed unsteadily. "But how could you be anyone else? I don't know what to think, or how to feel."

Hunter didn't flinch under her doubtful gaze. "If you don't accept me, go tell the others," he said. "It all rests on you. Without your support, I don't have a chance in hell of convincing anyone else of who I am."

Lara passed a hand over her moist forehead. She didn't want to make such a decision by herself, or to bear the responsibility for the mistake . . . if indeed it was a mistake. "We could wait for your mother to return from her travels," she said. "Once she learns about you, she'll come here as soon as possible. I will accept whatever she decides. A mother would certainly know her own son—"

"No." His face was like granite. "You decide. Am I your husband, Lara?"

"I suppose Mr. Young is right, that the evidence points to—"

"Damn the evidence. Am I your husband?"

"I can't be absolutely certain," she said, stubbornly refusing to give the yes or no that he wanted. "I never knew you very well. We weren't intimate in any way except physically, and even then . . " She faltered, her cheeks on fire.

"It was always impersonal," he acknowledged bluntly. "I had no damn idea of how to treat a wife in bed—I should have treated you like a mistress. I should have seduced you. The truth is that I was a selfish fool."

Lara dropped her gaze. "I wasn't the one you wanted."

"That wasn't your fault."

"You married me to have children, and I couldn't give you—"

"That has nothing to do with this," he interrupted. "Look at me, Lara." When she refused, he tangled his fingers at the back of her head, loosening the simple braided twist. "I don't give a damn if you conceive or not," he said. "It doesn't matter to me anymore."

"Of course it does—"

"I've changed, Lara. Give me a chance to show you how things can be between us." There was an endless moment of silence. Lara's gaze went to his firm, wide mouth, and she wondered in panic if he would kiss her again.

Suddenly he seemed to make a decision, and his hand swept down the front of her body in a caress so light and swift that she had no time to react. Her breast tingled from the fleeting brush of his palm. He lowered his mouth to her neck, his breath hot and soft on her throat. Lara gasped as he touched his tongue to her pulse. "You have skin like a child's," he whispered. "I want to undress you right here . . . hold you naked in my arms . . . love you the way I should have so long ago."

Lara's face flamed, and she tried to push him away, only to find that she had been caught securely against him in an unbreakable hold. His head moved, and he caught at the sensitive juncture of her neck and shoulder, biting gently through the cloth of her gown. Lara quivered at the erotic shock of it, her entire body arching. "Oh—"

"The Indians believe that a woman's life has no value or meaning without a husband," he said, pressing kisses over her throat and in the delicate hollow beneath her ear. A teasing note entered his voice. "They would consider you a very fortunate woman to have me return from the dead."

"I did very well without you," Lara replied, gripping his rock-hard shoulders as her knees wobbled.

She felt him smile against her ear. "In India you would have been burnt alive on my cremation pyre, to spare you the misery of living without me. It's called *sati.*"

"That's barbaric!" Her eyes closed as his hands found the tense curve of her buttocks through the folds of her skirts. "Please, I don't want—"

"Just let me touch you. It's been so long since I've held a woman."

"How long?" she couldn't help asking.

"More than a year."

She felt his palm slide up her spine in a savoring stroke. "What if a widow doesn't want to be burnt?" she asked breathlessly.

"She doesn't have a choice."

"Well, I was sorry to learn of your death, but I was hardly moved to commit suicide."

He laughed. "You probably considered yourself well off when you were told about the shipwreck."

"No," she said automatically, but to her horror, a guilty flush spread over her face.

Hunter drew back to look at her, and a wry smile touched his lips. "Liar," he said, before he took her mouth in a swift, glancing kiss.

"I really didn't—" Lara began uncomfortably, but he changed the subject with a speed that dazed her.

"I want you to have some new gowns made. I won't have my wife wearing rags."

Lara looked down at her black bombazine dress, gripping a loose fold of cloth. "But the expense," she said halfheartedly, thinking of how nice it would be to have some new clothes. She had become heartily sick of black and gray.

"The expense doesn't matter. I want you to dispose of every mourning gown you own. Burn them all, if you like." He fingered the material of her high neckline. "And order some negligees while you're about it."

In all her life, she had never worn anything but white cotton nightgowns to bed. "I don't need a negligee!" she exclaimed.

"If you don't have one made, I'll get it for you."

Lara pulled away from him and fidgeted nervously, plucking at her sleeves, her waist, her skirts. "I won't wear garments that are intended for seduction. I'm sorry if it displeases you, but . . . you must understand that I will never come to you of my own volition. I know it's difficult for a man to go without . . . and I know that you must have need of . . ." Lara felt herself blush until even her ears glowed. "I wish you would . . . that is, I hope . . ." She gathered whatever modicum of dignity was left at her disposal. "Please do not hesitate to go to another woman, to satisfy your masculine urges. I relinquish all claim on you, just as I did before you left."

Hunter wore a strange expression, as if he was insulted, amused, and annoyed all at once. "You won't be that fortunate this time, sweet. My masculine urges are going to be satisfied by one woman . . . and until you yield to me, I'll go without relief."

Lara lifted her chin in determination. "I will not be swayed on this point."

"Neither will I."

The air around them seemed to crackle with challenge. Lara's heart began a swift, heavy thudding, its rhythm resonating all through her. Her composure was further shaken when Hunter gave her a smile that held a disarming self-mockery.

She had never bothered to consider Hunter's attractiveness before. It hadn't mattered to her if he was handsome or not—he had been the match her parents had arranged, and she had accepted their judgment. Later the unhappiness of their marriage had eclipsed any consideration of his looks. But for the first time she realized that he *was* handsome, exceptionally so, with a trace of subtle charm that set her decidedly off-balance.

"We'll see how long either of us can last," he said. Lara's expression must have betrayed her thoughts, for Hunter laughed suddenly and slid her a provocative glance as he left the room.

Chapter 4

LATER THAT NIGHT, Hunter tried to focus on one goal—finding the journals—but his thoughts kept distracting him from the task at hand. Methodically he searched through the trunks that had been brought out of storage and set in his room. So far he had only discovered a few personal effects and some clothes that hung far too loosely on his lean frame.

He sighed tersely, his gaze sweeping over the ornate red and gold brocade that covered the walls. After the simple, sometimes primitive quarters he had occupied over the past year, including the sparsely furnished cabin on the endless voyage home, the overdecorated suite was an assault on his senses.

Stripping off his clothes, he donned a French brocaded silk robe he had discovered in one of the trunks. It had been tailored for a heavier man, but he folded back the wide front lapels and tied it snugly at his waist. Although it carried a stale smell from having been packed away so long, the fabric was soft and fine, made of woven brown and cream silk shot with gold stripes.

His attention returned to the tumbled contents of the trunks. He frowned, wondering where in hell the journals were. It was possible they had been discovered after his "death," and had either been destroyed or packed away somewhere else. He rubbed his jaw thoughtfully, scratching through the wiry bristle that had grown since that morning. He wondered if Lara had known about the journals.

There had been no sign of Lara since dinner. She had eaten little and retired early, darting away from him like a frightened rabbit. The servants had been remarkably unobtrusive, probably at the direction of the housekeeper, Mrs. Gorst. Most likely they all assumed that he was enjoying a long-awaited homecoming.

Unfortunately this would be the first of many nights to be spent in solitude. He would not force himself on an unwilling woman, no matter how badly he wanted her. It would take time and patience to win a place in Lara's bed. God knew she was worth the effort. Her response to his kiss that afternoon had been assurance enough on that point. She was decidedly reluctant, but not cold. For one moment she had responded to him with devastating sweetness and fire. Even now his flesh twitched and rose powerfully at the memory.

A grim smile curved his mouth as he struggled for self-control. One thing was clear—he'd been celibate for too long. At the moment any woman would have been sufficient to serve his needs, but he'd consigned himself to live like a monk, while his exquisitely beautiful wife slept only a few doors away.

He set his miniature of Lara on the semicircular table against the wall, and ran his finger lightly along the worn edges of the enameled frame. With an expert touch he opened the frame to reveal the delicate portrait inside. The familiar sight of her face soothed and refreshed him as always.

The portrait artist hadn't adequately captured the lushness of her mouth, the singular sweetness of her expression, the color of her eyes, like mist in a green meadow. No mere brush on canvas could have conveyed such things.

Lara was a rare woman with an unusual capacity for caring about others. Generous and easily entreated, she seemed to have a talent for accepting people with all their flaws. It would be easy for others to take advantage of her—she needed a man's protection and support. She needed a great many things he was all too willing to provide.

Experiencing a sudden urge to see her again, to reassure himself that he was really here with her, he left his room and went to the suite of three rooms adjoining his.

"Lara," he murmured, tapping the door lightly, alert to every sound and movement within. There was nothing but stillness. Repeating her name, he tested the door, discovering that it had been locked.

He recognized Lara's need to put some sort of barrier between them, but primitive masculine outrage sparked inside him. She was his, and he would not be denied access to her. "Unlock the door," he said, giving the knob a warning rattle. "Now, Lara."

Her response came then, in a higher-pitched voice than normal. "I-I don't wish to see you tonight."

"Let me in."

"You promised," she accused tautly. "You said you wouldn't force yourself on me!"

Hunter set his shoulder to the door and sent it bursting open, discovering that the small brass lock was more ornamental than useful. "There will be no locked doors between us," he said curtly.

Lara stood by the bed, her face stark white, slender arms wrapped tightly around herself. From her rigid posture, it was clear that she was using every ounce of self-control to keep from bolting. She looked like an angel, her body clad in layers of white muslin, her hair gathered in a dark shining stream over her shoulder. Remembering the firm tenderness of her breasts and hips in his hands, the sweetness of her mouth beneath his, Hunter felt a smoldering heat begin in his groin. He couldn't ever remember wanting a woman like this, craving the feel and scent and taste of her with every fiber of his being.

"Please leave," she said unsteadily.

"I'm not going to rape you, Lara," he said bluntly. "If that were my intention, I'd be on top of you now."

The crude words made her flinch. "Then why are you here?"

"I thought you might be able to tell me where the rest of my belongings are."

Lara considered the question for a moment. "Arthur sold or destroyed many of your things when he moved into the house," she said. "I wasn't in a position to object."

Hunter scowled, silently damning Arthur. He only hoped the bastard hadn't found the journals, or discovered the secrets they might contain . . . Better that they had been disposed of.

"I asked the servants to bring whatever was left to

your room," Lara murmured. "What are you looking for?"

He shrugged and kept his silence. There was a chance that the journals were hidden somewhere in the house. If so, he would rather not make Lara aware of their existence.

Wandering farther into the room, he noticed the way she backed away, preserving the distance between them. She looked lovely and wary, her small chin set defiantly. Her gaze darted over his robe, and she viewed the garment with such unease that he realized it had awakened some distasteful memory.

"What is it?" he asked gruffly.

A frown worked between her fine dark brows, pinching them together. "Don't you remember?"

He shook his head. "Tell me."

"You wore that the last time we . . . the last time you visited me." It was clear from her expression that the experience hadn't been particularly pleasant.

He heard himself mutter some sort of apology. They were bound in uncomfortable silence, while Hunter stared at his wife in a mixture of anger and regret, wondering how to erase the apprehension in her eyes.

"I told you it won't be like that again," he said.

"Yes, my lord," she murmured, though it was clear she didn't believe him.

Cursing beneath his breath, he paced across the Oriental carpet. He knew it would provide her with no end of relief if he left now, but he didn't want to just yet. It had been so long since he'd enjoyed any real companionship. He was lonely, and being in her presence was the only comfort he had, despite the fact that she had no great liking for him.

The room was decorated in the same florid style as his, only worse. The bed was a virtual monument, with carved and gilded end posts as thick as tree trunks, and valances heavy with gold and red beadwork. The ceiling was smothered in a pattern of golden shells and dolphin moldings ... not to mention a huge oval mirror framed with figures of bare-breasted mermaids.

Seeing where his attention wandered, Lara sought to break the tension with small talk. "Janet must have been very fond of her own reflection. Why would she want to watch herself going to sleep?"

Her innocence touched him. "I don't think sleeping was the activity the mirror was intended to reflect," he said dryly.

"You mean she wanted to look at herself during ..." Clearly the idea confounded Lara, and she turned scarlet. "But why?"

"Some people take pleasure in watching themselves during the act."

"But Janet doesn't seem to be the kind of woman who would ..."

"Never be surprised by what people do in the privacy of their bedrooms," he advised, coming to stand beside her.

He expected her to skitter away, but she held her ground and stared at him with those translucent green eyes. He sensed her curiosity, and the unvoiced suspicions in her mind. "Have you ever—" she began, and broke off abruptly.

"No, not beneath a mirror," he said matter-of-factly, though the notion stimulated him immensely. He imagined pushing Lara to the bed, lifting her nightgown, burying his head between her slim thighs while their entwined bodies were reflected overhead.

"I think it's a very silly idea," Lara said.

"My motto is, you shouldn't decide against something before you've even tried it."

A quick, almost reluctant laugh escaped her. "That motto could lead you into a great deal of trouble."

"So it has," he said ruefully.

Something about his expression told Lara that he was remembering some of his experiences in India, some of them not particularly pleasant. "Did you find what you were looking for in your travels?" she asked hesitantly. "The excitement and adventure you wanted so badly?"

"I found that excitement and adventure are damned overrated," he replied. "What I got from my travels was a new appreciation for home. For belonging somewhere." He paused, staring into her eyes. "For you."

"But how long will that last?" she asked quietly. "You'll become bored with this place and the people in it, and me, as you did before."

I'll want you forever, came a nagging, yearning voice from inside, startling Hunter with its insistence. He wanted this. He wanted her. He would take his place here and fight for it as long as he had breath left.

"Believe me," he said gruffly, "I could spend ten thousand nights in your arms and never grow bored."

She shot him a glance that was both uncomfortable and skeptical, and smiled. "After a year of celibacy, my lord, I think any woman would seem alluring to you."

She wandered to the dressing table and began to plait her hair, slender fingers combing through the smooth river of silk. It was a subtle signal for him to leave, but Hunter ignored it. Following her, he braced his shoulder against the wall and watched her. "Celibacy is an admired virtue among the Hindus," he remarked.

"Is it?" she responded with deliberate coolness.

"It demonstrates a man's mastery over himself and his environment, and brings him closer to true spiritual awareness. The Hindus practice self-control by covering their temples with erotic art. Visiting the temples is a test of faith and discipline. Only the most devout can view them without becoming aroused."

Lara concentrated on braiding her hair with scrupulous care. "Did you visit one of those places?"

"Naturally. I'm afraid I wasn't numbered among the devout."

"How surprising," Lara said in a gently acerbic tone that made him grin.

"I was informed by my companions that mine was the typical English response. The Hindus are far superior at mastering the limits of pleasure and pain, until they attain supreme control over their minds and bodies."

"Heathens," Lara said, finishing the braid.

"Oh, indeed. They worship many gods, including Shiva, Lord of Beasts and God of Fertility. I was informed that he has devised millions of sexual positions, although he's only told his followers of a few thousand."

"M-millions of . . ." Lara was sufficiently startled to turn toward him. "But there's only the one . . ." She stared at him, openly perplexed.

Hunter's enjoyment at teasing her faded, and he was suddenly at a loss for words, regarding her with an expression that must have matched her own. So that was what it had been like for her, a joyless, perfunctory act. No wonder she had welcomed him back with such reluctance.

"Lara," he said gently, "there were things I never showed you . . . things I should have done—"

"It's all right," she said uncomfortably. "Please, I don't wish to discuss our past—especially that part. I would like to go to sleep now. I'm very tired." She folded back the covers and linens, her small hands smoothing over the embroidered fabric.

Hunter knew he ought to leave then, but something impelled him to move forward and catch one of those slender hands. He brought it to his mouth, pressing her fingers over the contours of his mouth and chin, forcing her to accept the ardent kiss he placed in her palm. She quivered—he felt the vibrations that extended along her arm, but she didn't try to pull away.

"Someday you'll make a place for me beside you," he muttered, looking from her wide green eyes to the empty side of the bed. He released her slowly, and she rubbed her hand as if it were sore. "Did I hurt you?" he asked, frowning in concern.

"No, it's just . . . no." She held her hands to her sides, staring at him oddly.

Awareness caused a sharp pang inside him, and he shook his head with a rueful smile. He left the room at once, knowing that if he stayed a moment longer, he wouldn't be able to keep himself from taking her. As he closed the door behind him, he glimpsed her briefly as she stood without moving, her face a lovely mask.

Chapter 5

To Lara's consternation, the crowd of visitors they had received the previous day was nothing compared to the deluge that now overwhelmed Hawksworth Hall. It seemed that every one of the mansion's seventy-four rooms was filled to overflowing. Local political figures, gentry, and townspeople came to call, driven by curiosity and excitement over Hawksworth's return. Equipages with teams of four and six lined the long drive, while the servants' hall was filled with footmen and postilions in various shades of livery.

"Shall I turn them away?" Lara had asked Hunter in the morning, when the flood of guests was just beginning. "Mrs. Gorst can tell everyone that you are indisposed—"

"Send them in." He sat back in the library armchair with an air of anticipation. "I'd like to see some familiar faces from the past."

"But Dr. Slade prescribed rest and privacy for the next few days, until you adjust to being back home—"

"I've had months of rest and privacy."

Lara stared at him in bewilderment. Hunter, always protective of the family dignity, must be aware that it was only decent to keep themselves in seclusion for a few days and organize his reentry into society in a circumspect manner. "It will be a circus," she managed to say. "You can't let them all in at once."

Hunter wore a pleasant smile, but his tone was inflexible. "I insist on it."

He had proceeded to welcome any and all guests with a relaxed enjoyment that stunned Lara. Although Hunter had always been competent as a host, he had never seemed to take great pleasure in it, especially where the lesser gentry and plain townfolk were concerned. Dullards, he had referred to them contemptuously. Today, however, he had taken pains to welcome each of them with equal enthusiasm.

With easy charm, he regaled them with stories of his travels in India, carrying on two or three conversations at the same time, strolling through the gardens or the art gallery with a favored friend or two. As midday approached, he opened bottles of fine brandy and boxes of pungent cigars, while gentlemen gathered around him. At the back of the house, the kitchen clattered with the efforts of the staff as they labored to prepare refreshments for the multitude. Trays of delicate sandwiches, platters of preserved limes and figs, and plates of cakes were brought out and devoured eagerly.

Lara did her own share of entertaining, dispensing dozens of cups of tea and fielding questions from a gaggle of happily agitated women.

"What did you think when you first saw him?"

one woman entreated, while another demanded to know, "What were his first words to you?"

"Well," Lara said uncomfortably, "naturally it was a very great surprise—"

"Did you weep?"

"Did you faint?"

"Did he take you in his arms—"

Bemused by the onslaught of questions, Lara stared into her own cup of tea. All at once she heard her sister's dryly amused voice from the doorway. "I should think those things are none of our concern, ladies."

Lara glanced upward and felt close to weeping as she saw Rachel's sympathetic face. Rachel, more than anyone, understood what Hunter's return meant to her. Struggling to conceal her relief, Lara excused herself from the gossip circle and pulled Rachel out of the room. They stopped in the private corner beneath the grand staircase, and Rachel held Lara's hands in a comforting grip.

"I knew you'd have a surfeit of visitors," Rachel said. "I was going to wait until later, but I couldn't stop myself from coming."

"None of it seems real." Lara kept her voice low to avoid being overheard. "Things have changed so fast that I haven't had a moment to catch my breath. All of a sudden Arthur and Janet are gone, and I'm back here with Hunter . . . and he's a stranger."

"Do you mean 'stranger' in a figurative or literal sense?" Rachel asked gravely.

Lara gave her a startled glance. "You know that I wouldn't acknowledge him unless I believed him to be my husband."

"Of course, dear, but . . . he's not exactly the same,

is he." It was a statement, not a question.

"You've met him, then," Lara murmured.

"I happened to cross his path as he was walking with Mr. Cobbett and Lord Grimston to the smoking room. He recognized me on sight, and stopped to greet me with every semblance of brotherly affection. We drew aside and talked briefly, and he expressed his concern for all you've suffered in his absence. He asked after my husband, and seemed genuinely pleased when I told him that Terrell would come tomorrow." Rachel's face was wreathed in a perplexed pucker. "He seems to behave and react in a manner befitting Lord Hawksworth, but . . ."

"I know," Lara said stiffly. "He is not the same. It is only to be expected that he has been altered by his experiences, but there are things about him that I can't understand or explain."

"How has he treated you so far?"

Lara shrugged. "Very well, actually. He is trying to be agreeable, and . . . there is a sort of charm and perceptiveness about him that I don't remember from before."

"Odd, isn't it," Rachel commented thoughtfully. "I noticed the same thing—he's really rather dashing. The kind of gentleman that ladies swoon over. And he wasn't that way before."

"No," Lara agreed. "He's not like the man I knew."

"I'm curious as to what Terrell will make of him," Rachel said. "They were such close friends. If this man is a fraud . . ."

"He couldn't be," Lara said instantly. Her mind refused to accept the frightening possibility that she was living intimately with a consummate liar and actor the likes of which she had never encountered before.

"Larissa, if there is the slightest chance that he is an impostor, you could be in danger. You don't know what his past is, or what he might be capable of—"

"He is my husband." Lara remained resolute, though she felt herself turn a shade paler. "I'm sure of it."

"Last night, did he try to—"

"No."

"I suppose that when he holds you in his arms, you'll know whether he's the man you married or not."

As Lara tried to reply, she remembered the hot mist of his breath over her skin, the texture of his hair against her fingers, the spice of sandalwood in her nostrils. She had felt some strange, elemental connection between them. "I don't know who he is," she said in an uneasy whisper. "But I have to believe he's my husband, because that makes more sense than anything else. No stranger could know the things he does."

Evening approached and the guests lingered, despite Dr. Slade's misgivings. "He's had enough exertion for one day," the elderly doctor told Lara. Together they glanced at Hunter, who stood at a sideboard on a distant side of the drawing room. "It is time for him to rest, Lady Hawksworth."

Lara watched as her husband simultaneously poured a snifter of brandy and laughed at some quip one of his companions had made, and he seemed altogether comfortable ... until one noticed the faint strain around his eyes and the deepening brackets on either side of his mouth.

It had been a performance, she realized. A skillfully executed performance designed to win the support of the township . . . and it had been successful. He had been every inch the lord of the manor today: confident, hospitable, and polished. If his visitors had initially harbored suspicions as to his identity, very few of them doubted him now.

Lara felt a pull of compassion as she stared at him. In spite of the people surrounding him, he seemed very much alone. "He does look a bit fashed," she said to Dr. Slade. "Perhaps you could use your influence to coax him to retire."

"I've already made the attempt," the elderly man snorted, rubbing one of his long gray sideburns. "He's as bullheaded as ever. I expect he'll play the part of host until he drops from exhaustion."

Lara contemplated her husband. "He never has listened to anyone else's opinion," she agreed, feeling reassured that this, at least, was one thing that hadn't changed about Hunter. "However, I'll do what I can about the situation."

Adopting a pleasant smile, she approached Hunter and the three men standing with him. She started with the closest one, Sir Ralph Woodfield, a prosperous gentleman with a passion for hunting. "Sir Ralph," she exclaimed in delight, "it is a great pleasure to find you here!"

"Why, thank you, Lady Hawksworth," he responded heartily. "May I offer my congratulations on your good fortune? We've all sorely missed this fine fellow. I've no doubt you more than anyone are rejoicing over his return." A sly wink punctuated this sentence.

Lara colored at his effrontery. It was hardly the first of such remarks that had been made to her that day, as if the entire town of Market Hill considered her to be a love-starved widow. Concealing her annoyance, she smiled at him. "I am indeed blessed, sir. And so will others be, as soon as I tell you about the idea that came into my head recently. I am certain that you will adore it."

"Oh?" Sir Ralph cocked his head, her words seeming to penetrate the comfortable brandy-induced fog around him.

"I was thinking about your collection of Thoroughbreds, and the excellent care you give to your animals, and then it occurred to me . . . why doesn't Sir Ralph begin a home for old and crippled horses, right here at Market Hill?"

His jaw hung slack. "A-A home for—"

"A place for them to go when they become lame, ill, or otherwise unable to perform their duties. I'm certain it aggrieves you to know that so many loyal horses are needlessly destroyed after their years of service."

"Yes, but—"

"I knew you would be enthused about saving the lives of all those poor animals," she said. "You wonderful man. We will discuss this matter soon, and set out a course of action."

Clearly dismayed, Sir Ralph muttered something about going home to his wife, and bid them farewell as he slunk from the room.

Lara turned to the next gentleman, a confirmed bachelor of forty-five. "As for you, Mr. Parker, I've been lending your situation a good deal of thought."

"My situation," he repeated, his eyebrows converging until they formed a straight line across his forehead.

"I've worried, you see, over the fact that you're so bereft of companionship and all the care and comfort a wife provides . . . Well, I have found the right woman for you."

"I assure you, Lady Hawksworth, there's no need—"

"She's perfect," Lara insisted. "Her name is Miss Mary Falconer. The two of you are remarkably similar in character: independent, practical, opinionated . . . It's an ideal match. I plan to introduce you without delay."

"I am already acquainted with Miss Falconer," Parker said, his teeth grinding audibly. "An aging, ill-tempered spinster is hardly what I consider a perfect mate."

"Aging? Ill-tempered? I assure you, sir, Miss Falconer is an absolute angel. I insist that you reacquaint yourself with her, and you will see how mistaken you are."

Cursing beneath his breath, Parker took a hasty leave, throwing Hunter a dark look over his shoulder, as if commanding him to take his wife in hand. Hunter merely smiled and shrugged.

As Lara turned her benevolent attentions to the other guests, they suddenly found reasons to leave at once, quickly collecting hats and gloves and rushing to their carriages.

As the last visitor was taking his leave, Hunter joined Lara in the entrance hall. "You have a distinct talent for emptying a room, my love."

Not certain whether it was a compliment or complaint, she replied warily. "Someone had to get rid of them, else they would have stayed all night."

"Very well, you've banished our visitors, and you have me all to yourself. I'm interested to learn the rest of your plan for this evening."

Disconcerted by the teasing glint in his eyes, Lara twined her fingers in a knot. "If you would care to retire, I'll have a supper tray sent up to your room—"

"You're suggesting I go to bed early and alone?" His short grin both mocked and flirted with her. "I was hoping for a better offer than that. I believe I'll go to the library and write some letters."

"Shall I send your supper there?"

He shook his head briefly. "I'm not hungry."

"But you must eat something," she protested.

He regarded her with a smile that caused an odd, sweet flutter in her stomach. "It seems you're determined to feed me. All right, we'll have supper in the family parlor upstairs."

Thinking of the cozy area located so near to his bedroom, Lara hesitated and shook her head. "I would prefer the dining hall down here."

He scowled at the notion. "I would lose my appetite. I've seen what Janet did to the room."

Lara smiled ruefully. "An Egyptian motif is the latest craze, I'm told."

"Sphinxes and crocodiles," he muttered. "Serpents carved in the legs of the table. I thought the main hall was bad enough. I want everything restored to the way it was when I left. It's a damned strange homecoming when I can't recognize half the rooms here. Turkish tents, Chinese dragons, sphinxes . . . It's a nightmare."

Laura couldn't help laughing at his aggravated expression. "I thought so too," she confessed. "When I saw what they were doing to the house, I didn't know whether to laugh or cry . . . Oh, and your mother had a dreadful fit! She actually refused to set foot here again."

"I suppose that's one argument for keeping the place as it is," he said dryly.

Lara held her fingers to her mouth, but her merriment seeped out, the sound echoing against the marble walls.

Hunter grinned and took her hand before she had time to react. Clasping it lightly, he rubbed his thumb in her palm. "Come upstairs and have supper with me."

"I'm not hungry."

His hand tightened over hers. "You need to eat more than I do. I'd forgotten how tiny you are."

"I'm not tiny," she protested, tugging at her hand in the vain attempt to retrieve it.

"I could fit you in my pocket." He drew her a step closer, smiling at her discomfiture. "Come upstairs. You're not afraid to be alone with me, are you?"

"Of course not."

"You think I'll try to kiss you again. Is that it?"

Lara glanced around the entrance hall, afraid they would be overheard by a passing servant. "I don't care to discuss—"

"I won't kiss you," he said gravely. "I won't touch you. Now say yes."

"Hunter—"

"Say it."

A spurt of annoyed laughter escaped her. "All right, if it is so terribly important that we share a meal together."

"Terribly," he said softly, his teeth flashing in a triumphant smile.

Despite the changes Lord and Lady Arthur had made, they had kept the cook, for which Lara was grateful. The cook, Mrs. Rouillé, had been in the employ of the Hawksworths for more than a decade. Using French and Italian techniques, she prepared foods with a finesse that rivaled the best chefs in London.

Lara had become accustomed to the simple meals she had eaten in her cottage, or the pepper pots brought by a cook maid who had occasionally come from the village. It was a delight to sit down to a meal prepared at Hawksworth Hall once more. In honor of Hunter's homecoming, Mrs. Rouillé had prepared his favorite meal: spit-roasted partridge garnished with lemon, accompanied by creamed eggplant, boiled artichokes, and a steamed macaroni pudding covered with butter and shaved cheese.

"Oh, how I've missed this!" Lara could not help from exclaiming as the first course was brought to the table in the private parlor. She inhaled the heady aroma of fine cuisine and sighed. "I must confess, the greatest hardship was having to do without Mrs. Rouillé's cooking."

Hunter smiled, his face bathed in golden candlelight. It should have softened his countenance, but no trick of light or shadow could blunt the hard, elegant edges of his cheekbones or the insistent jut of his jaw. It disconcerted her to see her husband's face this way, so familiar and yet so altered.

Lara wondered if she had ever looked at him this closely, for this long, when they were married. She couldn't seem to avoid his gaze, so intense and restlessly searching, as if he were trying to learn every secret turn of her thoughts.

"I should have brought you some of the shipboard fare from my voyage home," Hunter remarked. "Salted dried meat, dried peas, and grog. Not to mention tough cheese and sour beer, and an occasional helping of weevils."

"Weevils!" Lara exclaimed in horror.

"They infested the hardtack." He laughed at her expression. "We learned to be grateful after a while— they carved perforations in the biscuit, which made it easier to break apart."

Lara made a face. "I don't want to hear about the weevils. You're going to spoil my supper."

"I'm sorry." He attempted to look contrite, reminding her of the mischievous boys at the orphanage. "We'll change the subject, then." His gaze fell to her bare left hand as she picked up a morsel of bread and broke it apart. "Tell me why you're not wearing the ring I gave you."

Lara stared at him blankly, then felt a quick shock of realization. "Oh, I . . ." She paused, stalling for time, while blood rushed to her cheeks.

"Where is it?" he prompted gently.

"I don't recall exactly . . ."

"I think you do."

Lara nearly choked on her guilt. The ring, a carved gold band, had been the only piece of jewelry he had ever given her. "It was wrong of me, but I sold it," she said in a rush. "I didn't have anything else of value, and I needed the money it would bring. I had no idea that you would ever know about it, or . . ."

"What did you need the money for? Food? Clothing?"

"Not for me, it was . . ." She took a deep breath and let it out in a controlled stream. "The children. At the orphanage. There are nearly forty of them, all different ages, and they need so many things. They didn't have enough blankets, and when I thought of the poor children shivering in their beds at night . . . I couldn't bear it. I went to Arthur and Janet, but they said . . . well, that doesn't matter. The fact was, I had to do something, and the ring was of no use to me." She looked at him apologetically. "I didn't know you were coming back."

"When did your involvement with the orphanage begin?"

"Just a few months ago, when Arthur and Janet were moving into Hawksworth Hall. They asked me to take up residence in the cottage, and I—"

"The title has only been theirs for two months."

Lara shrugged. "My insistence on staying would only have delayed the inevitable. And it was good for me to live in the cottage. I'd been sheltered and insulated for my entire life. When I was compelled to move out of Hawksworth Hall and live in humbler circumstances, it opened my eyes to the needs of the people around me. The orphans, and the elderly and ill, and those who are lonely—"

"I was told by more than one person today that you'd become something of the town matchmaker."

Lara colored modestly. "I've only helped in two

such situations. That hardly qualifies me as a match-maker."

"You were also described as a busybody."

"Busybody!" she exclaimed in indignation. "I assure you, I try never to intrude where I'm not wanted."

"Sweet Lara." There was a subtle flicker of enjoyment in his eyes. "Even your own sister admits that you can't resist trying to solve other people's problems. One afternoon a week you spend hours reading to a blind old woman—a Mrs. Lumley, I believe. You spend two full days at the orphanage, and another running errands for an elderly couple, and the rest of the time scheming and matchmaking, and prodding reluctant people into doing good works for others."

Lara was astonished that Rachel would have confided such things in him. "I wasn't aware that it was a crime to help someone in need," she said with as much dignity as she could marshal.

"What about *your* needs?"

The question was so intimate, so startling and yet unspecific, that Lara could only look at him in wide-eyed confusion. "I'm sure I don't know what you mean. I am fulfilled in every way. My days are filled with friends and interesting activities."

"Don't you ever want more?"

"If you mean have I desired to marry again, the answer is no. I have discovered that it is possible to lead a pleasant and productive life without being someone's wife." Some reckless inner impulse prompted her to add, "I didn't—I don't—like having a husband."

His face went smooth and serious. Lara thought

that he was angry with her, until he spoke in a tone filled with self-reproach. "My fault."

The flash of bitterness made her uncomfortable. "It was no one's fault," she said. "The truth is that we don't suit. We share none of the same interests, as you do with Lady Carlysle. Really, my lord, I think you should go to her—"

"I don't want Lady Carlysle," he said brusquely.

Lara picked up a fork and toyed with a morsel of partridge, but her former pleasure in the food had dissipated. "I am sorry about the ring," she said.

He waved the words away with an impatient gesture. "I'll have another made for you."

"There's no need. I don't want another." Lara sent him a discreet but steady glare, her entire body simmering in rebellion. Now he would command and crush her into compliance. But he held her gaze and sat back in his chair, contemplating her as if he found her a fascinating puzzle.

"I'll have to tempt you, then."

"I have no interest in jewelry, my lord."

"We'll see about that."

"If you desire to dispose of money—and I doubt that there is much left for you to spend—it would please me for you to make improvements to the orphanage."

He glanced at her left hand, her fingers clenched around the silver fork as if it were a weapon. "The orphans are fortunate to have such a dedicated patroness. Very well, make a list of what you require for the place, and we'll discuss it."

Lara nodded and removed the linen napkin from her lap. "Thank you, my lord. If you'll excuse me, I'd like to retire now."

"Before dessert?" He gave her a chiding glance, and grinned. "Don't tell me you've lost your sweet tooth."

Lara couldn't help returning his smile. "I still have it," she admitted.

"I asked Mrs. Rouillé to make a pear tart." Hunter stood and went to her chair, settling his hands on her shoulders as if to keep her there forcibly. Leaning close to her ear, he lowered his voice and murmured, "Stay for just one bite."

The velvet rasp of his voice made her shiver. He must have felt the tiny movement, for his fingers tightened on her shoulders. Something about his touch disturbed her profoundly, a gentle strength, a sense of ownership that she balked at. She made an automatic gesture to push him away, but as she felt the warm, hair-dusted backs of his hands, she paused. She couldn't seem to stop herself from exploring the shape of his long bones, the hard angles of his wrists. His fingers flexed, like a cat kneading its paws, and she drew her hands over his in a tentative sweep. The moment spun out, the silence deepening until the only sound that broke it was the tiny sputter of the candle flames.

From somewhere above her head, she heard Hunter's shaky laugh, and he pulled back as if she had burned him.

"I'm sorry," Lara said softly, her face reddening with surprise at her own actions. "I don't know why I did that."

"Don't apologize. In fact . . ." He knelt by her chair, staring at her. His voice was low and a bit unsteady. "I wish you would again."

She was mesmerized by the fire-swept darkness of

his eyes. He held very still, as if encouraging her to touch him, and she clenched her fist in her lap to keep from reaching out. "Hunter?" she asked in a whisper.

His face changed, the illusion of perfectly cast bronze dispelled by a crooked grin. "You always say my name as if you're wondering who I really am."

"Perhaps I am."

"Who could I be, then?"

"I don't know," she replied soberly in the face of his teasing. "Long ago I used to dream . . ." Her voice died away as she realized what she had been about to reveal. He had such a terrible power over her, making her want to tell him her secrets, to be vulnerable to him.

"What did you dream, Lara?"

She had dreamed of a man like the one he seemed to be . . . she had dreamed of being wooed, charmed, caressed . . . things she had never dared to confess even to Rachel. But those fantasies had faded when she had met Hunter, and she had learned the reality of marriage. Duty, responsibility, disappointment, pain . . . loss.

She didn't realize that her emotions showed on her face until Hunter spoke wryly. "No dreams left, I see."

"I'm no longer a young bride," she replied.

He gave a short laugh. "No, you're an ancient matron of twenty-four, who knows how to manage everyone's life but her own."

Pushing back from the table, Lara left her chair and faced him as he stood. "I've managed my affairs quite well, thank you!"

"So you have," Hunter said, all mockery gone.

"And I intend to do better this time. I'm going to make a settlement on you, so that if anything ever happens to me—again—you'll be provided for in a suitable manner. No more hovels and ill-fitting gowns and shoes with holes worn through them."

So he had even noticed the soles of her shoes. Was there anything that escaped his notice? She strode to the door and opened it, pausing to look back at him. "I shan't stay for dessert—I couldn't eat another bite. Good night, my lord."

To her relief, he didn't follow her. "Pleasant dreams," he murmured.

Her mouth curved in a forced smile. "For you as well."

She left quietly, closing the door behind her.

Only then did Hunter move, wandering to the portal, his large hand clasping the oval brass knob that she had just touched, searching for any remaining warmth her skin might have imparted. He leaned his cheek against the cool, glossy panel and closed his eyes. He craved her body, her sweetness, her hands on his body, her legs open to him, her throat tightening with feminine cries as he pleasured her . . . He shoved the thoughts away, but it was too late, he was left with a painful erection that wouldn't subside.

How long would it take for her to accept him? What the devil would she require? If only she would assign him some herculean task for him to accomplish and prove himself. *Tell me what to do*, he thought, emitting a slight groan, *and by God, I'll do it ten times over.*

Disgusted by his maudlin longing, he pushed away from the door and went to the Chippendale mahogany sideboard, its serpentine front adorned by delicate gilded swags and carved leaves. A silver tray had been placed on the top, laden with cut-glass decanters and snifters. He poured a healthy splash of brandy for himself and downed it at once. .

Hanging his head, Hunter waited for the smooth fire in his throat to spread through his chest. He braced his hands on the top of the mahogany cabinet, fingers curving over the edges . . . and then he felt it. A tiny, nearly undetectable hinge at his fingertips. Curiosity prickled along his nerves. Removing the silver tray and glasses, he set them on the floor and felt underneath the top of the sideboard in a search for hinges and latches. Locating an irregularity in the wood, he pressed inward, felt it give, heard a click. The top of the sideboard loosened, and he lifted it free.

A secret compartment—and what it contained made him sigh in sudden relief.

Just then a footman entered the room to remove the plates and bring dessert. "Not now," Hunter barked. "I want to be alone."

The servant closed the door with a muffled apology. Letting out an explosive breath, Hunter scooped up the pile of thin, leather-bound journals that had been stored in the sideboard's false top, carried them to the chair by the fire, and sorted them in the correct order.

He began to read, scanning the pages rapidly. As he absorbed the neatly written lines, he tore out the finished pages in sheaves of two or three, and fed them to the fire. The flames danced and crackled in anticipation, flaring up with each new addition. Every now and then Hunter paused thoughtfully, staring into the grate . . . watching the words that blazed and shrank into ashes.

Chapter 6

LARA ENTERED THE breakfast room and felt a stab of apprehension when she saw that Hunter was there. He sipped a cup of black coffee—the way he had always taken it—and set aside a copy of the *Times* as he beheld her. The footman in attendance brought Lara a cup of chocolate and a plate of strawberries, and left for the kitchen while Hunter seated her.

"Good morning," he murmured, his gaze sweeping over her face, not missing the shadows beneath her eyes. "You didn't sleep well."

Laura shook her head. "I lay awake for the longest time."

"You should have come to me," he said, his face innocent except for the devilish spark in his brown eyes. "I could have helped you to relax."

"Thank you, no," Lara said promptly. She lifted a strawberry to her lips, but before she tasted it, a sudden laugh choked her, and she set down her fork.

"What is it?" Hunter asked.

She pressed her lips together, but that only worsened her giggles. "You," she gasped. "I'm afraid you're in desperate need of a tailor."

80

Hunter had donned some of his old clothes, and he was swamped in folds of extra fabric, his jacket and waistcoat hanging loose, his baggy trousers held up by some miracle she didn't care to speculate on. An answering grin appeared on his face, and he spoke in a rueful tone. "I like to hear you laugh, sweet. Even when I'm the target."

"I'm sorry, I . . ." Lara dissolved in another burst of merriment. She pushed back her chair and went to him, unable to keep from investigating further. She pulled at the loose wads of material at his sides and waist. "We can't have you go about looking like this . . . Perhaps a few stitches here and there would help . . ."

"Whatever you suggest." He leaned back in his chair and smiled as she continued to fuss over him.

"You look a complete vagabond!" she exclaimed.

"I *have* been a vagabond," he said. "Until I came home to you."

Lara's gaze met his. His dark eyes gleamed with amusement. Her breath caught as she accidentally touched the hard surface of his midriff, his heat filtering through the thin linen shirt. She snatched her hand back at once. "Excuse me, I—"

"No." He caught her wrist swiftly, enclosing it in a gentle grip.

They stared at each other, frozen in a quiet tableau. Hunter exerted only a light tension on her wrist. It would be so easy for him to pull her forward, bring her tumbling into his lap, but he held still. It seemed as if he were waiting for something, his expression arrested, his chest rising and falling in a rhythm much faster than normal. Lara sensed that if she took one step toward him, he would pull her into his arms . . . Her nerves clamored with excited alarm at the prospect. She looked at his mouth, remembered the warmth and taste of him . . . Yes, she wanted him to kiss her . . . but before she could move her leaden feet, Hunter released her with a crooked smile.

Lara expected to feel relief, but instead she was flooded with disappointment. Troubled by her inexplicable reactions to him, she went back to her chair and bent her head over the plate of strawberries.

"I'll be leaving for London tomorrow morning," she heard Hunter say casually.

Startled, she glanced at him. "So soon? But you've only just arrived."

"I have business to take care of, including a meeting with Mr. Young and our bankers and solicitors." At her questioning expression, he added, "To arrange for some loans."

"We're in debt, then," Lara said gravely, not surprised by the news.

Hunter nodded, his mouth twisting. "Thanks to Arthur's mismanagement."

"But to arrange for more debt?" she asked hesitantly. "Won't that encumber the estate beyond all reason?"

He gave her a brief, reassuring smile. "It's the only way to climb out. Don't worry, madam—I have no intention of failing you."

The pucker on her forehead remained, but when she spoke again, it concerned a far different matter. "Is that the only reason you're going to London? I suppose you'll want to see some old friends as well." She paused and sipped at her chocolate in a show of unconcern. "Lady Carlysle, for example."

"You keep mentioning her name," he commented.

"It's hardly flattering, this desire of yours to push me into the arms of another woman."

"I was merely asking." Lara didn't know what had prompted her to bring up the subject. She forced herself to eat another strawberry as she waited.

"I told you I don't want her," he said flatly.

Lara struggled against a senseless feeling of gladness at the information. Her mind pointed out that it was to her benefit if Hunter renewed his affair with Lady Carlysle, thus sparing her from his unwanted attentions. "It is only to be expected that you would pay her a visit after having been gone for so long," she said. "At one time you cared for each other very much."

Hunter scowled and pushed back from the table. "If this is the direction of your breakfast conversation, I believe I'll occupy myself elsewhere."

As he stood up, there was a respectful tap on the door, and the senior footman's impassive face appeared. "Lord Hawksworth, there is a caller." At Hunter's nod, the footman brought a card on a silver tray.

Hunter read the card with an impassive expression. "Send him in," he said. "I'll receive him here."

"Yes, my lord."

"Who is it?" Lara asked as the footman departed.

"Lonsdale."

Rachel's husband. Lara stared at Hunter curiously, wondering why his reaction should be so matter-of-fact, even unenthusiastic. For years Terrell, Lord Lonsdale, had been one of Hunter's best friends, and yet Hunter's face was that of a man confronted with an unwanted duty. Hunter watched the door, and as soon as the sound of footsteps approached, a smile appeared on his lips . . . but it wasn't natural. It was the expression of an actor preparing himself for a performance.

Lord Lonsdale entered the room, his face glowing with anticipation and happiness—unusual for Lonsdale, who was known for his moodiness. There was no doubt of his genuine gladness to see Hunter again. "Hawksworth!" he exclaimed, striding forward to seize him in a brief, bearlike embrace.

The two men laughed and pulled apart to survey each other. Although Lord Lonsdale was above average height, he didn't quite reach Hunter's towering build. He was robust and muscular, though, and had a love of riding and sporting that rivaled Hunter's. Dark-haired and fair-skinned, with deep blue eyes inherited from an Irish grandmother, Lonsdale was a handsome and engaging man—when he wished to be. Other times he allowed his famous temper to explode out of control, frequently with unpleasant results. He always apologized afterward with a charm and sincerity that made everyone forgive him. Lara would have liked him much more if he were not married to her sister.

"My God, man, you're half the size you were!" Lonsdale exclaimed, laughing. "And as dark as a savage."

"And you're the same," Hunter replied with a grin. "Exactly the same."

"I should have known you'd cheat the devil his due." Lonsdale stared at him with open fascination. "You're so altered. I'm not certain I would have recognized you, except that Rachel told me what to expect."

"It's good to see you, old friend."

Lonsdale responded with a smile, but his penetrating stare did not waver from Hunter's face. Lara could understand the reason Lonsdale's pleasure suddenly seemed to dim. Lonsdale was no fool, and he was confronted with the same dilemma that everyone else faced. If this man was indeed Hunter, he was greatly changed . . . and if he was a stranger, he was an astonishingly convincing replica.

"Old friend," Lonsdale repeated cautiously.

As if sensing the man's anxious desire for proof, Hunter let out a coarse laugh that made Lara flinch. "Let's have a drink," he said to Lonsdale. "I don't care what the hour is. I wonder if there's a bottle of Martell 'ninety-seven left, or if my damned thieving uncle finished every drop."

Lonsdale was instantly reassured. "Yes, the Martell," he said with a bark of happy relief. "You remembered my liking for the stuff."

"I remember a certain evening at the Running Footman when your liking for the stuff nearly got us beaten senseless."

Lonsdale was nearly overcome with laughter. "I was as drunk as a mop! With quite an itch for that whore in the red gown—"

Hunter interrupted with a warning cough. "Let's save that reminiscence for a time when my wife isn't present."

Just then noticing Lara's presence, Lonsdale sputtered an apology. "Forgive me, Larissa . . . I was so shocked by the sight of Hawksworth, I'm afraid I took no notice of anything else around me."

"That is quite understandable," Lara said with a failed attempt at a smile. Witnessing the two men together recalled a host of unhappy memories. It seemed that they encouraged each other's worst traits: selfishness and a sense of masculine superiority that she found insufferable. She glanced uneasily at Hunter. If he wasn't her husband, he possessed a chameleonlike ability to become whatever others expected him to be.

Lonsdale gave her a deceptively solicitous smile. "My dear sister-in-law . . . tell me, how is it to have your dear departed come back home?" There was a mocking gleam in his blue eyes. He had, of course, known about their loveless marriage, and he had encouraged Hunter's infidelities.

Lara answered without looking at either of them. "I'm very pleased, of course."

"Of course," Lonsdale jeered. Hunter laughed with him, and their hearty amusement made Lara tense with resentment.

However, when she witnessed Hunter looking at Lonsdale in an unguarded moment, it seemed that he was none too fond of the man. What in heaven's name was going on?

Bewildered, Lara remained at the breakfast table and toyed with the remains of her meal while the men took their leave. Hunter would surely drive her mad. Was she to trust the evidence before her eyes, or her constantly shifting feelings? All of it was contradictory. She reached to his empty place and picked up his cup, touching where his hands had touched, her fingers curving around the delicate china.

Who is he? she thought, filled with frustration.

As he had indicated, Hunter left early the next day. He came to Lara's room just as she began to awaken, the morning sun slipping through a space between the closed drapes and stealing across her pillow. She started as she realized that she wasn't alone in the room, and jerked the covers high under her chin.

"Hunter," she said, her voice raspy from sleep. She shrank deep into her pillow as he sat on the edge of the bed.

A smile touched his dark face. "I couldn't leave without seeing you one last time."

"How long will you be gone?" She blinked uneasily, not daring to move as Hunter reached for the sable length of her braid.

"No more than a week, I expect." He pulled the braid across his palm as if enjoying the texture against his skin, and laid it back on the pillow with care. "You look so snug and warm," he murmured. "I wish I could join you."

The thought of him climbing under the covers with her made her heart contract in alarm. "I wish you a safe trip," she said breathlessly. "Good-bye."

Hunter grinned at her eagerness for him to leave. "Aren't you going to give me a farewell kiss?" He leaned over her, smiling into her startled face, and waited for a reply. When she remained silent, he laughed softly, his coffee-scented breath fanning over her chin. "All right. We'll put it on account. Good-bye, sweet."

Lara felt his weight leave the bed, and she continued to bunch the covers tightly under her chin until the door had closed behind him. In a few minutes she sprang from bed and hurried to the window. The Hawksworth equipage with its perfectly matched team of four and distinctive green and gold coachwork rolled away along the tree-lined drive.

There was a strange mixture of feelings inside her:

relief at his departure but also a touch of sadness. The last time Hunter had left her, she had somehow known that she would never see him again. How was it that he could have made his way back home?

Chapter 7

A STONE'S THROW away from the prosperous shopping area of the Strand, there was a series of alleys and courts that led to the slums of the London underworld. It was densely populated by a class of people with no homes, no regular means of supporting themselves, no recognition of marriage or family life or anything close to morality. The streets were sour with dung and littered with rats, their dark shapes slipping in and out of buildings with ease.

Night was falling fast, the last feeble rays of the sun disappearing behind the ramshackle structures. Grimly Hunter shouldered his way past prostitutes, thieves, and beggars, until the winding street led him to the marketplace he sought. It was a bustling place, featuring stolen carcass meat and other purloined goods. Costermongers hawked shrunken fruits and vegetables from barrows or primitive stalls.

A brief memory assailed him—wandering through an Indian market every bit as squalid, except the smells were different: the scents of peppery grain and spices, the fecund odor of rotting mangoes, the sweet whiff of poppy and opium, all underlaid with the peculiar pungency that belonged to the East. He didn't miss Calcutta, but he did miss the Indian countryside, the wide earth roads lined with swaths of elephant grass, the tangled forests and quiet temples, the sense of languid ease that permeated every aspect of life.

The Indians thought that the English were an unclean race, beef eaters, ale drinkers, filled with lust and materialistic desires. Casting a sardonic glance at the scene around him, Hunter couldn't suppress a quick grin. The Indians were right.

A drunken hag plucked at Hunter's sleeve, imploring him for a spare coin. He shrugged her away impatiently, knowing that if he showed any sign of mercy, all the beggars in the vicinity would throw themselves at him. Not to mention pickpockets, who were forming in groups and staring at him like jackals.

By necessity the market was opened under cover of night, though any police would have been insane to venture there. The area was lit with gas flares and smoking grease lamps, making the air thick and pungent. Hunter narrowed his eyes against the irritating haze and paused by an oddly dressed man seated on a rickety stool. The dark-skinned man, French-Polynesian in appearance, was dressed in a long blue velveteen coat with carved bone buttons. A strange design had been inked on his cheek, an exotic bird in flight.

Their gazes met, and Hunter indicated the mark on the man's face. "Can you do that?" he asked, and the man nodded.

"It is called *tatouage*," he replied in a liquid French accent.

Hunter reached in his coat pocket and pulled out a scrap of paper . . . the last remaining trace of the journals. "Are you able to copy this?" he asked brusquely.

The Frenchman took the design and examined it closely. "*Bien sur* . . . it is a simple design. It will not take long."

Picking up his stool, he carried it with him as he walked away, gesturing for Hunter to follow. They walked from the market to a streetside cellar, lit by guttering candles that filled it with a lurid orange glow. Two copulating couples were busy on rickety wooden cots. A few whores of varying ages lingered outside the cellar, beckoning to potential customers.

"Out," the Frenchman said briskly. "I have a customer." The whores cackled and cawed, moving away from the doorway. The Frenchman cast Hunter a vaguely apologetic glance while the couples inside finished their transactions. "It's my room," he said. "I let them use it in return for a share of the profits."

"An artist and a pimp," Hunter commented. "You're a man of many talents."

The Frenchman paused, clearly deciding whether to be amused or offended, and finally laughed. He led Hunter down into the cellar and went to a table in the corner, setting out an assortment of tools, pouring dishes of ink. "Where would you like the design?" he asked.

"Here." Hunter pointed to the inside of his upper arm.

The man raised his brows at the location, but nodded in a businesslike manner. "Remove your shirt, *s'il vous plaît*."

A group of four or five whores lingered in the cellar, ignoring the man's curt command for them to leave. " 'Andsome devil," a girl with garish red hair remarked, flashing him a friendly smile loaded with decaying teeth. "Care for a toss after Froggie's done?"

"No, thanks," Hunter said easily, though he was inwardly repulsed. "I'm a married man." That comment earned screams of delight and appreciation.

"Ohh, he's a darling!"

"I'll toss you for *free*," a large-breasted blonde offered, giggling.

To Hunter's discomfort, the whores stayed to watch him remove his jacket, waistcoat, and shirt. As soon as the baggy linen shirt was stripped away, they erupted in peals of admiration.

" 'Ere's a 'andsome bit o' beefsteak, dearies!" one of them cried, and ventured forward to touch his bare arm. "Jaysus, 'ave a look at those muscles. Built like a bloody bull, 'e is!"

"With a nice, tight breadbasket," another said, poking at his flat stomach.

"What's this?" The redhead had found the scar on his shoulder, another on his side, and the star-shaped one on his lower back. She made a cooing sound and examined the marks curiously. "Seen a bit o' action, 'ave ye?" she asked, favoring him with an approving smile.

Although Hunter kept his features emotionless, he felt a flush spreading over his face. Delighted by his obvious discomfort, the whores continued to giggle and tease, until at last the *tatouage* artist was finished with his preparations and ordered them out.

"I can't work with this noise," the Frenchman complained. "Out, girls, and don't come back until I'm finished."

"But where do I take the cock-stands?" one of them said plaintively.

"The alley wall," came the decisive reply, and the prostitutes filed out in a surly line.

The *tatouage* artist looked at Hunter assessingly. "You might find it more comfortable to lie on the cot while I proceed, monsieur."

Hunter glanced at the semen-stained ticking on the bed and shook his head in distaste. He sat on the stool and lifted his arm, bracing his shoulders back against the wall.

"D'accord," the Frenchman conceded. "But I warn you, if you move or flinch, the design will be flawed."

"I won't move." Hunter watched as the man approached him with two ivory instruments, one of them fitted with a short needle. After studying the drawing on the paper Hunter had given him, the Frenchman dipped the needle in a dish of black ink, placed it against Hunter's skin, and tapped it with the other instrument.

Hunter stiffened at the fiery sting. Once again the *tatouage* artist dipped the needle and tapped it into his skin, this time creating a long chain of pinpricks. It was the repetition that soon proved excruciating. Each sting in itself was nothing, but endless lines of them, accompanied by the maddening clicking of the bone instruments, made his nerves screech in protest. He felt sweat collecting on his forehead, stomach, even his ankles. Soon it felt as if his arm had been set on fire. He concentrated on breathing steadily, in and out, willing himself to accept the burn instead of fighting it.

The Frenchman paused, allowing him a moment of respite. "The pain makes most men weep, no matter how they fight it," he commented. "I've never seen anyone bear it so well."

"Just get on with it," Hunter muttered.

Shrugging, the Frenchman picked up the instruments. "*Le scorpion* is an unusual design to choose," he said, while the delicate click click of the needle resumed. "What meaning does it have for you?"

"Everything," Hunter said, his teeth clenching until his jaw ached.

The Frenchman paused as the needle hit a sensitive nerve that made Hunter twitch. "Please hold still, monsieur."

Hunter remained steady and dry-eyed. He thought of the future that beckoned before him—of Lara—and the work of the needle became welcome indeed. For what he wanted, this was a small price to pay.

Chapter 8

ACCORDING TO HUNTER'S instructions, Lara engaged the services of a designer, Mr. Smith, to change the interiors of Hawksworth Hall. Accompanied by the estate manager, Mr. Young, Lara showed Smith on a tour of the house.

"As you can see, Mr. Smith," she said with laughing dismay, "my claim that this will be the greatest challenge of your career is not far off the mark."

Smith, a heavyset gentleman with a long mane of gleaming silver-white hair, grunted noncommittally and scribbled in a small notebook with gilt-edged pages. Although his real name was Mr. Hugh Smith, he was known as "Possibility" Smith, having earned the nickname from his famous habit of saying, "This place has distinct possibilities." So far Lara had waited in vain for the magic phrase to appear.

She had taken him on a survey of the Egyptian dining room with its sarcophagus-shaped cabinets, the baroque entrance hall, the Chinese parlors filled with faux carved bamboo, and the Moroccan ballroom lined with marble blackamoors dressed in pink togas. With each new room he beheld, Possibility Smith's countenance became darker and his silence deepened.

"Is it worth saving, do you think?" Lara asked in a lame attempt at humor, "or shall we just burn the place to the ground and start over?"

The silver-maned head turned toward her. "For sheer bad taste, it is unrivaled by any residence I've ever had the misfortune of viewing."

Mr. Young interceded tactfully. "Let me assure you, sir, that Lady Hawksworth possesses exquisite taste, and had no hand in this decor."

"Let us hope not," Smith muttered, and sighed. "I must have another look at that ballroom. Then we'll visit the next floor." He wandered away, shaking his head in regal disapproval.

Lara put a hand over her mouth, stifling a laugh as she imagined his expression when he crossed the threshold of her multimirrored bedroom. Oh, she should have had the servants remove the one on the ceiling before he saw it!

Regarding her pinkening face, Mr. Young gave her a sympathetic smile. "Lord and Lady Arthur certainly left their mark, didn't they?"

Lara nodded, her eyes twinkling. "I'm afraid we can't afford the expense of changing everything . . . but how is anyone to live in such a horror?"

"I shouldn't worry about the expense for long," Mr. Young said comfortingly. "The earl discussed some of his plans with me, and I was quite impressed. With some reorganization of his properties, a much-needed loan, and a few sound investments, I believe the estate will be more prosperous than ever."

Lara's amusement faded, and she stared at him curiously. "Do you find the earl much as he was before, then?"

"Yes . . . and no. In my humble opinion he's improved. It seems to me that Hawksworth has a greater sense of responsibility and financial acuity than he once did. He was never much interested in his business affairs, you know. At least, not as much as he was in fox-hunting and grouse-shooting—"

"I know," Lara said, rolling her eyes. "But what is to account for his altered character? And do you think the change is permanent?"

"I believe it is only natural, after what he has been through," Mr. Young continued matter-of-factly. "To be reminded so forcibly of his mortality—to see what has become of his family and property in his absence—it is actually a great gift. Yes, I believe the change is permanent. The earl now realizes how much he is needed by all of us."

Rather than argue that she didn't need Hunter's presence in her life, Lara nodded shortly. "Mr. Young . . . are there any questions in your mind as to his identity?"

"No, not in the least." He seemed startled by the idea. "Don't tell me that you doubt him?"

Before she could reply, Possibility Smith rejoined them in the large hall. "Well," he said with a huge sigh, "let's get on with the rest of it."

"Mr. Smith," Lara commented wryly, "you seem rather aghast."

"I was aghast at least an hour ago. Now I'm horrified." He crooked his arm for her to take. "Shall we proceed?"

* * *

Mr. Smith and two assistants remained at the house for the rest of the week, sketching, conferring, littering the floors with books and fabric swatches. In the midst of the tumult, Lara found time to visit her friends at Market Hill, and more important, to go to the orphanage. Every problem and worry receded to the back of her mind as she saw a botany class of six children sketching plants in the garden under the supervision of a teacher, Miss Chapman. Lara felt a smile spread over her face as she walked toward them, heedless of the grass and mud that stained the hem of her gray skirt.

The children came to her at once, abandoning pencils and sketchbooks and eagerly calling her name. Laughing, Lara sank to her haunches and embraced them. "Tom, Meggie, Maisie, Paddy, Rob . . ." She paused and ruffled the last one's hair. "And you, Charlie . . . have you been behaving well?"

"I done awright." He ducked his head with a sly grin.

"He's tried very hard, Lady Hawksworth," the teacher said. "Not quite an angel, but close enough."

Lara smiled and hugged Charlie despite his squirming protest. After inspecting the drawings in progress, she drew aside to confer with Miss Chapman. The teacher, a small, light-haired woman close to her own age, regarded her with friendly blue eyes. "Thank you for the artistic supplies, Lady Hawksworth. As you can see, we're making good use of them."

"I'm glad," Lara replied with a rueful shake of her head. "I debated the wisdom of purchasing paint, paper, and books when clothes and food are always so badly needed."

"Books are as necessary as food, I think." Miss Chapman cocked her head and regarded her curiously. "Have you seen the new boy yet, Lady Hawksworth?"

"New boy," Lara repeated, startled. "I wasn't aware . . . How and when . . . ?"

"He arrived last evening, the poor mite."

"Who sent him?"

"I believe it was the doctor from Holbeach Prison. He sent the boy here as soon as his father was hanged. We're not quite certain what to do with him. There's not a single bed to spare."

"His father was hanged?" Lara's brow wrinkled in a frown. "For what crime?"

"I wasn't informed of the particulars." Miss Chapman lowered her voice. "The boy was living with him in prison. Evidently there was no other place for the lad to stay. Even the local workhouse refused to take him."

A queer, sick feeling came over Lara as she digested the news. An innocent child, living amongst hardened prisoners. What sane person would allow it? "How old is the boy?" she murmured.

"He appears to be four or five, though children in those circumstances are usually small for their age."

"I must see him."

Miss Chapman gave her an encouraging smile. "Perhaps you'll have better luck than the rest of us. So far he hasn't spoken a word to anyone. He turned vicious when we tried to bathe him."

"Oh, dear." Distressed, Lara took her leave of the botany class and headed to the old manor house. It was relatively quiet inside, the children engaged in various classes and activities. The cook, Mrs. Davies, was busy chopping root vegetables and dropping them into a large pot of mutton stew. No one seemed to be aware of the child's whereabouts.

"An odd creature, he is," Miss Thornton, the headmistress, remarked, emerging from a schoolroom as soon as she became aware of Lara's presence. "It's an impossible task to locate him. All I can be certain of is that he prefers the indoors. He seems to be afraid of going outside. Most unnatural for a child."

"Is there any room at all to spare for him?" Lara asked in concern.

Miss Thornton shook her head decisively. "He had to spend the night on a makeshift pallet in one of the schoolrooms, and I doubt he slept a wink. After the place he's lived in, I'm hardly surprised." She sighed. "We'll have to send him elsewhere. The question is, who will take him?"

"I don't know," Lara replied, troubled. "I'll have to think on the matter. In the meanwhile, would you mind if I search for him?"

Miss Thornton regarded her doubtfully. "Would you like for me to assist you, Lady Hawksworth?"

"No, please go on with your regular duties. I believe I can find him on my own."

"Yes, Lady Hawksworth," the headmistress said, clearly relieved.

Methodically Lara searched the house room by room, guessing that the boy would choose some quiet corner to hide in, away from the company of the boisterous children.

Finally she located him in the corner of a converted parlor, curled beneath a writing desk, as if the cramped space offered some sort of security. Lara saw him gather into a ball as soon as she entered the room. Silently he hugged his knobby knees and watched her. He was nothing but a small bundle of rags, topped with a thatch of long, dirty black hair.

"There you are," Lara said softly, sinking her to her knees before him. "You seem a little lost, darling. Will you come sit with me?"

He held back, staring at her, his intense blue eyes circled with dark smudges of weariness.

"Will you tell me your name?" Lara sat and smiled at him, while he stayed frozen before her. She had never thought the eyes of a child could be so wounded and suspicious. Noticing that one of his hands was buried in a tattered pocket, holding something protectively, she gave him an inquiring smile. "What do you have in there?" she asked, guessing that he held a small toy, a ball of string, or some other object that little boys cherished.

Slowly he pulled out a tiny, furry gray body—a live mouse, which peered at her over the edge of the boy's fingers with bright, beady eyes.

Lara held back a startled squeak at the sight. "Oh," she said weakly. "That's very . . . interesting. Did you find him here?"

The boy shook his head. "'E came with me." Gently he stroked the mouse between the ears with a grimy finger. "'E likes it when I pet 'is head like this." Growing bolder at Lara's close attention, he continued more warmly. "We do everything together, Mousie an' me."

"Mousie? Is that his name?" So the boy considered the rodent as something of a pet . . . a friend. Lara's throat was tight with laughter and pity.

"D'ye want to pet 'im?" the boy asked, extending the squirming creature to her.

Lara couldn't bring herself to touch the thing. "Thank you, but no."

"Awright." He stuffed the mouse back in his pocket and patted it lightly.

There was a strange, sweet constriction in Lara's chest as she watched him. The poor child had nothing—no family, no friends, no future to speak of—but in his own little way, he was taking care of someone . . . something. Even if it was just a prison mouse.

"You're pretty," the boy said generously, and surprised her by crawling into her lap. Startled, Lara hesitated before responding, her arms closing around him. He was bony and light, wiry like a cat. There was a sour smell wafting from his clothes and body, and the awful thought struck her that he was probably crawling with vermin above and beyond the little pet mouse. But he leaned back against her arm, tilting his head to look at her, and Lara found herself stroking his matted dark hair. She wondered how long it had been since he had known a maternal embrace. Such a small boy, he was . . . and so utterly alone.

"What is your name?" she asked. He didn't reply, only half closed his eyes, seeming to relax except for the grip of his grimy fingers on her sleeve. "My goodness, you need a bath," she said, continuing to stroke his hair back. "There must be a handsome boy underneath all this dirt."

Lara continued to hold him and murmur softly until she felt his head nod against her shoulder. He was utterly exhausted. It wouldn't be long before he fell asleep. Easing him from her arms, she stood and gestured for him to come with her.

"I'll take you to Miss Thornton," she said. "She's

a very kind woman, and you must promise to mind her. We'll find a home for you, sweetheart. I promise."

He went obediently to Miss Thornton's office, trotting beside Lara with his fist clutched in her skirt. They reached the small room and found Miss Thornton at her desk.

The headmistress smiled as she saw them. "You have a way with children, Lady Hawksworth. I should have known that you would find him." She approached the small boy and grasped his wrist. "Come with me, young sir. You've troubled her ladyship quite enough."

The boy huddled closer to Lara, snapping his teeth at Miss Thornton like a wild animal. "No," he said sharply.

The headmistress regarded him with surprise. "Well. It appears he can speak after all." She renewed her efforts to pull him away. "There's no need to carry on, lad. No one is going to harm you."

"No, *no*..." He burst into tears and clutched at Lara's legs and hips.

Distressed, Lara bent over to stroke his narrow back. "Sweet boy. I'll come back tomorrow, but you must stay here."

While the boy continued to howl and clutch at her, Miss Thornton left the room and reappeared with another teacher. "You're remarkable, Lady Hawksworth," she said, laboring with the other woman to pry him away. "Only you could call a child like that 'sweet' and sound as if you mean it."

"He's not a bad boy," Lara said, trying in vain to hush the crying child.

The teachers managed to jerk him away, and he

screamed in rage and misery. Lara stared transfixed at the sobbing boy, who was snarling and squirming like a wild cub.

"Don't mind him," Miss Thornton said. "I told you, he's odd and unnatural. Bless you, my lady, you've had enough to contend with of late without enduring a scene like this."

"That's all right. I . . ." Lara lost her voice, seized by anxiety as she saw them drag the little boy from the room. One of the teachers scolded him softly, gripping his arm to prevent him from escaping.

"We'll take care of him," Miss Thornton told Lara. "He'll be perfectly all right."

"Nooo!" he howled once more.

In the midst of the struggle, there was a scuttling movement as the mouse crawled from the child's pocket and landed on the floor. Catching sight of the rodent scooting along the polished wood, the teachers shrieked in unison and released the boy.

"Mousie!" he cried, dropping to his knees and scrambling after the escaping rodent. "Mousie, come back!"

Somehow the mouse found a hole in the seam of the wall and wiggled through, disappearing. Stupefied, the boy stared at the tiny hole and began to cry in earnest.

As Lara stared at the tearful child, the panicked teachers, and Miss Thornton's taut face, she heard herself speak. "Let me have the boy," she said impulsively. "I-I want him."

"Lady Hawksworth?" Miss Thornton asked cautiously, as if she'd taken leave of her senses.

Lara continued rapidly. "I'll take him with me for now. I'll find a place for him."

"But surely you don't mean—"

"Yes, I do."

The boy returned to the safety of Lara's skirts, his chest heaving with agitation. "I want Mousie," he sniffled.

She rested her hand on his back. "Mousie has to stay here," she said quietly. "He'll be fine, I promise you. Will you stay here as well, or would you like to come with me?"

He groped for her hand in answer, clinging tightly.

Lara glanced at the headmistress with a wry smile. "I'll take good care of him, Miss Thornton."

"Of that, I have no doubt," the headmistress responded. "I only hope he doesn't inconvenience you too greatly, milady." She bent down and stared sternly into the boy's reddened face. "I hope you realize what a stroke of luck you've had, young Master Cannon. If I were you, I'd try very, very hard to please Lady Hawksworth."

"Cannon?" Lara repeated. "Is that his name?"

"The family name, yes. But he won't tell us what they call him."

The little hand tugged at Lara's, and a pair of watery, bright blue eyes stared into hers. "Johnny," he said distinctly.

"Johnny," Lara repeated, squeezing his fingers gently.

"Lady Hawksworth," the headmistress cautioned, "in my experience it is better not to make much of a child in his situation, or he'll grow to expect it. I know that sounds cruel, but the world isn't kind to penniless orphans—he'd best know his place in it."

"I understand," Lara said, her smile fading. "Thank you, Miss Thornton."

* * *

The servants at Hawksworth Hall were clearly stupefied by the sight of Lara's small, shaggy guest, who never released his hold on her skirt. He seemed unaware of the overwrought grandeur of his surroundings, all his attention centered on Lara.

"Johnny is rather shy," Lara murmured to her personal maid, Naomi, whose overtures to the child had been quickly rebuffed. "It will take a little time for him to become accustomed to all of us."

Naomi's plump face regarded the boy doubtfully. "He looks as though he's been raised in the forest, milady."

Silently Lara reflected that the forest was a far more wholesome place than the diseased and dangerous environment Johnny had been living in. She drew her fingers lightly over the boy's matted hair. "Naomi, I want you to assist me in washing him."

"Yes, milady," the maid muttered, though she looked taken aback at the prospect.

While Lara's personal tub was painstakingly filled by a horde of housemaids carrying buckets up and down the stairs, she sent for a plate of gingerbread and a glass of milk. The child devoured every drop and crumb as if he hadn't eaten for days. When his appetite was satiated, Lara and Naomi brought him to her dressing room and removed his tattered clothes.

The difficult part was convincing Johnny to enter the water, which he regarded with the highest degree of suspicion. He stood naked by the tub, his body so frail as to be almost delicate. "I don't want to," he said stubbornly.

"But you must," Lara said, trying to suppress a laugh. "You're very dirty."

"Me pa says a bath'll make you die of ague."

"Your father was mistaken," Lara said. "I take baths all the time, and it's a lovely feeling to be clean. Get in while the water is still warm, Johnny."

"No," he said stubbornly.

"You must have a bath," Lara insisted. "Everyone who lives at Hawksworth Hall must bathe regularly. Isn't that right, Naomi?"

The maid nodded emphatically.

After a great deal of coaxing and persuading, they lifted him into the tub. The child sat rigidly, every knob on his spine prominent. Lara hummed a song to entertain him, while they washed him from head to toe. The water turned gray as they rinsed him repeatedly.

"Look at them rats," Naomi commented, touching one of the hopelessly thick tangles in his wet hair. "We'll have to cut 'em out."

"How fair he is," Lara said, marveling at his complexion. "You're as white as a snowdrop, Johnny."

He regarded his spindly arms and chest with interest. "A lot o' skin come off," he observed.

"Not skin," Lara said, laughing. "Just dirt."

Obeying their instructions, he stood from the water and allowed Lara to lift him from the bath. She wrapped him in a thick towel, blotting the water that streamed from his limbs. As she dried him, Johnny leaned close and tried to rest his head on her shoulder, soaking the bodice of her gown.

Lara hugged him tightly. "You did well, Johnny," she said. "You were very good in the bath."

"What shall I do with these, milady?" Naomi inquired, poking experimentally at the little heap of filthy clothes on the floor. "I think they'll fall apart if I tried to wash 'em."

"Burn them," Lara said, her gaze meeting the maid's as they both nodded in agreement. She reached for a clean shirt and a pair of drill trousers borrowed from the stableboy. Although the clothes were all that had been available on such short notice, they were far too large and baggy. "These will have to do for now," Lara commented, fastening a pur-loined dog collar at the boy's waist to keep the pants from slipping down. She reached down and wiggled one of the boy's bare toes, making him jerk back with a surprised laugh. "We'll have some shoes made for you, and some proper clothes. In fact—" Her brow wrinkled as she suddenly remembered that she had arranged for the dressmaker to visit this week—good Lord, it wasn't today, was it?

"Well, you always manage to surprise me," came her sister's voice from the doorway, interrupting her thoughts.

Lara looked up with a smile as she beheld Rachel. "Oh, dear. I forgot I had invited you over to help me choose dress patterns. I haven't kept you waiting, have I?"

Rachel shook her head. "Not in the least. Don't worry, I'm a trifle early. The dressmaker hasn't even arrived yet."

"Thank God." Lara pushed a damp lock of hair off her forehead. "I'm not usually such a jinglebrains, but I've been busy."

"So I see." Rachel ventured farther into the room, smiling at the little mop-headed boy. Johnny re-turned her inspection with silent awe.

Lara doubted the child had ever seen a woman like Rachel, at least not at this close distance. Rachel was especially lovely today, her dark hair curled in shining ringlets, pinned up to reveal the swanlike length of her neck. She wore a gown of cream-colored muslin embroidered all over with tiny pink rosebuds and green leaves, and a straw bonnet trimmed in pink ribbons and roses. Smiling in pride, Lara wondered if there was another woman in England who could equal her sister's delicate beauty.

"Larissa, you're a fright!" Rachel exclaimed, laughing. "I can see you've been grubbing with those children at the orphanage. How can you be the same girl who used to take such pains with her appearance?"

Ruefully Lara glanced down at her own dark, damp dress and made a futile effort to pin up the trailing strands of her board-straight hair. "The children don't care how I look," she replied with a grin. "That's all that matters to me." She sat the boy on a footstool and draped a towel around his shoulders. "Sit still, Johnny, while I cut your hair."

"No!"

"Yes," Lara said firmly. "And if you behave, then I'll have a forage cap made for you, with brass buttons on the front. Wouldn't that be nice?"

"Awright." Resignedly the child sat before her.

Lara began to cut his hair, snipping carefully through the unruly mass. Her progress was slow, as she stopped frequently to comfort Johnny, who was flinching with each snip of the scissors.

"Oh, let me," Rachel said after a few minutes. "I was always better at this, Lara. Remember, Papa used to let me cut his hair before he lost it all."

Lara laughed and relinquished the child to Rachel's expert hands. She stood back to watch as great clumps of snarled hair fell to the floor. "It's beautiful," Rachel murmured, carefully shaping the hair to the boy's head. "Black as ink, with just the hint of a curl. He's a handsome lad, isn't he? Hold still, my lad—I'll be finished in a flea's leap."

Her sister was right, Lara realized in surprise. Johnny *was* handsome, with strong features, a bold nose, glossy black hair, and bright blue eyes. He tried to return Lara's smile as he sat up straight on the stool, but his mouth stretched in an irrepressible yawn, and he swayed slightly.

"Imp!" Rachel exclaimed. "You mustn't move. I nearly snipped the tip of your ear off!"

"He's tired," Lara said, coming forward to remove the towel and pull the boy off the stool. "That's enough for now, Rachel." She carried Johnny to a nearby mahogany sofa with flowing lines and soft velvet upholstery. "Naomi, thank you for helping us. You may go now."

"Yes, milady," the maid said, dipping in a quick curtsy and leaving the room.

The child cuddled against Lara's side. It felt strangely natural to have his slight weight resting on her, his head bobbing in the crook of her shoulder. "Go to sleep, Johnny." She stroked his head, the dark hair soft and silky beneath her fingertips. "I'll be here when you awaken."

"D'ye promise?"

"Oh, yes."

That reassurance seemed to be all he needed. He settled harder against her and went limp, his breathing deep and even.

Rachel settled in a nearby chair, her wondering

gaze fixed on Lara's face. "Who is he, Larissa? Why have you brought him here?"

"He's an orphan," Lara replied, resting her hand on the child's back. "There's no room for him anywhere. He was sent over from Holbeach Prison, where his father was hanged."

"A convicted felon's son!" Rachel exclaimed, causing the boy to twitch in his sleep.

"Hush, Rachel," Lara said with a reproving frown. "It's not his fault." She bent over the child protectively, rubbing his back until he relaxed again.

Rachel shook her head in bewilderment. "Even with the way you usually carry on over children, I wouldn't have expected this. Actually bringing him to your home—what will Lord Hunter say?"

"I don't know. I'm sure Hunter won't approve, but there's something about this boy that makes me want to keep him safe."

"Lara, you feel that way about every child you encounter."

"Yes, but this one is special." Lara felt awkward and tongue-tied as she fumbled for a rational explanation. "When I first saw him, he had a mouse in his pocket. He had brought it from prison."

"A mouse," Rachel repeated, shivering suddenly. "Dead or alive?"

"Alive and kicking," Lara said ruefully. "Johnny was taking care of it. Isn't that remarkable? Locked away in that prison, facing horrors you and I could never imagine . . . and he found a little creature to love and care for."

Rachel shook her head and smiled as she stared at Lara. "So that's the attraction. The two of you share a habit of collecting strays. You're kindred spirits."

Overwhelmed by tenderness, Lara stared at the sleeping child. He had given her his trust, and she would die before failing him. "I know that I can't rescue every child in the world," she said. "But I can save a few of them. I can save this one."

"What are you planning to do with him?"

"I haven't thought of a plan yet."

"Surely you're not considering keeping him?"

Lara's defensive silence was answer enough.

Rachel sat beside her and spoke earnestly. "Dearest, I never knew Hunter very well—and even less now than before—but I know about the grief he caused you when you failed to conceive. He wants his own child, an *heir* . . . not some gutter-bred child who's come from a prison."

"*Rachel*," Lara murmured, astonished.

Rachel looked ashamed but resolute. "You may not like my choice of words, but I must be frank. You've become accustomed to making choices without the interference of a husband. Now Hunter has returned, and things are different. A wife must abide by her husband's decisions."

Lara set her jaw stubbornly. "I'm not trying to offer this boy as a substitute for the children I can't have."

"How else is Hunter to see it?"

"The way I do—that this is a little boy who needs our help."

"Dearest." Rachel's delicate mouth curved in a sad smile. "I don't want you to be disappointed. I don't think it is wise to cause problems between yourself and Hunter so soon after his return. A peaceful marriage is the greatest blessing imaginable."

Lara's attention was caught by the bleakness in her sister's expression. She looked closely at Rachel, suddenly noticing the lines of strain around her eyes and on her forehead, and the tension in her posture. "Rachel, what is wrong? More problems between you and Lord Lonsdale?"

Her sister shook her head uncomfortably. "Not really, it's just that . . . Terrell is so quick to take offense of late. He is bored and unhappy, and when he indulges in strong drink he becomes so agitated . . ."

"Agitated," Lara asked in a low voice, "or abusive?"

Rachel was silent, her gaze downcast. It seemed that she was making some unpleasant decision. After a lengthy pause, she took hold of the white lace chemisette covering the décolletage of her gown, and pulled it aside.

Lara stared blankly at her sister's bared throat and upper chest, where two large bruises and a pattern of four shadowed fingermarks showed prominently against the translucent skin. Lord Lonsdale had done this to her . . . but why? Rachel was the gentlest and mildest of creatures, always mindful of her duty, living for the comfort of her husband and all those around her.

Lara felt herself quiver with fury, tears springing to her eyes. "He's a monster!" she said sharply.

Hurriedly Rachel replaced the concealing lace. "Larissa, no, no . . . I didn't show you in order to make you hate him. I don't know why I showed you. It is my fault. I complained about his gambling and incensed him beyond his capacity to bear. I must try to be a better wife. He needs something I am not able to supply. If I could only understand him better—"

"When Hunter returns, I will have him talk to Lord Lonsdale," Lara said, ignoring her sister's protests.

"No! Not unless you want this to happen again—or something even worse."

Lara sat in miserable silence, fighting tears. She and Rachel had been brought up to believe that men were their protectors, that a husband was the superior, wiser half of a marriage. In her former sheltered innocence, she had not imagined that a man would be capable of striking his wife, or hurting her in any way. Why, of all people, was this happening to Rachel, the sweetest and gentlest woman she had ever known? And how could Rachel claim that it was her fault?

"Rachel," she managed to say unsteadily, "you have done nothing to deserve this. And Lord Lonsdale has proven that his word means nothing. He'll continue to inflict violence on you unless someone intervenes."

"You must not tell Lord Hawksworth," Rachel begged. "I would be so humiliated. Besides, if your husband took up the matter with him, I believe Terrell would deny everything and find some way to punish me later. Please, you must keep this a secret."

"Then I insist that you tell Papa and Mama."

Rachel shook her head hopelessly. "What would you have them do? Mama would cry and beg me to try harder to please Terrell. Papa would only brood in his study. You know how they are."

"Then I'm to do nothing?" Lara asked in anguished protest.

Rachel laid a gentle hand over hers. "I love him," she said quietly. "I want to stay with him. Most of the time he is very kind to me. It's only now and then, when he can't seem to control his temper, that things become . . . difficult. But those times always pass quickly."

"How could you want to stay with someone who hurts you? Lord Lonsdale is a selfish, evil man—"

"No." Rachel withdrew her hand, her beautiful face turning frosty. "Not another word against him, Larissa. I'm sorry. I shouldn't have burdened you with this."

A housemaid came to announce the dressmaker's arrival, and the two women prepared to meet her in the downstairs parlor. Rachel left the room first, while Lara lingered behind with the sleeping child. She laid a large embroidered shawl over him, tucking it at his neck, smoothing his soft, newly shorn hair. "Rest here for now," she whispered, kneeling by the sofa, staring into Johnny's small, peaceful face. He seemed absurdly helpless, left at the mercy of a large and uncaring world. Thinking of his plight, and of Rachel's, and the various problems of all her friends at Market Hill, Lara closed her eyes briefly.

"Dear Father in Heaven," she said under her breath. "There are so many who need Your mercy and protection. Help me to know what to do for them. Amen."

Chapter 9

IT WAS LAUNDRY day, a massive undertaking that occurred once a week and absorbed fully half the household. As had been her habit since the early days of her marriage, Lara supervised and participated in the washing, folding, and mending. In a house as large as Hawksworth Hall, it was necessary to sew cloth tickets on every pillowcase, featherbed, sheet, and blanket to determine where they belonged. Articles that were too worn or damaged to use were kept in a scrap bag to be sold to the rag merchant, the proceeds of which were divided amongst the servants.

"Bless you, milady," one of the maids said as they folded freshly laundered linens in the washhouse. "We've all missed the extra money we used to get from the ragman. Lady Arthur kept every shilling for her own purse."

"Well, now everything is back the way it used to be," Lara replied.

"Thank heaven," the maid said fervently, and went to collect another basket of laundry.

Lara frowned and began to retie the loose strings of her white apron. The air in the washhouse was humid, steam rising from huge iron vats that had been filled with soaking linens. She supposed she should be glad of having returned to her duties as mistress of the household. She had always experienced a fair amount of satisfaction in keeping Hawksworth Hall properly organized and efficiently managed. However, it seemed that her enjoyment in housekeeping and estate management had begun to pall.

Before "widowhood," she had always been too busy being the lady of the manor to notice much outside the borders of the estate. Now the time spent at the orphanage seemed far more important than anything she could accomplish here.

The strings of the apron slipped from Lara's fingers, and she fumbled for them. Someone approached her from behind. Before she could turn around, she felt warm masculine fingers tangle briefly with hers. She went still, her chest reverberating with the thudding of her heart. Until her dying day, she would recognize the touch of those hands.

Hawksworth tied the apron around her waist with meticulous care. Lara could feel the faint, hot puffs of his breath stirring in her hair. Although he didn't pull her against him, she sensed the towering height and strength of the body behind hers.

"What are you doing here?" she asked weakly.

"I live here," he informed her, his voice like a stroke of velvet down her spine.

"You know that I meant the washhouse. You've never set foot in this building before today."

"I couldn't wait to see you."

Out of the corner of her eye, Lara saw two maids pause uncertainly at the doorway as they saw that the master of the household was there. "You may come in, girls," she said loudly, beckoning to them to return to their chores, but they giggled and disappeared, evidently deciding that she needed a few moments alone with Hawksworth.

"You should have given me time to prepare myself," Lara protested as her husband turned her to face him. She was disheveled and red-faced, her hair straggling around her moist cheeks, her body swathed in a huge apron. "I would have at least changed my gown and brushed my ..." Her voice died away as she stared at him.

Hawksworth was astonishingly handsome, his dark eyes dancing with cinnamon lights, his sun-shot brown hair brushed neatly back from his face. He wore perfectly tailored clothes that displayed—no, flaunted—the power of his body. The snug-fitting beige pantaloons lovingly followed every muscular line of his legs, and emphasized his masculine endowments in a way that brought scarlet heat to Lara's cheeks. A blindingly white shirt and cravat, elegantly patterned waistcoat, and crisp dark blue coat completed the ensemble. The exotic dark hue of his skin only made him more striking. Lara had no doubt that the mere sight of him would make any number of women swoon.

In fact, her own insides were twisting in agitation. It definitely had to do with the way he looked at her—not a nice, respectful gaze, but the kind of look she imagined a man would give a prostitute. How was it that he could make her feel as if she were standing naked before him, when she was covered in layers of confining clothes and an apron the size of a tent?

"Did you have a pleasant stay in London?" she asked, trying to gather her wits.

"Not especially." His hands tightened at her waist as she tried to pull back. "It was productive, however."

"My time here was also productive," she said. "There are some things I must discuss with you later."

"Tell me now." Hawksworth slid an arm around her and began to pull her from the washhouse.

"I must help with the laundering—"

"Let the servants take care of it." He descended the two steps leading to the pathway that connected the building to the main house.

"I would rather talk to you at supper," Lara said, pausing at the top of the steps, so that their faces were level. "After you've had a few glasses of wine."

Hawksworth laughed and reached for her, making her gasp as he lifted her off her feet and swung her easily to the ground. "Bad news, is it?"

"Not bad," she said, unable to take her gaze from his wide, expressive mouth. "I would like to make some rather significant changes around here, and you may not approve."

"Changes." His white teeth gleamed as he smiled sardonically. "Well, I'm always open to bargaining."

"I have nothing to bargain with."

Hawksworth stopped before they reached the house, drawing her into a secluded nook of the hedges bordering the kitchen garden. The air was fragrant with herbs and sun-warmed flowers. "For what you have, sweet wife, I would lay the world at your feet.''

Realizing his intentions, Lara tried to twist away, only to find herself caught securely against him. His torso was as hard as iron, muscles protruding through the layers of clothing that separated them. And low against her abdomen and belly, the hot, leaping pressure of masculine flesh, instantly roused by her nearness. "My lord," she gasped, "Hunter . . . don't you dare—"

"You're not as shocked as you pretend. You're a married woman, after all."

"I haven't been for a long time." She pushed in vain at his chest. "Release me at once!"

He grinned, and his embrace only tightened. "Kiss me first."

"Why should I?" she returned frostily.

"I didn't touch a single woman in London," he said. "I only thought of you."

"And you expect a reward for that? I've done my best to encourage you to take a mistress."

He urged his hips against hers, as if she weren't already aware of his jutting arousal. "But I only want you."

"Haven't you ever been told that you can't have everything you want?"

That elicited a swift grin. "Not that I recall."

Despite his brutish strength, he seemed boyish and mischievous, and Lara realized that it wasn't fear that made her pulse beat so wildly. She was caught in a flurry of excitement, discovering for the first time the power of holding an aroused male at bay. Deliberately she withheld what he wanted, keeping her arms wedged between them, turning her face to the side.

"What will I gain if I kiss you?" Lara heard herself ask. The low, provocative tone didn't sound like her at all.

The question cracked his self-control enough to reveal that he wanted her badly, in spite of his teasing demeanor. His arms became as tight as barrel stays, his body hardening against hers. "Name your price," he muttered. "Within reason."

"I'm almost positive that you won't consider what I want is reasonable," she said ruefully.

Hawksworth sank his fingers into her disheveled hair and eased her head back. "Kiss me first. We'll talk about 'reasonable' later."

"One kiss?" she asked warily.

He nodded, his breath catching as Lara reached up to him. Her fingers slid around the back of his neck, and she pulled his head down, her own lips softening with anticipation—

"Lara! Lara!" A small figure came hurrying toward them, and Lara wriggled free to face Johnny. Anxiously he buried himself against her, small hands clutching at her skirts.

"What is it?" she asked, kneeling beside him, rubbing his narrow back as he held her tightly.

After a moment or two of consolation, Johnny lifted his dark head and stared at Hawksworth with a mixture of suspicion and dislike. "He was hurting ye!"

Lara pressed her lips together to keep them from quivering with sudden amusement. "No, darling. This is Lord Hawksworth. I was merely welcoming him home. Everything is all right."

Clearly unconvinced, the child continued to glare at the interloper.

Hawksworth didn't spare the boy a glance, but looked at Lara with all the annoyance of a hungry tiger just deprived of its prey. "I gather this is one of the 'changes' you mentioned," he said.

"Yes." Sensing that it would be a mistake to show any sign of doubt, Lara stood to face him and made her reply as firm as possible. "I wish I had been able to explain before you saw him . . . but I intend that Johnny shall live with us from now on."

The passion and heat faded from Hawksworth's eyes, his expression suddenly impenetrable. "An orphanage brat?"

She felt Johnny's little hand slip into hers, and she squeezed it reassuringly. Her gaze didn't move from Hawksworth's. "I will explain everything later in private."

"Yes, you will," Hawksworth agreed in a tone that chilled her.

Lara left Johnny in the care of the elderly gardener, Mr. Moody, who was cutting hothouse flowers and arranging them in urns and vases for various rooms at Hawksworth Hall. Lara smiled as she saw the child arranging his own little bouquet, sticking flowers in a small chipped pitcher. "Very good, lad," the gardener praised him, carefully stripping the thorns from a miniature rose and handing it to him. "You have an eye for color. I'll show you how to make a pretty nosegay for Lady Hawksworth, and we'll fit it in a little glass tube to keep the flowers fresh."

Johnny shook his head at the sight of the white rose. "Not that one," he said shyly. "She wants a pink flower."

Lara paused at the doorway, surprised and

pleased. So far Mr. Moody was the only person besides herself to whom Johnny had spoken.

"Does she now?" Mr. Moody's craggy face softened with a smile. He indicated the bowers of hothouse roses nearby. "Then find her the best bloom in the bunch, lad, and I'll cut it for you."

Lara was amazed by the strength of her feelings toward the little boy, as if a strong current of emotions that had been dammed up for years was suddenly allowed to flow free. In her resentment and shame at not having been able to give Hawksworth an heir, she had never acknowledged her own hunger for a child. Someone who could accept and return her love without limits or conditions—someone who needed her. She hoped that Hawksworth would not forbid her to keep Johnny. She was willing to defy him and anyone else who tried to separate her from the boy.

Sweating in her gray, high-necked muslin gown, Lara went upstairs to her suite and closed the door. What she needed was to change into a lighter, cooler gown, and strip off her itchy worsted stockings. She untied her apron, dropped it on the floor, and sat in a chair to unlace her serviceable leather shoes. A relieved sigh escaped her as she worked her toes free of the heavy encumbrances. Next she worked at the buttons of her wrists and the back of her neck. Unfortunately the gown fastened in the back, and she couldn't remove it without assistance. Fanning her perspiring face, she went to the tasseled bellpull near her bed, intending to ring for Naomi.

"Don't." Hawksworth's quiet voice made her jerk in surprise. "I'll help you."

Lara's heart thundered in her chest, and she

whirled toward the corner. Hawksworth lounged in a Hepplewhite chair with a shield-shaped back. "Good Lord," she gasped. "Why didn't you tell me you were here?"

"I just did." He had shed his coat and waistcoat, the thin linen shirt clinging fluidly to his broad shoulders and lean torso. As he came nearer, she caught the smell of his skin, mingled with the salt of perspiration, the tang of bay rum, and the faint but pleasant scent of horses.

Trying to ignore her own stirring attraction to him, Lara folded her arms around herself and regarded him with extreme dignity. "I would appreciate your leaving, as I am about to change my gown."

"I'm offering my services in lieu of your maid's."

She shook her head. "Thank you, but I would prefer Naomi."

"Are you afraid I'll ravish you if I see you undressed?" he mocked. "I'll try to control myself. Turn around."

Lara stiffened as he turned her away from him. He began on the back of her gown, unfastening the miniature hooks with maddening slowness. The air touched her overheated skin, making her shiver. The heavy gown fell away by degrees, until she clutched at the bodice to keep it from slipping down her front. "Thank you," she said. "That was very helpful. I can do the rest now."

Hawksworth ignored the stilted command and reached inside the back of her dress, unhooking her lightly boned stays. Lara swayed and closed her eyes. "That's enough," she said unsteadily, but he continued, pulling the gown from her grasp, pushing it down her hips until it dropped to the floor in a humid heap. The stays followed, and she was left only in her chemise and drawers and stockings. His palms hovered over her shoulders and upper arms, not quite touching, bringing goose bumps to her skin and making the fine downy hairs prickle. Her toes dug into the carpet.

She hadn't felt like this since she was a frightened young girl on her wedding night, not knowing what was expected of her, having no idea what he intended.

Still standing behind her, Hawksworth reached across her front to the mother-of-pearl buttons closing her chemise. For a man she had once considered rather ham-handed, he released the tiny buttons with surprising dexterity. The chemise sagged beneath his ministrations, cool air wafting over her exposed cleavage. The delicate cambric clung to the tips of her nipples, barely concealing them.

"Do you want me to stop now?" she heard him ask.

Yes, she wanted to say, but her unruly mouth wouldn't produce a sound. She was paralyzed with curiosity as he let down her hair, smoothing back the strands that clung to her moist, salty cheeks. His fingers slid under the dark silk and lightly rubbed her scalp, his touch so soothing and pleasurable that she felt a responsive moan welling up in her throat. Her back arched, and she fought the overwhelming temptation to lean against him and invite more.

He stroked the back of her neck, manipulating the taut muscles that ached from her labors of the morning, releasing pain and delight at the same time. He spoke close to her ear, making her shiver. "Do you trust me, Lara?"

She shook her head, still unable to speak.

He laughed softly. "I don't trust myself, either. You're too beautiful, and I want you too damn badly."

He stood so close, but the only place he touched her was her neck, his fingers compressing the sore nape with exquisite gentleness. She sensed rather than felt that he was aroused again. The thought should have made her bolt, but somehow she just stood quietly under his ministrations. She felt tipsy, off-balance, wild thoughts flitting through her mind. If only he would kiss her again the way he had before, his mouth so hard and delicious . . .

A sweet ache spread through her breasts, collecting at the tips. Lara bit her lip as she tried to keep from snatching at his warm fingers and pulling them to her body. Shamed, she kept still and prayed that he couldn't guess what she was thinking. She didn't realize she was holding her breath until it rushed between her lips in a quick gasp.

"Lara," she heard him murmur, and her heart stopped as he lifted the knee-length hem of her chemise, gathering it in handfuls until he reached the waist of her drawers. She began to tremble, her legs weakening until she was forced to lean against him for support. His chest was like a stone wall. His sex was huge and hard as it nestled against the pliant curve of her buttocks.

He pulled at the tape of her drawers, and they slipped down to her ankles. She heard his breathing change, felt the tremor in his hand as he rested it for one dizzying moment on her bare hip. Then he dropped the hem of her chemise, letting it cover her once more.

He picked her up with ridiculous ease, and she was swallowed in his strength. She kept her neck tense, refusing to lay her head on his shoulder, remaining stubbornly silent as he carried her across the room. The panicked question shot through her—was he going to make love to her? *Let him*, she thought suddenly. Let him do exactly what he had done all those times before. Let him prove that it was as awful as she remembered . . . and then she would be free of him. She would regard him with her old steadfast indifference, and he would have no more power over her.

To her surprise, he didn't carry her to the bed, but to the chair at her dressing table. He lowered her into the chair and knelt at her feet, his powerful thighs spread for balance. Light-headed, Lara stared into the handsome face so near hers. Sounds from outside the room penetrated the quietness . . . the muffled clang of a servants' bell, the low of animals grazing on the vast lawn, the bark of a dog, the rustling of servants going about their daily tasks. It seemed impossible that there was a busy world around them. All that existed was this room, and the two of them in it.

Hawksworth's gaze remained on her face as he touched her, his finger sliding up her stockinged ankle in a luxuriously slow ascent. Lara began to quiver, her legs stiffening as her husband urged her chemise up to her thighs. He found her knitted garter and untied it, and she couldn't prevent a little sob of alarm. He peeled back the itchy stocking, his fingers brushing the inside of her thigh, knee, calf, giving her a small, sweet shock each time he touched the tender skin. He turned his attention to her other leg, stripping the stocking away and dropping it to the floor.

Lara sat half naked before him, her fingers curled around the edges of the chair seat. She thought of the way it used to be between them, the rank smell of his breath when he had come to her after a drinking spree, the way he had climbed on top of her with few preliminaries and shoved himself inside her. Painful, embarrassing . . . and worse, the feeling she'd always had afterward, as if she had been used and discarded. According to her mother's helpful advice, she had always remained on her back for several minutes after Hawksworth had left her, giving his seed every possible chance of taking root.

Secretly Lara had always been glad when it didn't. She hadn't liked the idea of his child growing in her belly, overtaking her body, affording Hawksworth the opportunity of pointing to her as an example of his all-important virility.

Why had he never touched her then as he was doing now?

The tip of his forefinger brushed the top of one pale leg, where the garters had chafed her and made reddish marks. He reached past her for the blue Bristol glass jar on the dressing table, which contained a cream blended with extracts of cucumber and roses. "Is this what you use on your skin?" he asked in a low voice.

"Yes," she said faintly.

He opened the jar, releasing a fresh, flowery scent into the air. Scooping up a small amount of the cream, he spread it evenly between his palms, and smoothed his hands over her legs.

"Oh—" Lara's muscles twitched in reaction, her weight shifting in the chair.

He concentrated on his task, soothing the chafed

areas of her skin. Her gaze followed his long brown hands as they moved gently over her. The hem of her chemise rode up her legs, and she pushed it back down, trying to retain the last shreds of modesty. The attempt was futile. His hands glided rhythmically back and forth, higher and higher, making her breath stop each time he reached her inner thighs. She didn't understand the reactions of her own body, the urge to open and push herself against him, the sudden swelling warmth in her private place. His fingertips reached far up her legs, just brushing the edge of the nest of dark hair beneath her chemise.

Lara gasped and caught at his wrists. There was a silken ache in her loins, a peculiar surge of moisture. "Stop," she whispered shakily. "Stop."

He didn't seem to hear her at first, his gaze riveted on the shadow of curls beneath the thin cambric. His hands tightened on her flesh.

Stop. She asked the impossible, but somehow Hunter made himself do it. He closed his eyes before the sight of her drove him insane . . . the soft, pale skin, the fluff of dark hair that lured his fingers to dive beneath her chemise. She couldn't possibly understand how desperately he wanted to touch her, taste her, bite, devour, suck, kiss every sweet inch of her body. His muscles were as stiff as iron, not to mention the battering ram that surged against the tight fabric of his pantaloons. He was close to exploding.

When he was able to move, he took his hands from her and stood. Not paying much attention to where he was going, he crossed the room until he nearly walked into a wall. He braced his hands against it and concentrated on restoring his shattered self-control. "Cover yourself," he said brusquely, keeping his eyes fixed on the garishly papered wall before him. "Or I won't be responsible for what I do."

He heard her move like a startled rabbit, fumbling in the armoire for clothing. While she dressed, he breathed in a controlled pattern. The fragrance of the skin cream lingered on his hands. He wanted to go back to her, rub his rose-scented fingers over her breasts and between her thighs.

"Thank you." Her voice traveled to his ears.

"For what?" he asked, staring fixedly at the papered panel before him.

"You could have asserted your rights without regard to my wishes."

Hunter turned and braced his back on the wall, crossing his arms over his taut chest. Lara had donned a prudish white robe with rows of intricate tucks. The garment was shapeless and all-enveloping, but it did little to cool his desire. She was so lovely, her cheeks tinted with a delicate pink flush. He gave her a devil-may-care smile. "When I make love to you," he told her, "you'll be more than willing. You'll beg for it."

She laughed unsteadily. "You're too arrogant for words!"

"You'll beg," he repeated. "And you'll love every moment of it."

Alarm flitted across her features, and then she managed a look of cool disdain. "If it pleases you to think so."

Hunter watched as Lara went to the dressing table and sat before the mirror, brushing her long sable hair. She braided the dark locks and pinned them into a coil near the top of her head, her composure seeming to return. However, there was still a trace of chagrin that pulled at her forehead, making her look troubled. Any man would have given his fortune to have the chance of comforting her.

"Tell me about the boy," Hunter said.

The nimble movements of her fingers faltered. "Johnny was sent to the orphanage from Holbeach Prison. His father was a convicted felon. I brought Johnny here because there was no room for him, not even one spare bed."

"And you intend for him to live with us? As what? A servant? An adopted child?"

"There is no need for us to adopt him, if you don't wish it," Lara responded, her tone carefully neutral. "But with all the means at our disposal, I thought it would be possible to raise him as . . . part of the family."

Perplexed, annoyed, Hunter stared hard at her reflection in the mirror. "We're not talking about taking a relative's child into our home, Lara. It's likely he comes from a long-established line of thieves and murderers."

"Johnny's pedigree, or lack thereof, isn't his fault," she shot back, with a quickness that betrayed she had already considered this line of argument. "He's an innocent child. If he's brought up in a decent home, he won't be anything like his father."

"That's one theory," Hunter replied, unimpressed. "Tell me, then—are we to open our doors to every homeless child you encounter? There are too damn many orphans in England. I've no desire to be a replacement father to all of them. Or even to one, at this point."

"You don't have to act as his father." Lara's hands clenched in her lap. "I'll be enough for him. I'll take care of him and love him without letting it detract from my other responsibilities."

"Such as your responsibility to me?" He indicated the bed with a jerk of his head. "Let me know when you're ready to assume your wifely duties, and then we'll take up the matter of your latest protégé."

She gasped in outrage. "You can't possibly mean . . . Are you saying that you won't allow me to keep Johnny unless I agree to sleep with you?"

Hunter smiled mockingly, deciding that he would indulge her only up to a point. He would be damned if she would have everything her way and not have to pay some price. "As I said, I'm open to bargaining. But before we start setting terms, I want to point out something that you may not have considered. Raise the boy as one of the family, if you like. But he won't have the bloodlines to be accepted in good society, and he won't be a servant, and he'll be a damn sight too good for the lower classes he came from."

Lara compressed her mouth, stubbornly refusing to see the truth in his words. "That won't matter. I'll help him to find his own place in the world."

"Like hell it won't matter," he said savagely. "You don't understand what it's like to live between two worlds, and not fit in anywhere."

"How would you know what it's like to be a misfit? You've always been a Hawksworth, and had everyone bowing and scraping before you since the day you were born."

Hunter clenched his jaw until it vibrated. A torrent of words jammed inside him. She dared to defy him. She imagined him as a coldhearted bastard, and styled herself as the patron saint of all helpless creatures. Well, he was more than ready to answer her challenge.

"Fine," he said. "Keep him here. I won't stand in your way."

"Thank you." Her tone was wary, as if she sensed what was coming next.

"And in return," he continued silkily, "you can do something for me." He walked to the Hepplewhite chair and picked up a brown paper parcel beside it. Casually he tossed the featherlight package to her. She caught it in a reflex movement.

"What is this?" Lara asked. "A present?"

"Open it."

She complied slowly, as if suspecting some sort of trick—and it was, in a way. The present was for his benefit, not hers. Setting the brown paper on the dressing table, Lara extracted a delicate, slippery length of black silk and lace. Hunter had bought the negligee from a London dressmaker, who had created the garment as part of a large order for a celebrated courtesan. The customer would never miss it, the dressmaker had assured Hunter, eager for his future patronage.

The negligee was little more than a film of transparent silk, the bodice made of a web of sheer lace. The flowing skirt was slit to the waist in two places.

"Only a prostitute would wear this," Lara said in a stricken whisper, her green eyes huge.

"A very, very expensive prostitute, my sweet." Hunter wanted to laugh at her obvious horror.

"I could never . . ." Her voice trailed into silence, as if the thought of wearing it was too terrible to mention aloud.

"But you will," he said, enjoying himself. "You'll wear it for me tonight."

"You must be mad! How could I possibly wear something like this? It's indecent. It's . . ." She turned pink, a bright blush seeping down her neckline. "I may as well be naked!" she exclaimed.

"There is always that option," he said with a thoughtful expression.

"You . . . you devil! You degenerate, manipulative—"

"Do you want Johnny to stay?" he asked.

"And if I do wear it? What guarantee do I have that you won't . . ."

"Leap on you in a fit of lust?" he supplied helpfully. "Bull the cow, hoist the cock, play the hurdy-gurdy—"

"Oh, stop it!" She glared at him while her cheeks turned crimson.

"I won't touch you," he promised, a grin tugging at his lips. "Just wear the damn gown for one evening. Will it be so difficult?"

"No." She dropped the gown and covered her hot face with her hands, her small voice seeping out from between her fingers. "It will be impossible. Please, you must ask something else of me."

"Oh, no." There was nothing in the world he wanted more than to see her in the black negligee. "You've told me what you want—and I've reciprocated. You're getting off lightly, you know. The child will be here for years, whereas your part of the bargain will be over in one evening."

Lara lifted the frail wisp of a gown and regarded it with distaste. It was clear she would have preferred a hair shirt that would scrape off two or three layers of skin. Her snapping green eyes met his. "If you dare to touch me or make jest of me, I'll never forgive you. I'll find some way to make you sorry. I'll—"

"My love," Hunter interrupted softly, "you've already made me damned sorry. It's a constant source of regret to me, knowing that if I'd been kind to you all those years ago, I'd be in your arms right now. Instead I'm reduced to bargaining for just one glimpse of you."

Lara's defiant anger faded, and she regarded him with pained confusion. "It wasn't all your fault," she said unhappily. "I wasn't the one you wanted. And I don't enjoy intimacy of that kind. I think it's the way I'm made, or just some instinct I lack—"

"No, Lara. God. There's nothing wrong with you." Hunter closed his eyes, while the bitter taste of regret filled his mouth. He chose his words with excruciating care. "If you could just allow yourself to believe for one moment that it doesn't have to be painful or unpleasant—"

"Perhaps you could be more gentle than before," Lara said, her lashes lowering. "I believe it doesn't necessarily have to be painful. But even then, I don't think you could change my feelings about the act."

Her lovely face was so apologetic and dejected that it took all Hunter's strength to keep from going to her. "What feelings?" he asked gruffly.

Lara replied with obvious difficulty. "To me, what happens between a man and woman is so . . . sordid . . . shameful . . . and I'm such a failure at it. I have some pride, you know." She picked up the silk garment, which hung limply in her perspiring hands. "Making me wear this is a mockery, don't you see? It reminds me of my inadequacy as a wife."

"No," he said roughly. "The failure was your husband's, Lara. Never yours."

Lara stared at him with an arrested expression. The words he had chosen—*your husband's*—made it sound as if he were speaking of another man. Of course, he could be referring to himself in the third person, but it was an odd way to speak about himself. A touch of fear prodded her heart to beat more sharply, and she wondered if she should voice her suspicions. Before she could say anything, however, Hawksworth headed to the door.

He paused at the threshold and glanced back at her. "The bargain is set, Lara. If you want the child to stay, you'll have no objections from me. You know what I want in return."

Lara nodded stiffly, twisting the negligee in her hands as he left.

After Lara had changed into fresh linens and a light muslin gown, she emerged from her room to find Hawksworth waiting for her. There was an almost penitent look on his face, though she sincerely doubted that he regretted the bargain he'd made with her. "I thought you might take me around the house and describe the changes you're planning with Mr. Smith," he said.

"Perhaps you should consult with Mr. Smith and his assistants instead. I'm sure they are far better able to explain things than I, and if you don't approve of the schemes we've chosen, you can take it up with them directly."

"I approve of everything you've chosen." He took her hand and smiled at her, lightly playing with her fingers. "And I don't want to talk to Smith. I want you. So take me around the house . . . please." The last word was added with a cajoling smile she found hard to resist.

Lara hesitated while his fingertips drifted to the tender inside of her wrist. "All right," she said. "I'll tell you as much as I can remember, although Mr. Smith used many Italian words that I couldn't begin to pronounce."

Hawksworth laughed and kept her hand as they walked, threading his fingers with hers. It was an oddly pleasant feeling, her hand enclosed in his much larger one.

They began with the ballroom, where the Moroccan statuary would be replaced by rows of gleaming windows and marble colonnades. "They'll use *fleur de pêche* marble, I think," Lara said, stopping in the middle of the ballroom, the two of them standing alone on a sea of shining parquet. Her voice echoed slightly in the large room. "Mr. Smith said it contains many beautiful shades of amber. And over on that wall, they'll install ivory-colored paneling to make the room lighter." She turned to face him, seeking his reaction. His eyes were so dark and fathomless that she almost lost her train of thought. "As for the plasterwork . . ."

A long silence passed. "Yes?" Hawksworth prompted softly.

Lara shook her head, unable to remember a word she had been about to say. She kept staring at him, fascinated by his face, as thoroughly English and aristocratic as always . . . and yet . . . there was something different about him. It was more than the exotic copper hue of his skin and the startling whiteness of his teeth. It was a trace of foreignness, a sense that he didn't belong here in this civilized home discussing its interiors.

With an effort, Lara turned away and forced herself to continue. "They're going to strip away all the gilded plasterwork and replace it with a very subtle *basso-rilievo*." Her breath caught as she felt his hand settle at her waist. Moistening her dry lips, she managed to finish. "Two artists—*stuccatori*, Mr. Smith called them—will be sent from Venice to do the work."

"Very nice," he murmured.

He was so tall—he was standing close behind her, with the top of her head just reaching his shoulder. Suddenly she was tempted to lean back against him and press her head to his chest until she could hear his heartbeat. She had never liked very large men, feeling dominated in their company. But his strength now seemed inviting, and she realized in silent surprise that she no longer found his touch distasteful.

Lara stepped away from him with a nervous laugh. "I hope that Arthur and Janet will never take possession of the house again," she said lightly. "One wonders what new schemes they might come up with."

Hawksworth didn't share her smile. "They won't," he said seriously, following her, catching her easily. His warm hand slid to the small of her back. "There's nothing to fear from the Crosslands."

As he stared into her upturned face, he lifted his hand to the side of her throat and stroked her skin with the backs of his knuckles. Lara swallowed and stared at him, while his light touch made her shiver. "You know they must be planning some sort of legal action against you . . . us," she said.

"I'll deal with them when the time comes." His dark gaze captured hers. "I'll take care of you, Lara. Don't doubt it for a second."

"No, of course I . . ." She stopped and gasped as she felt him stroke her waist, sliding up until the heels of his hands brushed the sides of her breasts. To her bewildered dismay, she felt a responsive ache inside. "I wish you wouldn't touch me like that," she whispered. His head lowered, and she felt his mouth brush against her throat.

"Why not?" he asked, searching for the tiny hollow beneath her ear.

"Because it makes me feel so . . ." She groped for words, but as he pulled her closer, every rational thought flew from her head.

He cupped her breast with tantalizing gentleness, the soft weight fitting exactly in his hand. At the same time, he caught her earlobe with his teeth and touched it with his tongue. "How does it make you feel?" he murmured, but she only gasped and pressed herself against him in an unconscious plea for more.

He obliged her at once, capturing her lips in a long, slow kiss, his tongue gently probing and stroking inside her mouth. Skillfully he teased and caressed her, the kiss so compelling that she couldn't help responding. Her mind reeled with the improbability of the situation, finding such dizzying pleasure in her husband's embrace. They strained to be closer, her small hands clinging to his broad back, her body caught between his hard thighs. The sweeping excitement intensified, and she moaned and sagged against him until they were molded together from breast to thigh.

Only then did Hawksworth release her with an unsteady laugh, his lungs working hard for air. He stared at her swollen lips and flushed face, and a soft curse escaped his lips. "You make it hard to concentrate on panels and cornices," he muttered, his eyes bright with amusement.

Lara took a deep breath and tried to collect herself. She couldn't bring herself to look at him, afraid that if she did, she would be tempted to walk straight back into his arms. "Shall we continue with the tour?" she asked in a low voice.

Hunter approached her and slid his fingers beneath her chin, tilting her face upward. "Yes," he said with a rueful smile. "Just don't show me any of the bedrooms—unless you're prepared to deal with the consequences."

Chapter 10

THE EVENING MEAL was a long, drawn-out affair, attended by fourteen guests. Excited by the prospect of meeting the celebrated Possibility Smith, some gentry from Market Hill had angled for invitations, as well as the mayor, rector, Dr. Slade, and the Misses Withers, a pair of elderly sisters with a shared passion for gardening. As an afterthought, Lara had also invited Captain and Mrs. Tyler, a couple who had recently leased a manor house not far from town.

The guests began to arrive at seven o'clock and were shown into the drawing room, where Lara discreetly gathered them into appropriate pairs in preparation for the procession to dinner. The last to arrive were Captain and Mrs. Tyler. It appeared the Tylers were a well-matched couple, both of them small-framed and pleasant-faced. Having never met the Tylers before, Lara went to them immediately.

"Captain and Mrs. Tyler!" she exclaimed, greeting them warmly. "Welcome to Hawksworth Hall."

Mrs. Tyler murmured shyly and curtsied, while Captain Tyler, a dark-haired gentleman with a neatly trimmed black mustache, made their replies. "How do you do, Lady Hawksworth?" He bent smartly over her gloved hand. "We were honored by your invitation. It was a very great kindness for you to include us."

"Not at all. We are in dire need of new friends to enliven the neighborhood." She cocked her head and smiled at him inquiringly. "I had heard that you have recently returned from service in India."

"That is true," he acknowledged. "It's good to be back on English soil again."

"You'll have a great deal in common with my husband, then, as he lived there for a time."

"I'm afraid I never had the pleasure of making Lord Hawksworth's acquaintance, though I had heard of him. We moved in quite different circles." Although Captain Tyler was expressionless, Lara had the feeling that the last comment had been intended as a bit of censure. Being a military man, Tyler had probably disapproved of Hunter's lifestyle, living in a large household with at least fifty Indian servants, all of them devoted to one man's pleasure. No doubt Hunter had been a well-known roué, indulging himself freely in a land of beautiful women and sensual delights. The rumors of the endless parties and orgies held in Calcutta were rampant in London, and Lara was well aware that her husband had been no saint.

The thought of Hunter's sexual indulgences gave her a sour, unpleasant feeling, and she sought to cover it with a bland social smile. "If you haven't met Lord Hawksworth," she said, "we must rectify the matter immediately." Glancing around the room, she saw Hunter talking to Lord Lonsdale. No doubt the two of them were involved in some conversation about hunting, drinking, or other masculine pursuits. She caught Hunter's eye, and he excused himself from the private conversation in order to welcome the newcomers.

Dressed in a gleaming white waistcoat and cravat, cream breeches, and a chocolate brown coat with gilt buttons, Hunter looked every inch the aristocrat with centuries of breeding behind him. Only the deep tan of his skin and the tigerish grace of his movements distinguished him from the man he had been before. He approached them with the congenial smile of a host performing his duty . . . until he saw Captain Tyler's face. His steps slowed, and Lara thought she saw a flash of recognition in his gaze before his features were schooled into an inscrutable mask.

Captain Tyler wore the same impassive facade, but his face had turned pale, and his entire body was tense.

They knew each other—Lara was certain of it. She would have staked her life on it.

But they behaved as if they had never met. Stunned, Lara introduced them and witnessed their stiff attempts at conversation.

Captain Tyler stared at her husband as if he were seeing a ghost. "Congratulations on your miraculous return to England, my lord. It is the stuff of legend."

Hunter shook his head. "You're the legend, Captain, not I. Your accomplishments in India, particularly in suppressing the thuggees, are to be lauded."

The captain inclined his head. "Thank you."

Lara glanced at Mrs. Tyler, who seemed as bewildered as she. Why were the two men pretending to be strangers, when it was obvious there was some shared knowledge between them? They must have met each other in India, or perhaps they had some mutual friend or event that connected them in some mysterious way.

Although Lara looked at Hunter questioningly, he did not return her gaze. He disappeared behind a screen of impeccable politeness, betraying nothing of his true thoughts. The guests were led into the dining hall, all of them exclaiming with pleasure at the table laden with crystal, silver, candles, and flowers. Seated far away from her husband, Lara halfheartedly entertained the guests nearest her, enduring the Misses Withers's prattling about mignonette seeds and bedding plants, and Dr. Slade's accounts of his latest medical accomplishments.

The first course was brought out, a delectable array of soups and fish. It was followed by a course of venison, puddings, and vegetables, followed by another course of partridge, duck, and quail, cheesecakes and tarts, and so forth, until sweets, fruit, and biscuits were finally brought out. Wine flowed throughout the meal, the butler expertly opening bottles of Sauterne, Bordeaux and champagne, while footmen hastened to keep the guests' glasses filled.

Hunter was drinking a great deal, Lara saw with growing dismay. He had always been a heavy drinker, but this wasn't drinking for enjoyment's sake . . . this was deliberate. As if he were trying to assuage some inner pain that wouldn't abate. He raised his glass again and again, quiet except for an occasional biting comment that made the guests laugh. He spoke to Captain Tyler only once, when the conversation had turned to India, and Tyler was expounding on the idea that Indians were not fit for self-rule.

". . . history has shown that the natives are a corrupt lot and not to be trusted," Captain Tyler said earnestly. "Only through British intervention will the Indians be brought fully into the nineteenth century. And even then, they will always require the guidance and supervision of British officers."

Setting down his glass, Hunter sent a cool stare in Tyler's direction. "I knew a number of Indians who had the audacity to believe they could actually govern themselves."

"Did you?" There was a long pause, while Tyler's gaze suddenly acquired a malicious gleam. "How interesting. According to your reputation, you've rejected the idea of provincial autonomy for the natives."

"I changed my mind," Hunter snapped.

"The Indians have proved that they are not ready for such responsibility," Tyler rejoined. "A society which is rife with widow-burning, infanticide, brigandage, idol worship—"

"None of which have been helped by British intervention in matters that are none of our damned business," Hunter said, ignoring the gasps around the table at his profanity.

"What about Christianity? I suppose you're going to claim that the Indians haven't benefitted from that, either?"

Hunter shrugged. "Let them have their gods. They've done well enough with them. I doubt the average Hindu or Muslim is worse than any so-called Christian of my acquaintance."

The entire table was silent at the sacrilegious statement.

Then Captain Tyler burst out laughing, providing

relief from the tension, and smiles appeared as the group tacitly decided to treat the debate as a joke.

The rest of the dinner passed without incident, although Lara found it hard to keep from staring at her husband. She had rarely discussed politics with Hunter, as he'd had no interest in a woman's opinion on such issues. However, there was no doubt that he had once wholeheartedly approved of the British interference in India. How was it that he now apparently held the opposite view?

It took an eternity for the dinner party to end, with the rituals of after-dinner port and tea passing slowly, the guests staying until after midnight. Finally the last one had left, and the servants began to clear away the remaining plates and glasses and silver. Lara made an attempt to slip away to her room, reasoning that Hunter had drunk too much to notice or care where she went. Just as she reached the grand staircase, he caught her arm in one large hand, startling her.

Lara spun to face him, her heart jumping high in her throat. Hunter reeked of port, his eyes were glazed and his color was high, and he wasn't quite steady on his feet. "Drunk as an emperor," her father would have put it. Some men in that condition were as mellow as cattle, while others were loud and boisterous. Hunter was neither of those things. There was a sullen curve to his mouth and a dangerous moodiness in his expression.

"Where do you think you're going?" he asked, his grip firm on her arm.

With a stab of alarm, Lara realized that he had every intention of seeing their bargain satisfied that night. She would have to find some way of putting him off. With him in this condition, she was not about to display herself in a provocative negligee. The worst nights of her life had begun like this, with Hunter drinking heavily and forcing himself on her. "I thought I would leave you to enjoy another glass or two of port," she said, forcing her trembling lips into the semblance of a smile.

"And hope I would drink myself into a stupor," he finished for her, returning her faltering smile with a sardonic one of his own. "You won't be that lucky, sweet."

He began to pull her upstairs, like a tiger dragging its prey to a convenient location for snacking. Miserably Lara stumbled along beside him. "You haven't seemed yourself this evening," she ventured, then reflected inwardly that he *never* seemed himself—it was impossible to know what to expect from him. "Why did you take such an exception to Captain Tyler?"

"Oh yes, the Tylers." His voice was smooth and controlled, but somehow it stung like a whip. "Tell me, my sweet . . . how did they come to be at my table this evening?"

"They've leased Morland Manor," she said uneasily. "I'd heard that Captain Tyler had served in India, and I thought you would enjoy meeting him."

They reached the top of the stairs, and he jerked her to face him. Lara winced as his gaze raked over her face. He looked furious, accusatory, as if she had somehow betrayed him. "Hunter," she said softly, "what have I done wrong?"

After a moment some of the rage left him, though his eyes still contained a dangerous glitter, and he seemed to be battling ugly memories. "No more surprises," he muttered, giving her a little shake for emphasis. "I don't like them."

"No more surprises," Lara repeated, hoping that the storm had passed.

Hunter took a deep breath and let go of her. He scratched his head with both hands, dragging his fingers through his hair until the thick locks were a disheveled mass of sun-shot gold and brown. He seemed weary, and Lara thought suddenly that he might go to his bed in search of sleep.

Hunter punctured her budding hopes with one curt sentence. "Go and change into the negligee."

She was left stuttering. "I . . . but you couldn't possibly . . . I think another night would be . . ."

"Tonight." He smiled slightly, his face dark and satyric. "I've been waiting all day to have a look at you. A barrel of wine wouldn't be enough to stop me, much less a bottle or two."

"I'd rather wait," Lara said with a pleading gaze.

"Go now," he murmured. "Or I'll assume that you want me to help you change."

Quietly Lara took measure of his drunken determination and squared her shoulders. She would do it, if only to prove that she wasn't afraid of anything he could do to her. "Very well," she said evenly. "Come to my room in ten minutes."

He grunted in response, watching as she walked away from him with her spine held stiff and straight.

Lara struggled with a feeling of unreality as she entered her bedroom and closed the door. She wondered if she could really make herself stand before him in a gown that had been designed to flaunt a woman's body . . . a gown created to arouse a man. It was more provocative than nakedness. Hunter had never asked her to do something like this before. She supposed it was a result of the sexual experience he had gained in India, or perhaps this was merely a way of reasserting his control over her, to expose and shame her until she had no pride left.

Well, it wasn't going to work. He could humiliate her any way he chose, but he wouldn't touch the core of self-respect within her. She would put on the vulgar garment and despise him every minute that she wore it.

Trembling with outrage, Lara went to the armoire, where she had buried the negligee in a stack of chaste undergarments. Locating the garment, she drew it out with a grimace of distaste. The fragile web of lace and silk was so fine that she could have easily pulled it through a ring.

Awkwardly Lara undressed herself, having no desire for Naomi's assistance. She left her clothes and shoes in a heap on the floor. The negligee slid over her body in a cool whisper of silk, making her shiver. It fastened with tiny ribbons, which barely held the bodice and waist together. The skirt—if that was what it could be called—parted on both sides when she walked, exposing the entire length of her legs and part of her hips.

Should she let her hair down? She was tempted to unpin the braided coronet atop her head and brush the long locks until they helped to conceal her body. No . . . Hunter would only be amused by the cowardly attempt at modesty.

Lara went rigid as someone entered the room without knocking. Drawing close beside the armoire, half hidden by the massive piece of furniture, she peeked around it cautiously. Her husband sauntered to the

Hepplewhite chair, carrying a bottle of wine. He had removed his coat and cravat, the neck of his white shirt gaping to reveal his brown throat. Seating himself in a casual sprawl on the chair, he smiled insolently as he saw her tight-lipped face. Not bothering to hide his anticipation, he took a long pull on the bottle and gestured for her to come out of hiding.

The silent command increased Lara's furious agitation. After all, she was his wife, not some prostitute paid to perform on cue. "What shall I do?" she asked in a low, resentful voice.

"Walk toward me."

There was a fire in the grate, too far away for Lara to feel its heat. Goose bumps rose on her chilled skin. Gritting her teeth, she forced herself to obey, taking one step, then another, the fine Aubusson carpet prickling beneath her bare feet. As she came near him, the firelight shone through the transparent black silk. She knew he could see everything, the flashes of ivory skin, the shape of her body, the dark triangle between her legs.

Her face burned as she stopped before him.

Hunter sat like a statue, his face and hair dappled with light from the dancing flames. "Oh, Lara," he said softly. "You're so damned beautiful, I . . ." He stopped and swallowed, as if it were difficult for him to speak. His faint smile had died away, and he set aside the wine bottle as if his fingers had become nerveless. He barely seemed to breathe as his gaze swept from her bare feet to her breasts, lingering at the pink tips that strained against the delicate lace.

The room no longer seemed cold, but Lara continued to tremble.

"I made a promise not to touch you," he said

hoarsely, "but I'll be damned if I can keep it."

If he had grabbed or forced her in any way, she could have resisted. However, he reached for her so slowly, his fingers settling cautiously on her hips, as if he would frighten her with any sudden movement. His face was downturned, making his expression impossible to read. She heard his breathing, though, fast and scraping in his throat.

"I imagined this for so long," he said thickly, "seeing you . . . touching you . . ." His large hands slid down to her buttocks, fingers shaping to the taut curves. Exerting the slightest of pressures, he brought her closer between his spread knees. Mesmerized, Lara felt his hands begin a slow, careful sojourn over her body, gliding over her back, the indentations of her waist, the fullness of hips and thighs, even the hollows behind her knees. The heat of his palms sank through the thin barrier of silk as if it weren't even there.

Her heart pounded and she thought of pulling away, but her traitorous body wouldn't seem to obey. Hunter looked at her, his eyes filled with clear, dark heat, even as his hands began a slow upward slide to her breasts. He cupped their softness, lifting the pale weights encased in black lace. She gasped, her knees quaking until it took all her strength to keep from sinking into his lap. His fingertips stroked and lightly pulled the hardening centers, making the nipples stand in rosy peaks. He leaned forward, his breath like steam as it wafted over her skin.

His mouth covered the tip of her breast, surrounding her with heat and moisture that seeped through the screen of lace. She felt his tongue stroking, circling, sending ripples of pleasure through her aching flesh.

"Lara," he said, his voice gravelly. "I want you so much. Let me kiss you . . . taste you . . ." Haste made him clumsy, and he pulled at the bodice of her gown until her shoulder was bare and the lace was uncomfortably tight.

Lara whimpered, torn between indecision and excitement. "That's enough," she said, her hands fluttering against his shoulders. "You shouldn't . . . This isn't something I . . ."

But Hunter had found one of the silk ribbons and tugged it loose, the black lace spilling open to display her breasts. Filling his hands with the opulent curves, he spread greedy kisses over her tender skin. He captured a rosy nipple in his mouth and sucked greedily, while she shuddered and tried to push him away.

"Tell me you don't want this," he said fiercely.

Lara couldn't answer, couldn't speak with his tongue sliding between her breasts, his hands roaming over her naked skin. He jerked the second ribbon free, and the gown sagged to her hips. Growling in pleasure, Hunter kissed her belly, his tongue flickering around the rim of her navel before dipping delicately inside. Lara moaned in astonishment, jerking at the hot, moist touch, her fingers clutching at the rough silk of his hair.

Hunter pushed his head against her midriff with a tormented groan, and slid his arm around her waist. "Don't stop me," he breathed. "Please."

He picked her up as if she were a child, lurching toward the bed in a few drunken strides. Placing her on the mattress, he followed immediately, his large body levering over hers, his hands framing her face.

He kissed her hungrily, his tongue plunging and exploring her mouth, while she moaned in fearful delight. Tentatively she raised her arms around his neck, and his throat hummed with pleasure. His hand released its gentle clasp on her face and slid to the top of her thigh, where the thatch of dark curls was still veiled by the negligee.

"No . . . wait," Lara said, clenching her legs together.

To her surprise, he obeyed, resting his hand on the plane of her abdomen. He dropped his head beside hers, digging his forehead into the mattress. His lungs contracted with a great shuddering sigh.

They were both silent then, the heat of their bodies mingling. Hunter was so heavy next to her, his limbs stretching out well beyond hers.

Another time, long ago, he would have forced himself on her.

Filled with wonder and gratitude, Lara rested her hand on the heavy arm that crossed over her waist. She moved her palm over the hard curve of muscle, up to his shoulder. A wicked thought flashed through her mind, that she wished he had removed his shirt and exposed the tanned skin that intrigued her so.

"Thank you," she said, her voice a mere wisp of sound. "Thank you for not forcing me."

His silence emboldened her, and she stroked his shoulder in the first affectionate gesture she had ever dared to make toward him. "It's not that I find you unattractive," she murmured. A blush covered her face as she continued. "In fact, I think you're actually rather . . . appealing." She turned until her mouth was pressed furtively against the hot skin of his throat. "I'm glad you came back. Truly."

A soft snore rumbled near her ear.

Startled, Lara drew back and looked at him. Her husband's eyes were shut and his lips were parted like a slumbering child's. "Hunter," she said cautiously. He made a contented sound and snuggled against the counterpane. A raspy sigh escaped his throat, and the snoring resumed.

Lara bit her lip to hold back a sudden laugh. She disentangled herself from him and left the bed, kicking away the negligee as it tangled around her ankles. Hurrying to the armoire, she donned a fresh nightgown and robe. Hunter remained on the bed, a peaceful heap of long limbs and rattling snores.

Safely attired once more, Lara approached her husband. A wry smile curved her lips, and she reached for his feet, removing his shoes and stockings. She hesitated before unbuttoning his waistcoat, half expecting him to waken suddenly. He was lax and heavy, his muscles slack as she removed the well-fitted garment. Leaving him in his shirt and breeches, she pulled the side of the counterpane over him, protecting him from the chill of the night.

Before turning down the lamp, Lara paused to take one last glance at her husband. He was like some magnificent slumbering beast, all his alertness and vitality temporarily banked, his claws sheathed. But on the morrow he would be back in his usual form, mocking, argumentative, charming . . . and he would resume his efforts to seduce her.

What unnerved her was the realization that in some small way she was actually looking forward to it.

Frowning, Lara went to his bedroom to spend the night alone.

Chapter 11

JOHNNY SAT ON a chair next to Lara's, his seat augmented with a pile of books that elevated him to table height. The white napkin tied around his neck was splashed with chocolate, a treat that Lara guessed he had never tasted before. After gulping down a cup of the brew so quickly that she was certain he had burned his tongue, he repeatedly demanded another.

"First you must eat something," Lara said, nudging a little dish of eggs baked in cream toward him. "Try some of these—they're delicious."

Johnny eyed the gold and white splendor of the shirred eggs with open suspicion. "I don't want those."

"They'll help you to grow big and strong," Lara coaxed.

"No!"

Lara winced inwardly as she saw the disapproving look that flitted across the footman's face. Eggs were considered a luxurious treat by the servants, never to be wasted. Although they were too well trained to show open disapproval, some of the servants did not want to wait on a boy of Johnny's unsavory background. However, the boy could help matters by behaving himself and showing due appreciation for his new circumstances. If he could manage to endear himself to the servants—indeed, to the master—of the Hawksworth household, his position would be far more secure.

"I'm sure you could manage just one little bite," Lara coaxed, scooping up a bit of egg in a silver spoon.

Johnny shook his head violently. "More chocolate," he commanded, evidently having no plans to be endearing this morning.

"Later," Lara said firmly. "Here, take some of this toast. And a bite of ham."

His gaze met hers, assessing her determination, and he capitulated suddenly. "Awright." He held a piece of toast in both hands and bit off a corner, chewing enthusiastically. Eschewing the fork near his plate, he tore a chunk of ham with his fingers and stuffed it in his mouth.

Lara smiled, resisting the urge to lean over and crush him with a hug. For now she just wanted him to eat until his scrawny frame had filled out. The proper use of table utensils would be addressed later.

Even with the time she had spent at the orphanage, she had never been able to oversee a particular child's daily routine and enjoy interactions such as these. She found it unexpectedly satisfying. For the first time in her life, the burden of barrenness didn't seem so crushing. Even if she couldn't have her own flesh-and-blood child, she could create a family.

As Lara speculated silently on her husband's possible reactions to the idea of taking more children into their home, Hunter entered the breakfast room, looking uncharacteristically subdued.

"Good morning," Lara said cautiously.

Hunter made no reply, only cast a loathing glance at the sideboard laden with food. Looking pale beneath his tan, he turned to the waiting footman. "Tell Mrs. Gorst to make some of her witch's brew," he growled. "And bring a damned headache powder while you're at it."

"Yes, milord," the footman said, complying hastily. The recipe for a special "morning after" remedy had been in the family for years, but only Mrs. Gorst knew what was in it.

Johnny watched with wide eyes as Hunter poured himself a glass of water. The child looked at Lara questioningly. "Is 'e a duke?"

"No, darling," she replied, amused. "He's an earl."

Clearly disappointed, Johnny continued to stare at Hunter's broad back, and tugged at Lara's sleeve.

"What is it?" she murmured.

"Is 'e going to be my papa now?"

Hunter choked on a mouthful of water. Lara's lips quivered before she managed to reply. She stroked his black hair soothingly. "No, Johnny."

"Why doesn't 'e say nothing?" the boy piped in a voice that seemed to grate on Hunter's nerves.

"Hush, darling," she whispered. "I think he has a headache."

"Oh." Abandoning his interest in Hunter, Johnny looked down at the crumbs on his plate. He heaved a sigh. "I wonder how Mousie is."

Lara smiled, considering how to distract him from

thoughts of his lost pet. "Why don't you visit the stables today?" she suggested. "You can pet the horses and feed them a carrot or two."

"Oh, yes!" He brightened at the idea, and wriggled eagerly atop the pile of books.

"Wait," Lara cautioned, removing the napkin from around his neck. "First I'll send for Naomi, and she'll help you to wash your hands and face."

"But I washed yesterday," came the indignant reply.

Lara laughed and dabbed at his sticky face with the napkin. "You must remove the chocolate stains before you visit the stables, or you'll attract every fly in Market Hill."

After Johnny had been dispatched with Naomi, and the footman had brought a glass full of the mysterious remedy, Lara turned her attention to Hunter. "Do sit down," she invited. "Perhaps a slice of toast would help you—"

"God, no." The suggestion made Hunter wince. He sipped the remedy cautiously, and set it aside after finishing half the glass. Standing by the window, he cast Lara a brooding glance. It seemed that he had difficulty meeting her eyes, almost as if . . .

It couldn't be that he was embarrassed by his drinking spree of the previous night, could it? Lara rejected the idea immediately. There was no shame in a man drinking too much. In fact, Hunter and his peers considered it a masculine ritual to pour as much liquor down their throats as they could hold.

Puzzled, Lara stared at his averted profile. At first she had taken his mood for surliness, but on closer inspection he wore the expression of a man with an unpleasant duty to perform. Her curiosity grew until she finally gestured to the footman to leave, and he slipped from the room to allow them privacy.

Lara stood and wandered to the sideboard with an air of casual unconcern, while the silence thickened. It occurred to her that Hunter might be discomfited by the memory of intimacy between them, the things he had said, the way he had touched her . . . A bloom of heat spread over her face at the recollection.

"My lord," she remarked, "you seem rather quiet this morning. I hope that you are not distressed by . . . what happened last night." Her blush burned brighter as she waited for his reply.

After a moment, Hunter joined her at the sideboard, both of them staring steadily at the array of breakfast dishes. He took a deep breath. "Lara . . . regarding last night, I don't exactly remember what I . . ." He gripped the edge of the sideboard until his fingertips were white. "I hope . . . I didn't hurt you . . . did I?"

Lara blinked in amazement. He thought he had forced himself on her. What else was he to assume, upon waking in her bed with his clothes unfastened? But why would it trouble him now, when he had done it so many times before? She risked a quick glance at him. He appeared to be overcome with remorse.

How ironic, that Hunter had never felt a drop of guilt for the times he *had* hurt her, and then experienced such acute shame for something he hadn't done at all. Suddenly the situation struck her as irresistibly funny, and she turned away to hide her face.

"You were very much in your cups," she said,

struggling to sound dignified. "I suppose you didn't know what you were doing."

She heard a string of muffled curses, which only worsened her giggles, and she fought to contain them until her shoulders trembled.

"God, don't cry," Hunter said unsteadily. "Lara, please . . . you have to believe that I didn't mean to—"

Lara turned toward him, and his face went blank with astonishment as he saw her mirth. "You didn't," she gasped. "You fell asl—sleep—" She hiccuped with laughter, scooting away from him.

"You little devil," Hunter exploded, following her around the room. His relief was matched only by his annoyance. "I've gone through hell this morning!"

"Good," she said in blatant satisfaction, positioning herself on the far side of the table. "After making me wear that dreadful negligee, you deserved to feel a little discomfort."

Hunter tried to close the distance between them in a few strides, but she dodged him and retreated behind a chair. "I'm not sorry for making you wear the negligee—only that I barely remember seeing you in it. You'll have to put it on again."

"I most certainly will not!"

"It doesn't count if I don't remember."

"I remember enough for the both of us. I've never been so mortified!"

Abandoning the chase, Hunter braced his hand on the table and surveyed her with glowing dark eyes. "You were beautiful. That much I do recall."

She tried not to be disarmed and flattered, but it was difficult. The mood changed between them, becoming surprisingly comfortable. Lara sat at the table, while Hunter glanced at the crumb-scattered area Johnny had occupied. "Have you told the boy that he's to live with us from now on?" he asked abruptly.

A smile touched her lips. "Not in so many words. Actually, he seems to take it for granted."

"He's damned lucky. Any other child in his situation would have been dispatched to a workhouse—or worse."

Lara picked up a fork and toyed with the remaining scraps on her plate. "My lord," she murmured, "there is something I would like to discuss with you. I've been thinking about what happened to Johnny, having to live in prison with his father because there was no one to keep him, and ... I'm certain that he isn't the only one. If it occurred at Holbeach, it must happen in other prisons as well. Right now there may be many children residing with their parents behind bars, and I can't imagine a more appalling atmosphere—"

"Wait." Hunter pulled out a chair and sat facing her, reaching for her hands. He covered her fingers in a warm grip and stared directly into her eyes. "You're a compassionate woman, Lara. God knows you won't rest until every orphan, every beggar, and every stray dog and cat in the world is taken care of. But don't start a crusade just now."

Annoyed, Lara snatched her hands away. "I haven't proposed doing anything," she said.

"Yet."

"For now, all I want is to find out if there are other children in Johnny's circumstances. I've considered writing to various prison administrators and inquiring if they lodge any children of prisoners there, but I'm afraid that even if they do, they won't admit to it. Especially if the person asking happens to be a woman." She paused and stared at him expectantly.

"You want me to find out," Hunter said flatly, scowling. "Dammit, Lara, I have enough to attend to as it is."

"You once had many important political connections," Lara persisted. "If you asked some government officials or inspectors for whatever information they might have . . . or perhaps there is a reform society that might be able to supply—"

"There are at least three hundred prisons in England. Suppose we discover there are indeed children living with their convicted parents—ten, twenty, perhaps a hundred. What the hell would you be able to do about it? Adopt them all?" Hunter laughed without amusement, and shook his head. "Put it out of your mind, Lara."

"I can't," she said passionately. "I can't be as hard-hearted as you. I won't rest until I find out what I want to know. If necessary, I'll personally tour every prison I can find."

"I'll be damned if you'll set foot in even one of them."

"You can't stop me!"

They glared at each other, and Lara felt herself turn scarlet with a mounting rage that seemed out of proportion to the situation. If only she hadn't learned what it was like to live without a husband, if only she hadn't experienced the heady feeling of making her own decisions after he had left for India, then she might have been able to accept his judgment. But now the idea of being controlled and curtailed and *forbidden* to do something made her livid. Terrible words rose to her lips—she wished he were back in

India, or at the bottom of the sea, or any other place than in the same room with her. Somehow she kept silent, the effort making her eyes sting with furious tears.

She heard Hunter's low voice. "Lara. You're too precious for me to let you risk one hair on your head. So rather than tying you to a bedpost to ensure that you don't visit any damned prisons . . . I have a proposition for you."

Bewildered by his sudden tenderness, Lara lowered her head and concentrated on drawing invisible circles across the surface of her skirts. "Whatever your proposition involves, I am *not* going to wear that negligee again."

He reached over to squeeze her thigh. "Here's the bargain, my love . . . I'll get the information you require, but in the meantime you're not to go near Holbeach or any place like it. And when I find out what you wish to know, you won't take action of any kind without consulting me."

Lara looked up and opened her mouth to argue.

"I didn't object when you told me that Johnny was going to live with us," he reminded her. "You took matters into your own hands without saying a word to me. I chose not to stand in your way because I understood how badly you wanted to keep the boy. In the future, however, we'll act as partners. Agreed?"

Lara was hardly able to believe that Hunter Cameron Crossland, the sixth Earl of Hawksworth, had proposed being partners with her. He had always made it clear that she was nothing more than an extension of him, an appendage . . . a possession.

"Agreed," she murmured, and shot him a suspicious glance. "What are you smiling at?"

"You." He surveyed her with a look of masculine interest that was rapidly becoming familiar. The lazy smile remained on his lips. "I'll wager that everyone who knows you considers you to be soft, sweet, and accommodating. But you're not."

"What am I, then?"

Hunter's hand slid behind her neck, and he urged her forward until their lips were almost touching. Lara felt the warm touch of his breath, and her stomach turned over in excitement. "You're a lioness," he said, and released her without kissing her . . . leaving her to grapple with an absurd sense of disappointment.

The hallway echoed with the sounds of a child whimpering in frustration. Hunter's steps slowed. He paused in the arched opening, staring around the columns set against the wall. The boy was there, huddling on the floor with his back wedged in the corner. He wasn't crying, but he sniffled as if tears were imminent, and his cheeks were red. He stared up at Hunter and tugged nervously at his shorn black hair.

"Why are you sitting there?" Hunter asked in vague irritation, having no experience with children, or any understanding of their needs and wants.

"I'm lost," the child said miserably.

"Why isn't someone with you?" There should have been someone appointed to watch over the boy— God knew what sort of mischief he could get into. When that question elicited no response, Hunter tried another. "Where do you want to go?"

The tiny points of his shoulders moved beneath his oversized shirt as he shrugged. "I 'as to piss."

Hunter's mouth twitched in reluctant sympathy. "Can't find the privy? Well, I'll take you to one. Come with me."

"I can't walk."

"I'll carry you, then. But you'd best hold your water, I'm warning you." Gingerly Hunter picked up the mite and headed down the hallway. His load was surprisingly light. What strange eyes the boy had, a shade of blue so pure and dark it appeared to be violet.

"Are you married to milady?" Johnny asked, linking his arms around Hunter's neck.

"Yes."

"When I get big, I'm going to marry 'er."

"She can't be married to two men at the same time," Hunter replied, amused. "What will you do with me?"

"You can stay 'ere," the boy offered generously. "If milady wants it."

Hunter grinned into the small, serious face that was so close to his. "Thank you."

Johnny glanced downward as they walked. "You're tall," he said. "Ewen taller than my papa."

The remark sparked Hunter's interest. "Tell me, bratchet . . . why was your father hanged?"

"'E was a bug 'unter, Papa was. 'E killed someone, but 'twas an accident."

Bug hunters—the men who robbed drunks who wandered the streets at night. Hardly a top-drawer criminal . . . just one of the various scum that populated the London underworld. Hunter concealed his distaste and shifted the boy in his arms. "Where is your mother?" he asked.

"Mama's in 'eaven."

The boy had no one, then.

An innocent smile crossed the boy's face, as if he could somehow read Hunter's thoughts. "You an' milady got me now, aye?"

It was only now that Hunter began to understand Lara's attraction to the child. "Yes, I've got you," he found himself saying, without any trace of sarcasm. Well, the boy could do worse than have the knack of making people want to take care of him.

They reached a small room fitted up with a water supply, privy pan, and waste pipe, and Hunter set down his charge with care. "Here you go." He paused and asked uncomfortably, "Do you need help with, er . . . this sort of thing?"

"No, I can do it." The boy entered the little room and looked back anxiously. "You'll be 'ere when I come out?"

"I'll be here," Hunter replied, and stood staring at the door when it closed. He was unwillingly touched by the child, the small misplaced duckling brought to live among swans. Except that Hunter himself was no swan.

It wouldn't be comfortable to live with a child who unwittingly reminded him of his greatest weakness, day after day. A Hindu would shrug and say that it was the gods' will. *Each man is responsible for his own salvation,* a holy man had once instructed him—blasphemy to a Christian, but it had made sense to Hunter. *In some cases salvation will happen only when one breaks with society.* Johnny would come to the same understanding, if he was to survive in this corner of the world called England.

*   *   *

Captain Tyler sat heavily in a leather chair, the gentlemen's room lit only by a small fire in the grate. He held a glass of brandy in both hands, letting his palms warm the liquor. He sipped it slowly, in the manner of a man who deeply appreciated small luxuries.

Morland Manor, a small but well-maintained house, was poised on a hill like an elegant little bird that had established its preferred territory. The cloudless night loomed around them, vast and cool, making Tyler glad of his cozy sanctuary. The hour was late, and his attractive wife slept peacefully upstairs, her waist slightly thickened by a pregnancy in its early stages.

The joy of expecting his first child should have filled Tyler with contentment. And being back in England, something he had fiercely desired for eight years, should have given him the peace he had long expected. However, the well-deserved peace and contentment eluded him, driven away by a most unexpected turn of events.

"Damn you," Tyler murmured, gripping the brandy tightly. "Why didn't you stay in India?"

And then something amazing happened . . . something he would later acknowledge he should have expected. The shadows in the room seemed to shift and alter, and a dark figure emerged from the corner. Too stunned to react, Tyler watched as the current Earl of Hawksworth walked toward him.

"I had better plans," Hunter said softly.

To his credit, Tyler remained outwardly calm while he struggled to collect himself. The trembling of the glass in his hands was all that betrayed his agitation. "Cocky bastard," he said. "Only you would dare to accost me in my place of residence."

"I wanted to see you in private."

Tyler buried himself in his brandy, not stopping until he had drained it. "Until last night I thought you were dead," he said gruffly. "What the devil are you doing in England?"

"That's not your concern. I only came to warn you—don't interfere."

"You dare to give *me* orders?" Tyler turned purple. "What of Lady Hawksworth? That poor woman has a right to know—"

"I'm taking care of her," Hunter said, his voice softly menacing. "And I'll have your silence, Tyler . . . one way or the other. After all I've done for you, I deserve it."

Tyler seemed to swallow back a reprimand, while his conscience warred with a bitter sense of obligation. Eventually his shoulders sagged with defeat. "Perhaps you do," he muttered. "I'll have to think on it. For pity's sake, leave now. You remind me of things I'm trying damned hard to forget."

Chapter 12

To Lara's frustration, the promised report concerning English houses of correction did not come the next week, or the next. She was almost grateful for the refurbishing of the house, which occupied much of her attention as Possibility Smith and an army of craftsmen and assistants went about their work. She also visited her friends at Market Hill, and the orphanage. Most of her waking hours, however, were consumed by Johnny and the task of accustoming him to the new world he had been introduced to.

And of course, there was Hunter.

He managed the family's affairs, dutifully attended social events, and listened to his tenants' concerns. In addition, he managed the tricky and unorthodox strategy of involving the family more deeply in trade, when other peers were aspiring to do the opposite. A man had much higher social standing when he had completely withdrawn from mercantile concerns and concentrated solely on the aristocratic business of landowning. However, Hunter demonstrated a remarkable willingness to sacrifice pride in favor of practicality.

He was the husband Lara had once wished him to be: responsible, courteous, kind ... friendly. It was this last that caused her such unexpected annoyance. In a perplexing change of tactics, Hunter appeared to seek her friendship and little else. He barely seemed to notice her as a woman.

There had been a time when Lara would have been thrilled by this situation. She had all the benefits of a husband—security, comfort, companionship—without the physical demands she had disliked so much. Why, then, was she constantly on edge? Why did she wake in the middle of the night, empty, agitated, burning for a nameless something she couldn't identify? She craved her husband's company until she began to invent excuses to see him. And each time they were together, Hunter showed her the same maddening friendliness that caused her teeth to grind.

Lara didn't know what she wanted from him. She dreamed about his kisses, not the brotherly pecks he sometimes gave her, but the sweet, endless joinings of lips and tongues that set her world off balance. Yes, she wanted his kisses. More than that, she wasn't certain. If she allowed him to sleep with her, he would consider it his right to take her whenever he wanted. It was better to leave things the way they were. But why did Hunter have to treat her as if she were his younger sister?

In an impulsive moment, Lara sent word to the dressmaker to alter the gowns that were being made for her, and lower every neckline a full two inches. The collection finally arrived, a pastel rainbow of silk, muslin, and cambric, with matching bonnets trimmed in feathers or flowers ... silk scarves and gloves . . . shoes and ornamented slippers, fans of ivory, paper, and lace.

Filled with feminine pleasure in the new clothes, Lara dressed in a pale green gown that matched her eyes and made her skin seem to glow. Her breasts were pushed together by the plunging neckline, covered only by a translucent scarf. Knowing that Hunter was working alone in the library, she went to him straightaway. It was only polite, really, to thank him for his generosity.

Her husband sat at his desk, having removed his waistcoat and rolled up his shirtsleeves, the neck of his shirt open to catch any cooling breeze that might enter the room. He gave her a brief glance and a casual smile, and returned his attention to his work. In less than a second, however, his gaze flew back to her . . . and stayed.

"Is that a new gown?" he asked mildly, although he knew perfectly well that it was.

Lara ventured farther into the room. "Do you like it?"

There was no change in his expression, but his fingers clamped tightly around the quill until it threatened to snap. His gaze swallowed her, taking in every detail, combing restlessly over her slender body. "The fabric is very attractive," he replied in a monotone . . . but a warm current ran beneath his words, and her nerves tingled responsively. He still wanted her. She didn't know why that pleased her, but it did.

A teasing smile hovered on her lips. "The fabric is attractive? That's all you're going to say?"

A dangerous glint appeared in his eyes. "I would

compliment the design, but a large part of the bodice seems to have been omitted."

"A low-cut neckline is all the rage," she replied.

Hunter made a dismissive sound and returned his attention to the open ledger on his desk. Deliberately Lara approached his chair and feigned an interest in the book. She leaned closer, her breast brushing his upper arm. The touch was accidental, but a responsive thrill shot through her body, and she knew that Hunter felt it too. He inhaled sharply and dropped the quill, scattering drops of ink across the desk.

"I'm trying to work," he growled. "I can't think with your breasts hanging in my face."

Stung, Lara drew back. "You were the one who insisted that I have some gowns made. I merely wanted to show one to you. I had some misbegotten idea of thanking you."

"Yes, well . . ." He half laughed, half groaned, and reached for her before she could turn away. He caught her hips with one arm, clamping it hard around her buttocks. Pulling her between his thighs, he stared at her hungrily. "The gown is beautiful," he muttered. "And so are you. As a matter of fact, it hurts to look at you."

"Hurts?"

"My entire body is one large ache." Bringing her one step closer, he pulled at the silk scarf and dropped it to the floor. With a suddenness that left her stunned, he buried his face in her exposed cleavage, his half-open mouth dragging over her breast, tongue touching the cool ivory smoothness. "You're making me insane," he mumbled, the bristle of his jaw making her skin tingle. "No, don't pull away . . . let me—"

Lara jumped in shock as he found her nipple through the delicate muslin of her gown. "Stop it . . . stop!"

He released her with a frustrated snarl, standing to glare at her from his full height. "You knew full well what you were doing, coming in here dressed like that. Don't blame me for snapping at the bait."

Lara bent and fumbled for the fallen scarf. "I-I didn't ask to be mauled."

"Do you know what they call a woman who deliberately arouses a man and then withholds herself?"

"No," she said shortly.

"A tease."

"I wasn't trying to tease you. Perhaps I may have desired a kiss, or a compliment, but I hardly think—"

"My feelings for you don't stop at kisses. Dammit, do you think it's easy for me, living under the same roof, seeing you every day and never touching you?"

Lara stared at him in growing bewilderment and a vague sense of shame. She had misread him—she hadn't understood that he still wanted her, that it was difficult for him to live with her.

"I want to make love to you," he continued, his voice slightly hoarse. "I want to see you naked, kiss you everywhere . . . pleasure you until you beg me to stop. And wake in the morning with you in my arms. And hear your voice telling me—" He broke off and set his jaw hard, as if fighting to contain the words.

Lara fidgeted in agitation. "I'm sorry," she said softly. "I didn't realize that you still desired me."

"Here's a clue." He seized her once more, his fingers closing around her wrist, and pulled her hand right between his legs. Ignoring her squeaking protests, he molded her hand around the stiff, straining length of his erection, until the heat of him burned through his trousers and scorched her palm. With his other arm he pressed her body tightly against him. "This is what happens every time I'm in the same room with you. A stiff cock and blue balls are a fair indication that a man wants you."

The memories of all her old experiences with him seemed to cloud Lara's mind. She couldn't think of the throbbing hardness beneath her hand as anything other than a weapon. It wasn't difficult to recall the knifelike thrusts, the intimate battering that had left her sore, defeated, and shamed. Never, never again. "I don't care to discuss your private parts," she choked. She tried to jerk her hand free, but he wouldn't allow it.

"I'm a man, not a eunuch. I can't kiss and touch you, and never have you." He buried his mouth in the curve of her neck, making her shudder. "Let me come to you tonight. I've tried to be patient. I can't stand it any longer."

Close to tears, Lara finally managed to wriggle free, and tottered back a few steps. "I'm so sorry. I can't, I *can't*. don't know why I . . . Please, you must go to Lady Carlysle."

The mention of his former mistress seemed to be the last straw. Hunter's face twisted with furious contempt. "Maybe I will."

Lara was as still as a statue, watching as he went to his desk and snatched up a letter.

"By the way," Hunter snapped, "I've just received a letter from Lord Newmarsh—he served on a parliamentary committee to investigate prisons. Here's the information you wanted."

He tossed the letter to her, and she made a fumbling attempt to catch it. The folded paper fluttered past her fingers and slipped to the floor.

Striding from the room, Hunter threw one last jeer over his shoulder. "Go help the poor and needy, Lady Bountiful."

Lara scooped up the letter and turned to glare at the door as it slammed behind him. "Lecherous goat," she said, but a trickle of guilt seeped through her annoyance. Hunter had been right—she had known what she was doing. She had wanted him to admire her. She had wanted him to desire her. What had possessed her to provoke him when she had no wish to sleep with him? Why hadn't she been able to leave well enough alone and enjoy the distant but pleasant relationship they had developed?

She felt an overwhelming need to make peace with Hunter, but she suspected that at this point there was only one kind of apology he would accept, and that would involve crawling between the sheets with him.

Sighing, Lara went to the chair at his desk and seated herself. She touched the leather upholstery, which seemed to hold a lingering trace of warmth from his body. If she closed her eyes, she could almost detect his scent, the hint of sandalwood that was clean, fresh, and exotic at the same time. *I'm sorry*, she almost said aloud, though there was no one to hear. She was sorry for not being like other women who didn't seem to mind intimacy with men, and sorry for Hunter, who wanted more than she was able to give him. Remorse and loneliness knotted inside her.

Bending her head over the letter, she began to read.

*　　*　　*

Hunter left on horseback, giving no word as to where he was going, and stayed away all afternoon and evening. Lara waited in the family parlor, curled on the velvet-upholstered sofa. Her knees were covered with the red and blue lap blanket that had been knitted for her by some of the orphanage girls. The housemaids had replaced it at least three times with far more elegant embroidered and fringed blankets from the linen storage, but Lara had retrieved it each time. "I like this red and blue one," she had told Naomi, smiling into the maid's perplexed face. "I know it's not perfect, but every missed stitch or lumpy knot reminds me of the children who made it. And it's by far the most comfortable blanket in the house."

"If I were you, milady, I shouldn't want anything to remind me of when the Crosslands cast you out of the house," Naomi had dared to comment, eyeing the blanket with disfavor. " 'Twas a dark time for us all."

"I don't want to forget it." Lara had smoothed the blanket and folded it lovingly. "I learned some important things from that experience. I've been a better person since then, I hope."

"Ah, milady." Naomi had given her a warm smile. "You were always a jewel. We all thought so."

"What of Lord Hawksworth?" Lara had asked suddenly. "Do the servants like him better or worse since his return?"

Naomi had frowned thoughtfully as she replied. "He was always a good master—he was liked well enough. But now he takes more notice of the servants. Like the way he sent for the doctor when he saw that one of the housemaids had an abscess in her arm, or when he said that George the footman could have his fiancée to tea in the kitchen on his days off. He never did things like that before . . ."

Lara's thoughts were interrupted by the gentle peal of the longcase clock in the hall. Deciding to retire, she stirred sleepily on the sofa and pushed the blanket aside. At that moment, a dark figure shuffled past the door, and paused to investigate the source of lamplight.

The intruder, of course, was Hunter, with his clothes disheveled and his gait a little too loose-limbed. He had been drinking, though he didn't seem to be precisely drunk. He walked into the room with an obnoxious smile on his face—the smile of a teenaged boy who had misbehaved and was proud of it.

Lara drew her knees up and hugged them, her fingers lacing together tightly. "I hope you're feeling better," she said crisply. "From the smell of you—smoke and strong drink and heavy perfume—I gather you found some trollop to satisfy your needs."

Hunter stopped before her, his smile turning quizzical. "For someone who wants nothing to do with my private parts, you take an unseemly interest in where they've been."

"I'm only glad you heeded my advice and found a woman for yourself," she said.

"I went drinking with Lonsdale and some friends. And there were women. But I didn't tumble any of them."

"That's a pity," Lara said, though she couldn't help feeling a stab of relief at the information. "As before, I would be pleased if you took a mistress and spared me your attentions."

"Would you?" he asked, his tone deceptively mild. "Then why did you wait for me to return?"

"I wasn't waiting for you . . . I couldn't sleep. I can't stop thinking about the letter from Lord New-marsh, and the children who are in the same terrible circumstances Johnny was in—"

"Twelve," he interrupted. "There are twelve prison brats in all." One brow arched sardonically. "I suppose you want to do something about them now."

"We can discuss it tomorrow, when your mood is more amiable."

"A few hours of rest are not going to make me amiable." Hunter lowered himself to the opposite corner of the sofa, long legs arranged in a masculine sprawl. One large hand waved in an expansive gesture for her to proceed.

Lara hesitated, trying to gauge his mood. There was something puzzling about his expression—patient, watchful, like an animal at its favorite hunting grounds. He was waiting for an opportunity, and when it came, he would pounce on it. She couldn't begin to guess what he had in mind, but she strongly suspected she wouldn't like it.

"I am certain that the prisons would want these children removed from such terrible surroundings, if someone offered a suitable alternative," Lara began carefully. Hunter responded with an agreeable nod. "Obviously they must be brought to the orphanage at Market Hill," she continued, "but it is too small. A dozen children . . . well, we would need to enlarge the place, and hire more staff, and find a way to provide more food, clothes, and supplies . . . and that is quite an undertaking. I wish we had the means to accomplish all that—"

"We don't," he interrupted. "Not now, at any rate."

"Yes, I'm aware of that." Lara cleared her throat and arranged her skirts with exacting care. "Therefore we must solicit funds from other sources. With all of our friends and acquaintances, it shouldn't be difficult. If I—that is, if we—arrange some sort of benefit for the orphanage—"

"What kind of benefit?"

"A ball. A sizable one. We could use it as a means to attract donations for the Market Hill orphanage. And to ensure that everyone will come, we could also use it as an occasion to . . . welcome you home." She steeled herself not to wince at his steady dark stare. It was a good idea, actually. The *ton* would be so curious to see the mysteriously returned Lord Hawksworth and hear his incredible story that they would flock in droves to the ball. He was already the talk of London, and this would surely be the event of the Season.

"So you plan to exhibit me like a two-headed freak at the county fair, and use the proceeds to benefit your orphans."

"It wouldn't be like that—" Lara protested.

"It would be exactly like that." Slowly he sat up and leaned forward, all the while pinning her with that fathomless dark stare. "After what I've been through, now I'm expected to endure an evening of probing questions and scrutiny from a herd of shallow nitwits. And for what?"

"For the children," Lara said earnestly. "You'll have to face the *ton* sooner or later. Why not do it now, and arrange the time and place to your liking? Why not have the satisfaction of saving twelve children who deserve the chance to lead a decent life?"

"You overestimate me, sweet. I don't have a charitable bone in my body. I don't lose sleep at night thinking about orphans and beggars. I've seen too many of them. They're a fact of life—they'll never disappear. Save a thousand of them, ten thousand, and there'll always be more."

"I don't understand you," Lara said, shaking her head. "How can you be so kind to your own servants and so heartless to outsiders?"

"I can only afford to care for those who live under my roof. The rest of the world can go to hell."

"It appears you haven't changed after all." Sickening disappointment welled up inside her. "You're as heartless as always. For some reason I actually thought you would allow me to help those children."

"I haven't forbidden you to hold the ball. I'm only leading up to the conditions I'm going to impose."

"What conditions?" she asked warily.

"Ask me why I didn't tumble any of the whores I was with tonight," Hunter said. "I could have, easily. There was one with breasts the size of melons, and she kept sticking her tongue in my ear—"

"I don't want to know about that."

"Lonsdale and the other fellows were grinding the wenches on the tables, the floors, against the wall—but I left when all of it started, and came home to you. Do you know why?" Hunter smiled bitterly, as if he were about to tell a dirty joke. "Because I'd rather sit outside your door and moon over you while you sleep in your celibate bed. The mere act of holding your hand, or hearing your voice, or smelling your perfume, is more exciting than bedding a hundred women."

"You only want me because I'm a challenge," she said.

"I want you because you're sweet and pure and innocent," he said huskily. "In the past few years I've seen things more foul than you could imagine . . . I've done things you would never . . ." He stopped and let out a harsh sigh. "I want a few hours of peace. Of pleasure. I've forgotten how to be happy, if I ever did know. I want to sleep in my own bed with my own wife—and I'll be damned if that's a crime."

"What are you talking about?" Lara asked, bewildered. "What happened to you in India?"

He shook his head, a mask dropping over his face. "It doesn't matter. As things stand now, I've been reduced to bargaining for a night with you—and I'll be damned glad to get it."

"If you think that I'll sleep with you in exchange for—" Her eyes widened. "You couldn't possibly mean that you won't let me hold the benefit if I don't . . ."

"That's exactly what I mean. Make the arrangements and invite a thousand guests. I'm sure your efforts will be much admired, and the orphans will be grateful. Everyone will be pleased. Including me. Because at one o'clock on the night of the benefit, you're going to come upstairs with me, and get into my bed, and let me do as I wish with you."

"Can't you think of anyone or anything besides yourself?" Lara turned crimson. "How dare you use those poor children's misery in order to make me sleep with you?"

"Because I'm desperate." He smiled mockingly. "Do we have a bargain, my love?"

She didn't answer.

"It's not as if you haven't done this before," he reminded her.

Her lower lip protruded mulishly. "I hated it."

"You survived," he pointed out curtly. He sat there waiting, as stalwart and unbudging as a huge block of granite, impervious to her tiny barbs. There was nothing she could say, no counteroffer he would accept. Self-serving ass! How dare he turn a noble cause into a quest for his own sexual satisfaction? She longed to throw the bargain back in his face and assure him that nothing in the world would make her subject herself to *that* again. But the thought of twelve children like Johnny, suffering needlessly . . . and the thought of what she could do for them . . . it was more than she could bear.

Would it be so terrible to spend a night in Hunter's bed? He was right, she had survived the other times. She had managed to extinguish every emotion and sensation, and concentrate on other things, and ignore what was happening to her.

Lara's heart sank in her chest as she realized that she would have to do the thing she most disliked in order to get what she most wanted.

"All right," she said in a dull voice. "The night of the benefit. One time. And then . . ." She searched her mind for the appropriate epithet. "Then you can go to hell!"

He showed no sign of satisfaction, but she sensed the enormous pleasure he took in her surrender. "I'm already in hell," he said. "I just want one night of furlough."

* * *

Hunter left his pale, tightly strung wife, and somehow made his way to his own room. He fumbled with his boots and crawled onto the bed fully clothed. His brain was swimming with giddiness, partly because of the alcohol and partly because of the emotions that moved him. He had expected to feel triumph, but instead there was only relief. He imagined holding Lara, loving her, drinking in her sweetness like a soul in hell who had been granted a glass of cool water. "Thank God," he mumbled into a downy pillow. "Thank God."

"Oh my." Rachel's hazel eyes were round pools of amazement. "I've never heard of a husband negotiating with his wife in such a way. Of course, I've heard of the arrangements men make with their mistresses, but . . . you're not exactly . . ." She floundered and ended by saying lamely, "This is all very odd."

"Extremely odd," Lara agreed grimly. "After becoming a widow and allowing myself to believe I would never again be bothered with men and their distasteful urges, I find myself in the position of having to sleep with Hunter again." She curled herself into a tight ball on the chair and stared glumly at the fine, luxurious surroundings of Rachel's parlor. "It's even more dreadful to know about it so far in advance."

Rachel stared at her in a sort of fascinated sympathy. "Do you intend to keep your promise?"

"Of course not," Lara said promptly. "I want you to help me think of a plan. That's why I came to visit."

Obviously flattered and pleased that her older sister would value her ideas, Rachel set aside her needlework and concentrated on the problem. "I suppose you could make yourself so unattractive that he would no longer desire you," she said. "Or go catch the pox from someone, and hope it spreads over your face."

Lara wrinkled her nose. "I'm not especially fond of that idea."

Rachel began to wax enthusiastic about the project. "You could feign illness."

"That would only work for so long."

"Perhaps there is some way to render him impotent—some herb or powder we could give him."

Lara considered the suggestion doubtfully. "I shouldn't want to risk making him ill . . . and it seems a very tricky plan. I would be so nervous that I would end up giving the whole thing away."

"Hmm." Picking up a stray skein of blue silk, Rachel wound it around her finger. "Perhaps," she said hesitantly, "you should just give yourself to him for one night and be done with it."

"I won't be *used* that way," Lara said, suddenly fierce. "I won't be a convenience or a possession."

"I must disagree, Larissa. I don't know where you've gotten these strange ideas. Lord Hawksworth is your husband. You belong to him. You vowed to obey him."

"I did obey him. I followed his wishes concerning my behavior and the company I kept. I asked his permission for everything. I tolerated his adultery and I never once denied him my bed. But then he left for India, and for three years I only had myself to please . . . and I can't go back to the way it was."

"You may have to," Rachel murmured. "Unless we

can come up with a suitable plan to divert him."

They were both silent for a long time. Their un-spoken thoughts were underscored by the pounding of the heavy saturating rain outside as it splashed on the graveled drive and streamed down the window-panes. A gray, dolorous day, matching Lara's mood to perfection.

Finally Lara spoke. "The only thing that makes sense is to find someone else that Hunter will desire more than me. Then he'll be so besotted over his new discovery that he'll forget all about our bargain."

"But . . . didn't he say that you are the only woman he wants?"

"He didn't mean it," Lara said shortly. "I know from past experience that Hunter isn't capable of re-stricting himself to one woman. He likes variety. He enjoys the conquest."

"Whom are you going to find?" Rachel asked. "What kind of woman will be irresistible to him?"

"That's the easy part," Lara said, going to stand by the window, watching the sheets of rain whipping down from the sky. "You know, Rachel, I think this plan has half a chance of working."

Chapter 13

THE ROADS HAD turned to mud by the time Lara left the Lonsdale estate. The heavy chaise and four moved sluggishly through the mire, making slow progress past sodden pastures, farms, and prickly hedgerows planted to keep cattle from wandering. It seemed impossible that the rain should keep falling so heavily, but it struck the roof of the carriage as if someone were dumping buckets of water on them. Concerned for the comfort of the horses, driver, and footman, Lara wished that she had waited to visit her sister until the weather was clear. It had been ill advised to venture out during a spring rain—but who would have expected such a deluge?

She leaned forward in her seat as if she could will the carriage to reach its destination without mishap. The wheels dragged over the road, sinking into soft, mud-filled ruts while the horses strained to pull the vehicle forward. Suddenly the carriage gave a peculiar lurch and settled in a diagonal tilt, throwing Lara across the seat in a sprawl. She sat up and struggled to reach the door, wondering what had happened.

The door opened, water and wind blasting in as the footman's worried face appeared. "Are you injured, milady?"

"No, no, I'm fine," she said hastily. "What about you, George? And Mr. Colby?"

"We're all right, milady. There was a hole in the road—the carriage is stuck. Mr. Colby says we're not far from Market Hill, though. If it pleases you, we'll unhitch the horses, and I'll go to Hawksworth Hall for a lighter vehicle. Mr. Colby will stay here until I return."

"That sounds like a good plan. Thank you, George. Please tell Mr. Colby to wait inside the carriage with me, as he will be much more comfortable."

"Yes, milady." The footman closed the door, conferred with the driver, and returned in a minute. "Lady Hawksworth, Mr. Colby says he would prefer to stand watch outside. He has an umbrella and a greatcoat to keep the rain off, he says, and one never knows about the riffraff that travels the roads."

"Very well," Lara said ruefully, settling back against the seat. She suspected that it was her reputation and not her safety that the driver was concerned about. "You may tell Mr. Colby that I said he is a gentleman."

"Yes, milady."

Rain pounded on the disabled carriage, fat, aggressive drops that seemed to strike from every direction. Lightning shot across the sky, while rolls of thunder were punctuated by earsplitting cracks that made Lara jump. "What a misadventure," she said aloud, hoping that George and Mr. Colby didn't catch their deaths after being chilled and soaked through to the skin. She would hold herself to blame if either of them became ill.

The wait seemed interminable, but after a while there seemed to be some activity other than the storm outside. Lara stared out the window, but all she could make out were some blurry shapes moving through the grayness of the storm. She edged closer to the door and reached for the knob, intending to have a look outside. Just then the door was wrenched open, admitting a gust of wind and cold rain. Startled, Lara scrambled to the far side of the vehicle, while a huge, dark shape appeared in the open space.

The man, swathed in a black greatcoat, removed his hat. It was Hunter, a slight smile on his lips, his long lashes spiky and wet from the water that dripped down his face.

"I thought you were a highwayman!" Lara exclaimed.

"Nothing so romantic," he assured her. "Merely your husband."

A husband who was as dashing and unpredictable as any highwayman, she thought. "You didn't have to come out in this downpour, my lord. The servants are well able to bring me home."

"I had nothing better to do." Although Hunter's tone was offhand, he swept an assessing glance over her, and Lara realized that he had been concerned for her safety. The thought caused a little glow in her heart.

Busily she reached for a mahogany compartment underneath the seat and pulled out a set of pattens. It was the only way to keep the hems of her skirts from being ruined.

Hunter eyed the metal rings fitted on tiny stilts

with frank skepticism. "You don't need those," he said as she endeavored to buckle the leather fastenings around her feet.

"Yes, I do. Otherwise my skirts will become muddy."

That produced a hearty laugh. "I'm standing in ankle-deep mud at the moment, madam. You would sink up to your knees. Put those aside and come here."

Lara complied reluctantly, tying her bonnet ribbons in a neat bow. "You haven't brought a carriage?" she asked.

"And risk having a second one stuck?" He reached for her and swept her into his arms, carrying her out into the storm. Lara gasped and ducked her head against his shoulder as stinging pellets of rain struck her face. She saw that Mr. Colby was seated on horseback, holding the reins of Hunter's chestnut gelding as he waited for them.

Hunter lifted Lara into the empty saddle as if she weighed no more than a feather, and swung up behind her. The saddle was slick and smooth, with no pommel for Lara to hook her knee around. Instinctively she scrabbled for purchase, feeling herself slide across the horse's back. She was caught at once, a muscular arm locking around her.

"Relax," Hunter said close to her ear, his voice caressing. "Do you think I'd let you fall?"

Lara couldn't reply, blinking hard against the rain, shivering as it sank through her pelisse. With one hand Hunter unbuttoned his greatcoat and pulled her inside, enveloping her in a snug cocoon. It was warm against his body, and her shivers of discomfort changed to tremors of pleasure. Breathing deeply, she filled her nostrils with the smell of damp wool, and man, and Hunter's familiar spicy scent. She slid her arms around his hard midriff, feeling utterly safe, tucked inside his coat with the rain coming down around them. Evidently her bonnet annoyed him, for he jerked impatiently at the ribbon, pulled it off, and threw it aside as the horse began a bone-jarring trot.

Lara emerged from his coat in indignation. "That was my favorite—" she began, but a sheet of rain hit her face, and she ducked inside the greatcoat once more. The horse's gait evened into a swift, smooth canter. She had only ridden like this once before, when she was a small child and her father had taken her on horseback to the village shop and bought her an ell of ribbon for her hair. Her father had seemed so large and powerful to her, so capable of solving all her problems. As she had gotten older, her father had somehow shrunk into human proportions, and she had seen with disappointment the way he had withdrawn from both his daughters after they were married. As if she and Rachel were no longer his responsibility.

Lord Hawksworth is your husband, Rachel's voice echoed through her mind. *You belong to him . . .*

Hunter's arm was hard around her as he held her through the cloak, his thighs moving smoothly to control the horse. A nervous pang went through Lara's stomach as she thought of being at the mercy of this large, seemingly invulnerable man. He had promised to be gentle with her . . . but when a man was moved by his base desires, he had little control over his actions.

With those unhappy thoughts in mind, the proximity of Hunter's body no longer seemed pleasant, and she shifted uncomfortably. Somewhere over her head she heard him ask something, but the storm and the thudding of the horse's hooves made it impossible to hear.

Why had Hunter come after her himself? Once he wouldn't have considered her worth the bother. So much of his behavior was puzzling these days . . . the way he had bargained for her favors instead of simply forcing himself on her . . . the mix of mockery and endearments that never betrayed his true feelings . . . and now riding to her rescue when there was absolutely no need. As if he were wooing her favor. But why would he court her when he knew for a fact that she would sleep with him in a month's time?

Lara was so distracted by the unanswered questions that it was almost a surprise to find that they were on the drive leading to Hawksworth Hall.

They stopped before the front entrance, and servants rushed outside with umbrellas. Lara was both sorry and relieved when Hunter released her from his greatcoat and helped her from the horse. A footman held an umbrella overhead and escorted her to the entrance hall. Naomi hurried to divest Lara of the damp pelisse, while Mrs. Gorst dispatched a pair of maids to fill a bath for her. Lara stood shivering in her damp traveling gown, watching as Hunter removed his coat and hat.

He rubbed his dripping face and scrubbed his fingers through his partly wet hair, and slanted her a crooked smile.

Her own feelings confounded her. He was her adversary, but also her protector. He wanted her body, and in the process of pursuing it, he could very possibly break her heart. Heedless of the servants who might have seen them, Lara approached him hesitantly.

"Thank you," she said. Before he could reply, she stood on her toes, braced her palms on his hard chest, and pressed her lips to his smooth-shaven cheek. Hunter was very still, his breath catching slightly. The kiss was chaste by any standards, but when she drew back to look at Hunter, he wore an absorbed, intent look.

Their gazes met, and a wry grin twisted his lips. "For one of those I'd swim the channel," he said, and headed in the direction of the library.

Luxuriating in the large copper bath, Lara immersed herself up to her collarbone and closed her eyes in contentment. The heat of the water seemed to penetrate to her bones, while the lavender scent Naomi had sprinkled in the bath caused fragrant steam to rise in the air. A few long wisps of her hair fell from the topknot on her head and dangled in the water. As she splashed the water over her chest and throat, someone opened the door of the dressing room without knocking.

Lara tensed while Naomi went to intercept the visitor. "Oh, milord," Lara heard the maid say, "Lady Hawksworth is indisposed—that is—"

Hunter entered the dressing room and stopped at the sight of his wife in the bath, only her head and one bare foot visible. Lara's toes curled tightly over the rim of the copper tub.

"I thought you'd be finished by now," Hunter said, staring at her without blinking.

"As you can see, I'm in the middle of my bath,"

Lara replied, striving to sound dignified. "Naomi, please show Lord Hawksworth out."

"That's all right, Naomi." Hunter turned to the lady's maid with a considerate smile. "I'll attend my wife. Why don't you go downstairs and have some tea? Rest your feet. Take the rest of the afternoon off."

"Wait—" Lara began, frowning, but it was too late.

Giggling, Naomi accepted the invitation and disappeared, leaving the two of them alone together. The door closed behind her with a swift click of the latch.

Lara directed a reproving stare at her husband. "Why did you do that?"

He ignored the question. "You have eyes like a mermaid," he murmured. "Soft, pale green. Beautiful."

"I knew it was only a matter of time before you walked in during my bath," Lara said, trying to sound calm although her heart was pounding. "Your request to see me in that negligee made it quite evident that you're a shameless voyeur."

Hunter grinned. "I've been found out, it seems. But you can't blame me for it."

"Why not?"

"After more than a year of sexual deprivation, a man has to have some pleasure."

"You could expend your energy on something more productive," Lara suggested as he came closer to the bath. "Develop a hobby . . . collect something . . . take up chess or pugilism."

His eyes twinkled at her prim tone. "I do have a hobby, madam."

"Which is what?"

"Admiring you."

She shook her head with a reluctant smile. "If you weren't so annoying, my lord, you would almost be charming."

"If you weren't so beautiful, I wouldn't be annoying." He gave her an easy masculine grin. "But I plan to annoy you often, madam, and someday you'll like it." He took another step toward the tub. "Brace yourself—I'm coming closer."

Lara went rigid, thinking of covering herself, screaming, splashing him . . . but she did none of those things. She remained in the tub, stretched before him like a pagan sacrifice. Hunter made no obvious show of staring at her, but she knew that he took in every detail of her body as it shimmered beneath the scented water. "What do you want?" she asked. Her face felt hot, warmed no longer by the steam but by her own inner agitation.

If Hunter reached into the water right now, and pulled her out into his arms and took her to bed . . . she wasn't certain she would fight him. Part of her wanted him. Part of her wanted to be lost in him . . . and that thought didn't frighten her nearly as much as it should have.

Hunter seemed to have difficulty breathing. He reached out and fumbled for her hand, prying her fingers loose from their grip on the tub's edge. "Here. This is for you."

She felt him press a small object into her palm. Her fingers curled around it. "You could have waited until after my bath."

"And risk not seeing you like this?" He laughed unsteadily and backed away from the tub as if he no longer trusted himself.

Lara's wet fingers unfurled, and she looked down at the gold circlet in her hand, a heavy gold shank that supported a huge rose-cut diamond. The simple setting enhanced the fiery beauty of the water white diamond. "Oh," she said softly, staring at the stunning piece, unable to trust her own eyes.

"You never had a betrothal ring, as I recall," Hunter remarked casually.

Lara continued to stare at the sparkling gem in her hand. "But . . . is it wise to make such a purchase in our circumstances?"

"We can afford it," he said abruptly, sounding annoyed. "You leave those worries to me. If you don't like the thing, we'll have it exchanged for something you prefer."

"No, I . . . no. It's beautiful." Hesitantly Lara slid the stone, which weighed at least four carats, onto her finger. The ring fit snugly on the fourth finger of her left hand, looking unreal in its magnificence. It felt odd to wear a ring after leaving her hand bare for so long. Finally she dared to look at Hunter. He was expressionless, but his posture betrayed his tension. At the sight of her small smile, he seemed to relax.

"You've never given me anything like this before," Lara said. "I hardly know what to say."

"You can thank me later," Hunter replied, regaining his usual cockiness. "I believe you know how." He left the room with an arrogant male laugh, while Lara's shy pleasure turned into annoyance. She should have expected him to ruin the tender moment with a reminder of the hideous bargain they had made.

Settling back in the tub, she lifted her hand and

regarded the ring closely. The jewel was suitable for a queen. Why had he given her such a priceless gift? She suspected that the ring had been intended as a declaration of ownership . . . or perhaps he wanted to convince their peers that they were by no means financially destitute. Or was it possible he had merely wanted to soften her heart toward him? Shaking her head in wonder, Lara regarded the closed door and spoke her thoughts aloud. "I don't understand you, my lord. I never have . . . and apparently never will."

Possibility Smith's labors on Hawksworth Hall were far from over, but he had more than earned his sizable fee on the ballroom alone. Gone were the marble blackamoors dressed in pink togas, and the heavy, ugly giltwork. The room was now light and fresh, the walls covered in cream paint and crowned in delicate plasterwork, the row of long windows bordered by amber marble colonnades. Four huge chandeliers hung from the ceiling, strings of glittering crystal drops shedding light on the parquet floor below.

At Lara's instruction, the gardener, Mr. Moody, had made up massive arrangements of roses, lilies, and exotic blooms that had been placed around the ballroom. The heady fragrance spread through the air as a cool spring breeze blew through the open windows.

The night of the ball had come quickly . . . far too quickly for Lara.

She desperately wanted the evening to be a success. From the enthusiastic responses the invitations had garnered, it was sure to be heavily attended. She planned to use every means at her disposal to collect enough pledges for the orphanage to make certain that there would be no more children forced to live in an English prison. Hopefully Hunter would do his part by entertaining the guests with the tale of his miraculous return from India.

"Promise you'll try to be charming," Lara had pleaded with him earlier in the day. "And promise you won't mock anyone when they ask silly questions—"

"I know what to do," Hunter had interrupted grimly, his mouth curling with impatience with the entire affair. "I'll play my part to everyone's satisfaction. Just so long as you fulfill *your* obligations."

Knowing what he meant, Lara had bit the inside of her cheeks and flashed him a quick glare. It had been the first time in nearly a month that he'd had the bad taste to remind her of their bargain. She comforted herself with the knowledge that come one o'clock, Hunter would be far too busy with another woman to give her a thought.

With Naomi's help, Lara bathed leisurely in hot lavender-scented water and smoothed perfumed cream over her shoulders, arms, and throat. A faint dusting of pearl powder gave a translucent gleam to her face, while an application of rose-tinted salve made her lips dewy and pink. Naomi pulled Lara's hair into a braided coil atop her head, giving the effect of a sable crown, and adorned it with individual pearls sewn onto pins.

Lara's gown was simple yet beautiful, a delicate sheath of white overlaid with silvery gauze. The neckline swooped dramatically low, while the sleeves were nothing more than transparent bands of silver lace. It was an elegant gown, but a little too daring. Of course, it had been far more circumspect before she had mistakenly told the dressmaker to lower the neckline.

Lara stared at the mirror critically. "Thank heaven there is time for me to change."

"Oh, milady, you mustn't!" Naomi exclaimed. " 'Tis the loveliest gown I've ever seen, and you're a picture in it."

"The picture of indecency," Lara said, laughing as she tugged uncomfortably at the bodice. "I'm going to fall out of this thing at any minute."

"Lady Crossland wore gowns cut lower than that without batting an eye," Naomi said. " 'Tis the fashion."

Forbearing to point out that Janet was the kind of woman who had installed a mirror on her bedroom ceiling, Lara shook her head. "Bring out the pink gown, Naomi. I'll remove the pearls from my hair and fasten a rose there instead."

As the maid opened her mouth to argue the point, Johnny came bursting into the room with screams and yelps of delight. "Watch out! 'E's coming!" the boy cried, and dove against Lara's skirts.

Startled, Lara looked up as a tigerish roar resounded through the room, and Hunter came through the doorway. Moving with fluid swiftness, he approached Lara and snatched up the giggling boy. He lifted Johnny in his arms and pretended to snack on him like a starving beast, while the child squirmed and screamed and laughed.

"They're playing tiger-hunting in India again," Naomi said to Lara. "They've been at it all week."

Lara smiled as she watched the pair. In the past few weeks Johnny had begun to display a boisterous energy that equaled ten boys. He was a natural mimic and had responded well to Lara's efforts to teach him manners. He liked games of all kinds, and used his crafty intelligence to excel in them.

Dressed in a light blue short coat and dark blue trousers, his black hair covered with an ever-present forage cap adorned with brass buttons, Johnny could never be mistaken for a child who had come from the gutter. He was handsome, healthy, and adorable. And he was hers.

She didn't care what others thought of the situation, or how many disdainful eyebrows were raised. She would not care in the future, when others were sure to spread ugly rumors about Johnny's parentage, and insinuate that he was her bastard child, or Hunter's. How could any of that matter? She had been given the chance to take care of a child, to love him, and she intended to do just that.

What she hadn't expected, however, was Hunter's bond with Johnny. Despite his lack of experience with children and his initial resistance to Johnny's presence in their home, Hunter seemed to understand the boy far better than Lara did. He had quickly learned the mysterious language of frogs, mud cakes, sticks, rodents, and rocks that so delighted little boys. Games of chase and challenge, wrestling, off-putting stories ... Hunter knew endless ways to enthrall Johnny.

"I like the boy," he had admitted easily, when Lara had dared to mention his apparent attachment to the child. "Why shouldn't I? I'd prefer him to any of the delicate, passive creatures that are trotted out from most aristocratic nurseries."

"I expected you to resent him because he's not yours," Lara had said bluntly.

Hunter had smiled sardonically. "As you once pointed out, his lack of pedigree isn't his fault. And the mere fact of having Crossland blood doesn't ensure that a boy will turn out to be a paragon. I'm proof enough of that."

Squirming from Hunter's grasp, Johnny approached Lara. His blue eyes were round with interest and awe as he beheld her evening gown. "You look pretty, Mama."

"Thank you, darling." Lara bent down and hugged him, careful not to look at Hunter or Naomi. As Johnny had no memories of his own mother, he had tentatively begun to call her "Mama," and Lara did nothing to dissuade him. She knew it startled the servants, but none of them would dare mention it. As for Hunter's reaction, he kept his opinion to himself.

Johnny touched a fold of the silver fabric, rubbing it between his thumb and forefinger. "It looks like metal, but it's soft!" he exclaimed.

Lara laughed and straightened his cap. "It's almost bedtime. Naomi will help you wash and change into your nightshirt, and I'll come in a few minutes to say prayers with you."

The small black brows drew together in a frown. "I want to see the ball."

Lara smiled, understanding Johnny's curiosity about the strange proceedings. For the past few days he had watched the preparations for the event, the flowers and decorations being brought in, the chairs and stands set up for the musicians, and the laborious efforts of the kitchen staff. "When you're older you may have your own children's ball," she said. "And when you're an adult you may attend all the balls you wish—although by then I'm afraid you'll do your best to avoid them."

"I won't be an adult for years an' *years*," Johnny said fretfully, enduring Lara's smiling kiss and trailing after Naomi as she led him from the room.

Left alone with Hunter, Lara was finally able to turn her full attention to him. "Oh," she said softly, as she received the full impact of her husband in evening clothes—a remarkable sight to behold.

Straightening his cream marcella waistcoat and adjusting his crisp white cravat, Hunter glanced at Lara with a wry smile. His cream pantaloons were snug but not too tight, and his dark blue coat followed the lines of his broad shoulders and lean, well-exercised body with breathtaking precision. He wore his hair unpowdered, the short golden brown locks brushed back from his face. During the past weeks, his complexion had lightened from its startling copper tan to a smooth, light amber.

A well turned-out, utterly civilized man, one would think at first glance . . . but on closer inspection, there was something exotic and mysterious about him.

As she stared at him, she experienced a moment of doubt that frightened her.

He must be her husband, she told herself. He had the unmistakable look of the Crosslands. Besides, no stranger could have come this far, fooling Hunter's friends and family and his own wife, and daring to present himself to the *ton* tonight . . . It went beyond audacity. It bordered on insanity. He *must* be Hunter. Floundering in sudden anxiety, Lara could not look at him. "Very presentable," she said, her voice brittle and light.

He came to her, touched her, his fingers sweeping
over her bare upper arm, tracing the edge of her
neckline, stopping at the high curve of her left breast.
Lara couldn't stop the wild ascent of her heartbeat,
the uncontrollable response that made her want to
press her entire body against his. She held still, quivering slightly with the effort, baffled and yearning
and alarmed.

"You're the most beautiful woman I've ever seen,"
she heard him say. "More beautiful than anyone or
anything on earth." He leaned closer, and she felt his
mouth at her temple. "You need more pearls with
this gown, at your neck, waist, wrists . . . Someday I'll
cover you with them."

Lara's hands fluttered at her sides. She wanted to
rest them on him, touch him, but she clenched her
fists to keep them still. The diamond ring had turned
around on her finger, the rose-cut stone nestling
tightly in her palm. "You don't have to give me jewelry," she said.

"I'll give you half of England before I'm through.
I'll build back our fortune ten times over—you'll
have everything you've ever wanted. Jewels . . . land
. . . a dozen houses filled with orphans."

Lara looked up into his teasing dark eyes, and to
her relief, the shadow of doubt faded. She was still
nervous, of course, hoping that her plan to divert him
tonight would work, but the other matter . . . the suspicion over his identity . . . suddenly seemed ridiculous.

"Twelve orphans is all I'm asking for," she said.
"Although I want the orphanage enlarged sufficiently to accommodate twice that number. I have no

doubt we'll easily find children to fill the extra places."

Hunter smiled and shook his head. "God help anyone who stands in your way. Including me." He fingered one of the pearls in her hair and smoothed his fingertips over the shining braid. "Why have you become so passionate about children?" he murmured. "Is it because you're barren?"

Strange, that the word that had once wounded so deeply had now lost its power to hurt. In a way, Hunter's matter-of-factness seemed to absolve her of the guilt and unhappiness she had once felt. The barrenness was not her fault, and yet she had always felt responsible. "I don't know," she replied. "It's just that there are so many children who need someone to help them. And if I can't be a mother, I can at least be a sort of benefactress."

Hunter stood back and stared at her, his eyes so clear and deep that cinnamon lights seemed to flicker in the coffee-colored irises. "You remember what happens at one o'clock," he said quietly, with no taunting or mockery.

Lara's stomach seemed to flip, her nerves thrilling unpleasantly. She managed a slight nod, her chin dipping a half inch.

It seemed that he wanted to say something else, but the instinct to let well enough alone kept him silent. He returned her nod with a wary one of his own, and Lara realized that he expected her to welsh on the bargain. The thought interested her—what would he do if she simply refused to sleep with him? Would he be angry, demanding, sullen? Would he try to seduce her, ravish her, or simply wash his hands of her?

* * *

Carriages lined the long drive leading to Hawksworth Hall, while crowds of servants and footmen
worked with smooth efficiency to convey the mem-
bers of the *ton* from the vehicles to the entrance hall.
Lara and Hunter stood together, greeting and ex-
changing pleasantries with each new arrival. Hunter
performed his duties with competent charm, but Lara
was aware of a tension in him, a reined-in impatience
that betrayed his longing to be elsewhere.

The ballroom and surrounding halls echoed with
conversation and laughter, as guests exchanged wit-
ticisms with well-oiled ease. They swarmed around
the row of heavily laden buffet tables, filling china
plates with cold meats, puddings, eggs stuffed with
caviar, pastries and salads, exotic fruits and marzipan
sweets. The uncorking of wine and champagne bottles provided a steady staccato beneath the rapturous
hum of the guests, while lilting music drifted from
the musicians' bower in the ballroom.

"Lovely!" Rachel exclaimed, joining Lara when she
was finally able to move freely among the guests. It
occurred to Lara that her sister had lost weight recently. Her fine bones were too prominent. Even so,
Rachel was exceptionally pretty, her skin like rich
milk, her eyes a swirling mixture of green, brown,
and gold. The dark amber silk of her gown draped
softly over her slender figure, its scalloped folds
barely covering the little gold sandals on her feet.

Lara was amused to note that more than a few men
were staring openly at her sister, despite the fact that
she was a married woman. Of course, the so-called
gentlemen of the *ton* were rarely fazed by such insig-
nificant matters as marriage vows. She herself was

receiving a few admiring glances, though she ignored them coolly. The men who cast flirtatious comments and glances at her now were the same ones who had avoided her like the plague when she had been a poverty-stricken widow.

"I believe it's the grandest affair I've ever seen in Lincolnshire," Rachel said enthusiastically. "You've planned it brilliantly, Larissa. It seems you're as marvelous a hostess as ever."

"I've been out of practice for a while," Lara said with a self-deprecating shrug.

"One could never tell." Casting a surreptitious glance around them, Rachel lowered her voice before asking. "Has *she* arrived yet?"

There was certainly no need to ask whom she was referring to. Lara had been watching the door like a hawk for the past two hours. She shook her head with a frown. "No, not yet."

"Perhaps she won't come," Rachel suggested hesitantly.

"She *must*," Lara replied grimly. "She would out of curiosity, if nothing else."

"I hope so."

Their conversation was interrupted by the approach of Lord Tufton, a shy young viscount who had once offered for Rachel's hand, but had been eclipsed by Lonsdale's greater fortune and position.

Lonsdale had resembled a prince, with his athletic build and dark handsomeness and his aura of virility. Tufton, by contrast, was a small, bookish sort of man, far more comfortable in intimate gatherings than large ones. He was gentle and intelligent, and his near-worship of Rachel seemed not to have dimmed in the years since her marriage to Lonsdale. Back then Lara had believed along with everyone else that Lonsdale was the better match for her sister. Now she reflected sadly that Rachel would have been much happier with this shy, sweet man than with a brute like Lonsdale.

After greeting them both, Tufton turned a hopeful smile toward Rachel. "Lady Lonsdale," he murmured, "would you do me the honor . . . that is, I hope you would consider . . ."

"Are you asking me to save a dance for you, Lord Tufton?" Rachel asked.

"Yes," he said with patent relief.

Rachel smiled. "My lord, I would be very pleased to—"

"Hello, darling." To all of their dismay, Lord Lonsdale's voice interrupted Rachel's reply. He slid his arm around her waist, his grip tightening until Lara saw her sister wince. His hard gaze bored into Tufton's mild brown eyes. "My wife has saved all her dances for me, Tufton—tonight and every night thereafter. Save yourself the embarrassment of rejection by refraining to approach her ever again. And tell that to any other man who wishes to pant and drool over her."

Lord Tufton flushed and stammered excuses as he made a strategic retreat to the other side of the room.

Lara turned a questioning stare toward Lonsdale, wondering what had caused such crude behavior. "Lord Lonsdale," she remarked coolly, "it's perfectly normal for a married woman to indulge in a harmless dance or two."

"I'll handle my wife as I see fit. I'll thank you not to interfere. Excuse me . . . ladies." Lonsdale gave them a mocking glance, as if the word were hardly applicable to such a pair, and left after one last remark to Rachel. "Try not to behave like a tart, will you?"

The sisters were frozen in silence as he walked away.

"Did Lonsdale just call you a tart?" Lara managed to ask, white-faced.

"It's only that he's jealous," Rachel murmured, staring at the floor. She seemed like a wilted flower, all her lovely glow evaporated.

Lara seethed with fury. "What does Lonsdale have to be jealous of? Surely he would never dare to accuse you of infidelity, when you are the sweetest, most honorable woman who ever lived, while he's a great rutting hypocrite—"

"Larissa, *please*. Lower your voice, unless you wish to cause a scene at your own ball."

"I can't help it," Lara replied. "I hate the way he treats you. If I were a man, I'd beat him to a pulp, or call him out, or—"

"I don't want to discuss it. Not here." Wreathed in artificial calmness, Rachel walked away as if she were unable to tolerate another word.

Boiling in frustration, Lara retreated to the corner of the room where she could simmer in private. She accepted a glass of champagne from a passing footman and downed it too quickly, causing a fit of hiccups. Champagne was not a beverage easily guzzled.

As she twirled the empty glass in her fingers, she saw her husband coming toward her. Hunter wore the same bland smile he'd had two hours ago. As he had predicted, he was prominently on display. Old and new acquaintances alike were clearly fascinated by him, and they didn't hesitate to fawn and question and annoy him like so many gnats.

"Are you enjoying yourself?" Lara asked, though she already knew the answer.

His thin social smile didn't falter. "Immensely. There are packs of idiots everywhere I turn."

"Have some champagne," Lara advised, disliking the feeling that had suddenly come over her, a sort of camaraderie, as if the two of them shared an understanding that excluded the rest of the world. "It makes everything a little easier." She gestured with her glass. "At least, that's what I'm hoping."

"I don't like champagne."

"Have some punch, then."

"I'd rather have you."

Their gazes met, locked, and Lara found that the teasing comment affected her far more strongly than the champagne. She felt unsteady, giddy, endangered. He was waiting, she realized, minute by minute, biding his time until one o'clock when she would be helpless in his arms. Every instinct prompted her to turn and run . . . but there was no sanctuary available. She took a deep breath and still felt suffocated.

Gently Hunter removed the glass from her nerveless fingers, gestured for a servant who seemed to appear from nowhere, and placed it on a silver tray. "Another?" he asked, and Lara nodded stiffly.

Her gloved hand curled around the stem of a new glass, and she drank it as rapidly as the first, with the same results. The sparkling bubbles seemed to float into her brain, and she covered her mouth with her fingers to suppress another attack of hiccups.

Hunter's brown eyes gleamed with amusement. "It's not going to work, my sweet."

"What's not going to work?"

"You can drink until you're corned, pickled, and salted . . . but I'm still going to hold you to our bargain."

She gave him a glance of seething annoyance. "I had no such plan in mind. However, I'll drink as much champagne as I want. After all, I can't recall a time when you ever came to my bed sober."

His gaze evaded hers, and his mouth tightened in what was either anger or regret. "I'm sorry about that," he said gruffly, glancing about the room as if she had made him uncomfortable. "Lara, I—"

Something caught his attention, and he stopped in midsentence. He didn't seem startled so much as . . . intent . . . as if he were suddenly occupied with solving an important riddle. Lara followed his steady gaze, and her entire body twitched in reaction as she realized whom he was looking at.

A tall woman stood near the doorway. Her attractiveness was the kind people usually called handsome rather than beautiful. She was lean and large-boned, her arms lightly muscled from a devotion to outdoor activities such as hawking, hunting, and archery. A man's woman. Her strong, almost stern features were balanced by rich chestnut hair, sherry-colored eyes, and a pleasantly curved mouth. A cream-colored gown draped over one shoulder and left the other bare, falling over her statuesque body in the style a Greek goddess would favor.

Lara was puzzled by the lack of obvious recognition on Hunter's face. He glanced around the room and took note of the slew of curious gazes fastened on him, the way everyone watched for his reaction.

Then he looked back at the woman, who gave him a faintly tremulous smile.

Suddenly the woman's identity seemed to dawn on him, and he shot Lara a glance of black rage. "Damn you," he breathed, and left her as he headed toward his former mistress, Lady Carlysle.

Lara felt hundreds of gazes on her as the scene unfolded. The rush of gossip—amused, pitying, fascinated—threatened to drown out the musicians. Shaken, she was barely aware of her sister coming to her side.

"All going according to plan," Rachel remarked, trying to look as though nothing unusual were happening. "Try to smile, Larissa—everyone is watching."

Lara obediently curved her lips in an imitation of a smile, but her mouth felt stiff and numb.

"Why do you look so strange, dearest?" Rachel asked softly. "He's gone to her, just as you planned. It's what you wanted, isn't it?"

Yes, it was what she had wanted . . . but how could she explain that everything seemed horribly wrong? How could she explain the awful moment in which Hunter hadn't seemed to recognize his former mistress? It must be that he had been shocked by the unexpected sight—that and the fact that he hadn't seen Lady Carlysle for more than three years. It had taken him several seconds to recover.

Lara took a deep breath, trying to calm herself, but the ache in her chest remained. She had accomplished her goal, bringing Hunter and Lady Carlysle together. Now their old passion would reignite and Lara would be left alone once more. Exactly what she wanted.

Why, then, did she feel so betrayed? Why did she feel as if she had made a terrible mistake?

"Here, give me that." Rachel took the empty champagne glass from her. "You're about to snap the stem in two." She stared closely into Lara's face. "Dearest, what is wrong? How can I help you?"

"It's too hot in here," Lara said thickly. "I don't feel well. Act as hostess for me, Rachel, just for a few minutes. Make certain everything goes smoothly until I return."

"Yes, of course." Rachel squeezed her gloved hand. "Everything will be all right, dear."

"Thank you," Lara whispered, not believing her for a moment.

Chapter 14

HUNTER HAD SEEN the unmistakable guilt on Lara's face, and realized in an instant what she had done. He was filled with outrage at having been manipulated by his own wife. More than that, he was aware of a wry realization that he should have expected such a maneuver. Lara was an intelligent and stubborn woman who would do anything rather than surrender to him. It had been a clever idea to stage a public reunion with his former mistress, and Lara's timing couldn't be faulted. No doubt she expected him to be occupied with Lady Carlysle in one way or another for the rest of the evening.

He couldn't wait to enlighten his wife on a few important points.

In the meantime, however, he would have to deal with Lady Carlysle—something he had tried to avoid ever since coming to England. A grim smile touched his lips. "You'll pay for this, sweetheart," he said under his breath, and squared his shoulders as he reached Lady Carlysle.

"Esther," he said, bending over her hand, holding

it a second longer than was strictly proper. Lady Carlysle's gloved fingers were long and strong, her grip uncommonly firm. He could easily see the appeal of this straightforward woman, who would never require a man to be a hero, only a companion. Except ... every man had the urge to be a hero once in a while, to offer a woman his strength and protection ... and thousands of years of civilization would never breed that out.

"You heartless knave," Lady Carlysle murmured, though her brown eyes were warm with affection. "Why haven't you come to me? I've been waiting ever since I learned of your return from the East." She gave his fingers a light squeeze and withdrew her hand.

"I would have chosen a more private moment than this," he said with a slight smile.

"The time and place wasn't of my choosing. Our dear Larissa persuaded me, by means of a charming letter, to come here tonight."

"Did she," Hunter remarked pleasantly, longing to find his meddling wife and throttle her. "What exactly did she write, Esther?"

"Oh, something along the lines of wanting you to be happy after all you had been through—and believing that I was necessary to your happiness." Her gaze met his, her height making it nearly unnecessary for her to look up at him. "Was she right, my lord?" Coming from another woman, the question might have been coy, but she infused it with a quiet earnestness that touched Hunter.

To hell with the ball and the avidly watching guests, he thought suddenly. He would be damned if he'd hurt this woman in front of them all. He had already provided more than enough entertainment for them, and at his own expense.

"Let's talk," he said bluntly, taking her elbow and pulling her from the ballroom.

Lady Carlysle gave a low laugh of pleasurable anticipation, accompanying him willingly. "We're already talking, my dear."

Hunter took her to the library and closed the doors, surrounding them both in the comforting ambience of oiled wood, the smell of books, leather, and liquor. Turning the key in the lock, he fought a leaden feeling of dread. Silently he cursed Lara for maneuvering him into this situation.

"Esther . . ." he said, facing her.

She smiled and held out her arms to him. "Welcome home. Oh, it's been too long."

Hunter hesitated and went to her. She was an attractive, pleasant woman, but he tensed at the feel of her arms closing around him, her long body matched against his. She wasn't the one he had desired and dreamed of, and he wouldn't satisfy himself with anyone other than Lara.

Thankfully Lady Carlysle didn't attempt to kiss him. She tilted her head back and smiled at him. "You're too lean," she accused. "I miss the way your arms used to feel. It was like being held by a great brawny bear. Promise me you'll eat beefsteak every night until you've filled out again."

Hunter didn't return the smile, only stared at her seriously as he sought the words to tell her he had no more interest in her. God, it would have been easy if he disliked her, but the reluctant respect she inspired was a definite hindrance.

As it turned out, explanations weren't necessary.

Lady Carlysle read it all in his expression, or lack thereof. Her friendly grasp loosened, and then her arms fell away. "You don't want me, do you?" she asked incredulously.

There was a welter of confusion and pain in her eyes, but somehow Hunter forced himself to meet her gaze. "I want to make a new start with my wife," he said gruffly.

"With Lara . . . ?" Her mouth dropped open. "If you want to be rid of me, Hawksworth, you have only to say so. But don't insult me with lies."

"Why shouldn't I want my own wife?"

"Because she is the last woman you would ever want! I remember the countless times we used to make sport of her. You used to despise such delicate creatures—you said Lara was as spineless and cold as a jellyfish! And now you expect me to believe that you have some sort of feeling for her? She wouldn't last five minutes with you—she never could!"

"Things have changed, Esther."

"I should say so," she retorted. "I . . ." She stared at him and began to look rather queer, the healthy glow of her skin undercut by an ashen paleness. "Oh, no," she whispered. "Oh, I should have known . . ."

"What is it?" Moved by concern, Hunter reached for her, but she twisted away with a sickly gasp. She threw a desperate glance at the door, briefly contemplating escape, but made her way to a chair instead. She sat down abruptly, as if her legs had been cut from beneath her.

"A drink," she said, staring at him in open horror. "Please."

Hunter knew he should have felt remorse for her obvious distress, but instead he was aware of a biting impatience. *Damn you*, he thought savagely, *how much trouble are you going to make for me?* Snatching up a glass from the sideboard, he poured a large brandy and brought it to her, not bothering with the courtesy of warming the snifter between his palms.

Receiving the drink, Lady Carlysle sipped it until the color had returned to her face. "My God," she said, staring at him over the rim. "I don't know why I was fool enough to hope. He didn't survive the shipwreck. He's dead. And somehow you've taken his place." Tears glimmered in her eyes, but she dashed them away impatiently. "You're not Hawksworth. You're not half the man he was."

The accusation filled him with cold fury, but he kept his reply quiet and calm. "You're distraught."

"And you're damned convincing," she shot back. "But Hawksworth would never have chosen Lara over me. He loved *me*, not her."

"Sometimes love doesn't last," Hunter said, his initial liking for her fading rapidly. It was hard to understand why she was so certain of her superiority over Lara.

Lady Carlysle's grief was suppressed in another deep pull on the liquor, and she leveled a cold stare at him, the kind that men exchanged over pistols at dawn. "Who the hell are you?"

"I'm Lord Hawksworth," he said, as if he were speaking to the village simpleton.

She laughed bitterly. "Does Lara believe you? I'll wager she does, the featherbrain. She never understood Hawksworth, or gave a fig for him. It would be easy enough to convince her, especially given such a remarkable similarity of appearance. But I knew Hawksworth better than anyone on earth, and I could prove in less than a minute that you're a fraud."

"Try," he invited.

Suddenly she looked almost admiring. "What nerve you have! I would, had I anything to gain from it. But the only thing in the world I want is Hawksworth, and you can't give him back to me. I suppose there would be some satisfaction in hearing you admit that you're an impostor—"

"You'll never hear that," he assured her. "Because it isn't the truth."

"I suspect, my lord, that you wouldn't know the truth if it bit you in the ballocks." She stood and set the empty glass aside, her balance uncertain. "Good luck," she advised, though it was clear that she wished him anything but. "You're a talented charlatan, and anyone who believes you deserves whatever he—or she—gets. Fool them all, if you can. But you haven't deceived me, and it will be a cold day in hell when you manage to convince the dowager countess that you're her son. She'll put an end to this charade when she returns from her travels."

"You don't know what you're talking about."

"Oh, but I do. And here's something else for you to ponder—Larissa is nothing but a pretty wax doll. You won't get any more satisfaction from her than Hawksworth did. There's nothing beneath the surface, do you understand? No warmth, and precious little intelligence. Bedding her isn't worth the bother."

"Esther," he said softly, "I think it's time for you to go home."

"Yes." She nodded, looking furious, disappointed, and weary. "I think so too."

*   *   *

Filled with agitation, Lara sat alone in the guest parlor off the entrance hall. She relived the scene in the
ballroom a dozen times, and wondered what Hunter
and his former mistress were doing right now. The
pair hadn't been seen for some time. Surely they
wouldn't have the bad taste to arrange a tryst on the
spot. On the other hand, they were passionate lovers
who hadn't seen each other in over three years.

A strange feeling bubbled up inside her—jealousy
that left an acid taste in her mouth. The image of
Hunter with Lady Carlysle, his hands roaming her
body, his dark head bent over hers . . . oh, it was unbearable! Why couldn't she feel the relief she had so
eagerly expected?

Groaning, Lara stood and left the parlor. She
would have one more drink, and then she would return to the ballroom and act as if she were delighted
by the situation. She would toss her head and laugh,
and dance until her slippers were worn through. No
one, not even her husband, would be able to guess
at her turmoil.

Wandering into the great hall, she paused to
exchange pleasantries with a pair of women who
were strolling toward the downstairs gallery. It was
a frequently trafficked area, filled with paintings,
sculptures, and long marble benches. The women
wandered away arm in arm, chatting animatedly,
while Lara decided to head to the library. She knew
that Hunter kept the sideboard well stocked with a
variety of wines and spirits. One small glass of something bracing, and she would rejoin her guests in the
ballroom.

To her dismay, she saw Hunter enter the hall at

the same time she began to cross it. They both stopped and stared at each other, separated by perhaps ten or fifteen yards.

Hunter's face was as smooth and hard as granite . . . but the black glitter of his eyes revealed the barely contained violence inside him. Driven by a strong instinct for self-preservation, Lara turned to flee. Hunter closed the distance between them in rapid strides and caught her easily. His fingers closed over her gloved arm, and he hauled her away unceremoniously. His pace obliged her to run beside him, while she sputtered protests with every step.

"My lord . . . what are you . . . Stop, I can't . . ."

Hunter dragged her into the dark corner beneath one side of the double staircase . . . the convenient place where the maids sometimes consorted with their followers, or the footmen stole kisses from their sweethearts. Lara had never imagined herself being accosted in the same corner. In spite of her breathless objections, she was pinned against the wall by fourteen stone of anger-charged male. One of his hands sank into her sleek coiffure, while the other gripped her hip through the soft fabric of her gown.

Hunter's voice was filled with fury. "Somehow I don't recall having seen Lady Carlysle's name on the guest list."

Lara winced as his hand tightened in her hair. "I thought I was doing you a kindness."

"Like hell. You thought you were getting rid of me and my unwanted attentions."

"Where is Lady Carlysle?"

"She decided to leave after I explained that I have no interest in her. And now the only question left is what to do with you."

"We should return to the ball," Lara managed to say. "People will wonder where we are."

"You weren't so concerned about appearances when you arranged for my reunion with Lady Carlysle in front of everyone."

"P-perhaps I could have been more discreet—"

"Perhaps you could have minded your own bloody business. Perhaps you could have believed me when I told you I didn't want her."

"I'm sorry," she said in an effort to placate him. "I apologize. It was very wrong of me. Now if we could return to the—"

"I don't want an apology." He forced her head back and glared at her, his eyes glowing like hot coals in the shadows. "By God, I could wring your neck," he muttered. "But I have another way to punish you—something I'll enjoy a hell of a lot more."

More than a little alarmed, Lara gasped as he gathered her closer. The hard, swollen ridge of his erection pressed against her, while the solid wall of his chest nearly flattened her breasts. "Not here," she said urgently, panicked by the thought that a servant or guest would pass by. "Please, someone will see—"

"Do you think I give a damn?" he growled. "You're my wife, *mine*, and I'll do as I want with you." He bent his head and sealed his mouth over hers, kissing her hard, sending his tongue deep. Lara struggled only for a moment, until the fear of being caught under the stairs disappeared in a sudden shock of pleasure.

Hunter kissed her as if he would devour her, his mouth hungry and searching, while his hands cupped the back of her head and held her steady. The kiss tasted of brandy and the spicy essence that was uniquely him. Lara's gloved hands knotted into fists as she struggled to keep from responding, but her defenses crumbled as he possessed her mouth with deep, delicious kisses. Moaning, she clung to his broad shoulders and arched her body against his. Just one more minute, and then she would push him away. One more kiss, one more touch . . .

Tearing his mouth from hers, Hunter tugged off his right glove with his teeth and dropped it to the floor. He spread his fingers over her throat, savoring the delicate skin, and dipped inside the edge of her neckline. He pulled at the fabric of her bodice so roughly that she feared it would tear, until her breast slid free of the shallow covering, her nipple hardening in the open air. He cupped her breast and captured the sensitive peak between his fingertips, pulling and stroking until she smothered a cry against his coat. "Not here . . . not now," she gasped.

He didn't listen to her, only bent and took her nipple into his mouth, while his hand lifted her gossamer skirts and delved beneath them. A grunt of satisfaction escaped him as he discovered that she wasn't wearing drawers, and his large hand clasped the curve of her bare bottom. Lara jumped in shock. The music and voices from the ball were audible, reminding her of the imminent danger of being discovered. She began to struggle in earnest, succeeding only in disarranging her clothes further.

He crushed her mouth in another ravenous kiss and slid his hand between her thighs, his fingers combing through the triangle of protective curls. She choked and writhed and moaned in protest, until he parted the soft thatch and stroked the delicate line of closed lips. Lara shuddered and went still, her nerves shattering at the intimate touch. She couldn't breathe, couldn't speak as he stroked deeper, finding a humiliating trace of moisture. Hunter lifted his mouth from hers and whispered thickly near her ear.

"I'm going to kiss you there tonight."

The image shocked her, made her flush all over, and she leaned hard against him as her legs threatened to collapse. He opened the feminine folds and explored her with just one fingertip, sliding through the moisture, circling the entrance to her body, then caressing a tiny place of intense, burning sensation. Her arms wrapped around his neck, one hand gripping the opposite wrist until her nails bit into her own skin. She had never imagined he would touch her this way, the movement of his fingertip delicate and sure, using the moisture of her own body as lubrication. He stroked and teased until she began to move against his hand with small, urgent nudges of her hips.

Hunter kissed her throat, working his way to the fragile hollow at the base. "Do you want more?" he asked, his rasping voice barely penetrating the roar of her heartbeat.

"I . . . don't know what you mean."

"Do you?"

"Yes, *yes*." She was beyond shame or reason, not caring what he did to her, as long as he didn't stop. Her body moved in a voluptuous quiver as she felt his finger nudge inside her. "Oh . . ."

He stroked the slippery silk of her body, at first advancing an inch or two, then sliding the entire length of his finger inside. Lara's head fell back, eyes closed, while the pleasure threatened to uncoil in a way that would surely make her faint. Or worse, scream. Struggling to suppress the moans that kept rising in her throat, she clamped her teeth on her lower lip. His finger moved in a delicious pattern of advance and retreat, and Lara realized that he was mimicking the movements of lovemaking. Her hips thrust in helpless response, delighting in each slow penetration, her inner muscles grasping at him hungrily.

"Kiss me," she said shakily, craving his mouth on hers. "Please, now . . ."

Hunter lowered his head, but his lips remained a teasing inch away from hers, their panting breaths mingling in swirls of heat. His body was tense and aroused, his skin covered with a fine, hot mist.

"This is your punishment, Lara," he whispered. "To burn as I do."

Her breath caught as she felt his finger slip away from her trembling body. Gently he reached around his neck and unlocked her taut arms. Letting go of her, he bent to retrieve his glove from the floor. Lara leaned against the wall and watched him. He was going to leave her. "No," she said faintly. "Wait, I . . ."

He gave her one scorching glance and walked away, leaving her alone in the shadow beneath the stairs. Lara stared after him . . . angry . . . aghast. "How could you?" she heard herself whisper. "How could you?" After a minute, she fumbled with her clothes in an effort to restore them, but her fingers were strangely clumsy. She couldn't keep her mind on any subject other than her husband, and the exciting, mortifying things he had just done to her.

*   *   *

Lara never quite knew how she survived the rest of the evening. Somehow she was able to produce a sociable manner, an agreeable smile, an air of calmness that concealed the chaos within. There was only one moment when she feared her facade would crack, when it was time for the dancing to begin. Leading the first dance was a duty she might have found enjoyable if not for the fear that everyone could somehow see what had transpired between them.

"I can't," she whispered as Hunter came to her and pulled her hand through the crook of his arm. To her mortification, she felt a tide of red sweep over her chest and face. "Everyone is watching."

"You were the one who invited my ex-mistress here," he muttered with an indecipherable expression. "You can't blame them for being curious as to the state of affairs between us."

"The gossip will be ten times worse after you and I retire early," Lara said. "They'll assume that we're either arguing or—"

"Or humping ourselves into exhaustion," he finished for her, the corners of his mouth lifting in a taunting smile.

"Must you be so crude?" she asked tightly.

Hunter responded by treating her with an exaggerated politeness that was almost worst than crudity. Nodding to the musicians to begin a sprightly quadrille, he led Lara to the middle of the ballroom and waited for the other guests to join them. A multitude of couples fell in rapidly, and soon Lara was whirled into a pattern of sashaying, skipping feet. She had always loved dancing, and it had been a long time since she had led a quadrille, but there was painfully little enjoyment in this one.

She felt awkward and terribly exposed, unable to escape the memory of what they had just done beneath the stairs . . . She nearly stumbled when she thought of her husband's gentle hands on her breasts and between her thighs.

Midnight came, and the minutes crowded upon each other in rapid succession, until the appointed hour was nearly upon her. Lara glanced around the crowded ballroom for her husband, but there was no sign of him. Perhaps he was already upstairs . . . waiting. She felt as desperate as a criminal facing the moment of execution. But the moment under the stairs was still with her, the shameful delight lingering like strong perfume.

Nearly one o'clock . . . Hunter had chosen the time well. The guests were moving in an inebriated, self-entertaining swarm, and her absence would scarcely be noticed. Discreetly she extricated herself from a conversation and slipped from the ballroom.

By the time the longcase clock in the upstairs hall resonated with a single chime, Lara had reached her room. She managed to undress herself, twisting and tugging at the back of her gown, letting it fall to the floor. After adding underclothes and stockings to the heap, Lara opened the armoire and found the black negligee. It settled over her body in a shimmering rustle, light as mist.

Her fingers were unsteady as she removed the pearls from her hair and unpinned the long braid from its neat coil. She ran a brush through the rippling tresses until they were smooth, and glanced at herself in the dressing table mirror. Her eyes were huge and her skin was bloodless. She pinched her cheeks to give them color, and took a breath so deep that her lungs ached from the pressure.

It wouldn't be as terrible as before, she thought. She believed that Hunter, in spite of his annoyance, would try to be gentle, and in return she would be as accommodating as possible in the hopes that he would finish quickly. Then it would be over, and on the morrow things would go back to the way they had been. With that thought in mind, she left her bedchamber and padded quickly down the hall to his suite.

Shaking with nerves, Lara entered Hunter's room without knocking. The lamp had been turned low, a quiet glow of light barely encompassing the huge bed. Hunter sat on the corner of the mattress, still dressed in his evening clothes. His dark head lifted, and a murmur left his throat as he saw her in the black negligee. He was very still as she came to him, his smoldering gaze taking in everything: the white flashes of her bare feet, the roundness of her breasts encased in black lace, the sable fall of her hair.

"Lara," he murmured, touching a lock of her unbound hair with unsteady fingers. "You look like an angel in black."

She shook her head. "My actions of this evening have proved that I'm far from an angel."

He didn't argue the point.

Seeing that his earlier anger had abated, Lara began a careful apology. "My lord, about Lady Carlysle—"

"Let's not speak of her. She doesn't signify."

"Yes, but I—"

"It's all right, Lara." He released her hair and

touched the side of her throat. "Sweet . . . go back to your room."

Stunned by his words, Lara stared at him silently.

"It's not because I don't want you," Hunter said, standing to remove his coat. He draped the garment around her shoulders and closed it over her front. "In fact, the sight of you in that negligee is more than I can bear."

"Then . . . why?" she asked in bewilderment.

"Because I realized tonight that I can't play games and claim your body as the prize. I thought I could, but . . ." He stopped and gave a huff of self-mocking laughter. "Call it a scruple I never knew I had."

"I want to fulfill the bargain—"

"I don't want you this way, as if you owe me something. You don't."

"Yes, I do."

"I'll be damned if the only way I can have you is through coercion. So . . . go back to your room. And lock the door."

The moment was a revelation. Lara's amazed stare seemed to make him uncomfortable. Hunter turned and went back to the bed, hoisting himself onto the corner and waving her to leave with an abrupt gesture.

Lara didn't move. A new feeling of trust unfurled inside her as she realized that he would never again force himself on her, no matter what the circumstances, no matter how badly he wanted her. She had always been a little afraid of Hunter, his dominating and callous nature, but he had somehow changed the rules between them, and now . . .

She felt as if she were on the edge of a chasm,

suspended in the breathless instant before she threw herself over.

It would be easy to take the escape he offered. Lara stared into her husband's expressionless face. As he had once pointed out, she had survived other nights with him. This could certainly be no worse. Perhaps it would even be a great deal better. Hesitantly she pulled the coat from her shoulders and went to her husband.

"I want to stay with you," she said.

When he made no move to touch her, she crawled onto the bed beside him.

Hunter's dark, questioning gaze locked on her face. "You don't have to."

"I want to." Nervous but determined, she touched his face, his shoulder, encouraging him to take her in his arms. Hunter remained motionless, perplexed, staring as if she were an apparition from a dream.

She slid her fingers into the space where heat collected between his shirt and cream silk waistcoat. Her hands flattened over the broad cage of ribs and muscle. His stillness encouraged her, and she moved to the carved mother-of-pearl buttons, freeing them one by one until the waistcoat gaped open. She tugged at the knot of his cravat then, finding the starched linen difficult to loosen. Although she sensed him staring at her face, she concentrated on the task before her, finally managing to unwind the length of white cloth.

The points of his collar sagged open, revealing skin that was humid and chafed from the confining cravat. Lara tossed the starched linen aside and slid her hand to the nape of his neck, rubbing it softly. "Why do men wear their cravats so high and stiff?" she asked.

His eyes half closed at her touch. "Brummell started them," he muttered. "To hide his swollen neck glands."

"You have a very fine neck," Lara said, drawing a fingertip down the length of his brown throat. "It's a shame to hide it."

The stroke of her finger made Hunter inhale sharply, and he caught her wrists with startling swiftness. "Lara," he warned unsteadily, "don't start something you can't finish."

With her wrists still imprisoned, Lara leaned forward. She drew her lips over his in light, repeated brushes, tempting, offering, until he caught her with a lush openmouthed kiss. She answered the pressure and welcomed the touch of his tongue, exploring his mouth with growing curiosity.

Hunter released her arms and lowered her to the bed, kissing her mouth and cheeks and throat. Lara reached around his neck, staring at the silhouette of his head and shoulders above her. "Don't stop kissing me," she said, craving the taste of him.

Hunter cradled the back of her head in his hands. His mouth covered hers in a deep, compelling kiss that made her heart race and her knees draw upward as if she could curl herself around him.

She couldn't precisely remember the last time he had made love to her, only that it had been perfunctory, accomplished without a single word or caress. How differently he touched her now, his fingertips moving over her like butterfly wings. He drew the hem of her negligee up to her knees, then bent to her legs and kissed them . . . the arches of her feet, the tender inside of one ankle. Lara let him pull her leg higher, wider, and her body jerked as she felt the nip of his teeth in the sensitive hollow behind her knee.

"Do you like that?" he asked.

"I . . . no . . . I don't know."

He pressed his face against the inside of her thigh, until she felt the prickle of his beard through the thin silk of her gown. "Tell me what you like," he said, his voice muffled. "Or what you don't like. Tell me anything you want."

"When I came to you tonight," she said, "I thought I wanted you to finish this quickly."

He laughed suddenly, his hands gripping the sides of her legs. "I want to make it last as long as possible. I've waited for this night . . . God knows when I'll get another." The heat of his mouth sank through the negligee as he kissed her thigh.

Lara tensed and strained her legs against him, her knees bumping into the wall of his chest as he moved higher. Her gown was a slippery midnight veil between them. He strung kisses higher on her leg, while his hands kneaded her hips and slid beneath her bottom.

His mouth moved to the verge of a private, forbidden place, and Lara reacted without thinking, trying to push his head away. Undeterred, he caught one of her hands and kissed her taut fingers, and bent his head once more to her shrinking body. She felt his tongue through the silk, a wet, voluptuous stroke right between her thighs, where the sensitive flesh wasn't protected by curls. She whimpered at the intimate sensation, and her husband settled more heavily over her, pushing her legs wider. He licked again, wetting the thin fabric, his tongue sinuous and teasing, sending paralyzing pleasure all through her.

She gasped out something, not knowing if it was

protest or encouragement, and Hunter lifted his head. "Shall we try it without the gown?" he asked huskily.

"No!"

He laughed at her quick response and levered himself upward until they were face-to-face. "Take the gown off," he coaxed, pulling the negligee from her white shoulder.

"First turn down the lamp."

"I want to see you," he said, kissing the delicate skin he had revealed, nudging at the soft crease of her underarm. "I want you to see me."

Lara looked at him warily. It would be easier in the dark. Easier to separate her ordinary self from the one who participated in events that were too intimate to dwell on in the daytime. She didn't want to see what was happening between them. "No," she said plaintively, but he heard the indecision in her voice.

"Sweet darling," he whispered against her shoulder. "Try it this way just once."

She lay unprotesting as Hunter slid the gown from her shoulders and eased it down her legs, leaving her vulnerable in the shallow pool of lamplight. He pulled her against him, her bare skin clasped against his fully clothed body. "Help me," he said.

Obediently Lara worked at the buttons on his shirt, the linen crumpled and warm from his skin. Although he waited patiently, his muscles were taut and trembling from eagerness, and his lungs worked hard to draw in badly needed oxygen. As Lara fumbled to unfasten his French cuffs, his hand clenched into a fist.

"I want you," he said hoarsely. "More than anything in my life."

Before she could finish the cuff, he pushed her down and crouched over her, his open shirt falling on either side of her naked body. His gaze slid over her, greedily absorbing every detail. He kissed her, his weight supported on his elbows and thighs, his muscle-banded chest right above her. There were so many things about him she could not remember, had never dared to investigate. Hesitantly she touched his bare chest, so hard and smooth beneath her palms, the brown points of his nipples, the long stretch of his waist. His body had once been so sturdy and well padded, so different from this springy, lean animality.

He slid lower on her body and played with her breasts, cupping them high in his hands, circling the peaks with his fingers. His mouth opened over the center of one plump mound, drawing the nipple inside, catching it between his teeth. Lara moaned, riveted by the sight of his dark head hovering over her chest, while he tugged and suckled, first one breast, then the other. She felt strange, feverish . . . Something was loosening inside her, every defense falling away. His hand moved over her stomach, and she opened her legs to invite his touch, his penetration, anything he wanted.

Sensing her sudden abandon, Hunter dragged his mouth everywhere, tasting and kissing her waist, tummy, thighs . . . kissing the soft curls between them, breathing in the intimate fragrance. He used his fingers to separate the curls, gently parted her flesh to find the spot he wanted, and pressed his tongue against it. She arched against a blaze of pleasure, sharp and terrifying, while her eyes burned with salt tears. He licked in small circles of fire that made her gasp and quiver, and then she felt his tongue slide lower, deeper, invading her with exquisite softness. He used the weight of his chest to pin her legs wide, while his tongue nurtured the sensation to savage intensity.

Lara struggled upward, raising on her elbow, using her free hand to touch his head, fingers tangling in his thick hair. Her heart pounded against her ribs, her vision blurred, and all awareness and feeling centered in the place his mouth covered. He worshiped, consumed, devastated her, until the twisting pleasure became too much, and she spasmed endlessly, groaning with the force of her release.

After the last contraction had faded, Hunter raised himself to look directly into Lara's wet, bewildered eyes. His expression was serious as he used his fingers to brush away the tear-tracks on her cheeks. She touched his mouth with trembling fingers, his lips damp from the liquor of her own body.

He urged his knee between her thighs, and she parted them at once, trusting him with every last part of herself. He fumbled with the openings of his pantaloons, and there was a blunt, heavy pressure against the soft cove of her body. She braced herself against it, knowing that now the pain would come. He entered her slowly, pushing into the yielding flesh so gradually that there was no discomfort, only the feeling of being stretched and deliciously filled. Her body accepted the massive intrusion, the thrust penetrating deeper until she moaned in astonished delight.

Now fully joined with her, Hunter paused and buried his face in the fragrant curve of Lara's shoulder. She felt his large body shaking as he struggled to contain an eternity of pent-up passion. "It's all right," she murmured, drawing her hand down the long plane of his back. Her hips tilted in an encouraging lift, and he gasped at the small movement.

"No, Lara," he said thickly. "No, wait . . . God, I can't . . ."

She pushed upward again, managing to take more of him inside, and the silken undulation was his undoing. He groaned and climaxed without even thrusting, his body coursing with pleasure.

A long, shivering minute later, he rolled to his side, bringing her with him. Still panting for breath, he kissed her roughly, his mouth flavored with salt and a provocative essence that was not at all unpleasant.

Lara was the first to speak, her face pressed against his smooth chest. "*Now* may I turn down the lamp?"

His laughter rumbled beneath her cheek. He obliged her and left the bed for a moment, removing his clothes and reaching for the lamp. When all trace of light had been extinguished, he came back to her in the darkness.

Lara awakened from a dream about Psyche, the maiden who was sacrificed to a winged serpent and was carried away instead by Eros . . . the unknown husband who came to her at night and made love to her without being seen. Rolling to her back and stretching, Lara was almost startled to feel a man's body beside her. Instantly she reached for the sheet, which had fallen to her waist. A large hand covered hers.

"Don't," came Hunter's low murmur. "I like to see the moonlight on your skin."

He had been awake, watching her. Lara glanced

down at her body, gilded by the bluish white light shining through the half-open window, and she continued to tug at the sheet.

Hunter removed the linen from her grasp and pulled it completely away from her. He touched the tips of her breasts, the silvery curves leading down to the shadowed hollow between. She turned toward him, seeking his mouth, and he gave her a kiss so satisfying and enticing that she felt her pulse quickening once again. His hands slid to her bottom, cupping the round shapes in his palms, gripping and pulling her closer.

The hard length of his arousal pressed against her stomach, no longer a weapon to be feared but an instrument of pleasure. Lara reached for it cautiously, encircling the shaft with her fingers, sliding them along the hot silken skin. Her touch made him shiver, his body responding eagerly to the caress. She sensed that there were things he wanted to show her, teach her, but for now he let her explore him as she liked. She moved down to the pouch between his legs, testing the pendulous weight, and slid her fingers up the shaft to the smooth, broad tip. He groaned and lowered his mouth to her throat, kissing her, telling her in guttural murmurs how much he wanted her.

Pushing her knees upward and apart, he settled in the lee of her thighs and took her, sheathing himself in a deep slide. Lara gasped and wriggled to accommodate him. There was only an instant of discomfort before her body accepted him in dewy welcome. He began a steady rhythm, driving straight and sure within her, angling himself to press against her sex with each stroke. She lifted herself up to him, cradling him with her hips, her hands gripping the dense muscles of his back. He was hard, delicious, riding her just as she wanted, covering her with his masculine weight, plunging deeper, deeper . . . The pleasure of it was overwhelming.

She cried out at the height of it, her body filled with a liquid rush of delight, a shudder of satisfaction. It was equally pleasurable to share Hunter's fulfillment, to hold him in her arms and feel him shake with sensations he could no longer control.

He remained inside her for a long time while his mouth covered hers, caressing and tasting. Dreamily Lara stroked his thick hair and found the place behind his ear where the skin was soft and downy like a child's. She felt his weight shift as he prepared to move off her, and she moaned in protest.

"Oh, don't . . ."

"I'll crush you," he whispered, rolling to his side.

His thigh intruded between hers, and he played idly with the moist patch of hair, his fingers soothing and arousing at the same time. "Is this what you had with Lady Carlysle?" she asked, staring into his shadowed face.

"I've never had this with anyone."

Pleased by his answer, Lara snuggled closer and rested her cheek on his chest. "Hunter?"

"Mmm?"

"What did Lady Carlysle say to you earlier tonight?"

The movements of his fingers stopped. She felt a new tension enter his body, and his voice was laced with exasperation as he replied. "Esther was disappointed when I made it clear that I had no interest in resuming our affair. So disappointed, in fact, that she claimed I couldn't be the real Hawksworth."

"Oh." Lara kept her face pressed to his chest. "Do you think she intends to make any sort of public accusation?" she asked carefully.

His shoulders moved in a slight shrug. "I doubt it. The *ton* will assume any such claim would arise from wounded vanity. And Esther has no desire to make herself appear foolish."

"Of course." Lara blinked, her lashes tickling his chest. "I'm sorry."

"For what?"

"For making the evening such a trying one."

"Well..." His fingers entered the cleft between her thighs with a gentle twist that made her quiver. He reached far inside the depths of her, exploring with subtle, diabolical knowledge. "You'll make it up to me," he murmured. "Won't you?"

"Yes   yes..." And her lips parted against his chest in a sigh of pleasure.

"Mama. Mama."

Lara yawned and opened her eyes, squinting as the early morning sunlight assaulted her. To her dismay, she saw Johnny standing beside the bed, his small face level with her own. He stood in his nightshirt and dirty bare feet, while shocks of black hair stuck out at the top of his head.

Realizing the child had found her in Hunter's bed, Lara glanced behind her and saw her husband beginning to awaken. She kept the covers pulled high and turned back to Johnny. "Why are you up so early?" she asked.

"The chickens are hatching."

Groggily she remembered the nest of hen's eggs

they had been watching for the last several days. "How do you know that, darling?"

"I just went out to look at 'em." His innocent gaze passed from her to Hunter, who sat up and rubbed his own disheveled hair, the sheet falling to his waist.

"Good morning," Hunter said calmly, as if the situation were an everyday occurrence.

"Good morning," Johnny replied cheerfully, and returned his attention to Lara. "Mama, why aren't you in your own bed?"

Wincing at the question, Lara decided that the simplest explanation was best. "Because Lord Hawksworth invited me to sleep here last night."

"Where is your nightgown?"

Her cheeks pinkened, and she steadfastly avoided looking at Hunter as she replied. "I was so sleepy last night, I must have forgotten to put it on."

"Silly old Mama," he said, giggling at her oversight.

Lara smiled back at him. "Go find your robe and slippers."

As the child disappeared from sight, Hunter reached for Lara, but she rolled away and slipped from the bed. Finding his discarded shirt on the floor, she snatched up the garment and used it as a temporary cover for her nakedness. She held the front closed and looked at the long sprawl of her husband's body as he stretched on the bed. Their gazes met, and they exchanged a tentative smile.

"How are you?" Hunter asked softly.

Lara didn't answer for a moment, struggling to name the feeling that seemed to saturate her from head to toe. It was a strange, warm gladness, more complete and certain than anything she'd felt before.

She didn't want to leave him even for a minute, wanted to spend the day with him, and tomorrow, and every day after that until she had learned everything about him.

"I'm happy," she said. "So happy that I'm afraid."

His eyes were as dark and soft as molasses. "Why afraid, my love?"

"Because I want so badly for it to last."

Hunter gestured for her to come to him, but she ventured close enough only for a quick, glancing kiss, and then danced out of his reach.

"Where are you going?" he asked.

Lara paused at the doorway and smiled back at him. "To get dressed and see the chickens, of course."

Chapter 15

SOMETHING HAD TO be done with the prison children while the orphanage was being enlarged. Leaving them in their current circumstances was out of the question. Lara couldn't abide the thought of any of them spending one more night in the foul, dangerous places they had been consigned to live in. The only solution was to convince the people of Market Hill to take the children into their homes until the orphanage was ready to receive them. Unfortunately that idea was met with a general reluctance that astonished her.

"How can they be so coldhearted?" Lara complained to Hunter after she had made a morning of calls, during which her requests on behalf of the children had been politely refused. Wandering farther into the library, she removed her bonnet and tossed it to a chair, and fanned her overheated face. "The only people I've asked to take in a child or two are families with more than enough means to support them—and it's only for a matter of months! Why won't anyone lift a finger to help? I was so certain I could count on Mrs. Hartcup, or the Wyndhams—''

"Practical considerations," Hunter replied matter-of-factly, pushing his chair back from his desk. He pulled Lara to his lap and began to unfasten the detachable ruff from around her neck. "All charitable impulses aside, my sweet, you have to recognize that you're not asking them to take in ordinary children. The good citizens of Market Hill regard the prison orphans as criminals in training—and who could blame them?"

Lara stiffened in his lap and shot him a glance of displeasure. "How can you say that when Johnny has been such an angel?"

"He's a good lad," Hunter acknowledged, smiling wryly as he cast a glance toward the window. It was only then that Lara heard a snapping, popping noise and realized that Johnny was outside indulging in his favorite pastime, pounding tiny gunpowder caps with rocks, or firing them in his toy pistol. "But Johnny is the exception," Hunter continued. "Many of the other children need special care and attention. Some of them can't be trusted any more than if they were wild animals set loose in the town. You can't expect the Hartcups or Wyndhams or anyone else to take on such a responsibility."

"Yes, I can," she said obstinately, frowning into his sympathetic face. "Hunter, what is to be done?"

"Wait for the new wing to the orphanage to be finished and additional teachers to be hired," he said.

"I *can't* wait. I want the children out of prison immediately. I'll bring them all here and take care of them myself if I have to."

"What about Johnny?" Hunter pointed out evenly. "How will you explain it when all your time and attention are devoted to a dozen other children and there's none left for him?"

"I'll tell him ... I'll simply say ..." Lara stopped with a frustrated groan. "He won't understand," she admitted.

Hunter shook his head in the face of her obvious misery. "Sweet darling," he murmured. "I would advise you to harden your heart just a little ... but somehow I don't think you can."

"I can't leave those children in prison for months," she said.

"All right, dammit. I'll see if I can do something, though I doubt I'll have any more luck than you."

"You will," Lara said, instantly hopeful. "You have a talent for getting people to do what you want."

Hunter grinned suddenly. "I have another talent that I intend to demonstrate tonight."

"Perhaps," she said provocatively, and scooted from his lap.

Hunter became an unexpected ally, making calls, coaxing, bargaining, and bullying with all his considerable charm until he had found temporary homes for all twelve children. Having been the object of one of Hunter's campaigns, although for a far different cause, Lara knew exactly how difficult it was for the townspeople to refuse him.

She would never regard him in the same way after their night together, the first time she had ever experienced pleasure and fulfillment in a man's arms. Even more surprising than the physical satisfaction had been the realization that she could trust him.

Hunter was a kind man, Lara thought with some amazement. Her husband, *kind*, not only to her but

to the others around him . . . She didn't know what
had caused such a change, but she was deeply grateful for it. Although he didn't approve of her philan-
thropic meddling in other people's lives, he seemed
to understand it, and he indulged her as much as he
thought reasonable.

Hunter had always been busy, but his pursuits
were far different from in the first years of their marriage. He had once been a standard figure at every
hunt or sporting event, not to mention a visible fix-
ture at gaming clubs. Lara suspected his old com-
rades were sorely disappointed to discover that
Hunter had returned from India with a new sense of
responsibility toward his dependents. He developed
the Crosslands' interests in shipping, trading, and
manufacturing companies, and acquired a brewery
that returned a steady profit each month. Taking an
interest in the workings of his own estate, he paid
close attention to the harvest and farming, and un-
dertook to make improvements the tenants had long
requested.

As a young man accustomed to privilege and filled
with a sense of invulnerability, Hunter had once believed the world existed only to give him pleasure.
The only time he had ever been denied anything was
when he had been confronted by Lara's infertility,
and he had handled it poorly. Now he seemed im-
measurably older and wiser, taking nothing for
granted, shouldering the responsibilities he had once
done his best to avoid.

Not that Hunter was a saint . . . There was a touch
of the rascal about him that Lara enjoyed. He was
seductive, tricky, teasing, encouraging her to lay
aside her morals and romp with him in a manner she

would never have believed herself capable of. One evening he visited Lara's bedroom with the stated intention of enjoying the ceiling mirror before it was removed by Possibility Smith and his assistants. Ignoring Lara's mortified protests, he made love to her beneath their reflections, and laughed as she dove under the covers immediately afterward. He took her to a dignified musical evening and whispered outrageous passages from Indian love texts in her ear ... accompanied her on a private picnic and seduced her beneath the open sky.

He was the husband she had never dared to hope for: compassionate, exciting, and strong. She loved him—it was impossible not to—although some tiny flicker of fear kept her from admitting it aloud. In time she would tell him, when she felt safe in doing so. Some part of her heart was waiting for him to prove himself, offer a signal or sign or key that would allow her to relinquish every last part of herself to him.

Lara covered herself in a large apron and stood at the corner of the kitchen worktable, crushing linseed in a small marble mortar. Carefully she scraped the oily powder from the bowl and dropped the linseed into a cup of melted beeswax. It was an old family recipe for a poultice that would ease the gout—an affliction that had lately tormented a resident of Market Hill, Sir Ralph Woodfield. Although Sir Ralph was a proud man who hated to ask a favor of anyone, he had sent a servant over that morning to request a batch of the treatment.

Enjoying the fragrance of the cooling beeswax, Lara poured another half cup of linseed into the mortar and began to grind it with circular strokes of the pestle. The cook and two kitchen maids stood at the other end of the worktable, kneading great piles of bread dough and shaping it into perfect oblong loaves. They were all entertained by one of the maids' cheerful warbling of a love song that was currently popular in the village. Her fingers plowed deftly into the dough, keeping time with the melody.

> *"Oh, the lad who has me must have pockets of gold,*
> *A horse and carriage, and a silver watch too*
> *And well for him if he's handsome and bold,*
> *With curly brown hair and eyes so blue . . ."*

The song went on extravagantly extolling the virtues of the imaginary lad, until every woman in the kitchen was chuckling. "As if a man like that could be found in Market Hill!" the cook exclaimed.

Amid the general amusement, Naomi slipped into the room, the skirt of her walking dress dusty from the walk to the village. She came to Lara at once, removing a straw bonnet to reveal a troubled frown.

"Naomi," Lara said, pausing in her work. "It's your day off—I thought you were going to spend the day in the village with friends."

"I had to come back at once, milady," Naomi murmured, while the others continued to sing and chatter. "I don't know what to believe, or if there's a bit of truth in it, but . . . I heard something in the village."

Lara set aside the pestle and stared questioningly at the maid.

" 'Tis about Lady Lonsdale," Naomi continued. "I'm friends with her lady's maid, Betty, you see, and we fell to talking . . ." Clearly uncomfortable, Naomi took a deep breath and finished quickly. "And-Betty-said-'twas-a-secret-but-Lady-Lonsdale-is-ill."

Aware that the others were listening, Lara pulled the maid to the corner of the kitchen and whispered rapidly. "Ill? But that couldn't be . . . Why wouldn't I have been told?"

"Betty says the family doesn't want anyone to know."

"How ill?" Lara asked urgently. "Naomi, did Rachel's maid tell you . . . did Lonsdale do my sister some violence?"

The maid's eyes lowered. " 'Twas a fall down the stairs, Lady Lonsdale said. Betty wasn't there to see it, but she says it looks worse than a simple fall. She says Lady Lonsdale is in a bad way, and they haven't even sent for the doctor."

Horror, turmoil, and most of all rage . . . Lara trembled from a torrent of emotions. Lonsdale had beaten Rachel again. She was certain of it. And as with the other times, he had been remorseful afterward—and too ashamed to send for a doctor when Rachel needed medical attention. Lara's mind clicked with plans . . . She had to reach Rachel, take her from Lonsdale, bring her to a safe place, make her well.

"Milady," the maid said tentatively, "please don't tell anyone as how you found out. I wouldn't want Betty dismissed on account of this."

"Of course I won't," Lara replied, somewhat amazed by her own calmness when all was chaos inside. "Thank you, Naomi. You did well to tell me."

"Yes, milady." Seeming relieved, Naomi gathered her bonnet and left the kitchen.

Not looking at the cook and kitchen maids, who

had begun to whisper, Lara wandered in a daze until she found herself in the gentlemen's room. The walls were covered with an assortment of stuffed and mounted game Hunter and his father had shot. Eerily shining glass eyes were set in somber animal faces. The aura of smug masculine victoriousness, bred through generations of Hawksworths, seemed to fill the room.

Springing into action, Lara went to the cabinets beside the long row of gun cases and opened them furtively, finding bags of shot, cleaning implements, powder horns, and mahogany boxes of pistols cushioned in velvet. Pistols with handles of pearl, wood, silver ... carved, engraved, adorned as lavishly as religious artifacts.

Lara had never actually fired a pistol before, but she had seen Hunter and other men of her acquaintance with them. The loading and operation of them seemed simple enough. Fueled by rage that worsened with each passing minute, she hardly noticed that someone had entered the room until Hunter spoke.

Having returned from an inspection of new fence that had been built on the estate, Hunter was dressed in riding clothes. "Is there going to be a duel?" he asked lightly, coming forward to remove a pistol from her unsteady grasp. "If you're going to kill someone, I insist on knowing in advance."

Lara resisted him, hugging the weapon against her midriff. "Yes," she said, her anguished fury breaking forth as she stared into his taut face. Tears spilled from her eyes. "Yes ... I'm going to kill your friend Lonsdale. He's done it to Rachel again, *again* ... I don't know what condition she's in, but I intend to take her away from that place. I should have done it long ago! I only hope Lonsdale is there when I arrive, so I can put a bullet in his heart—"

"Hush." Hunter's large hand closed around the pistol and he took it from her, setting it on a side table with care. He turned back to Lara, his alert gaze raking over her tearful face. Somehow the solid reality of his presence eased her panic. He folded her in his arms, anchoring her against his chest, murmuring quietly into her hair.

Sniffling, Lara reached inside his waistcoat until her palm rested over the steady beat of his heart. The sensation of his warm breath sinking down to her scalp made her quiver. It was so terribly intimate, crying in his arms . . . even more personal than making love. She hated feeling so helpless. But he had never felt so much like a husband to her as he did in this moment. Quieting, she inhaled his familiar scent and let out a shaking sigh.

Hunter located a handkerchief and wiped her sodden face. "All right," he said gently, blotting her nose. "Tell me what happened."

Lara shook her head, knowing he would not be of any help, not where Lonsdale was concerned. They had been friends for too long. To men like Hunter and Lonsdale, friendship was more sacred than marriage. A wife, as Hunter had said long ago, was an inevitable necessity. All other women were for recreation. A man's friends, however, were carefully chosen and cultivated for life.

"You mentioned Lonsdale," Hunter prodded as Lara remained silent. "What happened?"

Lara struggled out of his arms. "I don't want to discuss it," she said. "You'll only defend Lonsdale, as you have in the past. Men always side with each other in matters like this."

"Tell me, Lara."

"Naomi heard a rumor in the village today that Rachel is ill. Something about Rachel being injured after a fall down the stairs. Knowing what I do about my sister and her husband, I am convinced that something much more despicable has happened."

"It's only gossip, then. Until it's confirmed by evidence—"

"Can you doubt it?" Lara cried. "Lonsdale uses any excuse to vent his temper on my sister. Everyone knows it, but no one dares to interfere. And Rachel will go to the grave before admitting it. She'll never leave him, or say one word against him."

"She's a grown woman, Lara. Leave her to make her own judgments on the matter."

Lara glared at him. "Rachel is not fit to make decisions about Lonsdale. She believes along with everyone else that a wife is a husband's property. A man can kick his dog, whip his horse, or beat his wife—it all falls within his rights." Lara's eyes welled with fresh, raw tears. "I don't know how badly he's hurt Rachel this time, but I think something is terribly wrong. I'm not asking you to do anything, as I'm well aware of your friendship with Lonsdale. All I require is that you stand aside while I do what I must."

"Not when you start pawing through my pistol cabinet." He caught her as she reached for another mahogany box. "Lara, look at me. I'll ride to the Lonsdale estate and find out if there's cause for concern. Will that satisfy you?"

"No," she said stubbornly. "I want to go, too. And

no matter what the state of Rachel's health, I want her brought here."

"You're not making sense," he said in a hard voice. "You can't interfere in a man's marriage and forcibly remove his wife from her own house."

"I don't care about the law. I only care about my sister's safety."

"And what do you suggest we do to keep her here when she wants to go home?" he jeered. "Lock her in a room? Chain her to the furniture?"

"Yes!" Lara burst out, though she knew it was illogical. "Yes, anything to keep her away from that monster."

"You're not going," Hunter said grimly. "If Rachel is ill, you'll only make it worse by distressing her."

Lara wrenched free of him and went to a gun case, pressing her hands on a cool glass panel and smudging the pristine surface. "You have no brothers or sisters," she said, swallowing the tears that kept pooling in her throat. "If you did, you would understand how I feel about Rachel. Ever since she was born I've wanted to take care of her." She scrubbed at her stinging eyes. "I remember one time when we were little, and Rachel wanted to climb a large tree in our yard. Even though Papa had forbidden it, I helped Rachel to climb up with me. We were sitting on one of the limbs, swinging our legs, when suddenly she lost her balance and fell. She broke her arm and collarbone when she hit the ground. I was too slow to save her. All I could do was watch her fall through the air, and my stomach flipped over and dropped as if *I* were the one falling. I would have given anything to put myself in her place. That's how I feel now, knowing that something terrible is happening to her while all I can do is watch."

Lara's chin quivered violently, and she clenched her jaw to keep from crying again.

A long time passed. The room was so still that she might have thought Hunter had left, except that part of his reflection shone in the smudged glass. "I know you can't do anything," Lara said stiffly. "You don't want to make an enemy of your closest friend, and that's what will happen if you dare to interfere."

Hunter gave a curse that raised the hairs on the back of her neck. "Stay here, damn you," he said gruffly. "I'll bring Rachel to you."

She spun around and stared at him in round-eyed amazement. "You will?"

"I swear it," he said curtly.

Relief swamped her. "Oh, Hunter . . ."

He shook his head, scowling. "Don't thank me for doing something I have no damned desire to do."

"Then why—"

"Because it's bloody obvious you won't give me a moment's rest otherwise." He looked as though he wanted to throttle her. "Unlike you, I have no overwhelming need to save the world—I'd just like to find a bit of peace for myself. After this little episode, I'd appreciate a few days of not worrying about orphans or old people or otherwise unfortunate creatures. I want an evening or two of privacy. If that's not too much to ask."

Lara's searching gaze meshed with his furious one. He didn't want to appear the chivalrous knight, she realized, and he was trying to make it clear that his motives were more selfish than benevolent.

But it wasn't working. Nothing could disguise the fact that once again Hunter was doing the right thing.

Silently Lara marveled at how he had changed. "I must confess something," she said.

"What?" he asked icily.

"Once, years ago . . . I actually envied Rachel because . . ." Her gaze dropped from his wrathful face and fixed on the carpet. "When Rachel married Lonsdale, she thought herself to be in love with him. Lonsdale seemed so dashing and romantic, and when I compared the two of you in my mind, you came off rather . . . worse. You were so infinitely serious and self-absorbed, and you had little of Lonsdale's charm. Certainly it's no surprise that I didn't love you. My parents arranged our marriage and I accepted it as a sensible choice. But I couldn't help thinking, when I saw the affection between Rachel and Lonsdale, that she had made the better match. I never intended to admit such a thing to you, it's only that now—" Lara twisted her hands into a tight, white knot. "Now I see how wrong I was. You've become so . . ." She stopped and flushed, before gratitude and some deeper, more dynamic emotion forced her to finish. "You're more than I hoped you could be. Somehow you've changed into a man I can trust and rely on. A man I could love."

She didn't dare look at him, having no idea whether her admission was something he wanted or not. Hunter walked past her, his boots moving across the edge of her field of vision, and he went through the half-open doorway . . . leaving her alone with the echo of her own impetuous confession.

Chapter 16

IT SEEMED THAT the servants of the Lonsdale estate had chosen sides by gender, the males supporting the master while the females were in sympathy with the lady of the manor. A pair of footmen and a stoic butler did their best to prevent Hunter from entering the Lonsdale mansion, while the housekeeper and lady's maid hovered nearby, watching anxiously. Hunter sensed that the women were more than willing to show him to his sister-in-law's room.

Hunter made his face expressionless as he locked stares with the butler, an elderly man who had given decades of loyalty to the Lonsdales. No doubt he had seen or helped to conceal many a misdeed committed by the family. The man was polite and dignified as he greeted Hunter, but a flicker of uneasiness in his eyes revealed that something was not as it should be. He was flanked by a pair of towering footmen who seemed prepared to carry Hunter bodily from the mansion.

"Where is Lonsdale?" Hunter asked tersely.

"The master is away, my lord."

"I've been told that Lady Lonsdale is ill. I came to ascertain her condition for myself."

The butler spoke with the requisite hauteur, but it seemed that his color heightened slightly. "I cannot confirm any details regarding Lady Lonsdale's health, my lord. Naturally it is a private matter. Perhaps you could take it up with Lord Lonsdale when he returns."

Hunter glanced at the footmen and the two women by the stairs. Their frozen expressions made him realize that Rachel was ill indeed.

The situation reminded him of an occasion in India when he visited the house of a dying friend and found the place filled with relatives from both sides of the family. Their silent despair had hung in the air like a haze of smoke. They had all known that if the man died, his wife would be burned alive with his corpse. Hunter remembered the red-paint handprint the bereaved wife had left on the doorway just before going to fulfill the ancient tradition of *sati*. The mark was all that had remained to remind the world of her existence. To Hunter's sickening frustration, he could do nothing to help her. The Indians felt so strongly about *sati* that they were apt to kill a foreigner who dared to interfere.

How little a woman's life was valued in so many cultures. Even in this one, supposedly so modern and enlightened. Hunter hadn't been able to argue with Lara's assessment that in the eyes of English law a man's wife was his property to do with as he saw fit. Judging from the anxious gloom hovering in this place, the unfortunate Lady Lonsdale was about to fall victim to society's callous disregard. Unless someone intervened.

Hunter spoke to the butler, though his words were directed to all of them. "If she dies," he said quietly, "you'll likely be charged as accomplices to murder."

He could feel, even without looking, how the comment affected the group. A current of fear, guilt, and concern rippled through the room. They all remained motionless, even the butler, as Hunter went to the stairs. He stopped before the plump housekeeper. "Show me to Lady Lonsdale's room."

"Yes, my lord." She ascended the stairs with such swiftness that Hunter was obliged to take them two at a time.

It was dim and still in Rachel's bedroom, a sweet, dry note of perfume in the air, the velvet curtains closed except for a six-inch space that allowed a hint of sunlight. Rachel reclined on large lace-trimmed pillows, her hair long and loose, her fragile body swathed in a white gown. There were no bruises apparent on her face or arms, but she had a strangely waxen complexion, and her lips were chapped and bloodless.

Becoming aware that someone was in the room, Rachel opened her eyes and squinted at Hunter's dark shape. A whimper of fright escaped her, and he realized that she thought he was Lonsdale.

"Lady Lonsdale," he said quietly, coming to her side. "Rachel." He looked down at her as she tried to shrink away. "What happened to you? How long have you been ill?" He took her thin, cold hand in his large one and gently chafed her fingers.

She stared at him with the eyes of a wounded animal. "I don't know," she whispered. "I don't know what happened. He didn't mean to do it, I'm certain . . . but somehow I fell. Rest . . . that's all I need. It's just that . . . it hurts dreadfully . . . I can't seem to sleep."

She needed a hell of a lot more than rest, starting with a visit from Dr. Slade. Hunter had never taken much notice of Rachel, thinking of her only as an attractive but less interesting imitation of Lara. However, seeing the faint resemblance she bore to his wife, and her obvious suffering, he was aware of a twist of pity in his chest. "Lara sent me for you," he muttered. "God knows you shouldn't be moved, but I promised her—" He broke off abruptly, filled with frustration.

Lara's name seemed to pierce through Rachel's pain-fogged nightmare. "Oh, yes . . . Larissa. I want Larissa. Please."

Hunter cast a sideways glare at the housekeeper, who stood nearby. "What the hell is going on?"

"She's been bleeding, sir," the housekeeper replied softly. "Ever since the fall. Nothing we do seems to stop it. I wanted to send for the doctor, but the master forbade it." Her voice dropped until it was barely audible. "Please, sir . . . take her away from here before he comes back. There's no telling what might happen if you don't."

Hunter looked back at the listless figure on the bed, and pulled the covers back. There were rusty splotches of dried blood on Rachel's nightgown, and more beneath her. Gruffly he ordered the housekeeper to assist him, and together they pulled a soft cambric robe around the ailing woman. Rachel tried to help, gamely lifting her arms into the sleeves, but even the smallest movement seemed to cause her agony. Her lips were blue and tightly compressed as the housekeeper buttoned the front of the robe.

Hunter leaned over and slid his arms beneath her, speaking as if she were a small child. "Good girl," he murmured, lifting her easily. "I'll take you to Larissa, and you'll be better soon." He tried to be gentle, but she moaned in pain as he cradled her against his chest, her bare feet dangling. Swearing silently, Hunter wondered if moving her would result in her death.

"Go on, milord," the housekeeper urged at his hesitation. "It's for the best—you must believe me."

Hunter nodded and carried Rachel from the room. Her head dropped on his shoulder, and he thought she had fainted, but as he brought her down the stairs, he heard a feeble whisper. "Thank you . . . whoever you are."

The pain and blood loss must have made her delirious, he thought. "I'm Hawksworth," he said, trying not to jostle her as they continued down the staircase.

"No, you're not," came her faint but certain reply . . . and her thin fingers touched his cheek in gentle benediction.

The carriage ride to Hawksworth Hall was torturous, Rachel white-faced and ill, gasping every time the wheels hit a rut or hole in the road. She lay curled on the length of the velvet seat, cushioned by pillows and blankets that did little to ease her misery. After a while Hunter found himself flinching at Rachel's quiet moans, her pain affecting him more than he expected.

Like everyone else, Hunter had wanted to ignore Lonsdale's past treatment of Rachel, reasoning that what transpired between a married couple in the pri-

vacy of their own home was not his concern. He had
no doubt that many people would say that he was
going too far in removing Rachel from the Lonsdale
estate. Damn them all, he thought savagely, as Rachel
whimpered in misery. It was the fault of everyone in
Market Hill and all the Lonsdales' friends and relatives—they had collectively allowed the situation to
come to this.

It seemed almost miraculous that Rachel didn't die
during the hideous carriage ride. They finally arrived
at Hawksworth Hall, and Hunter carried her into the
house with great care. He found old Dr. Slade already there, waiting with Lara. His wife did not seem
surprised by her sister's condition, and he guessed
that her imaginings had led her to expect the worst.
At Lara's direction, Hunter brought the patient to his
wife's own bedroom and settled her on the linen
sheets. While maids bustled about and Lara bent over
Rachel, and the doctor rummaged through his case,
Hunter wandered from the room.

His part was done. He supposed he should feel
some sort of satisfaction at having fulfilled his promise, but instead he was troubled and restless. He went
to the library and closeted himself there, drinking
slowly, wondering how the hell he would deal with
Lonsdale when he arrived. No matter how remorseful Lonsdale appeared, Hunter knew that he couldn't
allow him to take his wife back. How could Lonsdale
convince any of them that he wouldn't harm Rachel
again—how could they be certain that he wouldn't
eventually kill her?

Lonsdale wouldn't change, Hunter reflected, starting on his second brandy. People never did. He
thought of what Lara had said to him earlier: *Some-*

*how you've changed into a man I can trust and rely on.
A man I could love.* The earnest confession, spoken
with such gentle hope, had filled him with bitter
longing. He hadn't known how to respond, still
didn't. He wanted Lara's love. He would do anything
to have her, though he might prove as destructive to
her in his own way as Lonsdale was to Rachel.

A servant came to tell him that the doctor was
ready to leave, and Hunter set aside his brandy. He
reached the central hall just as Lara and Dr. Slade
did. The old doctor's face was grave and dark with
displeasure, his wrinkles more prominent than usual,
giving him the look of a surly bulldog. Lara seemed
composed but brittle, her facade concealing a welter
of emotion.

Hunter looked from one of them to the other, waiting for the news. "Well?" he asked impatiently.

"Lady Lonsdale had a miscarriage," Dr. Slade replied. "It seems she wasn't aware of her condition
until the bleeding began."

"How did it happen?"

"Lonsdale pushed her down the stairs," Lara said
quietly, her eyes filled with fire. "He'd been drinking
again, and he was in a temper. Rachel claims he
didn't know what he was doing."

Dr. Slade frowned heavily. "A nasty business,
this," he commented. "I never thought I would say
this, but it's a blessing old Lord Lonsdale isn't alive
to see what's become of his son. I remember the pride
he used to take in that boy—"

"Will she be all right?" Hunter interrupted, sensing that a long reminiscence was about to begin.

"I believe Lady Lonsdale will recover fully," the
doctor replied, "provided she receives adequate rest

and care. I would suggest that no one disturb her, as she is in a fragile state. As for her husband..." He hesitated and shook his head, silently acknowledging the matter was beyond him. "One hopes he can be persuaded that this sort of behavior is not acceptable."

"He will be," Lara said steadily, before Hunter could reply. She turned without looking at either of them, and went back up the stairs to her sister's sickroom. Something about the rigidity of her spine and the regal tilt of her head made Hunter feel vaguely guilty, as if he and the doctor had been tarnished by Lonsdale's actions. As if they both had been judged and convicted of participating in some great male conspiracy against women.

"Damn Lonsdale," he muttered, scowling.

The doctor reached up and patted the side of his shoulder gently. "I understand, my lad. I'm well aware of the affection you bear for your friend. But if an old man's opinion means anything to you, I am pleased that you took Lady Lonsdale under your protection. It shows a compassion that has sometimes been in short supply in the Crossland family. No offense intended."

Hunter's mouth twisted ironically. "I can't take offense at the truth," he said, and sent for a carriage to take the old man home.

Lara held vigil at Rachel's bedside through the night, until she began to doze in the chair while still sitting upright. She jerked awake as she sensed a large shape moving through the room. "What—"

"It's me," Hunter murmured, finding her in the darkness, his hands settling on her shoulders. "Come

to bed, Lara. Your sister is sleeping—you can attend
to her in the morning."

Lara yawned and shook her head, wincing at the
knifelike pain of her strained neck muscles. "No. If
she awakens . . . if she needs something . . . I want to
be here." She couldn't explain the irrational feeling
that she must not leave her sister alone, that Rachel
needed constant protection from monsters both real
and invisible.

His fingertips swept along her throat in a tender
stroke. "You won't do her any good by exhausting
yourself," he said.

Lara turned the side of her face in to his hand and
sighed. "I want to do something, even if it's only
watching her sleep."

His thumb caressed her temple, and he leaned over
to press his mouth on her head. "Go to bed, sweetheart," he said, his voice muffled in her hair. "I'll
watch over her now." Despite her reluctance, he
pulled her from the chair and urged her from the
room, and Lara made her way to her own bed like a
sleepwalker.

Lonsdale came to Hawksworth Hall the next afternoon. At first Lara was unaware of his arrival, having
secluded herself in Rachel's room for most of the day.
She had managed to coax Rachel into taking some
soup and a spoonful of blancmange, and administered a dose of the medicine Dr. Slade had left. Silent
and exhausted, Rachel seemed to welcome the obliv-
ion the medicine offered. She fell asleep quickly,
holding Lara's hand with a childish trust that broke
her heart.

Carefully Lara disengaged her hand and smoothed

her sister's long brown hair. "Sleep well, dear," she whispered. "Everything will be fine."

She left the room, silently debating how and when to tell her parents about what had happened to Rachel. It would be unpleasant, to say the least. She expected them to deny everything. Lonsdale was a fine man, they would say, and perhaps he had made a mistake that required everyone's understanding and forgiveness.

Lara knew that Hunter's support was essential if she was to keep Lonsdale away from Rachel. She would have no recourse if Hunter changed his mind. He was all that prevented Lonsdale from taking his wife back and doing exactly as he wished with her. Lara was grateful for what Hunter had done so far, but she couldn't help fearing that his long friendship with Lonsdale would ultimately prevail. She couldn't quite imagine her husband denying Lonsdale access to his own wife. And if Hunter gave in to his friend's demands . . . Lara wasn't certain what she would do.

As increasingly despondent thoughts ran through her mind, she neared the top of the stairs leading down to the great hall. The sound of masculine voices drifted to her, laced with alarming intensity. She scooped up a handful of her skirts, lifting the hem away from her feet, and descended the stairs quickly. As she reached the last step, she had a clear view of Hunter talking to Lonsdale.

The sight of her brother-in-law, well dressed and boyishly handsome, filled Lara with rage. Lonsdale appeared relaxed and charming, as if nothing were wrong. She would be damned if he would ever put his hands on Rachel again—she would shoot him herself, if it came to that.

Although Lara made no sound, Hunter sensed her presence. He turned and skewered her with a glare. "Stay there," he said roughly. She obeyed, her heart hammering violently, while Hunter returned his attention to Lonsdale.

"Hawksworth," Lonsdale murmured, seeming bewildered by his cold reception. "Good God, man, how long are you going to keep me standing here? Invite me in, and we'll talk over a friendly drink."

"This isn't the occasion for a friendly drink," Hunter said curtly.

"Yes, well . . . the reason I'm here is obvious." Lonsdale paused and asked in patent concern, "How is my wife?"

"Not well."

"I don't pretend to understand what's going on. Rachel had an accident, and instead of allowing her to recover at her own home, you drag her across the countryside . . . all to satisfy some whim of Lara's, no doubt. I understand Lara's reaction—she's like all women, with the sense of a peahen—but *you* . . ." Lonsdale shook his head in amazement. "What possessed you to do it, Hawksworth? It's not like you to bother about another man's business, especially when that man is the best damned friend you've ever had."

"No longer," Hunter said softly.

Lonsdale's blue eyes crinkled in bewilderment. "What are you saying? You're like a brother to me. No dispute over a mere woman can come between us. Just let me have Rachel, and we'll be on the upsides again."

"She can't be moved."

Lonsdale laughed incredulously at the refusal.

"She will be moved if I say so. She's my wife." He sobered as Hunter continued to stare at him implacably. "Why are you looking at me like that? What the devil is going on?"

Hunter didn't blink. "Leave, Terrell."

An anxious frown crept over Lonsdale's face. "Tell me how Rachel is!"

"She was pregnant," Hunter said flatly. "She lost the baby."

Lonsdale's color seemed to drain away, and his mouth moved in a convulsive twist. "I'm going to see her."

Hunter shook his head, refusing to step aside. "She's being taken care of."

"She lost the baby because you brought her here while she was ill!" Lonsdale cried.

Lara bit her lip in an attempt to remain quiet, but somehow her voice came bursting forth. "Rachel had a miscarriage because you pushed her down the stairs! She told me and Dr. Slade all about it."

"It's a lie!"

"Lara, shut up," Hunter growled.

"And you wouldn't even send for a doctor," Lara continued recklessly, ignoring him.

"She didn't need one, damn you!" Lonsdale's temper exploded, and he started for her with a dark flush climbing his face. "You're trying to poison everyone against me. I'll close your mouth for you, you bitch—"

Lara retreated automatically, forgetting the stairs were just behind her. She fell backward with a gasp, sitting down hard on the second step. From there she could only watch in wide-eyed horror as Hunter seized Lonsdale like a hound with a hapless fox.

"Get out," Hunter said, swinging his former friend toward the door.

Lonsdale wrenched free and came toward him with both fists flying. Lara expected Hunter to react in a similar manner, adopting the traditional pugilist's stance. Both men shared a keen interest in the sport, having attended countless prizefights together in the past, and practiced at fisticuffs with their aristocratic friends.

But what happened before Lara's bewildered gaze was not what she or anyone else could have expected. Hunter moved in a strange, fluid blur, using his knee and the heel of his hand in a way that somehow sent Lonsdale to the floor in a groaning heap. It seemed to be accomplished without thought. Hunter ended up crouched over Lonsdale, his arm drawn back in preparation for one last blow. A fatal blow, Lara realized suddenly, trying to gather her wits. She saw from Hunter's taut, strangely blank face that he was more than ready to kill the man beneath him. His reason was gone, replaced by pure lethal instinct.

"Hunter," she said desperately. "Hunter, wait."

The use of his name seemed to break through the fog that surrounded him. He glanced at her alertly, his arm lowering an inch or two. Lara nearly recoiled from what she saw in his eyes, a bloodthirst that went far beyond this situation. He was fighting to keep from sliding into some dark abyss that he had no wish to return to. There were many things she didn't understand, but she knew without doubt that she must help him by restoring normalcy as quickly as possible.

"That's enough," Lara said, while servants seemed to come from all directions, their bewildered gazes

pinned on the two men in the center of the hall. "I
believe Lord Lonsdale wishes to leave now." She
stood and brushed at her skirts, and spoke to a footman who waited nearby. "George, please assist Lord
Lonsdale to his carriage."

The footman separated himself from a gaggle of
staring servants, all of them clearly wondering what
had occurred. Seeming to understand Lara's unspoken wishes, Mrs. Gorst dispersed the small audience.
"On your way, now," the housekeeper said briskly.
"There's work aplenty to be done, and little time for
gawking and gaping."

Hunter didn't move as the stupefied Lonsdale was
removed from the hall. Two footmen half dragged
and half carried him to the waiting vehicle. Coming
to stand by her husband's side, Lara touched his arm
tentatively. "My lord," she said gratefully. "Thank
you for protecting my sister. Thank you."

He shot her a gaze of hot black intensity. "Thank
me in bed," he said, barely audible.

Lara stared at him, startled. "Now?" she whispered, feeling her cheeks prickle with heat. Hunter
didn't reply, only continued to stare at her in that
alarming way.

She didn't dare look around them, suspecting that
anyone present could discern what her husband
wanted from the way he gazed at her. The thought
of refusing him went through her mind. After all, she
was perfectly justified in claiming that her worry
over Rachel had fatigued her. It was the truth. But
Hunter had never made a request in this way before.
The other times they had made love, he had been
seductive, teasing, encouraging . . . but never desperate . . . as if he needed her to save his soul.

Daunted by his intensity, she lowered her lashes and turned toward the stairs. Hunter followed instantly, not allowing more than a foot of space between them. He didn't try to rush her, only kept pace as if he were stalking her. She could hear him breathing, light and quick, not from exertion but from appetite. Lara was nearly dizzy from the rapid beat of her heart. She paused at the top of the stairs, uncertain if they should go to his bedroom or hers. "Wh-where?" she asked softly.

"I don't care," he said in a low voice.

She led the way to his room, which was somewhat more secluded than her own. Hunter closed the door roughly. His hungry gaze returned to her. He removed his waistcoat and shirt without the appearance of haste, but she knew what seethed just beneath his self-control. Unnerved, she reached behind her neck to unfasten her gown. She had only managed the first two buttons when he strode to her and took her head in both hands, as if he feared she would try to escape him. He kissed her, his mouth hard and eager, his tongue searching deeply.

She reached out for him, grasping at the heavy bunched muscles of his torso. His skin was feverishly hot beneath her hands. His long fingers tightened on her skull, and he kissed her with scorching violence, the pleasure mounting until she moaned in excitement.

Trembling with fierce desire, Hunter finally tore his mouth from hers and pushed her to the bed. Lara stumbled in confusion, but his hands were there to guide her, steadying her hips and bending her face down over the edge of the mattress. Her thoughts scattered as she felt him pulling her skirts up to her waist. There was a jagged sound as he tore her chemise and pushed the sides apart.

"What are you doing?" she asked, beginning to push up from the bed. He pinned her back down, and she felt his fingers slide between her thighs.

"Let me," he muttered. "I won't hurt you. Hold still for me." He pushed past the tangle of dark curls, one finger slipping inside the swollen entrance of her body, reaching deep into the warmth and moisture. Lara quivered and gripped the covers until they bunched in her hands. "You're ready for me," he said hoarsely, reaching back to unfasten his trousers.

Realizing that he meant to take her like this, from behind, Lara closed her eyes and waited, her pulse thrumming with fear and eagerness. She felt his heavy shaft against her, searching, pressing, and he entered her with a long thrust that made her cry out. Her flesh closed tightly around the invading hardness, gripping firmly as he slid even deeper.

Holding himself inside her, he grasped the back of her gown, ripping it apart, sending delicate buttons flying across the bed and floor. Her chemise received the same treatment, the fragile muslin giving way to his aggressive hands and falling away from her body. She felt his warm mouth on her back, kissing the tender skin of her nape, sliding along her spine, and she writhed at the exquisite sensation.

"Now," she begged, wanting more, and her buttocks pushed against him.

He answered the movement, grinding his hips in small circles until she moaned and clutched even larger handfuls of the counterpane.

"I want to touch you," she gasped. "Please, let me—"

"No." He licked the edge of her ear, flicked his tongue inside it, muttered softly in the moist hollow.

Lara trembled at the maddening pleasure, feeling him inside her, all around her, but not being able to touch or see him. "Let me turn around. Hunter, please—"

He used his legs to widen the spread of her thighs. His hand slid around her front, down her taut belly and into the thatch of curls. Finding the sensitive bud where all pleasure centered, he stroked her gently. Caught between his teasing, tickling fingers and the deep thrusts of his hips, Lara sobbed his name. Her body was helplessly stretched and pinned beneath him, his rhythm increasing in pace, driving the pleasure higher and higher until all her senses opened and the rush of release began.

Shaking in delight, she muffled her cries in the counterpane, and felt his face press hard against her back. He was lost in his own climax now, clenching her hips hard in his palms, pouring himself into her with a groan of satisfaction.

In the glow of aftermath, Lara was nearly too weak to move. She stirred drowsily as she felt Hunter strip away the remains of her clothes. He removed his trousers and climbed onto the bed naked, holding her against his long body. She relaxed and slept for a time, though it was impossible to tell whether minutes or hours had passed. When she awakened, Hunter was watching her with eyes like dark velvet.

"You're the last woman I'll ever make love to," he said, stroking her breast, toying with the rosy peak.

She stroked his sun-streaked hair and the hard nape of his neck, loving the feel of him against her. "Good," she whispered.

"Keep me with you, Lara. I don't want to leave you."

Bewildered, she slid her arms across his broad back, her fingertips not quite reaching the center. Why would Hunter worry about leaving her? Was it possible he feared some accident, some unforeseen catastrophe that would part them once again? The thought was truly awful. It hadn't been so long ago that she'd been told that he was dead . . . and to her shame, she hadn't really mourned him. But if something happened again, if they were somehow separated . . . dear Lord, she couldn't bear it now. She didn't want to live without him.

She stared at him with glistening eyes, and her thighs opened willingly as he pushed his knee between them. "Then stay with me," she said simply. "We won't think about the past anymore."

"Yes. God, yes." He sheathed himself inside her and groaned. Lara stared into his face, the lean features gleaming with sweat, his jaw clenching. He made love to her slowly, making it last an eternity, until pleasure rippled through her in endless waves, and she felt somehow as if he were staring into her soul and showing her a glimpse of his own, all secrets burned to ashes.

"Do you love me?"

"Yes, yes . . ."

She didn't know who asked, or who replied . . . only that the answer was true for each of them.

Chapter 17

FOR THE NEXT few days there was an ominous silence from Lord Lonsdale, who made no further attempt to visit Hawksworth Hall. Finally a short, stilted note arrived from Lonsdale, asking to be informed of his wife's condition. Lara hesitated to reply, feeling that Lonsdale had no right to know anything about Rachel after he'd caused her such harm. However, the decision was not hers to make. Reluctantly she approached her sister with the letter, as Rachel relaxed on a sofa in the family parlor.

Dressed in a white nightgown with a lace-trimmed blanket covering her lap, Rachel looked as fragile as a porcelain figurine. A novel lay open in her lap while she stared out the window with a blank gaze.

"Is that not to your liking, dearest?" Lara asked, nodding to the book. "I can bring up something else from the library—"

"No, thank you." Rachel gave her a tired, fond smile. "I can't seem to keep my attention on anything. After a minute of reading, the words stop making sense."

"Are you hungry?"

Rachel shook her head. "Johnny brought a peach from the garden not long ago. He claimed it was a magic peach that would make me all better, and he insisted on staying while I ate it."

Lara smiled at the child's imagination. "What a darling," she said.

"At times I could almost swear he's yours," Rachel continued. "With his collection of turtles and the little animals he brings in from outdoors, he's very much like you."

"After the way he behaved during Dr. Slade's last visit, rummaging through his medical bag and asking a hundred questions, I wouldn't be surprised if he wanted to study medicine someday."

"It would be convenient to have a doctor in the family," Rachel said, then leaned her head back with a barely perceptible sigh.

Lara knelt by her and covered her sister's cool hand with her own. "Rachel . . . Lonsdale has written to inquire about your condition. Shall I reply, or remain silent?"

Rachel's face went blank, and she shook her head. "I have no idea."

They were both silent, while Lara continued to hold Rachel's hand in quiet support. Finally she dared to tell her sister what she had wanted to say ever since the miscarriage. "Rachel . . . you don't have to go back to him. Ever. You may stay with us, or take a house anywhere you'd like."

"No husband, no children, none of the things that make a woman's life worthwhile," Rachel said bleakly. "What choice is that? I must go back to Lonsdale and hope that he will change."

"You can fill your life with many worthwhile things, Rachel—"

"I'm not like you," her sister interrupted quietly. "I don't have your independence. I couldn't do what you did after Hawksworth's death, and carve out a new life that doesn't include a man. If I had been in your place, I would have started searching for a new husband right away. I've always wanted my own family, you see. It's true that Lonsdale has his faults. I realized long ago that I must learn to accept his limitations—"

"He nearly killed you, Rachel," Lara said. "No, don't try to argue. In my opinion, Lonsdale's refusal to send for a doctor was nothing short of attempted murder. He is abominable in every regard, and I will do everything in my power to prevent you from returning to him."

"He was not kind," Rachel agreed, "and I cannot defend him on every point. However, if I had realized my condition and told him, he might have become more considerate, and the accident would not have happened."

Lara became so agitated that she released Rachel's hand and sprang to her feet. She paced in a circle, fuming. "After this so-called accident, I am certain Lonsdale will be contrite for a while. And then he will revert to his true self . . . condescending, selfish, and cruel. He will not change, Rachel!"

Rachel's hazel eyes, usually so soft, were cool and keen as she stared at Lara. "Your husband did," she pointed out. "Didn't he?"

Lara was bewildered by the hint of challenge in her sister's tone. "Yes," she said warily, "Hunter has become a better man. But I frequently remind myself that the change may not be permanent."

Rachel regarded her for a long moment. "I think it is," she murmured. "I think Hawksworth has become a different man altogether. The day he came to fetch me from Lonsdale House, I hardly recognized him. The pain had become quite severe, and I wasn't thinking clearly, and then he appeared . . . I thought he was some kind, dear stranger. I could not fathom that he was actually Hawksworth. I thought, quite literally, that he was an angel."

"He has his moments," Lara admitted, while the phrase "different man altogether" echoed oddly in her mind. She stared at her sister's downturned face. "Rachel, I have the feeling you are hinting and talking around something—" She stopped and gathered her nerve before asking, "Are you trying to say that you don't believe my husband is really Hawksworth?"

Rachel's penetrating gaze locked with hers. "I choose to believe he is Hawksworth because *you've* chosen to believe it."

"It is not a matter of choice," Lara said, profoundly disturbed. "All the facts support his identity—"

"The facts are not absolute. One could argue endlessly over them." Rachel's composure only underscored Lara's inner turbulence. "The heart of the matter is, you have accepted him for reasons only you understand." She smiled wryly. "Dearest, you are the least self-aware person I've ever known. All your thoughts and energies are turned outward and expended on others. You make decisions impulsively, instinctively, without ever examining your motives. And you involve yourself in other people's problems as an excuse to keep from looking too closely at your own."

"What are you saying?"

"I'm saying that . . ." Rachel's voice trailed away, and she stared at Lara in loving concern. "Forgive me. I'm distressing you when there's no need. All I mean to convey is, I have chosen to believe that by some miracle your husband has come home to you, because I want your happiness so badly. And in return you must allow me to return to Lonsdale when I'm ready, and hope for a miracle of my own."

Lara lay on her stomach, her naked body stretched on the bed, while her husband spread scented oil between his palms. The fragrance of lavender filled the air with drugging sweetness. She stiffened as she felt Hunter's warm hands on her back. A gentle *ohhhh* escaped his lips, the sound soothing her, and she lay still beneath his ministrations.

He displayed astonishing knowledge of her body, finding the knotted muscles of her shoulders and the coiled places all down her back, releasing the pain with such precision that Lara couldn't prevent a groan of pleasure. "Oh, that feels so . . . oh, yes, *there*."

His thumbs fanned the sore muscles on either side of her spine in half-circular strokes that worked up to her shoulders. "Tell me what's wrong," he said after several minutes, when she was relaxed and pliant beneath him. His hand settled on the nape of her neck, fingers compressing the knotted muscles.

Suddenly Lara found it easy to confide the worry that had made it impossible for her to eat during supper. Despite Hunter's coaxing, she had remained miserably silent, hunched over the plate of untouched food, until he had finally brought her to the privacy of their room. "I talked to Rachel about Lonsdale today," she said. "She wants to return to him when she's able. Naturally I objected, and we quarreled. If only I could find the right words to convince her that she mustn't go back. I have to think of something—"

"Lara," he interrupted, his fingers working at the base of her neck. There was a smile in his voice. "As always, you want to charge forward with a solution and settle everything to your satisfaction. But that won't work this time. Let Rachel rest. Don't press her for answers she's not ready to give. She's not going anywhere for a while."

Recognizing the wisdom of his advice, Lara slumped beneath him. "I'm too impatient," she said, berating herself. "I should never have mentioned Lonsdale so soon. When will I learn to stop meddling?"

Hunter turned her over and smiled, his lavender-scented hand splayed over the frame of her collarbone. "I love your impatience," he murmured. "I love your meddling."

Lara gazed uncertainly at the dark face above hers. "Rachel said that I involve myself with other people's problems as a way of avoiding my own. Do you agree with her?"

"Not entirely. Do you?"

"Well . . ." She drew her knees up and crossed her arms over her breasts. "I suppose it's easier to see what needs to be fixed in someone else's life than to take a hard look at my own."

His head lowered, and he kissed her cheek. "I

think you thrive on the satisfaction of helping someone else," he whispered. "And there's nothing wrong with that." Gently he pulled her arms away from her body. "Why do you always try to cover yourself?" he asked. "Still shy after all we've done?"

Lara blushed as Hunter stared intently at her nakedness. "I can't help it. I'll never feel comfortable without my clothes on."

"Oh yes, you will." His lightly oiled fingers drew over her stomach in a circling stroke that made the muscles tighten. "I happen to know of a cure for shyness."

"What is it?" She listened as he murmured to her, her eyes widening. Before he had even finished describing his "cure," she was sputtering in a mixture of amusement and disbelief. "Have you ever done that?" she asked.

"I've only heard of it."

"I'm sure it's not even possible."

Hunter's teeth flashed in a grin. "We'll have to find out, won't we?" Before she could manage a reply, he covered her mouth with his, and gathered her against his aroused body.

In a town such as Market Hill, gossip spread like the ripples from a pebble thrown in a pond. Secrets, illnesses, troubles of every kind were discovered, discussed, and soon resolved or forgotten . . . The community processed an endless amount of such information. It did not take long for the latest news of Captain Tyler and his wife to reach the residents of Hawksworth Hall. Evidently Mrs. Tyler, who was expecting her first child, had recently experienced pains that had led Dr. Slade to prescribe bed rest for the remainder of the pregnancy.

Lara reacted to the news with sympathy and concern. The idea of being confined to a bed for four or five months was dreadful. Physical discomfort aside, the sheer boredom would be enough to drive any woman mad. Obviously she must do something for poor Mrs. Tyler, even if it was only to bring a few novels that might help the days to pass more swiftly.

However, there was a difficulty to the situation. Lara still remembered her husband's reaction to the unexpected presence of the Tylers at the dinner she had given after his homecoming. He had been uncomfortable, cold, unaccountably angry. And there had been that strange moment when Lara could have sworn that Hunter and Captain Tyler knew each other quite well but pretended to be strangers. Ever since then Lara had kept her distance from the Tylers, sensing that to approach them would cause problems between her and Hunter.

On the other hand, pleasing her husband took second place to the promptings of her own conscience. The captain's wife had been consigned to lie helpless in bed for months, and Lara could not ignore her plight. She resolved to visit Mrs. Tyler discreetly, and if Hunter discovered her activity, she would just have to deal with the consequences.

On the day that Hunter left to conduct business in London, Lara set out for Morland Manor. She had packed a basket with puddings and choice peaches from the Hawksworth orchard, as well as a stack of novels that might help Mrs. Tyler pass the time. During the hour-long journey across the countryside, Lara stared through the carriage window at fertile green land divided into neatly fenced pastures. Fat sheep and brown-coated cattle grazed peacefully, scarcely pausing to lift their heads at the passing of the carriage.

Although the vehicle was luxurious by any standards, Lara was uncomfortable. She shifted position several times, rearranged her skirts, and became aware of a pressing need to visit a privy. A rueful smile curved her lips as she considered her impending arrival at Morland Manor. It was hardly good manners to rush in unannounced and search for the nearest place to relieve one's needs, but that was evidently going to be the case. Strange, that her bladder had become so undependable of late.

Lara's smile faded as she continued to ponder her own physical condition, something she had neglected in her worry over Rachel. Her body had been temperamental of late, becoming a bit heavier in spite of her physical activity, prone to twinges and minor aches . . . and shouldn't her menses have occurred by now? She had never been irregular in her life.

The realization astonished her. Yes, she was late . . . two weeks late. For once in her life, the monthly flow that occurred with stubborn regularity had failed to appear. In any other woman, she would have acknowledged this as evidence of pregnancy. *But not me*, she thought, her breath turning shallow with distress. *Never me.*

Lara reached for the stack of books, intending to distract herself. However, once the thought had presented itself, it was impossible to ignore. How many times during her early marriage to Hunter had she longed to conceive? The guilt, the inadequacy, the yearning . . . they had been unbearable. Finally she had accepted that she would always be a childless woman. It was ironic that Hunter, of all people, had now helped her to come to terms with barrenness and recognize her value beyond the ability to produce children.

But what if . . . ? She was afraid to hope. If only it could be true, if only . . . Lara closed her eyes and kept her hands over her stomach, and whispered a swift prayer. She wanted to carry Hunter's child, to bear a part of him within her. It seemed an impossible miracle that she could be gifted with what seemed so ordinary to the rest of the world. Lara screwed her eyes shut, but a tear squeezed out in spite of her efforts. She was almost sick with yearning.

She managed to collect herself by the time the carriage reached Morland Manor. Half hidden in a grove of woodlands, the Tudor manor was fronted with half timbered walls and red brickwork that gave it an air of mellow charm. Outwardly poised, Lara directed a footman to convey the basket of delicacies and the parcel of books to the entrance hall. She was kept waiting at the door for less than a minute before Captain Tyler appeared to greet her.

"Lady Hawksworth!" the captain exclaimed, seeming more perplexed than pleased. "It is a most unexpected honor—"

"Forgive me if I've come at an inconvenient time," Lara replied, giving him her gloved hand. "I only wish to give my regards to you both, and deliver a few gifts for Mrs. Tyler."

"How kind of you." His momentary bewilderment was replaced by gratitude. "Please come in and take some refreshment. I'll send a servant upstairs to inquire if Mrs. Tyler is resting, and perhaps she'll be able to see you."

"You mustn't disturb her on my account. I won't stay long." Lara accompanied him inside and removed her gloves and traveling bonnet. It was a warm day, and she pulled a lace-trimmed handkerchief from her sleeve to blot her moist forehead and cheeks.

Welcoming Lara into a small visitor's parlor, the captain showed her to a scroll-backed sofa covered in flowered chintz. Lara arranged her skirts and regarded him with a smile as he occupied a mahogany chair. Her initial impression of him was unchanged; he seemed a pleasant if serious man. But something about his intent gaze disturbed her, as if he were keeping an uneasy silence on a matter that concerned her.

"Lady Hawksworth," he said carefully, "I hope it will not offend you if I ask after your sister's health?"

"She is very well, thank you. And of course I would not be offended by your kind concern. Why should I?"

Tyler's gaze lowered. "The circumstances of your sister's illness make it rather awkward . . ."

"Yes, it is a scandal," Lara said softly. "No doubt everyone in Market Hill has some opinion about it. But the shame of the situation belongs entirely to Lord Lonsdale."

Tyler folded his hands together, his fingers forming a temple. "Unfortunately this is not the first time I have learned of such dastardly behavior on the part of a husband toward his wife, nor, I fear, will it be the last." He hesitated before adding tactfully, "I only hope that Lady Lonsdale will enjoy happier circumstances from now on."

"So do I," Lara replied. They continued the conversation for a few minutes, touching on neutral subjects before reaching the more personal one of Mrs. Tyler's well-being.

"Dr. Slade assures us that if we follow his instructions, my wife and the babe will both have an excellent chance," Captain Tyler remarked. "And one can hardly disbelieve a man of his experience and wisdom. Nevertheless I do worry. I am excessively fond of Mrs. Tyler. She has been a faithful companion through all the trials I have brought on her, most especially the years in India."

Touched by his devotion to his wife, Lara dared to mention the question that had bothered her for some time. "Captain Tyler," she said cautiously, "your mention of India reminds me of something I have wondered about."

"Yes?" He was immediately wary, his black mustache twitching like the whiskers of a nervous cat.

Lara proceeded with care. "When you attended the dinner at Hawksworth Hall some months past, and you and Lord Hawksworth met . . . I somehow had the idea that you were already acquainted with each other."

"No, my lady."

"Oh." She made no attempt to hide her disappointment. "There are so many events connected with India that my husband refuses to discuss. For some reason I hoped you could shed some light on his experiences there."

"I never met Hawksworth in India." Tyler looked directly at her. An endless pause followed, and Lara sensed that a carefully maintained pretense was suddenly falling away. "However . . ." he said slowly, "your husband reminds me in some ways of a man I knew there."

The statement seemed innocuous, but something warned her that it was an invitation to discovery. The hairs on the back of Lara's neck prickled. The subject must be dropped at once, came the urgent thought.

"Indeed?" she murmured softly.

Captain Tyler regarded the woman before him speculatively. Such a gentle, unguarded face she had, with a luminous prettiness he had seen only in Rembrandt paintings. From all accounts she was a kind, well-liked woman, passionate in her concern for those who were less fortunate than she. Of all people, she did not deserve to be used and betrayed . . . but that was the way of the world. Predators always sought out the weak and the vulnerable.

Tyler had known about the deception being practiced on Lady Hawksworth, but there hadn't seemed a clear choice to make. For a man in his position, there were often no right choices, merely ones between lesser and greater evils. And he had found that his greatest mistakes had always resulted from decisions made in haste.

In this particular matter of the Hawksworths, Tyler had sensed that his duty would present itself gradually as things unraveled—and he'd known without a doubt that the situation *would* unravel.

Without doubt, he owed his loyalty to the man known as Hunter, Lord Hawksworth. The man had once saved his life, and Tyler hated to repay him with betrayal. At the same time, this kind, innocent woman deserved the truth, and it was left to him to tell it. Had she not come here today, Tyler knew he would have put the matter off indefinitely. But she *was* here, and it almost seemed that fate had arranged for the two of them to be here together with time and privacy enough to talk.

"The man I refer to was a mercenary, actually," Tyler said. "I first discovered him when he was employed as a factor in the East India Company. He was an extraordinarily intelligent fellow who kept to himself and seemed to have no particular ambitions. Although he was English by birth, he was brought up among the Indians by a missionary couple."

Tyler's narrative was interrupted by a servant bearing a tray of refreshments. "Sandwiches? Biscuits?" he asked.

Lara refused the offer of food but accepted a glass of lemonade, welcoming the sour shock of it on her tongue. She regarded the small, delicate engraving on the upper bowl of the glass, depicting a shepherdess in a pastoral setting, and wondered why the captain was bothering to tell her so much about a man who meant nothing to her.

"It occurred to me to make use of him in a force of a half dozen men who would assist me in restoring order to recently annexed territories. As you can imagine, there were—are—conflicts of every kind when barbarians are brought under the protection of the British lion."

"No doubt many Indians are reluctant to accept the British lion's 'protection,'" Lara said dryly.

"Eventually they realize it is for the best," Tyler replied gravely, missing the touch of irony in her comment. "In the meanwhile, their rebellion takes on many ugly forms. Murder, attacks, robberies, all happening in such volume that we were forced to restore order without the usual process of British law. Much as I hate to acknowledge it, there was also a strain of corruption among our own officials. Therefore I created a small unit to accomplish special and highly secretive tasks. Four of the men were already in my command, while two were brought in from outside the regiment. And this particular man I speak of, as it turned out, was ideal."

"Because of his intelligence and his understanding of the natives," Lara said.

"Precisely. But there was something else about him . . . a unique ability to change himself as a situation required. I've never known such a chameleon. He could become anyone, anything, at will. He was able to adopt any appearance, accent, or mannerism. I saw him mingle with the natives as if he were one of them, and later attend an ambassador's ball as a proper Englishman, causing no hint of suspicion. He was as stealthy as a tiger, and quite as remorseless. Most importantly, he had no fear of death, which made him remarkably effective in his duties. I used him as a spy, an investigator, and at times even as . . ." Tyler paused, looking distinctly uncomfortable. "As a weapon, one might say," he finished quietly.

"Did he execute people for you?" Lara asked in revulsion.

The captain nodded. "When it had to be done quickly and without show. I believe he did it in the manner of the thuggees, using a coin knotted in a handkerchief—they're quite particular about not spilling blood, you know." Seeing from Lara's pale face that he had gone too far, he frowned apologetically. "Forgive me, my lady. I shouldn't have been so explicit—but I did wish to convey the character of this man."

"Character," Lara repeated with a humorless laugh. "It seems to me that he had a complete *lack* of character."

"Yes, one could say that."

"What happened to him?" Lara asked without much interest, eager to be done with the distasteful reminiscence. "Is he still prowling around India under someone else's command?"

The captain shook his head. "He simply disappeared one day. I assumed that he had been killed, or perhaps even taken his own life. He hadn't much to live for, as far as I could tell. In any event, I never saw him again. Until . . ."

"Yes?" she prompted.

Captain Tyler waited so long that she thought he might not continue. "Until I came to England," he finally said. "And attended the dinner party at Hawksworth Hall. And saw him at your side." He blotted his perspiring forehead with his sleeve and stared at her with blatant pity. "My lady, the unpleasant truth is . . . he has taken the place of your husband."

Lara felt herself shrinking, dwindling, until the parlor loomed large around her, and Captain Tyler seemed to be speaking from very far away. She could only hear a faint, tinny echo of his words. ". . . should have said before . . . obligations . . . not certain what to . . . please believe . . . assist you any way . . ."

She shook her head, feeling as if someone had struck her. Dazed, she made an effort to breathe, but something heavy was pressing on her chest, making it impossible to draw in enough air. "You're mistaken," she managed to say. She sensed his concern, heard him asking her to stay and collect herself, have something to drink—

"No, I mustn't stay." To her relief, she was able to marshal a sort of brittle dignity that allowed her to speak more or less clearly. "My sister needs me. Thank you. You're wrong about my husband. He's not at all the man you described. Good day."

She left on shaking legs. She felt so very odd, and it was an incredible relief to walk on the arm of her own footman, and escape into the familiar interior of her carriage. Sensing that something was terribly wrong, the footman asked if she was all right. "Take me home," Lara wheezed, staring blindly ahead.

Chapter 18

LARA SAT IN the carriage as stiffly as a wax doll, while thoughts and voices chattered in her head.

The unpleasant truth is . . .

Keep me with you, Lara.

. . . he has taken the place of your husband.

I don't want to leave you.

Do you love me?

Yes, yes . . .

The cruelty of it was stunning. She had finally learned to trust a man, given her heart and soul into his keeping . . . and it had all been an illusion.

A chameleon, the captain had said. A man with no conscience and no capacity for remorse. A cold-blooded murderer. He had come to her, manipulated, seduced, and impregnated her. He had stolen Hunter's name and money and property and even his wife. What contempt he must have for the people he had deceived.

Any other woman would have recognized her own husband, Lara thought numbly. But she had accepted his lies, because in her heart she had wanted to believe.

Remembering Janet Crossland's hateful accusations—*How eager you are to climb between the sheets with an absolute stranger!*—Lara wanted to die of shame. It had been the truth. From the very beginning she had wanted him, instinctively, impetuously. Everything inside her had been drawn to him. And so she had let it all happen.

Humiliation and fury and anguish rippled through her. The pain was too great to contemplate. She shivered and held still, like a terrified child, and wondered why she wasn't crying. Nearly everything that mattered had just been ripped away from her. A blaze of feelings was trapped inside her, but nothing broke through the shroud of ice.

Feebly she tried to gather her sanity. She had to make a plan. But rational thoughts kept eluding her, like slippery fish darting through her fingers. She wanted the carriage to keep going, the wheels rolling, the horses to pull its weight until they reached the edge of the earth and toppled over. She couldn't go home. She needed help. But the one person she wanted to turn to had betrayed her.

"Hunter," she whispered in wild grief. But the real Hunter was dead, and the man she had come to think of as her husband . . . She didn't even know his name. A hysterical laugh bubbled in her throat, but she suppressed it, afraid that if she started to laugh, she might never stop, and end up in some lunatic asylum. Which didn't sound all that unappealing, actually. She could appreciate a place where one could scream and laugh and hit the walls with one's head as much as one liked.

By sheer force of will she kept silent, calm, waiting with unnatural patience for the carriage to reach

Hawksworth Hall. She had no sense of time—it could have been minutes or hours until the vehicle stopped and the door opened to reveal the footman's concerned face.

"Milady." He escorted her carefully into the house. Lara knew there must have been something strange about her expression. It was obvious from the way the servants treated her, with the deference they might have shown to a sickly old woman.

"Milady," Mrs. Gorst asked carefully, "is there ought I can do? You seem rather—"

"I'm only a little tired," Lara said. "I want to rest in my room. Please see that I'm not disturbed."

She made her way up the stairs, gripping the balustrade to pull herself along.

Catching a glimpse of herself in the upstairs hall mirror, Lara realized the source of the servants' concern. She looked feverish, her eyes bright and stricken. Her face gleamed with the burnished color she might have gotten from a sunburn. But the hot red blush was caused by the shame and fury inside, not from any external source.

Slightly short of breath, Lara headed toward her room but found herself at Rachel's door instead. She tapped gently and looked inside, and saw that her sister was seated by the window.

"Larissa," Rachel said, a smile crossing her face. "Do come in and tell me about your visit with the Tylers." As she stared at Lara, her forehead creased with lines of perplexity. "What is it? What is wrong?"

Lara shook her head, unable to express the enormity of what she had discovered. Her throat seemed to be filled with sand. She swallowed several times,

struggling to speak. "Rachel," she managed sheep-
ishly, "I wanted to bring you here so I could take
care of you, but ... I'm very much afraid ... you'll
have to take care of me instead."

Rachel's gentle hands lifted in entreaty. It was a
reversal of their usual roles, with the younger sister
offering comfort to the elder, but Lara went to her
without hesitation.

She sank to the floor and laid her head in Rachel's
lap. "I'm such a fool," she gasped. The story began
to spill out in broken phrases, many of them incom-
prehensible, but somehow Rachel seemed to understand. Lara confessed everything, every humiliating,
soul-wrenching detail, while Rachel's slim fingers
smoothed over her hair repeatedly. Finally she was
able to cry, with sobs so ugly and rending that she
shook from the force of them, but her sister was
steady amidst the storm. "It's all right," Rachel murmured over and over. "It's all right."

"No," Lara choked, drowning in despair. "Nothing will ever be all right again. I think I'm going to
have his baby. His baby, do you understand?"

Rachel's fingers trembled in Lara's hair. "Oh, my
darling," she whispered, and fell silent while Lara
continued her wretched confession.

"Captain Tyler may be mistaken," Rachel said at
one point. "How can anyone know for certain who
Lord Hawksworth is?"

Lara let out a shuddering sigh and shook her head.
"The real Hunter is dead," she said dully. "It's no
good to pretend otherwise. This man is not my husband. I think I've known it all along, but I didn't
want to face the truth. I let it happen because I
wanted him. What does that make me, Rachel?"

"You are not to blame," her sister said resolutely. "You were lonely. You had never been in love be- fore—"

"There is no excuse for what I've done. Oh God, I'm so ashamed! Because the truth is that I still love him. I still don't want to let him go."

"Then why must you?"

The sheer audacity of the question, coming from a principled soul like Rachel, took Lara's breath away. She stared at her sister in wonder before replying shakily. "A thousand reasons . . . but none of them matter as much as the fact that everything he has said and done has been a lie. I'm nothing to him except as a means to an end."

"He has behaved as though he truly cares for you."

"Only because it's been convenient for him to do so." Suddenly Lara's entire body was immersed in a scarlet glow. "Oh, when I think of what an easy con- quest I was . . . the poor love-starved widow . . ." She buried her face against Rachel's knees and began to sob again. "I never understood until now how shel- tered I've been. Even Hunter's death didn't affect me as it should have. He was as much a stranger to me two years after we married as he had been before. But this man came to me like something from a dream, and insinuated himself into every part of my life . . . and I loved him. Every moment with him. And when he leaves, he'll take my heart with him. He's ruined me for anyone else."

She talked and wept without interruption until ex- haustion overcame her. Her head dropped in her sis- ter's lap, and she actually dozed for a few minutes. When she awoke, still sitting on the floor, her spine and neck were unbearably stiff. It seemed for a moment that she had been lost in a nightmare, and for a moment her heart thudded with hope. But one look at Rachel's face revealed that the nightmare was true.

"What will you do?" Rachel asked softly.

Lara rubbed her bleary eyes. "I must send for Lord and Lady Arthur," she said. "The title must be restored to them. It is rightfully theirs. I owe them whatever assistance I am able to provide. As for Hunter—" She stopped, nearly choking on the name. "He'll return from London tomorrow," she said. "I'll advise him to flee to avoid prosecution. Otherwise I've no doubt he'll be hanged, not only for what he's done to me, but for the fraud he's committed in my husband's name. Contracts, investments, loans... Oh, Lord, not one of them is valid."

"What about the baby?" came her sister's soft question.

"No one must know," Lara said instantly. "Especially not him. It has nothing to do with him now. The baby is mine, and only mine."

"Will you keep it?"

"Oh, yes." Lara covered her stomach with her hand, and fought to suppress a fresh flow of tears. "Is that wrong, to want this child in spite of everything?"

Rachel stroked her disheveled head. "No, dearest."

After a night of broken sleep, Lara awoke to face the next day with weary resolution. She felt the need to put on mourning, as if someone had died, but instead she dressed in a circumspect blue gown adorned with silk braiding at the bodice and hem. The house seemed wreathed in gloom. She knew she would have to explain something to the servants, to friends

and acquaintances in Market Hill . . . and to Johnny.
How could she make a child understand what had
happened, when she didn't understand it herself?
The thought of all that lay ahead filled her with in-
describable weariness.

When all of this was over, she promised herself,
when Hunter was banished from her life and the
Hawksworth title was restored to Arthur and Janet,
she would leave this place for good. Perhaps she
would make a new life in Italy or France. Somehow
she might even convince Rachel to go with her. But
the notion of starting anew only made her want to
cry again.

She counted the time since "Hunter"—she didn't
know how else to think of him—had come to her.
Three months. The most fulfilling time of her life,
when she had tasted the kind of joy that few people
ever knew. She had blossomed under the spell of his
gentle, passionate, loving presence. Were the pain not
so great, she might have considered it worth the
price.

Groping for words, Lara tried to prepare some sort
of speech for when Hunter returned from London.
Something dignified, calm, circumventing distasteful
arguments and accusations. But all she could come
up with were questions. With her emotions writhing
beneath a blanket of ice, she went into the garden in
search of solitude. She sat on a bench and hugged
her knees, and stared at a small, splashing cherub
fountain. A mild breeze rustled through the neatly
trimmed yews and stirred flowers potted in great
stone urns. She breathed in the hot, sweet smell of
the grass, and rubbed her temples in an effort to ease
the throbbing ache in her head.

Like a nightmare descending, she became aware of two figures approaching. Arthur and Janet Crossland. So soon, she thought gloomily. But of course they would jump on the chance to regain the title, like scavengers hovering over a freshly scrapped kill. They were as tall and blond and smug as ever, wearing identical smiles as they reached her.

Janet spoke before Arthur had the chance. "It took you long enough to come to your senses," she said acidly. "I gather your little escapade is now concluded, and we may have back what is rightfully ours."

"Yes," Lara said tonelessly. "The escapade is over."

Arthur bent to take her lifeless hand, and pressed it in a show of concern. "My dear niece. I sympathize with what you've suffered. You've been deceived, betrayed, humiliated—"

"I'm perfectly aware of what I've been through," Lara interrupted. "There's no need to recount it all."

Seeming surprised by her quiet rebuke, Arthur cleared his throat. "You're not yourself, Larissa. I'll overlook any rudeness on your part, as I know you're distraught and confused."

Janet folded her bony arms over her chest and regarded Lara with a cold smile. "She doesn't look confused to me," she remarked. "More like a sullen child who's been deprived of her candy."

Arthur turned toward his wife and muttered something under his breath. Although the words weren't clear, it served to silence her temporarily. He looked back at Lara with a reptilian smile. "Your sense of timing can't be faulted, dear Larissa. It was just the thing to wait until *he* was off the estate and then send for me. I made certain that he was arrested in London. Although I would have preferred him to be imprisoned, I had to settle for placing him under guard in the Hawksworth town house until he's brought to trial. The thing will eventually have to be settled in the House of Lords, of course, as he must be tried by his peers . . . though they'll quickly discover that he is not one of them!''

Lara tried and failed to imagine the man she had come to think of as her husband placed under guard. Surely any restraints on his freedom would drive him mad. And worse, the idea of him being tried before every influential lord in London . . . She stifled a small cry of anguish. He had so much pride. She didn't want to see him torn to pieces that way. "Must he be tried in the Lords?'' she asked dully.

"First the lord chancellor will receive our depositions in a private session. Unless he decides to discharge the case—which is entirely unlikely—there will indeed be a trial at the Lords.'' Arthur smiled in malicious pleasure. "Oh, we'll have our pretend Hawksworth dancing on the end of a rope before long. I'll ask them to make certain his neck is *not* broken, so he'll gasp and turn blue as the noose crushes his throat. And I'll be there to enjoy every moment as he slowly strangles—'' He stopped as Lara made an inarticulate sound. Immediately he adopted a look of solicitous concern. "My dear, we'll leave you in private to continue your reflections. But really, you'll come to see that this is all for the best.''

Lara bit her lip and made no reply, while everything inside her cried out in protest. Surely this was the right thing, the moral thing to do. How could one go wrong by upholding the truth? But logical arguments only seemed to muddle everything. She was supporting the Crosslands and their claim to the title because it was her duty, and yet it brought her only misery. They would most likely drain the family fortune and be condescending and selfish, and everyone abiding on the Hawksworth estate would suffer. And Johnny would be deprived of the secure future she had intended for him. How could that be right?

A single hot tear rolled down her cheek, and Janet regarded her with a vicious smile. "Cheer up, my dear," she said gently. "You've had an exciting adventure, haven't you? And your temporary husband was a handsome fellow indeed. No doubt he was most entertaining in bed. At least you have that to be thankful for."

Arthur grabbed his wife's thin arm and jerked her aside. This time Lara heard his muttered words "Shut up, you sharp-tongued bitch. Provoke her enough and we'll lose the title. We need her testimony, do you understand?" He looked back at Lara and smiled reassuringly. "Don't worry about anything, Larissa. This will all be over soon, and you'll finally be at peace. In the meantime there are only a few difficulties to get through, and I will help you every step of the way."

"Oh, thank you," Lara said softly.

He stared at her, clearly wondering if he had imagined the note of sarcasm in her reply. "I do expect civility from you, Larissa. Remember, we are all family, with one shared goal in mind. Furthermore, I expect you to be civil to Lord Lonsdale when he arrives this afternoon, regardless of the discord which seems to have sprung up between you."

"No!" Lara shot to her feet, her face whitening.

"Why in God's name would you invite Lonsdale here?"

"Calm yourself," Arthur said gently, his gaze hard. "Lord Lonsdale has information that is extremely helpful to our case, which I intend to discuss with him. He also wishes to collect his wife, for which I can hardly blame him. After the way you stole your sister away from her own home—"

"I forbid Lord Lonsdale to set one foot on this estate," Lara said in a steely tone. "I won't have it, do you understand?"

"You *forbid* it?" Arthur asked incredulously, while Janet laughed nastily. "Remember, niece, that you are no longer the lady of the manor. You have no right to remark on any of my decisions, much less to forbid anything."

"Nevertheless, I do," Lara said, her eyes narrowing. "And if you cross me in this, you will not have my testimony against Hunter. I will withdraw my help, and swear to the heavens that he is and always has been my husband . . . unless you promise me here and now to keep Lonsdale away from my sister."

"For how long?" Arthur asked, staring at her as if she were a madwoman.

"Indefinitely."

He exploded with disbelieving laughter. "Keep a husband away from his own wife indefinitely . . . I'm afraid you ask too much, my dear."

"He is a violent, abusive husband. Rachel nearly died from his last beating. You have only to ask Dr. Slade."

"I'm sure you exaggerate," Arthur countered. "I've always found Lonsdale to be a likable fellow," Janet remarked. "Besides, if he did strike Rachel, she may have deserved it."

Lara shook her head slowly as she stared at Janet. "For such a remark to come from another woman . . ." she started, but her voice trailed away as she realized that Janet was too callous to be reasoned with. She returned her attention to Lord Arthur. "Your promise, sir, in exchange for my testimony."

"You're asking me to do something that's not only immoral but illegal," Arthur protested.

"I'm sure that shouldn't trouble you too greatly," Lara said coolly. "You won't have my support any other way. And I expect your word to be upheld even after the trial. I only hope that you're enough of a gentleman to keep it."

"You stubborn, irrational, insulting— " Arthur said, his lean face coloring with rage, but Janet interrupted him with a touch of feline enjoyment.

"Remember, darling . . . we need her testimony."

Arthur closed his mouth, the muscles of his face twitching and contorting as he labored to control his wrath. "All right," he snapped, glaring at Lara. "Enjoy this small victory. I vow it shall be your last." He stormed away with Janet at his heels.

Lara's alarmed fury took a long time to fade. She sat down again, her knees trembling, and buried her face in her hands. Tears leaked from her eyes and through her fingers, and she let out a shaking sigh. "Oh, Hunter," she whispered miserably. "Why couldn't you have been real?"

From then on, events passed with bewildering speed. Although Hunter had apparently refused legal assistance, Mr. Young had ignored his instructions. He engaged the family solicitor, Mr. Eliot, His Majesty's attorney at King's Bench and Common Pleas, who in turn had hired a barrister, Serjeant Wilcox.

Correspondingly, Lord and Lady Arthur had hired a lawyer to conduct the prosecution, although there was little that he or Serjeant Wilcox were required to do. The lord chancellor had sent a pair of clerks to Market Hill to collect depositions from anyone who had valid testimony to offer. The clerks were kept frantically busy for two days, copying down statements and opinions from what seemed to be nearly everyone in the county. Lara was almost grateful for the way Lord Arthur sheltered her from the flood of callers. He managed to keep everyone at bay, informing all acquaintances that Lara was too distraught to receive visitors.

However, Lara did consent to visit with Mr. Young, the estate agent, when he returned from London. She knew he had seen Hunter, and in spite of her efforts to be indifferent, she longed for some news of him.

Young appeared to be haggard from a lack of sleep. His gentle brown eyes were bloodshot and troubled. Lara welcomed him into the family parlor and closed the door, mindful of Janet's habit of eavesdropping. Here they had at least a chance of privacy.

"How is he?" Lara asked without preamble, seating herself and gesturing for him to join her.

Young perched on the edge of the sofa beside her, his bony knees and elbows making sharp points against his rumpled clothes. "His health is good," he replied somberly, "but as to his emotional condition, I couldn't say. He speaks very little, and he shows neither anger nor fear. He seems peculiarly indifferent to the entire process, actually."

"Does he need anything?" Lara asked, her throat tight. She had the terrible urge to go to Hunter, to offer him her comfort and support.

"If you do not mind, my lady, I should like to bring him some fresh clothes and a few personal items when I return to London tomorrow."

Lara nodded. "Please see that he has whatever he wants."

"Lady Hawksworth," the estate agent said tentatively, "I assure you, Dr. Slade and I would never have brought Lord Hawksworth to you in the first place were we not absolutely convinced of his identity."

"We all wanted to believe in him," Lara murmured. "He knew that, and he made use of it."

"My lady, you know that I have the deepest respect for your judgment . . . but I can't help believing that you're acting under the influence of your uncle. It is not too late to change your mind." The urgency of his tone deepened as he continued. "Do you understand what will happen to your husband if you do not retract your accusations?"

Lara smiled sadly as she looked at him. "Did he send you here to say that?"

Young shook his head. "Hawksworth refuses to offer one word in his own defense. He will not confirm or deny his identity, only says that the entire matter must be decided by you."

"The matter must be settled by each of us adhering to the truth as best we can. All I can do is state my beliefs, whether or not I like the consequences."

The estate agent's disappointment was obvious. "I

understand, Lady Hawksworth. However, I hope
you will not be distressed if Dr. Slade and I lend our
support to Lord Hawksworth."

"Quite the contrary," Lara said, fighting to keep
her voice from breaking. "It would make me happy
if you would help him in every way possible, as I
am unable to do so."

"Yes, milady." He gave her a sorrowful smile.
"Please forgive my rudeness, but I must be off now.
I have many tasks to accomplish on Lord Hawks-
worth's behalf."

She stood and gave him her hand. "Do your best
for him," she said softly.

"Of course." Young frowned regretfully. "The two
of you are a star-crossed pair, it seems. I should think
you would have every reason to be happy, but fate
keeps throwing obstacles in your way. I never
dreamed it would all come to this."

"Neither did I," Lara whispered.

"I've never considered myself a romantic," he said
awkwardly, "but my lady, I do hope that you and
he—"

"No," she said gently, leading him to the door.
"Don't hope."

The nursery walls were lined with dolls and toys,
and hung with pictures of children at play. Lara had
tried to make the room a comforting haven for
Johnny, but it seemed there was painfully little she
could protect him from. She slid a book into its place
on a blue-painted shelf, and resumed her seat on the
edge of Johnny's bed. He seemed absurdly small as
he lay back on the pillows, his black hair still damp
from his bath.

The boy's reaction to the events of the past few days was almost worse than the tears Lara had expected. He had responded to Hunter's absence with unshakable solemnity, all of his smiles and boyish energy extinguished. Lara hadn't explained the specifics of the situation to him, knowing it would overwhelm a child of his tender years. Instead she had told him simply that Hawksworth had behaved wrongly and had been arrested until a judge could sort out everything.

"Mama," Johnny asked, staring at her with huge blue eyes, "is Lord Hawksworth a bad man?"

Lara smoothed his hair. "No, darling," she murmured, "I don't think he's really bad. But he may have to be punished for some things he's done in the past."

"Lord Arthur says they'll hang him like they did my papa."

"Did he?" Lara asked gently, concealing a flash of anger toward Arthur. "Well, no one knows for certain what will happen until after we've met with the lord chancellor."

Johnny turned on his side, propping his head up on one small hand. "Mama, will I go to prison someday?"

"Never," Lara replied firmly, bending to press her lips on his dark head. "I will never let that happen to you."

"But if I grow up to be a bad man—"

"You're going to be a good, fine man," Lara said, staring at him intently, filled with tenderness and fierce love. "You mustn't worry about such things. We're going to stay together, Johnny, and everything will be fine."

The boy snuggled into the pillow, his face still grave and uncertain. "I want Lord Hawksworth to come back," he said.

Lara closed her eyes, holding back the pressure of sudden tears. "Yes, I know." After letting out an unsteady breath, she drew the covers up to the child's narrow shoulders.

Lara arrived in London the evening before the scheduled meeting with the lord chancellor. She had decided to stay in the Hawksworth town house, the Park Place residence where Hunter was being held under guard. The gleaming white town house, fronted by tall bay windows and a classical pediment with four pilaster columns, had been fitted up with elegant and tasteful restraint. The interiors were all wainscoted with gleaming dark oak and painted in soothing colors of stone, beige, and a rich olive that had been invented exclusively for the Hawksworths fifty years earlier. Made by combining specific amounts of Prussian blue and ocher, that particular shade of olive had caused a rage all through England when it had first appeared, and was still widely popular.

Lara was swamped in trepidation as she approached the town house. The thought of spending the night under the same roof with Hunter, albeit in separate rooms, made her tremble uncontrollably. She wanted to ask him the questions that had been tormenting her night and day. She wasn't certain she could bring herself to face him, however. Not without breaking down before him—and the humiliation of that was something she couldn't live through.

To Lara's relief, Lord and Lady Arthur had elected

to stay in their own London house, preferring its garish familiarity to the Hawksworth address. Quietly she bade the servants to unpack her trunks in her customary bedroom, only to be informed by the butler that the room was already occupied.

"By whom?" Lara asked warily.

"By the dowager countess, milady."

Hunter's mother was here? Lara's lips parted in amazement, and she stared at the butler blankly. "When . . . ? How . . . ?"

"I arrived only this afternoon," came the dowager's voice from the top of the stairs. "After one of the letters you had sent all over Europe finally reached me, I came to London straightaway. My plan was to travel to the estate tomorrow and sort through this strange muddle myself. Instead I discovered my purported son under guard here. Obviously I came not a moment too soon."

Lara had started up the stairs before her mother-in-law had finished speaking. As always, Sophie, the Dowager Countess of Hawksworth, was slim and attractive, with a regal pile of silver curls atop her head and her signature ropes of pearls cascading down her front. An intelligent, practical woman who refrained from showing emotion in even the direst circumstances, Sophie was difficult to love, but very easy to like.

"Mother!" Lara exclaimed, embracing her at once.

Sophie tolerated rather than returned the affectionate gesture, and gave Lara a fond smile. "Well, Larissa . . . it seems you would have been better off accepting my invitation to share my travels. You've had a difficult time of it, haven't you?"

"Yes," Lara said, returning the smile with a wobbly one of her own, and her eyes stung.

"There, there," Sophie said, her face softening.
"We'll sort through this, you and I, and make some
sense of it. A bottle of wine and a good long talk . . .
that's what the situation needs."

After giving a few crisp instructions to the servants, Sophie took Lara's arm, and they went to the
lavender room, a parlor Sophie had decorated herself. The sole exception in an otherwise masculine
home, the room was exclusively frilly and feminine.
It was filled with shades of mauve and lavender,
with plum-colored accents and small gold-finished
tables, and painted glass windows featuring violets.
The scent of violets clung to Sophie's hair and wrists,
having been her preferred fragrance for decades.

Lara wondered which room Hunter was imprisoned in, and what he might be thinking, and if he
knew she was there. "Have you seen him?" she
asked Sophie nervously.

The dowager took her time about replying, seating
herself with care in a plush velvet wing chair. "Yes,
I've seen him. We spoke at some length."

"He looks a great deal like Hunter, doesn't he?"

"Naturally. I would be surprised if he didn't."

Startled, Lara sat in her own chair and stared at
her mother-in-law. "I'm sure I don't know what you
mean."

Their gazes locked for a frozen moment. Lara had
never seen Sophie look quite so perturbed. "I see,"
the dowager finally murmured. "You haven't been
told, then."

"Told what?" Frustration bubbled up inside Lara.
"Good Lord, I'm weary of being surrounded with

secrets!" she exclaimed. "Please, *what* can you reveal about the man who is under guard downstairs?"

"To begin with," the dowager replied acerbically, "he and my son Hunter were half brothers."

Chapter 19

UNFAZED BY LARA'S stricken stare, Sophie waited patiently as a footman arrived with a bottle of red wine and a pair of glasses with diamond-shaped cuts incised in the stems. Another servant attended to the ceremony of opening the bottle. Lara bit her lip to keep silent, watching the servants proceed with maddening slowness.

Lara gripped the stem of her wineglass until the diamond pattern made red marks on her fingers. She waited until the servants had left before speaking. "Please tell me," she said softly.

"My husband, Harry, had a weakness for attractive women," Sophie said. "I tolerated it because he was discreet, and because he always came back to me. No man is perfect, Larissa. They each have some unpleasant feature or habit that must be tolerated. I loved Harry in spite of his infidelities, and they never posed a great problem for me . . . until one of his relationships resulted in his paramour's unwanted pregnancy."

"Who was she?" Lara asked. She took a sip of wine, the acrid flavor filling her mouth.

"An ambassador's wife. She had been pursued by nearly every man in London. Harry thought her quite a prize, I'm certain. Their affair lasted for nearly a year. When she conceived, she informed Harry that she would not keep the child. It would be his to do with as he wished."

"But he didn't want it?"

"Oh, Harry wanted the babe very much. He intended for it to abide with us, or at least to be raised in a place where he could visit it from time to time. However, I wouldn't hear of it. As you know, we hadn't much luck in bearing healthy children. Our first three did not survive infancy. Then we had finally been blessed with Hunter. I suppose I feared that my husband's interest in a bastard son might lessen his devotion to his legitimate child. I was quite protective of Hunter's interests. Therefore, I insisted that the bastard be given to a missionary couple who would take him so far away that we would never see him again."

"India," Lara said. Each word fell on her ear like the soft clicks of puzzle pieces snapping into place.

"Yes. I knew it would undoubtedly result in a hard life for the child, with no means or social position, and no proximity to his father. My husband was quite reluctant to send the baby away, but I was insistent." Sophie rearranged her skirts with undue care. "I've tried for thirty years to forget about what I had done, but he's remained in the back of my mind every day . . . haunting me, you could say."

Lara set aside her wine, staring at her mother-in-law without blinking. "What was his name?"

Sophie shrugged. "I wouldn't allow his father to

choose a name. I've no idea what his surrogate parents called him."

"Did your real son know that he had a brother?"

"No. I saw no reason to tell him. I never intended for Harry's bastard to interfere in our lives." The feathery wrinkles at the corners of Sophie's mouth stretched in a wry smile. "The irony of this is priceless, is it not?"

Being in no mood to appreciate irony, Lara did not return the dowager's smile. She felt victimized by a chain of events that had started long before her own birth. Harry's womanizing, the ambassador's wife's callous rejection of her own child, Sophie's repudiation of the bastard infant, Hunter's selfish irresponsibility . . . and finally, the stranger who had invaded Lara's life and seduced her with his lies.

Lara had no influence over any of this, and yet she was the one who had ultimately been punished for their collective actions. She would have to deal with the lifelong consequences . . . an illegitimate child of her own. By keeping it, she would place herself outside of good society for the rest of her life. Although Lara was tempted to tell Sophie about her pregnancy, some burgeoning maternal instinct kept her silent. The only way to protect her child's interests was to keep him a secret.

"What are we to do now?" she asked in a low voice.

Sophie sent her an assessing glance. "That's for you to decide, Larissa."

Lara shook her head in protest. "I'm in no state of mind to think sensibly."

"I suggest that you go to the downstairs guest suite where your lover is being held, and talk to him directly. After that, I suspect you'll know how you wish to proceed."

Your lover . . . It seemed inappropriate to call him that. Even now he seemed to be very much her husband, despite their relationship having been exposed for the illicit liaison it was. "I don't know if I can face him," Lara murmured.

"Oh, come now," Sophie chided gently. "If I could summon the nerve to face him after thirty years, surely you can."

Lara changed from her traveling clothes, donning a simple muslin gown printed with tiny pink flowers and pale green leaves. She brushed her hair and pinned it in a tight coil atop her head, and checked her appearance in a mirror. She looked pale and frightened . . . but it wasn't Hunter she was afraid of, it was herself.

Squaring her shoulders, she vowed silently that no matter what transpired between them, she would not give in to tears or anger. She would preserve her dignity at all cost.

She went to a door that was flanked by two guards, and quietly asked permission to visit the prisoner. To her relief, they were respectful and courteous, one of them bidding her to call out if she wanted assistance. Her blood raced with alarm and excitement as she walked through the door, and she knew her cheeks were stippled with bright color.

And there he was.

He stood in the center of the windowless room, his hair the same antiqued gold and brown as the heavy gilded picture frames that covered the walls. The guest suite was small but luxurious, the walls covered with rich olive and gold damask, the plaster painted soft gray. A pair of folding glass sash doors separated the receiving room from the bedchamber. He seemed perfectly at home in his elegant surroundings, an English gentleman in every regard. One would never guess who he was, or where he had come from. A chameleon indeed.

"How are you?" he asked, his gaze arrowing to her face.

The question sparked a flare of anger. How dare he affect concern for her after what he had done? But part of Lara couldn't help responding. She wanted to go to him and feel his arms close around her, and lay her head on his hard shoulder.

"Not well," she admitted.

The ease and intimacy that had existed between them was still there. She was suddenly filled with the dizzying pleasure of being near him, and worse, the feeling of completeness that she would never experience with anyone else.

"How did you find out?" he asked gruffly.

"I spoke with Captain Tyler."

He nodded slightly, showing no trace of surprise or anger. He had never expected it to last, Lara realized. He had always known that the charade as Lord Hawksworth was temporary at best. Why do it, then? Why risk throwing his life away for a few months of pretending to be Hawksworth?

"Please," she said, hearing her own voice as if she were speaking from a dream, "help me to understand why you've done this to me."

He didn't reply for a moment, watching her with the concentration of a man solving a mathematical problem. Then he turned partially away from her, his profile hard, his thick lashes lowering.

"The people who raised me—" He wouldn't call them parents. They had been caretakers at best, and damned negligent ones at that. "They never made a secret of who I really was. I grew up wondering about the father that didn't want me, and the half brother who most likely didn't know I existed. When I realized that Hawksworth had come to India and taken a house in Calcutta, I wanted to find out more about him. For a while I watched him from a distance. Then one evening I slipped into his house while he was away."

"You looked through his belongings," Lara said rather than asked, moving to sit on a small couch with scrolled ends. Her legs were suddenly unable to render any meaningful support.

He remained standing on the other side of the room. "Yes."

"And you found the miniature of me."

"Yes. And the letters you'd sent to him."

"My letters?" Lara tried to remember what she had written to Hunter about. Mostly she had described her daily activities, her interactions with people in the village, and news of family and former friends. Nothing of love or longing, nothing about her inner life. "I can't think why Hunter would have saved them. They were so very ordinary."

"They were lovely," he said softly. "I found them in a drawer—he kept them there along with his journals."

"Hunter never kept journals," she said coldly.

"He did," came the calm reply. "From the way they were numbered and dated, I knew there had to be more here. I found them soon after I arrived, and destroyed them after taking what information I needed."

Lara shook her head, bewildered by this revelation about her husband. "What did Hunter write in these journals?"

"He filled them with what he imagined were important secrets, political intrigues, social scandals . . . rubbish, most of it."

"Did he mention me?" she asked hesitantly. "What did he . . ." She fell silent as she saw from his face that Hunter had not written fondly of her.

"It was obvious the marriage was not a good one."

"He was bored by me," Lara said.

Hearing the defeated note in her voice, he looked at her with sudden intensity. "Hunter wanted Lady Carlysle. He married you because you were young enough to give him children."

And she had turned out to be barren. "Poor Hunter," she whispered.

"Poor stupid bastard," he agreed. "He was too thickheaded to see what he could have had. I read your letters, and I knew what kind of woman you were. I understood exactly what he had thrown away. He'd easily discarded the life I had wanted— a life I believed I deserved." His eyes half closed. "I took the miniature and kept it with me. I thought every moment of what you might be doing . . . if you were taking a bath . . . brushing your hair . . . visiting your friends in the village . . . sitting alone reading . . . laughing . . . crying. You became an obsession."

"Did you ever meet my husband?" Lara asked.

He was silent for a long moment. "No."

"That's a lie," she said softly. "Tell me what really happened."

He stared at Lara, so beautiful and obdurate, her fragility transformed into a stern, delicate strength that vanquished him. He could withhold nothing from her now. It seemed that his soul had cracked open, and every last secret was spilling out. He wasn't aware of moving, but he found himself in a corner of the room, leaning his forehead against the cool damask wall covering.

"It was March, festival time . . . Holi and Dhuleti, they call it. The festival of colors. Bonfires are lit everywhere, and the whole city goes mad with celebration. Everyone knew Hawksworth was giving the largest party in Calcutta . . ." He continued to speak absently, almost forgetting Lara was there.

He had wandered the streets in front of Hawksworth's palace amid the riotous crowd, while people laughed and screamed and threw colored powder and paint from the rooftops. Young women used pistons of bamboo sticks to spray perfumed water and silver or red paint at passersby, while young men smeared makeup on their faces and impishly donned saris to dance in the streets.

A horde of people wandered through Hawksworth's huge manor, an opulent home of classical design that proudly overlooked the green bank of the Hugli River. It was covered with ivory chunam stucco polished as slick as marble, while its front was adorned by a line of slender colonnades. The sea of English faces seemed identical to him, all of them splotched with colorful paint, their eyes glazed from strong drink, their cheeks sticky from gorging on delicacies of sugar and dried fruits.

Heart pounding, he entered the manor and moved among the revelers. He had worn a hooded robe of dark red cotton, similar to the other flamboyant garments the guests had donned. The luxury of the house was breathtaking, the rooms fitted with chandeliers and filled with Titian paintings and Venetian glass.

As he walked from room to room, tipsy women threw themselves at him, infected by the orgiastic mood of the crowd. He pushed them aside dismissively. None of them even seemed to notice the rejection, merely giggling and going in search of new prey.

The only sober faces in the crowd were those of the Indian servants, bringing forth platters of food and drink that were instantly devoured. He asked one of the servants where Hawksworth was, and was met with a shrug and a blank stare. Searching stealthily through the manor, he came to what appeared to be the library. The door was half open, affording a view of a tall mahogany bookcase topped with a collection of marble busts, and a set of library steps fitted with a carved handrail.

Hearing muted voices, he approached the doorway. There was a soft laugh, a gasp, a low groan . . . the unmistakable sounds of a couple having sex. His brow worked with a frown, and he faded back from the door to became part of the shadows. Soon all was quiet, and a dark-haired woman left the room. She was flushed and pretty, a smile on her lips as she rustled the crisp silk skirts of her pomegranate-colored gown into place and adjusted her breasts in the scooped bodice. Satisfied with her appearance, she hurried away without noticing the man in the shadowed corner.

He entered the room quietly and saw a tall, broad-shouldered man facing away from him, jerking his trousers closed. The man's head turned to reveal a distinctive profile, long nose, well-defined chin, forehead partially obscured with a thick swipe of dark hair. It was Hawksworth.

Hawksworth went to a pedestal desk topped with green leather and picked up a glass filled with amber liquid. Seeming to sense that he was not alone, he turned and looked directly at the intruder. "Damnation!" he exclaimed in startlement. "Who are you to come sneaking up behind me like that? Explain yourself!"

"I'm sorry," he replied, finding it difficult to speak. He pulled off his robe and stood facing Hawksworth, riveted by the face that was eerily similar to his own.

The resemblance was not lost on Hawksworth. "Sweet Christ," he muttered, setting aside his drink and coming closer to him. Two pairs of dark brown eyes gazed at each other in fascination.

They were not identical . . . Hawksworth was darker, beefier, and he had the expensive, well-tended look of a Thoroughbred. But anyone seeing the two of them together would have known instantly that they were related.

"Who the hell are you?" Hawksworth snapped.

"I'm your half brother," he replied quietly, and watched the complex play of emotions on Hawksworth's face.

"My God," Hawksworth muttered, and snatched up the drink once more. He downed it rapidly and coughed, and regarded the stranger with a reddened face. "My father's by-blow," he said hoarsely. "He once told me about you, though he wouldn't say what had become of you."

"I was brought up by missionaries in Nandagow—"

"I don't give a damn about your life," Hawksworth interrupted, bristling with angry suspicion. "I can guess why you've come to me. Believe me, I have enough bloody hangers-on tugging at my coat. Is it money you want?" He bent and fumbled in the desk drawer, and unearthed a cash box. Thrusting his hand inside the unlocked box, he withdrew a fist full of coins, and scattered them before the stranger. "Take it and leave. I assure you, it's all you'll get from me."

"I don't want money." Humiliated and angry, he stood frozen amid the glittering coins.

"Then what is it?" Hawksworth demanded.

He couldn't answer, just stood there like a miserable fool while all the questions he'd had about his father and his past died inside him.

Hawksworth seemed to read his thoughts. "What did you think would happen if you came here?" he asked with biting contempt. "Should I throw my arms around you and welcome the long-lost sheep into the fold? You're not wanted or needed. You have no place in the family. I should think that needs no explanation after the way my parents shipped you out of England. You were a mistake that needed getting rid of."

As he listened to the jeering words, he couldn't keep from silently questioning the unfairness of fate. Why should this self-important jackass have been born as lord of the manor? Hawksworth had been given a family, land, title, fortune, a lovely young wife, and he valued it all so little that he had left England for frivolous reasons. Whereas he, born a bastard, had nothing.

He understood Hawksworth's hostility all too well. Hawksworth had been brought up to consider himself the Crosslands' only son, legitimate or otherwise. The family had no use for a bastard offspring who would only cause them embarrassment. "I didn't come to make a claim on you," he murmured, interrupting Hawksworth's tirade. "I only wanted to meet you."

The words did nothing to mollify the irate man. "Now you've achieved your objective. I advise you to leave my home, or there'll be the devil to pay!"

He had left Hawksworth's manor without touching a single coin on the floor, and felt a certain satisfaction in knowing that he still possessed the miniature of Lady Hawksworth. He would keep that one small piece of his brother's life for his own.

". . . I continued my service under Captain Tyler's command for a time, until I learned that Hawksworth's ship had wrecked." he said tonelessly. "He was gone, and I knew that everything he had—everything I wanted—was here waiting for me. I resolved to do whatever was necessary to have you, if only for a little while."

"So you took his place in order to prove yourself the better man," she said.

"No, I . . ." He paused, forcing himself to be truthful. "That was part of it at first," he admitted. "But I fell in love with you . . . and soon you became the only thing that mattered."

"You gave no thought to the consequences of what

you were doing," Lara said, anger pouring through her. "You've destroyed any possibility of my trusting anyone ever again. You stole another man's life, and hurt me unforgivably, and now you'll likely hang. Was it worth all of this?"

He gave her a look that seemed to scorch her very soul, his eyes black with yearning and fierce love. "Yes."

"You selfish wretch," she cried, her mouth trembling.

"I would become anyone, anything for you. I would lie, steal, beg, kill for you. I'm not sorry for what I did the past few months. My life would have been nothing without them."

"What about my life?" she choked. "How can you claim to care for me when you've done nothing but lie and take advantage, and make me into the biggest fool that ever lived?"

"You're not a fool, Lara. I made it easy for you to believe that I was Hunter. I knew that you would ignore your own doubts if you wanted to believe in me—and you did."

"None of it was real," she said, tears beginning to slide down her face in heavy streaks. "Everything you said to me, every time you kissed me . . . it was all a lie."

"No," he said hoarsely. He made a move to come to her, then checked himself as he saw her shrink back.

"I don't even know your name. Oh, why did you have to pretend you were Hunter?"

"Could I have had you any other way?" he asked, his voice raspy. It was acute torture to see her cry and not be able to comfort her. "If I'd come to you with the truth about who I was, would you have let me near you?"

Lara was silent for a long time. "No," she finally said.

He nodded, her answer confirming what he had already known.

"I can't lie for you," Lara ventured after a moment of introspection. "I couldn't go through the rest of my life—"

"No," he muttered. "I wouldn't expect that."

Lara's entire body went rigid as he walked toward her. He moved carefully, as if he thought a sudden movement might cause her to bolt. He stopped within an arm's length of her and sank to his haunches. "I could never tire of looking at you," he said huskily. "Your beautiful green eyes. Your sweet face." He stared at her with such naked need that she felt scorched by the dark fire of his gaze. "Lara, there's something you have to understand. The past few months with you . . . the time we've had together . . . it's worth dying for. If it's all I can have, it's enough. So it doesn't matter what you choose to say tomorrow, or what happens to me from now on."

Lara couldn't speak. She had to escape him before her tears became uncontrollable. Standing jerkily, she ducked her head and made her way to the door. She thought he said her name, but she couldn't stop, couldn't bear his presence without falling apart.

Sophie was waiting for her, her gaze arrowing to Lara's ravaged face. "You're in love with him," she said simply, curving an arm around Lara's shoulders. Together they walked up the stairs.

"I'm so sorry," Lara said with a broken laugh.

"You must despise me for feeling this way, when I never gave my love to the man who was truly entitled to it."

As a pragmatist who was fond of reducing any situation down to a skeleton of unvarnished fact, Sophie was not moved to agree. "Why should I despise you? I don't know that my son was entitled to your love. Did he ever make a sincere effort to win your heart?"

"No, but—"

"Of course he didn't. Hunter was too enamored of that Lady Carlysle, though God only knew what he saw in that mannish creature. He was mad over her, and he should have married her. To my regret, I advised him to marry you instead and keep her on the side. He could run with the hare and hunt with the hounds, I told him. It was a mistake on my part. I hoped your charms would grow on Hunter, and you would influence him for the better."

"Well, that didn't happen," Lara said. Although she hadn't intended the comment to be amusing, the dowager emitted a dry laugh.

"Obviously." She sighed, her face sobering as they reached the family parlor. "My poor son," she said. "I know full well that he wasn't a good husband to you. He never had a sense of responsibility. Perhaps it was that he grew up so spoiled, everything coming easily to him. He could have done with a few of the hardships that mold a man's character. But I couldn't help doting on him. He was all I had. I encouraged him in his selfishness, I'm afraid."

Although Lara was tempted to agree with Sophie, she held her silence. They sat close together, as before, and she rubbed her tired eyes.

"Have you decided what you will do tomorrow?" the dowager asked briskly.

"What choice is there? I have a responsibility to tell the truth."

"Nonsense."

"What?" Lara asked faintly.

"I've never understood why honesty is always considered to be the highest virtue. There are more important things than truth."

Taken aback, Lara stared at her with wide eyes. "Pardon, but that seems a very odd thing to say."

"Is it? You've always been too conventional, Lara. Have you no concern for the dependents whose fate is being determined by the outcome of this? And is your own well-being of no consequence?"

"You sound as if you want this stranger to take the place of your son," Lara said incredulously.

"My son is gone," the dowager said. "All I can do now is take stock of the situation as it is. Arthur and his wife have proved that they will not safeguard the Hawksworth inheritance. They will do everything in their power to disgrace the title. On the other hand, legitimate or no, this young man *is* my husband's issue, and he seems to have performed adequately in the role of Hawksworth. To my way of thinking, he has as much right to the title as Arthur. Added to that, he seems to have won your affection. I did wrongly by him all those years ago. It was because of me that he had a very poor start in life, and yet he seems to have made himself into a capable man. Of course, I don't approve of what he has done. However, one can argue that his actions are not those of an evil man but merely a desperate one."

"Are you saying that he has your support?" Lara exclaimed numbly.

"Only if you wish it. Because it is you, my dear, who will have to live with a lie for the rest of your life . . . you who will bear his children and act as his wife in every way. If you are willing to take him as your husband, then I am willing to take him as my son. Mind you, if we establish him now as Hawksworth, there will be no turning back."

"Could you actually betray the real Hunter in this way?" Lara whispered. "Would you be able to accept another man in his place?"

"My feelings about Hunter will remain my concern and no one else's," the dowager said with great dignity. "The question is what you desire, Larissa. Will you save this man or send him to the devil? Shall he go on as Lord Hawksworth, or will you return the title to Arthur? You must decide tonight."

Lara was confounded by her mother-in-law's reasoning. Never in a thousand years would she have expected Sophie to take such an outlandish position. It didn't seem right at all. She had expected Sophie to react with the appropriate outrage at having her son impersonated by another man, not supporting the charade and proposing that it continue.

As thoughts whirled through her head, Lara recalled Rachel's voice saying, *The facts aren't absolute. One could argue endlessly over them.* And added to this impossible tangle, there were these facts to consider: The man downstairs . . . whoever he was . . . had been good for her. He had made her happy. He had taken care of Johnny and Rachel and everyone on the estate. No matter what he had done in the past, Lara knew that he was a good man. And she loved him down to the deepest corners of her soul.

"But . . . how can I love a man I don't really know?" she asked, speaking more to herself than to Sophie. "And how can I trust that he loves me? He is a chameleon, just as Captain Tyler said. I'm not convinced he'll ever be capable of honesty. He'll always be on guard, hiding his thoughts, never allowing anyone to see him for the man he truly is."

"A troubled soul," the dowager said, with a smile that combined irony and affection and a hint of challenge that bewildered Lara. "Well, that is your forte, is it not?"

Chapter 20

KNOWING THAT CAPTAIN Tyler had been called to London to give his deposition, Lara had sent for him early in the morning. To her vast relief, he came at once to the Park Place town house. He was dressed in uniform, a short scarlet coat fronted with thick gold braid, gleaming white trousers, immaculate black boots, a sash, and a plumed black hat tucked beneath his arm.

"Lady Hawksworth," he said respectfully, striding into the parlor and bending over her proffered hand.

"Thank you for coming so quickly," she said.

"I only hope I can be of service to you, my lady."

"So do I," Lara said gravely, seating herself on a plump velvet chair and leaning against the carved, scrolled mahoghany back. Obeying her gesture, the captain seated himself on an identical chair nearby. "You're in London to give your deposition to the lord chancellor, of course," she said.

"Yes, my lady." His neat black mustache twitched in discomfort. "May I again apologize for withholding the truth from you for so long, and for the distress I caused you when last we met? I will always regret my actions in this matter, and I hope that someday you will forgive my unaccountable silence—"

"There is nothing to regret, or forgive," she assured him sincerely. "I understand your silence concerning Lord Hawksworth, and in a way I'm grateful for it. As a matter of fact . . ." She drew a deep breath and looked directly into his face as she continued. "The reason I wanted to see you this morning is to ask for your continued silence."

He showed no emotion save a fluttering blink of his dark eyes. "I see," he said slowly. "You're asking me to perjure myself before the lord chancellor today. You wish for me to deny knowledge of the man masquerading as Lord Hawksworth."

"Yes," she said simply.

"May I ask why?"

"After much reflection, I have come to believe that it would be in the Crosslands' best interests, including mine, for this man to continue as the head of the family."

"My lady, I may not have successfully conveyed the character of this man to you—"

"I am fully cognizant of his character."

Sighing, Captain Tyler rubbed his thumb over the thick gold braiding on the sleeve of his coat in a repeated motion. "I should like to agree to your request, as it would fulfill a debt I have longed to repay. Yet . . . to allow him to have a position entailing such power and responsibility . . . to let him steal another man's life . . . it doesn't seem right."

"What debt do you owe him?" Lara asked curiously.

He explained stiffly. "He saved my life. We—the Crown, I mean—were establishing new towns further along the Ganges, and trouble arose in the Cawnpore territory. Thuggees would lie in wait along the roads and attack travelers, killing them without mercy. Even women and children weren't spared. When they realized we weren't going to be driven away, the devils became more aggressive. Many of the men in my company were hunted and slaughtered, some in their own beds. I myself was beset one night whilst returning from a visit to Calcutta. I was suddenly surrounded by a half dozen thugs who killed a young ensign and another escort, and were about to make short work of me." He paused, breaking out in a sweat at the memory. "And then *he* came out of the night like a shadow, felling two of my attackers so swiftly that the others eventually fled, shouting that he was the messenger of some wrathful god. That was the last time I saw him . . . until his reincarnation as Lord Hawksworth."

"The scar on the back of his neck . . ." Lara said in a flash of intuition.

Tyler nodded. "During the fray, one of the thugs took possession of my sword. Your 'Hawksworth' was fortunate not to have been beheaded. Luckily for him, he's quite agile in combat." He reached inside his coat for a handkerchief and blotted his brow. "He's not an ordinary man, my lady. If I agree to your request, I cannot be held responsible for the future pain and unhappiness he may cause you."

Lara smiled at him steadily. "I believe he is worthy of my trust. I have no doubt that he will lead an exemplary life if only he is given a chance."

He regarded her as if she were either a saint or a

lunatic. "Forgive me, but your trust is rather too easily given, Lady Hawksworth. With all my heart, I
hope this man will prove it well founded."

"He will," she said, impulsively taking his hand
and pressing it hard. "I know he will, Captain."

Lara had been kept waiting in an antechamber to the
lord chancellor's offices for only an hour, but it had
seemed like forever. Sensitive to every muffled sound
that occurred in the rooms and halls around her, she
sat on the edge of a hard wooden chair and tried to
interpret what was happening. Finally a clerk appeared in the antechamber and escorted Lara to the
hall outside the lord chancellor's office. Her heart
leapt as she saw the captain exiting the office. Their
gazes caught, hers questioning, his reassuring. Then
in response to her unspoken plea, he gave her a slight
nod. *It's all right,* his eyes seemed to say, and some
of her terrible tension eased.

Gathering her confidence, Lara accompanied the
clerk to the chancery chambers. Sunbury, the lord
chancellor, rose from a chair set at a heavy mahogany
table, and waited until Lara was seated before lowering himself onto the brown leather upholstery. Sunbury cut an impressive figure in a glowing scarlet
robe, his jowly face framed with a long silvery wig.
As he toyed with a pocket-sized terrestrial globe covered with tiny painted maps, Lara saw that his right
hand was heavy with the weight of three massive
gold rings.

Sunbury's gray eyes were small but piercing, staring lucidly out from a fleshy face. He had an innate
look of importance that would have been evident
even without the trappings of wealth and office. Lara

wouldn't be surprised to see him on Judgment Day,
positioned at the heavenly gates to assess the quali-
fications of aspiring angels.

Like a magnet, her gaze was drawn to Hunter. He
was seated at the far end of the long table, his head
silhouetted in the glimmering light from the window.
He almost seemed unearthly in his austere handsomeness, his face remote, his lean body clad in
cream breeches, a black waistcoat, and a coat of dark
green striped velvet. He didn't return Lara's gaze,
merely watched the lord chancellor with the unblinking gaze of a wild creature.

The room was filled with other occupants . . . a
clerk to copy the spoken depositions onto paper, the
attorneys Eliot and Wilcox, the prosecutor whose
name Lara didn't recall, Sophie, Arthur and Janet . . .
and a familiar face that made Lara stiffen in bewildered outrage. Lord Lonsdale, dressed to the nines
in a satin waistcoat embroidered with butterflies,
shoes with ornate buckles, and a diamond pin in his
cravat. He smiled at her, his blue eyes sparkling with
malicious pleasure. What was he doing here? What
information could he possibly have that would merit
his presence before the lord chancellor?

Questions and protestations burned on the edge of
her lips, but Lara managed to keep silent. She looked
at Sophie, who toyed idly with a long strand of pearls
that cascaded along the lace front of her peach gown.

"*Now* the truth will out," Arthur said triumphantly, giving Lara a commanding stare. He spoke
to her as if she were a small child. "Just answer the
lord chancellor's questions as honestly as you can,
Larissa."

Resenting his patronizing tone, Lara ignored the

direction and focused her attention on Sunbury.

The lord chancellor spoke in a rumbling tone. "Lady Hawksworth, one can only hope that you will be able to shed some light on this perplexing situation."

"I will try," she said softly.

Sunbury rested his beefy hand on a thick sheaf of paper. "I have been presented with a score of depositions from people who vigorously insist that this man is, to the best of their knowledge, the Earl of Hawksworth. The Dowager Countess of Hawksworth, no less, affirms that he is indeed her son." He paused and glanced at Sophie, who gave him a short, impatient nod. "However," Sunbury resumed, "some contradictory opinions have been offered— most notably from the gentleman in question. He has insisted that he is *not* Lord Hawksworth, though he has refused to explain more. Tell me, my lady . . . who exactly is this man?"

The room was deadly silent as Lara moistened her lips. "He is Hunter Cameron Crossland, the Earl of Hawksworth," she said in a clear, steady voice. It was slightly unnerving to speak and watch a clerk take down every word as it left her lips. "He is my husband, he has always been, and it is my dearest hope that he always will be."

"*What?*" Arthur exclaimed, while Janet catapulted from her chair.

"You lying bitch," she screeched, striding toward Lara with her fingers curved into claws. Lara flinched in reaction. Before Janet reached her, Hunter leapt from his chair and caught her from behind, snatching her flailing wrists. Janet reacted like an enraged cat, twisting and yowling in a way that seemed to alarm everyone except for Arthur, who merely looked disgusted.

"Out!" the lord chancellor thundered, his jowly face mottled with outrage. "I insist that this creature be removed from my chambers at once!"

The pandemonium was slow to subside.

"She is lying!" Arthur exclaimed. "Larissa, you double-tongued witch, I'll see you in hell for this—"

"Silence!" The lord chancellor stood, his scarlet robes swirling about his large body. "I will not have my chambers disgraced by profanity and violence. Remove your wife, sir, and if you are not capable of controlling yourself henceforth, do not return!"

Turning purple, Arthur wrested Janet's writhing body from Hunter's grasp.

Hunter went to Lara, his gaze raking over her. Ascertaining that she had not been injured, he gripped the arms of her chair and leaned over her. His face was close to hers, and suddenly the rest of the room was blocked out, and all that existed was the two of them. His dark eyes simmered with anger. "Why are you doing this?" he asked harshly. "Tell them the truth, Lara."

Her chin lifted, and she returned his gaze obstinately. "I won't let you go."

"Dammit, haven't I done enough to you by now?"

"Not nearly," she said softly.

Her words seemed to infuriate rather than please him. He released her chair with a muffled sound of frustration, and crossed the room in a few swift strides. The atmosphere was fraught with unexpected antagonism.

Arthur returned for a hastily muttered conference with the prosecutor, who then approached the lord chancellor. Words were exchanged, and Lara saw the prosecutor's mouth press into a thin line of disapproval. Unhappily he returned to his seat, waving Arthur to do the same.

"Now, then," Sunbury barked, staring hard at Lara. "I hope you will enlighten us further, Lady Hawksworth. You claim that this man is your husband, yet he insists that he is not Lord Hawksworth. Which one of you is telling the truth?"

Lara focused an earnest stare on him. "My lord, I believe my husband feels unworthy of me because of a past indiscretion. His well-known affair with a certain . . ." She paused as if it were painful to mention the name.

The lord chancellor nodded, the rolls of his silver wig slipping over his shoulders. "Lady Carlysle," he supplied. "I received her deposition earlier."

"Then I'm certain you've been informed about her liaison with my husband," Lara continued, "a relationship that has caused me no small amount of grief. In his remorse over the affair, I believe my husband's intention is to punish himself in this most drastic manner, by denying his very identity. However, I wish to make him understand that I forgive him for everything." She glanced at Hunter, who stared stonily at the floor. "Everything," she repeated firmly. "I want to begin again, my lord."

"Indeed," the lord chancellor muttered, scrutinizing Hunter's closed face, and Lara's resolute one. He returned his gaze to Hunter. "If what Lady Hawksworth claims is true, my good fellow, it's going a bit far to renounce your own name. A man makes mistakes now and again. It is up to our wives, with their superior virtue, to make up for us." He chuckled at his own joke, heedless of the fact that no one shared his amusement.

"Claptrap!" Arthur exclaimed as he glared at Lara. "My lord, this woman is suffering from mental derangement. She has no idea what she is saying. This cunning impostor has somehow convinced her to side with him, when only yesterday she was denouncing him!"

"What have you to say to that, Lady Hawksworth?" Sunbury inquired.

"I have made a terrible mistake," Lara acknowledged. "I can only beg forgiveness for the trouble I've caused. I brought the suit against my husband in a fit of anger over his affair with Lady Carlysle, and I was influenced adversely by my uncle. I'm not usually so weak-minded . . . but I'm afraid my condition has made me somewhat irrational."

"Your condition?" Sunbury repeated, while everyone in the room stared at her openmouthed, including Hunter and Sophie.

"Yes . . ." Lara flushed as she continued, hating the necessity of using her pregnancy this way. However, she intended to use every weapon at her disposal. "I'm expecting a child, my lord. I'm certain you understand the instability of a woman's temperament when she is in the family way."

"Indeed," the lord chancellor murmured, stroking his chin thoughtfully.

Hunter's face was pale beneath its golden tan. From the way he looked at her, Lara knew he thought she was lying. "Enough, Lara," he said hoarsely.

"More lies!" Arthur cried, standing and shaking off his attorney's restraining hand. "She's as barren as the desert. Everyone knows that she is incapable of producing a child. My lord, she's faking a pregnancy and will no doubt fake a miscarriage as soon as it's convenient!"

Lara began to enjoy the sight of her uncle's apoplectic countenance. With the faintest of smiles, she turned to the lord chancellor. "I will submit to any physician of your choosing, my lord, if you so desire. I have nothing to fear."

Sunbury regarded her with a long, measuring glance, and though his face was grave, an answering smile appeared in his gray eyes. "That won't be necessary, Lady Hawksworth. It seems congratulations are in order."

"Excuse me," came Lonsdale's dry voice. "I hate to puncture Lady Hawksworth's pretty story, as I enjoy a good tale as much as the next fellow. However, I can prove in less than a minute that this man is a fraud—and that our charming Lady Hawksworth is a liar."

The lord chancellor's thick gray eyebrows lifted. "Oh? And how may that be accomplished, Lord Lonsdale?"

Lonsdale paused for theatrical effect. "I have information that will surprise all of you—secret information about the real Lord Hawksworth."

"Let us have it, then," Sunbury replied, passing the pocket globe from one heavy palm to the other.

"Very well." Lonsdale stood and made a show of straightening his satin waistcoat. "The real Hawksworth and I were not only the closest of friends, but also fellows in an exclusive society. The scorpions, we call ourselves. I don't feel it is necessary to explain our purpose except to say that we have certain political aims. Although each of us has taken an oath to keep our affiliation a secret, I feel compelled to reveal it, and thereby prove that this so-called Hawksworth is an impostor. You see, just before he left for India, Hawksworth and the rest of us had a certain mark placed on the inside of the left arm. A permanent mark made with ink embedded beneath the skin. I have this mark, and so do the others. Only the true Earl of Hawksworth would have it."

"And this mark, I suppose, is shaped like a scorpion?" Sunbury inquired.

"Precisely." Lonsdale made a move to shed his coat. "If you'll allow me but a minute or two, my lord, I will show you the mark—"

"That won't be necessary," the Lord Chancellor said dryly. "It would be more to the point for Lord Hawksworth to display *his* arm."

All gazes turned to Hunter, who pinned Sunbury with a mutinous glare. "There's no need," he muttered. "I'm not Hawksworth."

The lord chancellor returned his hard stare without blinking. "Then verify it by removing your shirt, sir."

"No," Hunter said through his teeth.

The flat refusal caused Sunbury's color to rise. "Shall I have it removed for you?" he asked gently.

Lara breathed hard in agitation. She couldn't remember having seen any kind of mark on Hunter's arm. The thought that one small patch of ink would send all her hopes and dreams plummeting . . . She clenched her fists in her skirts and twisted them tightly. "I give you my word the mark is there," she cried.

The lord chancellor smiled sardonically. "With all due respect, Lady Hawksworth, in this instance I would prefer solid proof to your word." He returned his gaze to Hunter's face. "The shirt, if you please."

Arthur began to laugh in wild glee. "Now you're done for, you damned charlatan!"

The lord chancellor began to reprove him for the profanity, but his attention was soon diverted as Hunter stood. Scowling, Hunter set his jaw and stared at the floor, and pulled his coat off, yanking hard at the sleeves. Discarding the coat, he began on the buttons of his black waistcoat. Lara bit her lip in silent anguish, trembling as she saw dark color spread over Hunter's averted face. He set aside his waistcoat and pulled his shirt free of his breeches. Midway through the fastenings of the shirt, he paused and looked at the lord chancellor. "I'm not Hawksworth," he growled. "Listen to me for one damned minute—"

"Make him continue," Arthur snapped. "I insist on it."

"You may speak your piece, sir," Sunbury informed Hunter, "after I examine your arm. Proceed."

Hunter didn't move.

Enraged by the hesitation, Arthur sprang forward, grabbed a loose fold of the shirt, and yanked at it until they all heard the screech of rending linen. The shirt tore away, shreds hanging from the cuffs to reveal a lean body rippling with muscle, the tanned skin marked in places by scars not unlike the old hunting wounds her husband had suffered while pursuing boar and other wild game. Transfixed by the sight of Hunter's body, and the dreadful knowledge of what was about to happen, Lara held her breath.

Arthur shoved Hunter toward the lord chancellor.

338 LISA KLEYPAS

"There," he sneered. "Show him your arm, you lying bastard."

Hunter's fist clenched as he raised it behind his head and lifted his arm.

From where she was sitting, Lara had a perfect view. There, a few inches above the patch of dark hair that furred his armpit, was a small design of a scorpion inked in blue.

Lonsdale, who had come around to see, staggered backward in amazement. "How can it be?" he asked hoarsely, his gaze darting from the mark to Hunter's taut face. "How the hell did you know?"

Lara's mind was occupied by the same question. She pondered in bewildered silence, until it occurred to her that the only way he could have reproduced the scorpion design was if he had seen it in her husband's journals.

Arthur was incoherent with fury, Sputtering and gasping, he made his way to the nearest chair and collapsed.

Sophie regarded Hunter with a strange look of perplexed admiration, while she addressed her words to the lord chancellor. "I should think this settles the matter quite neatly, Lord Sunbury."

Lonsdale's face twisted with murderous fury. "You won't win," he hissed at Hunter. "I'll see you dead first!" He fled the room with a torrent of curses, slamming the door with a force that seemed to shake the building.

The lord chancellor rolled his eyes and turned his attention to the pocket globe in his hands. He snapped it open to reveal a tiny map of the constellations, and drew his finger along a trail of painted stars. "Well, my lad," he murmured, sliding a glance at Hunter's sullen face. "I'm rather inclined to believe your wife. Trying to punish yourself for an indiscretion, eh? Is that the case? Well, even the best of men sometimes struggle with that particular weakness. And in the event that you *aren't* the Earl of Hawksworth . . . I'm not inclined to argue with the majority of people who say you are. It seems reasonable to settle the question immediately in favor of Lord Hawksworth being, er . . . Lord Hawksworth, and I'll discharge the case forthwith." He glanced at Hunter hopefully. "I trust you will not persist in arguing, my lord? I should very much dislike to be late for my midday meal."

"Where is he?" Lara exclaimed in frustration, striding across the parlor floor under Sophie's disapproving gaze. "I can't leave London without seeing him, but I must return to Rachel and Johnny. Oh, what could have gotten into his head, to vanish like this?"

During the tumult that followed the lord chancellor's decision, Hunter had disappeared. Lara had no choice but to return to the Hawksworth town house and wait for him. It had been four hours, and there was no sign of him. She wanted desperately to talk to him, but she felt an urgent need to leave at once for Lincolnshire. Her instincts warned that she must return to Rachel as quickly as possible. There was no telling what Lonsdale might do in his fury—Lara was certain he meant to collect his wife without delay, by force if necessary.

An awful thought occurred to her, and she stared at Sophie in dawning horror. "You don't think Hunter has disappeared for good, do you? What if he never comes back?"

Uncomfortable with displays of volatile emotion, Sophie frowned reprovingly. "Don't carry on so, Larissa. I promise you, he'll find you when he's ready. He isn't about to disappear after the surprise you dropped at the hearing until he discovers if it's true or not. Which leads to the question . . . *are* you expecting or not?"

"I'm certain that I am," Lara said shortly, too occupied with her worry over Hunter to share Sophie's evident pleasure in the news.

The dowager settled back with a wondering smile. "Praise be. Harry's line will continue after all, it seems. A virile creature, your errant lover. He certainly had no problem in starting you breeding."

"Husband," Lara corrected. "We'll refer to him as my husband from now on."

Sophie shrugged nonchalantly. "As you prefer, Larissa. Do calm yourself. You're far too agitated. It can't be good for the babe."

"I don't think he believed me about the child," Lara murmured, standing at the window and recalling Hunter's stunned expression in the lord chancellor's office. He must have thought it was yet another lie to save him. She pressed her palms and her forehead against the cool, misty glass panes, while her chest ached with the fear that he might never return.

Chapter 21

Lara's carriage reached Hawksworth Hall late in the evening, when most of the household was asleep. She was grateful to be spared the task of explaining an inexplicable situation to Johnny and Rachel and the others tonight. She was weary of talking and traveling and trying to ignore the thoughts buzzing in her head. With each turn of the carriage wheels that conveyed her from London, she had felt increasingly defeated and hopeless. She wanted to lose herself in sleep.

"Lady Hawksworth," Mrs. Gorst asked quietly, welcoming her inside, "shall Lord Arthur be returning?"

"No," Lara replied with a shake of her head. "The case was discharged by the lord chancellor."

"I see." A genuine smile covered the housekeeper's face. "That is very good news, my lady! Shall we expect Lord Hawksworth to arrive soon?"

"I don't know," Lara said, her dejected manner seeming to dampen Mrs. Gorst's good spirits.

Forbearing to ask further questions, the house-

keeper directed a footman to bring Lara's trunk upstairs, and a maid to unpack it.

While the servants were thus engaged, Lara hurried up two flights of stairs to the nursery where
Johnny slept. Entering the room carefully, she set a
single candle on the painted blue dresser. The sound
of the little boy's breathing, soft and serene, made
her heart contract in sudden gladness. This, at least,
was something she could count on . . . the trust and
innocent love of a child. His head was snuggled deep
into the downy surface of a pillow, the babyish
roundness of one cheek glowing in the candlelight.

Lara bent low to kiss him. "I'm home," she whispered.

Johnny stirred and murmured, black lashes lifting
to reveal slitted blue eyes. Satisfied to see her, he produced a drowsy smile before falling asleep once
more.

Lara retrieved her candle and crept from the nursery, going to her own room. It seemed very empty,
even with the maids busily unpacking her belongings
and turning back the covers on the bed. When they
had finally departed, she changed into her nightgown and left her clothes in a heap on the floor. After
extinguishing the lamps, she crawled into bed and
lay on her back, staring blindly through the darkness.

Her hand smoothed the empty space beside her.
She had lain with two different men in this bed, one
out of duty, one out of passion.

Lara knew in her heart that Hunter did not intend
to come back to her. He meant to atone for the
wrongs he had done her. He had believed her when
she told him that she could not lie for him the rest

of her life. He thought it would be easier, better for her, if he disappeared once again.

The reality was, she loved him too much to let him go. She wanted him as her husband, regardless of what the world might think. She loved him far more than propriety and duty and even honor.

She fell into a turbulent sleep, her head filled with disquieting images. In her dreams the people she loved were walking away from her, not seeming to see or hear her. She ran after the shadowy figures, pleading, pulling at them, but they were impervious to her cries. One by one they began to vanish, until only Hunter was left ... and then he, too, faded. "No," she cried, searching frantically for him, "*noooo . . .*"

A scream tore through the silent house.

Lara sat upright, her heart thudding. At first she thought the cry might have been her own, but as she listened intently, she heard it again.

"Rachel," she breathed, and sprang from bed, galvanized into action by the sound of her sister's muffled cries. She ran from the room in her bare feet, not bothering with slippers or a robe. As she reached the top of the grand staircase, she saw a man halfway down the stairs, tugging and dragging Rachel along with him. One of his fists was tangled in her long braid, while the other was clamped around her arm.

"No, Terrell, *please*," Rachel said, fighting him every step of the way.

He hurled her forward, sending her tumbling down three or four steps until she collapsed in a heap on the first landing.

Lara let out a shriek of alarm. Lonsdale ... She hadn't expected he would dare to come in the middle of the night and snatch Rachel from her bed. He was flushed from drink and self-righteous rage. A sneer twisted his mouth as he looked upward and saw Lara.

"I'm taking back what's mine," he said in a slurred voice. "I'll teach you to cross me! You'll never see my wife again. If I ever find the two of you together, I'll kill the both of you." He grabbed Rachel by the hair and hauled her to her feet, seeming to relish her sob of pain. "You thought you could get away from me," he snarled. "But I own you, and I'll break and bend you to my will, you faithless bitch. The first lesson starts tonight."

Weeping violently, Rachel looked up at Lara. "Don't let him take me, Larissa!"

Lara charged after the pair as Lonsdale continued to haul her sister away. "Don't you touch her," she cried, her bare feet flying down the stairs until she reached them. She took hold of Lonsdale's arm and tugged wildly. "Let go of her, or I'll kill you!"

"You'll do *what*?" he asked with an ugly laugh, and flung her away with frightening ease. The force of his arm threw her back to the landing. The back of her head struck the wall with a sharp crack. For a moment the world tipped sideways, and her mind was covered in a thick gray cloud. Blinking hard, she raised her hands to her head, becoming aware of an annoying, piercing ringing that wouldn't abate. Beneath the deafening sound, she heard Rachel's distant pleas.

Struggling to a sitting position, Lara realized that Lonsdale was dragging her sister across the great hall, while Rachel stumbled and sobbed beside him. Despite her physical weakness, Rachel fought valiantly, pulling hard at her captured arm. Annoyed by her resistance, Lonsdale hit her on the head with some object in his hand. Rachel staggered and nearly collapsed. She moaned in pain and followed him docilely, her entire body shuddering.

The servants had been awakened by the furor. A few of them appeared in the hall, staring at the spectacle in disbelief.

"Stop him!" Lara cried, gripping the balustrade and lurching to her feet. "Don't let them leave!"

But none of the servants moved, and she suddenly realized why. The object in Lonsdale's hand was a pistol. In his enraged condition, he wouldn't hesitate to use it.

"Open the doors," Lonsdale snapped, gesturing to a footman with the weapon. "Now!"

The footman hastened to comply. He darted to the entranceway, fumbled with the door handles, and sent the heavy portals swinging gently outward.

To everyone's startlement, a high-pitched voice echoed through the great hall. "Stop!"

Lara's gaze switched to the top of the stairs, where Johnny stood in his little white nightshirt, his dark hair ruffled all about his head. He held a toy pistol in his hand, the one that could be loaded with a harmless gunpowder cap.

"I'll shoot you!" the boy shouted, pointing the pistol at Lonsdale.

Reflexively Lonsdale lifted his own weapon and took aim at the small figure.

"Don't!" Lara screeched to Lonsdale. "It's only a toy!"

"Let Auntie Rachel go," Johnny cried, and fired.

The toy emitted a feeble pop, the sound causing everyone to freeze.

Realizing the tiny pistol was harmless, Lonsdale began to laugh incredulously, his mocking gaze fastened on the small, furious boy at the top of the stairs.

All at once a shadowy figure moved through the open doorway with a lithe, animal-like spring.

"Hunter," Lara breathed, while he launched himself at Lonsdale with an impact that sent both men crashing to the floor.

Rachel was thrown aside from the force of the collision, and she rolled once, twice, before her body went limp from pain and shock. She closed her eyes and fainted, her arms flung out like a discarded rag doll's.

The men fought viciously for the gun, swearing and grunting as they pummeled each other. Lara turned and clambered up the stairs as fast as she could move. She reached Johnny in a matter of seconds and pulled him to the ground, sheltering his body with her own.

The boy gasped with confusion, his cheeks wet with tears. "Mama, what's happening?" he asked plaintively, and she hugged him tightly.

She risked a glance at the scene below, where Hunter twisted and grappled for the weapon. Biting her lip in terror, Lara fought to keep silent. The two large men were locked in deadly combat, rolling across the polished floor . . . and then the air was shattered by a thunderous explosion.

Both men were still.

Lara gripped Johnny, her wide eyes focused on the two long bodies and the pool of ruby red blood that seeped around them. She made a strangled sound in her throat, and covered her mouth with her hand to hold in an anguished scream.

Hunter moved slowly, disentangling himself from the other man and pressing his large hands over the gaping wound in Lonsdale's midriff. Breathing heavily, Hunter looked at the servants nearby. "Send for Dr. Slade," he growled at a footman, "and have someone else fetch the sheriff." He motioned to the butler with a jerk of his head. "You—take Lady Lonsdale upstairs before she wakens." His curt voice seemed to make sense of the chaos. They all rushed to obey, grateful for his leadership.

Trembling with relief, Lara took Johnny's hand and pulled him away from the scene. "Don't look, darling," she murmured as he strained to glance over his shoulder.

"He's come back," Johnny said, gripping her fingers fervently. "He's come back."

It was almost dawn by the time the sheriff departed, after the prolonged questioning of the Hawksworths and the servants. The sheriff had shown no great surprise at the turn of events. As he had remarked laconically, everyone knew of Lonsdale's habitual drunkenness and violence. It had only been a matter of time before he received his comeuppance.

Although it appeared the matter would be set aside with no charges made, Hunter couldn't dismiss it easily. Grimly he scrubbed himself in a hip tub in his room. A thick application of soap removed every trace of dirt and blood, but he still didn't feel clean.

For most of his life he had been able to ignore his conscience. In fact, he had been fairly certain he didn't possess one. But he was deeply troubled about the consequences of bringing Rachel to Hawksworth Hall. If he hadn't, Lord Lonsdale would probably still be alive. On the other hand, if Hunter had left Rachel to her husband's mercy, she would likely be dead. Had he made the right choice? Had there been a right choice to make?

He dressed and combed his wet hair, and thought about Lara. There were still things left to be said between them . . . painful things that he didn't want to say and she would not want to hear. Groaning, he dug the heels of his hands into his sore eyes. He considered how all of this had started, with his overwhelming wish to become Hunter Cameron Crossland. The surprise of it all was how natural it had felt. He had made the name his own, until even he had trouble remembering that he was living a stolen life. His other bleak existence had been closed away like a dusty attic room he had no wish to visit.

And Lara, for some motive he couldn't begin to understand, had made it possible for the charade to continue. Perhaps she was trying to think of him as one of her many charity cases, and save him from what he was.

But he couldn't allow Lara to become part of the lie. He couldn't bear to corrupt her any more than he already had.

Filled with dread and longing, he went to tell Lara good-bye.

Lara sat in a chair before her bedroom hearth, shivering as the heat of the coals wafted over her bare toes. Rachel was fast asleep in her own room, drugged by a dose of laudanum the doctor had administered. Johnny had been tucked away in the nursery, soothed by a glass of hot milk and a story. Although Lara was exhausted, she stayed resolutely awake, afraid that if she fell asleep, Hunter would leave her once again.

Her body gave a little jump as the doorknob turned, and Hunter entered the room without knocking. She stood automatically. After one look at his remote face, she held back and wrapped her arms around her middle, hugging herself.

"I thought you had left me after the depositions in London," she said quietly. "I thought you weren't going to come back."

"I wasn't. But then I thought of you here alone with Rachel, and I realized what Lonsdale would do." He made a sound of self-disgust. "I would have come sooner if I'd been thinking clearly."

"You came in time," Lara said, her voice cracking. "Oh, Hunter . . . downstairs . . . for a moment I thought you were hurt . . . or dead . . ."

"Don't." He held up a hand in a silencing gesture.

Utterly miserable, Lara held her tongue. How could they have been so intimate only a few days ago, and now stand before each other as strangers? She loved him whatever his name was, no matter whose blood ran in his veins, no matter what he believed or wanted. Just so long as he wanted her. But as she stared into his fathomless dark eyes, it seemed an impossible task to convince him.

"Stay with me," she said, extending a beseeching hand. "Please."

He looked as though he hated himself. "Don't ask that, Lara."

"But you love me. I know you do."

"That makes no difference," he said bleakly. "You know why I have to go."

"You belong with me," she persisted. "For one thing, you have a duty to take care of the child you helped to create."

"There is no child," he said flatly.

Lara approached him, closing the distance between them. Carefully she reached for the large hand that was held so stiffly at his side, and tugged it to her stomach. She pressed his palm there, as if she could make him feel the truth of her words. "I'm carrying your baby."

"No," he whispered. "You can't be."

"I wouldn't lie to you."

"Not to me," he agreed bitterly, "only to the rest of the world. For my sake." His other arm slid around her, and he held her as if he couldn't stop himself. A shiver went through his body, and he dove his face into the loose sheaves of her hair. She heard his breathing change, and she realized his mask was shattering, revealing the despair and frustrated love beneath the surface.

"Lara, you don't know what I am."

"Yes, I do," she said urgently, reaching around his back to hold him tightly. "You're a good man, even though you don't realize it. And you're my husband in every way that matters."

A shuddering laugh broke from his throat. "Dammit. Don't you understand that the best thing I can do for you is get out of your life?"

Lara drew back and pushed at his head, forcing him to look at her. His dark eyes were glittering with tears, and his mouth shook with the emotions he had always suppressed until now. She drew her hands over his beautiful hair, his beloved face, as if she could heal him with her touch.

"Stay with me," she said, trying to give his massive shoulders a shake. His large body wouldn't budge. "I won't hear another word about it. I don't see why we should live apart and suffer when we have the chance to be together. If you don't feel worthy of me, you can work on improving yourself during the next fifty years." She gripped the loose folds of his shirt and pulled herself hard against him. "I don't want a perfect man, anyway."

Hunter looked away, struggling to control himself. "You damn well haven't got one."

Lara gave him a wobbly smile, hearing something in his voice that gave her a flicker of hope. "I'm offering you a life you want," she said. "A life of meaning and purpose, and love. Take it. Take *me*." She pressed her lips to his hard mouth, stealing a swift kiss, and another, coaxing and enticing until he groaned in response. He crushed his mouth over hers with a raw desire that suddenly raged out of control. He searched her with his tongue, a primitive masculine sound coming from his throat, and pulled up her nightgown in frantic handfuls.

Lara twined a bare leg around one of his, offering herself with a willingness that seemed to drive him wild. He scooped her in his arms and carried her to the bed, and Lara's weariness vanished as her blood raced with excitement. "I love you," she said, pulling him down to her, and she felt the responsive tremor that ran through him. He tugged at her nightgown until it tore from her body. His lips sealed over her nipple and sucked firmly, while his fingers spread over her belly and hips.

Lara moaned and cradled him with her arms and legs, needing him more than she had thought humanly possible. He raised himself higher and took her mouth again, in deep searching kisses that stole her breath away. Gasping, she tugged at his clothes and tried to unbutton his shirt.

"I can't wait," he muttered, reaching down to his trousers and jerking them open.

"I want to feel your skin," she whimpered, still struggling with his shirt.

"Later . . . oh God . . ." He spread her legs wide and drove inside her with a demanding push. The heavy, sweet pressure filled her until she cried out, her body overcome with exquisite sensations that raced along every nerve. She arched upward and trembled in pleasure as he moved gently inside her, prolonging the delight. His thrusts deepened, a sliding, teasing rhythm of impact and withdrawal. He made love to her as if he were feasting on her, every movement carnal and deliberate. Lara reached beneath his shirt and grasped the hard muscles of his back, urging him to finish quickly. He took his time, however, seeming to relish her low moans.

"I can't . . . I'm too tired," she said. "Please, not again—"

"Again," he said hoarsely, deepening his thrusts until she writhed in another climax, this one almost painful in its intensity. Hunter buried himself inside her and let her inner contractions bring him to his own release, his teeth clamping together as the storm raged through him.

Shivering and breathing erratically, they relaxed in a tangle of bedclothes. Lara sank into a peaceful lethargy, turning her face toward Hunter as she felt him stroking her hair. Daylight threatened to intrude in the quiet room, but the heavy curtains kept it at bay.

"Even if you had left me," Lara said drowsily, "you wouldn't have been able to stay away for long."

He made a rueful sound. "Because I need you," he said, pressing his warm lips to her forehead.

"Not nearly as much as I need you."

He smiled, his hands moving gently over her body. But when he spoke, his tone was serious. "How do we go on from here after all that's happened?"

"I don't know." She settled her head in the crook of his shoulder. "We'll just start again, that's all."

"Every time you look at me," he said, "you'll remember that I took his place."

"No," she said, laying her fingers over his lips, determined that no ghost from the past would haunt them now. "I suppose I'll think of him sometimes . . . but I never really knew him. He didn't want a life with me, nor I with him."

She felt his mouth twist wryly. "That's all I've ever wanted," he muttered.

Lara moved her hand to the steady thud of his heart. "When I look at you," she said, "I see only you." She nuzzled closer against his side. "I know you," she added throatily.

The comment drew an unwilling laugh from him, and Hunter rolled to his side to stare down at her. It was clear that he was prepared to argue the point, but as he gazed at her small face, his expression changed to one of extraordinary tenderness. "Maybe you do," he said, and gathered her close.

Epilogue

AFTER TOURING THE orphanage and seeing the improvements that had just been completed, Lara was filled with satisfaction. They were ready to admit the new children now, only ten instead of the expected twelve, as two families in Market Hill had become so fond of their temporary guests that they had decided to keep them. It would be easy enough to fill the extra beds at the orphanage, Lara thought. There were always far too many children who were in need of a decent place to live.

As she stepped from the carriage and entered Hawksworth Hall, Lara's mind was so busy with plans that she scarcely noticed the man who waited for her.

"Lady Hawksworth . . . forgive me, my lady . . ."

A gentleman's cultured voice repeated her name until Lara stopped and turned with an inquiring smile.

The visitor was Lord Tufton, the shy, gentle man who had courted Rachel before her marriage to Lonsdale. He was an intellectual rather than a sportsman, with a kind, earnest manner that Lara had always liked. She had heard recently that Tufton had come into an unexpected fortune at the death of his uncle,

which would undoubtedly make him sought after by
many ambitious young females.

"Lord Tufton!" Lara exclaimed with sincere pleasure. "How nice it is to see you."

They conversed amiably for a minute, and Tufton
gestured lamely to a magnificent arrangement of
roses that had been set on the table by the entrance.
"I brought these for your family to enjoy," he remarked.

"How lovely they are," Lara said warmly, suppressing a smile as she realized that the flowers were
really for her sister. However, it wouldn't have been
proper for Tufton to give them exclusively to Rachel,
as she was in mourning. "Thank you. We will all
enjoy them—especially my sister. She is quite fond
of roses, you know."

"Yes, I . . ." He cleared his throat nervously.
"Might I inquire after her health, my lady?"

"She is quite well," Lara assured him. "Although
. . . she is rather quiet and downcast these days."

"That is only to be expected," he remarked gently,
"after the tragedy she has experienced."

Lara surveyed him with a thoughtful smile. Rachel
had not received visitors in the two months since
Lonsdale's death, but somehow Lara was certain that
Tufton's face would be a welcome sight. "Lord Tufton . . . my sister is always out in the garden at this
time of day, taking a long stroll. I'm sure she would
enjoy walking with a companion."

He looked both eager and hesitant at the prospect.
"Oh, I shouldn't like to bother her . . . if she desires
solitude . . ."

"Come with me," Lara said, tugging him through
the great hall with relentless determination. She led

him to the French doors that opened to the garden, and caught a glimpse of Rachel's black dyed bonnet as she walked among the hedges. "There she is," Lara said triumphantly. "Go right along and join her, Lord Tufton."

"But I don't know if—"

"My sister will be delighted, I assure you." Lara opened the door and ushered him outside, and watched as he made his way through a flower-strewn parterre.

"Mama!" Hearing Johnny's voice, Lara turned with a smile. The boy was dressed in miniature breeches and a blue jacket in preparation for a riding lesson.

"Darling, where is the nanny?" she asked.

"She's coming down from the schoolroom," Johnny said, slightly breathless. "But she can't run as fast as me."

Lara straightened the boy's cap. "Why are you always in such a hurry?" she asked.

" 'Cause I don't want to miss anything."

Laughing, Lara returned her attention to the window, watching as Lord Tufton and Rachel came into view. Her sister was holding Tufton's arm as they strolled together. Beneath the brim of the black mourning bonnet was the first real smile Lara had seen on Rachel's face in far too long.

"Who is that with Auntie Rachel?" Johnny asked.

"I believe he's going to be her next husband," Lara replied thoughtfully, and glanced at the boy with a conspiratorial smile. "But that's our secret for now."

This turn of thought led to consideration of another secret they shared, and Johnny tugged at Lara's skirts. "When can we tell everyone you're going to have a baby, Mama?"

"When I begin to show," Lara replied. At his look of confusion, she explained with a slight blush, "When my tummy gets bigger."

"Will it get as big as Sir Ralph's?" he asked, naming a stout gentleman of their acquaintance.

Lara couldn't hold back a laugh. "Good Lord, I hope not."

His face turned sober. "Will you still love me after the baby comes, Mama?"

Smiling with perfect happiness, Lara knelt and put her arms around his slim, straight body. "Oh, yes," she murmured, hugging him hard. "Always, Johnny."

In the early evening, Hunter arrived from an errand in Market Hill and found Lara just as she finished changing for dinner. He came to her and pressed a quick, hard kiss on her lips.

"I have them," he replied in response to her questioning glance.

Lara smiled, smoothing his lapels with her fingertips. "I thought you might have forgotten what we planned for tonight."

Hunter shook his head. "I've thought about it all day."

"Shall we have dinner first?" she asked softly.

"I'm not hungry. Are you?"

"No."

He caught her small hand in his and pulled her along with him. "Then let's go."

*   *   *

He took her to the outskirts of Market Hill, driving
a curricle with a matched pair of chestnuts. They
reached a small stone church tucked in a grove of
small trees near the rectory. The quaint little building, with its thatched roof and round Saxon tower
topped with a belfry, looked like something out of a
fairy tale.

Lara smiled in anticipation as Hunter swung her
down from the vehicle. He used a carriage lantern to
light their way along a small path, and held Lara's
elbow lightly, guiding her across the uneven stones.
They entered the quiet church, and Lara surveyed the
interior as Hunter lit a pair of candles by the altar. A
simple wooden cross on one wall and a circular
stained-glass window were the building's only
adornments, save for the carving on the sides of the
four pews.

"It's perfect," Lara said.

Hunter shot her a skeptical glance. "Lara, I
wish . . ."

"This is more than enough," she interrupted, her
face glowing in the candlelight. "We don't need an
elaborate church, or a congregation, or a minister to
hold a proper ceremony."

"You deserve so much more," he grumbled.

"Come here." She stood by the altar and waited,
her lips curved with a smile.

Hunter approached her and reached in his pocket,
extracting a tiny velvet pouch. Gently he shook the
contents into his hand. Lara's breath caught as she
beheld the geminal ring, two gold bands fitting together into one. "It's lovely," she said, watching as
he deftly twisted the bands apart and set them on the
altar.

Moved by the sweet serenity of their surroundings, Lara bent her head and prayed silently, her heart filled with hope and joy. She looked up to find Hunter's bright dark gaze on her.

"Whatever amount of time I have with you," he said huskily, "it's not enough."

Wordlessly she held out her hand, and Hunter took it in a solid clasp. He held it for a moment, then picked up a gold band and slid it onto her finger. "I promise," he said slowly, staring into her eyes, "to give you my whole self, body and soul . . . to take care of you . . . to respect and honor you . . . and most of all to love you until the day I die . . . and even after that." He paused and added with a flare of tender laughter in his eyes, "And I won't complain about all your charitable projects . . . as long as you remember to spare some time for me."

Lara's hand trembled a little as she slid the other band onto his finger "I promise to be your helpmate, friend, and lover," she said softly. "I promise to give you all my love and trust, and build a life with you . . . and help you to forget about the past and cherish each day we have together."

"And you'll give me children," he said, placing a gentle hand over her stomach.

"Ten," she said ambitiously, making him laugh.

"Now I see your plan. You'll keep me in bed all the time, laboring to produce them."

"Complaining?" Lara asked.

He grinned and pulled her close in an ardent hug. "God, no. I'm just thinking . . ." He took her mouth in a string of passionate kisses. "We'd better . . . start practicing."

Her hands slid around his head, and they kissed

lavishly until they were both breathless.

"Tell me your name," Lara whispered. "Your real one."

She had asked him many times before, and as always, he refused. "No, my curious cat," he said softly, stroking her hair. "That man doesn't exist anymore."

"Tell me," she demanded, and tugged at the front of his coat.

He broke her imperious grip by tickling her, making her collapse against his chest with a giggle. "Never," he said.

Lara wrapped her arms around his neck. "I'll make you tell me someday, you realize," she informed him, pressing her lips to a sensitive spot on his throat and making him shiver suddenly. "You haven't the slightest hope of resisting me."

"Not the slightest," he agreed huskily, bending over her mouth once again.

THE WORLD OF
AVON ROMANCE SUPERLEADERS

*Cross-promotion and rebate offer in the
back of every book!*

MEET THE MEN OF AVON ROMANCE . . .
They're fascinating, they're sexy—they're irresistible! They're the kind of men you definitely want to bring home—but not to meet the family. And they live in such romantic places, from Regency England to the Wild West. These men are guaranteed to provide you with hours of reading pleasure. So introduce yourself to these unforgettable heroes, and meet a different man every month.

AND THE WRITERS WHO CREATE THEM
At Avon we bring you books by the brightest stars of romantic fiction. Christina Dodd, Catherine Anderson and Pamela Morsi. Kathleen Eagle, Lisa Kleypas and Barbara Freethy. These are the bestselling writers who create books you'll never forget—each and every story is a "keeper." Following is a sneak preview of their newest books . . .

Enter the world of New York Times *best–selling author* **Catherine Anderson.** *This award–winning writer creates a place where dreams really do come true and love always triumphs. In April, Catherine creates her most memorable characters of all in* **Forever After.**

County Sheriff Heath Masters has a hard enough time managing small–town crime, and he doesn't need any complications—especially ones in the very attractive form of his new neighbor, Meredith Kenyon, and her adorable daughter, Sammy. But when Heath's giant of a dog causes trouble for Merry, he finds himself in trouble, too . . . of the romantic kind.

FOREVER AFTER
by Catherine Anderson

HEATH VAULTED OVER the tumble-down fence that divided his neighbor's patchy lawn from the adjoining cow pasture, then poured on speed to circle the house. He skidded to a halt about fifteen feet shy of a dilapidated woodshed. A child, dressed in pink pants and a smudged white T-shirt, stood splayed against the outbuilding. Her eyes were so wide with fright they resembled china-blue supper plates.

Fangs bared and frothing at the jowls, Goliath lunged back and forth between the child and a young woman Heath guessed to be her mother.

"Stay back!" he ordered.

At the sound of his voice the woman turned around, her pinched face so pale that her dark brown eyes looked almost as large as her daughter's. "Oh, thank God! Help us! Do something, please, before he hurts us!"

Heath jerked his gaze back to his dog. If ever there had been an animal he would trust with a child, Goliath was it. Yet now the rottweiler seemed to have gone berserk.

Heath snapped his fingers. "Goliath, heel!"

At the command, the rottweiler whirled toward Heath, his usually friendly brown eyes glinting a demonic red. For an awful instant Heath was afraid the dog might not obey him.

What in the hell was wrong with him? Heath's gaze shot to the terrified child.

"Goliath, *heel*!" He slapped his thigh for emphasis.

The rottweiler finally acquiesced with another frenzied bark followed by a pathetic whine, massive head lowered, legs stiff, his movements reluctant and abject. The second the dog got within reach, Heath grabbed his collar.

"Sammy!"

The woman bolted forward to gather her child into her arms with a strangled cry. Then she whirled to confront Heath, her pale, delicately molded face twisting with anger, her body quaking.

"You get that *vicious*, out-of-control dog *off* my property!"

The blaze in her eyes told Heath she was infused by the rush of adrenaline that often followed a bad scare.

"Ma'am, I'm really sorry about—"

"I don't want to hear it! Just get that monster out of here!"

Damn. Talk about starting off on the wrong foot with someone. And wasn't that a shame? Heath would have happily fixed this gal's plumbing late at night—or anything else that went haywire in the ramshackle old house she was renting.

Fragile build. Pixieish features. Creamy skin. Large caramel brown eyes. A full, vulnerable mouth the delicate pink of barely ripened strawberries. Her hair fell in a thick, silken tangle around her shoulders, the sable tendrils curling over her white shirt like glistening ribbons of chocolate on vanilla ice cream.

Definitely not what he'd been picturing. Old Zeke usually rented this place to losers—people content to work the welfare system rather than seek gainful employment. Even in baggy jeans and a man's shirt this lady had "class" written all over her.

*Nationally best-selling author **Pamela Morsi** is known for the trademark wit and down-home humor that enliven her enchanting, memorable romances that have garnered rave reviews from critics and won national awards. This May experience the charm of Pamela Morsi in* Sealed With a Kiss.

When Gidney Chavis jilted Pru Belmont and left Chavistown, the nearly wed bride was devastated, the townsfolk scandalized . . . and Chavis was strongly discouraged from showing his face again. But now he's back, a bit older, a whole lot wiser . . . and rarin' to patch things up with Pru.

SEALED WITH A KISS
by Pamela Morsi

THE COWBOY ALLOWED his gaze to roam among the customers. There was a table full of poker players intent upon their game. One tired, sort of half-pretty woman looked up hopefully and pulled her feet out of the chair next to her. He didn't even bother to meet her glance. A couple of rowdy farmhands seemed to be starting early on a weekend drunken spree. A few other men drinking quietly. No one that he recognized for certain.

At the near end of the bar a dandied-up gentleman in a plaid coat and summer derby sat alone, his traveling bag at his feet.

The cowboy almost smiled. If there was anyone more certain not to be a local, it was a drummer in a plaid coat. Without any appearance of haste or purposeful intent, he casually took the seat right next to the traveling bag.

"Afternoon."

The little man looked up eagerly.

"Good afternoon to you, sir," he answered and in true salesman fashion, offered his hand across the bar. "Arthur D. Sattlemore, Big Texas Electric Company."

The cowboy's only answer was an indecipherable grunt as he signaled the barkeep to bring him a beer.

"Hot weather we've been having."

The cowboy nodded. "A miserable summer," he agreed. "Good for cotton."

"You are a farmer, sir?" Clearly the drummer was surprised.

"No," the cowboy answered. "But when you're in Chavistown, it's hard to talk about anything here without mentioning cotton."

The drummer chuckled and nodded understanding. He leaned closer. "You have the right of it there, sir," he admitted. "I was asked to come present my company to the Commercial Club. I've been here a week and haven't been able to get a word in edgewise. The whole town is talking cotton and what will happen without old man Chavis."

The cowboy blanched. "He's dead?"

The drummer shook his head. "Not as of this morning, but without him to run the gin and the co-operative, the farmers are worried that their cotton will sit in wagonloads by the side of the road."

"Ginning time has just begun," the cowboy said. "Surely the old man will be up and around before it's over."

The drummer shook his head. "Not the way they're telling it. Seems the old man is bad off. Weak as a kitten they say, and the quacks warn that if he gets out of bed, he won't live to see winter."

"Doctors have been wrong before," the cowboy said.

The drummer nodded. "The whole town hopes you're right. The old man ain't got no one to take over for him. The gin's closed down and the cotton's just waiting."

The cowboy nodded.

"They had a meeting early in the week and voted to send for young Chavis, the old man's son."

"Is that so?"

"Young Chavis created some bit of scandal in this

town eight years ago," the drummer explained. "No-body's seen so much as his shadow since."

The cowboy listened quietly, intently.

"So they sent for their son and they're hoping that he'll come and save their biscuits," the little man said. "But for myself, I just wouldn't trust him."

"No?"

The traveling man tutted and shook his head. "They say he was all but married to a local gal and just left her high and dry."

"Is that what they say?"

The drummer nodded. "And I ask you, what kind of man blessed with plenty of money, an influential name, a fine place in the community and an innocent young sweetheart who expects to marry him, runs off with some round-heeled, painted-up saloon gal?"

The cowboy slowly picked up his beer and drank it down in one long swallow. He banged the glass on the bar with enough force to catch the attention of every man in the room.

"What kind of man, indeed," he said to the drummer.

Best-selling author **Kathleen Eagle's** *marriage to a Lakota Sioux has given her inspiration to write uniquely compelling love stories featuring Native American characters. She's won numerous awards, but her most gratifying reward was a note from a reader saying, "You kept me up all night reading." This June, stay up all night with* **The Night Remembers.**

Jesse Brown Wolf is a man living in the shadows who comes to the rescue of kids like Tommy T, a street-smart boy, and

Angela, a fragile newcomer to the big city. Jesse rescues An-
gela from a brutal robbery and helps nurse her back to health.
In return, Angela helps Jesse heal his wounded soul.

THE NIGHT REMEMBERS
by Kathleen Eagle

HE HADN'T BEEN this close to anyone in a long
time, and his visceral quaking was merely the proof.
He sat on a straw cushion and leaned back against
the woven willow backrest and drank what was left
of the tea. He didn't need any of this. Not the kid,
not the woman, not the intrusion into his life.

A peppering of loose pebbles echoed in the air
shaft, warning him that something was stirring overhead. He climbed to the entrance and waited until
the boy announced himself.

"I had a hard time gettin' the old grandpa to come
to the door," Tommy T reported as he handed the
canvas bag down blindly, as though he made regular
deliveries to a hole in the ground. "Some of this is
just, like, bandages and food, right?"

"Right."

The boy went on. "I said I was just a runner and
didn't know nothin' about what was in the message,
and nobody asked no questions, nothin' about you.
You know what? I know that old guy from school."

"A lot of people know him. He practices traditional
medicine."

"Cool." Then, diverting to a little skepticism, "So
what I brought is just roots and herbs and stuff."

"It's medicine."

"She might be worried about her dog," the boy said, hovering in the worlds above. "If she says anything, tell her I'm on the case."

"You don't know where she lives."

"I'll know by morning. I'll check in later, man." The voice was withdrawing. "Not when it's daytime, though. I won't hang around when it's light out."

On the note of promise, the boy left.

The night was nearly over. The air smelled like daybreak, laden with dew, and the river sounded more cheerful as it rushed toward morning. Normally, he would ascend to greet the break of day. The one good thing about the pain was the relief he felt when it lifted. Relief and weariness. He returned to the deepest chamber of his refuge, where his guest lay in his bed, her fragile face bathed in soft candlelight.

He made an infusion from the mixture of herbs the old man had prepared and applied it to the tattered angel's broken skin. He made a paste from ground roots and applied it to her swollen bumps and bruises, singing softly as he did so. The angel moaned, as though she would add her keening to his lullaby, but another tea soon tranquilized her fitful sleep.

Finally he doused the light, lay down beside her, closed his eyes, and drifted on the dewy-sweet morning air.

When you open a book by New York Times *best-selling* author **Lisa Kleypas**, *you're invited to enter a world where you can attend a glittering ball one night . . . and have a secret rendezvous the next. Her sensuous, historical page-turners are delicious treats for readers. In July, don't miss her latest gem,* **Stranger in My Arms.**

All of England believed that Hunter, the Earl of Hawksworth, had disappeared in a shipwreck, leaving a large estate and a grieving widow. But now, a man claiming to be Hunter had arrived at Hawksworth Hall—handsome, virile . . . and very much alive. And Lara, Hunter's wife, must decide if he is truly her husband—or a very clever impostor.

STRANGER IN MY ARMS
by Lisa Kleypas

HE WAS so much thinner, his body lean, almost raw-boned, his heavy muscles thrown into stark prominence. His skin was so much darker, a rich bronze hue that was far too exotic and striking for an Englishman. But it *was* Hunter . . . older, toughened, as sinewy and alert as a panther.

"I didn't believe . . ." Lara started to say, but the words died away. It was too much of an effort to speak. She backed away from him and somehow made her way to the cabinet where she kept a few dishes and a small teapot. She took refuge in an everyday ritual, fumbling for a parcel of tea leaves, pulling the little porcelain pot from its place on the shelf. "I—I'll make some tea. We can talk about . . . everything . . ."

But her hands were shaking too badly, and the cups and saucers clattered together as she reached for them. He came to her in an instant, his feet swift and startlingly light on the floor. Hunter had always had a heavy footstep—but the thought was driven away as he took her cold hands in his huge warm ones. She felt his touch all through her body, in small, penetrating ripples of sensation.

A pair of teasing dark eyes stared into hers. "You're not going to faint, are you?"

Her face was frozen, making it impossible to smile, to produce any expression. She looked at him dumbly, her limbs stiff with fright and her knees locked and trembling.

The flicker of amusement vanished from his gaze, and he spoke softly. "It's all right, Lara." He pushed her to a nearby chair and sank to his haunches, their faces only inches from each other.

"H-Hunter?" Lara whispered in bewilderment. *Was* he her husband? He bore an impossibly close resemblance, but there were subtle differences that struck sparks of doubt within her.

He reached inside his worn black broadcloth coat and extracted a small object. Holding it in his palm, he showed it to her. Eyes wide, Lara regarded the small, flat enameled box. He pressed the tiny catch on the side and revealed a miniature portrait of her, the one she had given him before his departure to India three years earlier.

"I've stared at this every day for months," he murmured. "Even when I didn't remember you in the days right after the shipwreck, I knew somehow that you belonged to me." He closed the box in his hand and tucked it back into his coat pocket.

Lara lifted her incredulous gaze to his. She felt as if she were in a dream. "You've changed," she managed to say.

Hunter smiled slightly. "So have you. You're more beautiful than ever."

Barbara Freethy's poignant, tender love stories have garnered her many new fans. Her first Avon romance, Daniel's Gift, was called "exhilarating" by Affair de Coeur and Romantic Times said it was ". . . sure to tug on the heartstrings." This August, don't miss Barbara's best yet, **One True Love.**

Nick Maddux believed he'd never see his ex-wife, Lisa, again. Then he knocked on the door to his sister's house and Lisa answered—looking as beautiful, as vulnerable as ever. Nick soon discovered that, despite the tragedy that lay between them, his love for Lisa was as tender—and as passionate—as ever.

ONE TRUE LOVE
by Barbara Freethy

NICK MADDUX WAS surrounded by pregnant women. Every time he turned around, he bumped into someone's stomach. Muttering yet another apology, he backed into the corner of his eight-by-twelve-foot booth at the San Diego Baby and Parenting Fair and took a deep breath. He was hot, tired and proud.

His handcrafted baby furniture was the hit of the show. In some cases, it would be a challenge to have his furniture arrive before the stork, but Nick thrived on challenges, and Robin Wood Designs was finally on its way to becoming the profitable business he had envisioned.

Nick couldn't believe how far he'd come, how much he'd changed.

Eight years ago, he'd been twenty-five years old, working toward getting his contractor's license and trying to provide for a wife and a child on the way. He'd kept at it long after they'd gone, hammering out his anger and frustration on helpless nails and boards.

Two years had gone by before he ran out of work, out of booze and out of money. Finally, stone-cold sober, he'd realized his life was a mess.

That's when he'd met Walter Mackey, a master craftsman well into his seventies but still finding joy in carving wood. Walter made rocking chairs in his garage and sold them at craft fairs. Nick had bought one of those chairs for his mother's birthday. She'd told Nick he'd given her something that would last forever.

It was then Nick realized he could make something that would last forever. His life didn't have to be a series of arrivals and departures.

Nick had decided to focus on baby furniture, because something for one's child always brought out the checkbook faster than something for oneself. Besides that mercenary reason, Nick had become obsessed with building furniture for babies that would nurture them, keep them safe, protect them.

He knew where the obsession came from, just not

how to stop it. Maybe Robin would be proud of all that he'd accomplished in her name.

Nick felt himself drawn into the past. In his mind he saw Lisa with her round stomach, her glowing smile, her blue eyes lit up for the world to see. She'd been so happy then, so proud of herself. When she'd become pregnant, they both thought they'd won the lottery.

He closed his eyes for a moment as the pain threatened to overwhelm him, and he saw her again.

"I can't believe I'm having a baby," Lisa said. She took his hand and placed it on her abdomen. "Feel that? She's kicking me."

Nick's gut tightened at the fluttering kick against his fingers. It was the most incredible feeling. He couldn't begin to express the depth of his love for this unborn child, but he could show Lisa. In the middle of the baby store, he kissed her on the lips, uncaring of the salespeople or the other customers. "I love you," he whispered against her mouth.

She looked into his eyes. "I love you, too. More than anything. I'm so happy, it scares me. What if something goes wrong?"

"Nothing will go wrong."

"Oh, Nick, things always go wrong around me. Remember our first date—we hit a parked car."

He smiled. "That wasn't your fault. I'm the one who wasn't paying attention."

"I'm the one who distracted you," she said with a worried look in her eyes.

"Okay, it was your fault."

"Nick!"

"I'm teasing. Don't be afraid of being happy. It's not fatal, you know. This is just the beginning for us."

It had been the beginning of the end.

Award-winning author **Christina Dodd** *is known for capti-*
vating characters and sizzling sensuality. She is the author of
twelve best-selling romances, including **A Well Pleasured**
Lady *and* **A Well Favored Gentleman.** *Enjoy an excerpt*
from **That Scandalous Evening.**

Years earlier, Jane Higgenbothem had caused a scandal
when she'd sculpted Lord Ransom Quincey of Blackburn in
the classical manner. Apparently everything was accurate
save one very important part of Lord Blackburn's body.
Jane retired to the country in disgrace, but now she has come
back to London to face her adversary.

THAT SCANDALOUS EVENING
by Christina Dodd

London, 1809

"CAN YOU SEE the newest belle?" Fitz demanded.

"No."

"You're not even looking!"

"There's nothing worth seeing." Ransom had better things to do than watch out for a silly girl.

"Not true. You'll find a diamond worth having, if
you'd just take a look. A diamond, Ransom! Let us
through. There you go lads, you can't keep her for
yourselves." The constriction eased as the men

turned and Fitz slipped through the crowd. Ransom followed close on Fitz's heels, protecting his friend's back and wondering why.

"Your servant, ma'am!" Fitz snapped to attention, then bowed, leaving Ransom a clear view of, not the diamond, but the profile of a dab of a lady. Her gown of rich green glacé silk was *au courant*, and nicely chosen to bring out the spark of emerald in her fine eyes. A lacy shawl covered her slight bosom, and she held her gloved hands clasped at her waist like a singer waiting for a cue that never came. A mop cap covered her unfashionable coil of heavy dark hair and her prim mouth must have never greeted a man invitingly.

Ransom began to turn away.

Then she smiled at the blonde with an exultant bosom beside her. It was a smile filled with pride and quiet pleasure. It lit the plain features and made them glow—and he'd seen that glow before. He jerked to a stop.

He stared. It couldn't be her. She had to be a figment of his wary, suspicious mind.

He blinked and looked again.

Damn, it *was* her.

Miss Jane Higgenbothem had returned.